Death in Cold Type

Death in Cold Type

C.C. Benison

Signature
EDITIONS

© 2005, C.C. Benison

All rights reserved. No part of this book may be reproduced, for any reason, by any means, without the permission of the publisher.

Cover design by Terry Gallagher/Doowah Design.
Photo of C.C. Benison by James Hammel Photography.
This book was printed on Ancient-Forest-Friendly paper.
Printed and bound in Canada by Hignell Book Printing.

Acknowledgements
Many minds make light work. Well, light*er* work. My thanks to the following for their comments, contributions, expert advise, and commiseration: Esme Langer, Bernie Chodirker, Tim Ingles, Rita Kurtz, Tom Moffatt, Lenore Richards, John ("Shelterbelt") Whiteway, Jim Hammel, Michael Phillips, Rorie Bruce, Jackie Mitchell, Jim Sutherland, Annalee Greenberg, Sarah Burton, and Susan Falk. Thanks to the Manitoba Arts Council for its generous support during the writing of this book.

We acknowledge the support of The Canada Council for the Arts and the Manitoba Arts Council for our publishing program.

Library and Archives Canada Cataloguing in Publication

Benison, C.C.
    Death in cold type / C.C. Benison.

ISBN 1-897109-03-2

    I. Title.

PS8553.E5135D436 2005   C813'.54   C2005-903089-5

Signature Editions, P.O. Box 206, RPO Corydon
Winnipeg, Manitoba, R3M 3S7

Winnipeg (CP) – Author C.C. Benison today dedicated his new novel *Death in Cold Type* to four women – Barbara Huck, Hope Kamin, Marilyn Mackinnon and Barbara Robson. The dedicatees were unavailable for comment at press time.

This is a true story.
Only the people and events aren't true.

Book 1

Tuesday, September 27

1

Birds

Stevie gripped the banister.

Was she alone? Had only one car left? Or both?

She couldn't remember. Everything was hazy.

And if only one car, which one?

At least the carpet on the staircase muffled sound. But the texture: to her bare feet the plush was as smooth as a blanket of butter. In the state she was in, it was all she could do to keep from careening to the bottom of the stairs and landing—sound unmuffled—in a heap under the front hall table.

There would be no escape then.

She groped her way to the bottom of the stairs, her ears alert to the slightest noise. But the only sound was that of her own blood pumping past her ears, her heart pounding in her chest. Her mouth was dry. God, was it dry. Then her feet hit the cold tile of the hall and she nearly cried out. Sucking in her breath, she tiptoed past the arched entranceway into the living room. In the morning light, filtered by ivory silk drapes, the furniture lay heavy and grey, like hippos dying beside some African water hole, the stillness broken only by some obnoxious bird screeching outside the window. Stevie's head throbbed. She took a few soft steps forward. If she could get to the kitchen, then...

But the dining room lay in between. And if anything lurked, it would lurk there.

She stopped. She strained to listen.

All quiet.

Two cars must have left.

She was alone. A reprieve. Stevie's heartbeat settled into normal rhythms. She pushed aside an obstructing ottoman with one foot and turned the corner to the dining room. Here, the drapes had been pulled back and she caught a glimpse of the elms along the river before a shaft of hazy autumn sun pierced her eye and brought a spasm of pain. She leaned away from the light.

Then her heart jerked.

Only one car *had* left that morning.

A figure, caught in a ray, stood sentry by the sideboard, cloaked in black. An arm came up, and an arrow of light glanced off something metallic, piercing Stevie's eye anew.

"What time do you call this?" Kathleen Lord glanced at her watch, then resumed pushing a hoop of silver into one of her earlobes.

"Morning, Mother." Stevie's voice emerged as a croak.

"It's 9:30."

Stevie sighed and tightened the belt of her bathrobe. She had been home for five months, not doing much of anything—and enjoying it, by and large—but she was beginning to dig herself into a hole of guilt. Her mother—worried, she knew—was beginning to act like the mother of a teenager. Lately, if she'd been out in the evening and rose as her mother was leaving for work, she was in for what she and her two older brothers referred to as the Standish Inquisition, Standish being her mother's maiden name.

"You must have got in very late. You weren't with Michael, were you?"

"I had a mini-reunion with some of the girls I graduated with at Balmoral Hall. We had a few drinks…somewhere. I forget." A few too many margaritas at Grapes, she remembered very well. Her head throbbed.

"I thought it was Michael you were seeing."

"Tonight. I'm seeing him tonight." Stevie declined to catch her mother's eye.

Kathleen pushed a hoop through the other ear. "There's an envelope for you." She motioned with her head toward the dining room table on which lay, besides the usual breakfast things, the leavings of Canada Post.

"It feels odd," she added.

Feels odd? Stevie glanced with dismay from her mother's avid expression to the stationery as she passed the table. She noted it was not the official letter she had been expecting. Even more dismaying, the envelope bore both a familiar return address and familiar handwriting, which declared that the correspondence was for Stevie Sangster—the last name heavily underlined—not Stevie Lord, which was who she was now.

And forever, if she had anything to do with it.

"Mailman's early."

"Well? Aren't you going to open it?"

"Don't you have a patient waiting?"

Kathleen tapped her fingers along the top of the tablecloth, her diamond rings flashing as they caught the light—the same light, Stevie figured, against which her mother had tried to scrutinize the contents of the envelope not moments before.

"I think another few minutes won't kill her."

"I hope this one's not suicidal."

"Stevie...!"

"Mother, that letter is addressed to *me*. I'll open it when I damn well feel like it."

"Which will be thirty seconds after I leave this house."

"Or less, even." Stevie smiled fondly at her mother. She pondered the creamy stationery a moment. "Or maybe more. Anyway, it's my decision. Now, is there any coffee?"

"If you like coffee four hours old. Your father was up at 5:00, you know, and I was..."

Stevie disappeared into the kitchen. Of course he was up at 5:00. He had a surgery to perform at Health Sciences Centre. He was up at 5:00 and she was up at 9:30. She sighed, opened a cupboard and reached for a mug.

"All right, I'm leaving now, Stevie." Her mother's voice came through the door in a kind of steely singsong. A discreet click signalled a briefcase closing.

"Byeeeeee," Stevie began to sing back, but her voice died in another croak. Her throat constricted. She couldn't remember the last time she'd felt even a little hungover.

She stood before the coffee maker, noted the time on the inset clock (9:37) and waited for the sound of the front door to close.

Then for the fainter grinding noise of the garage door opening.

Then for the car ignition.

Stevie waited a little longer.

9:39.

It wasn't above her mother to feign starting the car, then, as it idled, dart back into the house under the pretext of having forgotten something to try to catch Stevie opening the envelope. A file (unlikely—she had a mind like a steel trap). Her umbrella (it hadn't rained in ages). Stevie opened the connecting door to the dining room a notch and pushed one ear through. The throb of the Saab's diesel engine grew loud a moment. And then fainter, pitch falling. Good old Doppler effect.

Stevie returned to the coffee maker (9:41), poured herself the dregs, then shuffled back into the dining room and settled herself at the table. Next to the pile of mail lay folded the Winnipeg *Citizen*. She sipped the hot molasses-like brew and glanced at the headline. "Our Day of Shame," the sky-is-falling type size shrieked. "Ben Johnson stripped of gold after positive test for drugs."

Stevie yawned. Ben Johnson, poor boob. She glanced down the paper's index.

Ann Landers	32
Bridge	34
Business	43
Classifieds	47
Comics	41
Crossword	42
Deaths	2, 50
Editorials	10
Horoscope	35

Thirty-five, she muttered to herself, and began flipping through the pages, flicking a glance at the buff-coloured envelope on top of the pile as she did so.

Feels odd? What did her mother mean, *feels* odd?

Stevie set aside the *Citizen*, lifted the envelope, and weighed it in her hand. It was plump. Heavy. She fingered the surface. It did feel odd. Lumpy. No, that wasn't the word. *Textured*. That was the word.

She tossed the thing back on the pile, disgusted. *What now*? What was David, her bastard of a soon-to-be-ex-husband, pray god, playing at now? She sipped her coffee, wondered if there was any Aspirin in the kitchen, and flipped through the newsprint to page thirty-five. She furiously folded the paper into a manageable square.

Just then, a key rattled in the back-door lock. Startled, Stevie called out.

"Just me," a voice said as the hollow thump of something plastic hit the floor.

Sharon Bean, once the star pupil of their grade ten Latin class at BH, now sole proprietor of Bean Cleans, came Tuesday mornings at 10:00 for four hours. Overkill for three people, Stevie thought, but what the hell, I'm not paying for it.

"How are you?" she shouted and felt a pain shoot through her head.

"Fine." Sharon popped her head through the door from the kitchen. Her hair was in a chignon so tight her eyebrows were locked in permanent surprise. She had once been one of her mother's patients. Hated doing social work, she told Kathleen Lord, Psy.D.(Berkeley) in despair. Hated the human misery. Hated the bureaucracy that manipulated so much human misery in order to save its own skin. Loved to clean things. Wanted to clean things.

So clean things, Kathleen had advised, presenting her with a potential client list.

"I'd suggest you have some coffee before you start," Stevie offered. "But you'd have to make a fresh pot."

"Can't stop. Has your mother left?"

"Omnia vincit labor," Stevie responded airily. She had been a Latin star too.

Sharon laughed and passed back through the kitchen door.

Work does conquer all, Stevie reflected, and I should go and look for some, if I'm not going back to Toronto. Or am I? She turned to the horoscope.

Taurus (April 21– May 21)
   Something you have been working on for months will bear fruit today. Others may say you are lucky, but the fact is, you have worked hard and long to get this far and deserve the good things now coming your way. A letter may contain a surprise.

"Oh, for god's sake," she sputtered.

"Something the matter?" replied the kitchen.

"Oh, nothing."

Stevie thought: There are twelve signs of the zodiac and about five-and-a-half billion people on Earth. That means—she calculated quickly, the way she might if she were sizing square-footage for an impatient client—some four hundred and fifty million people can expect to learn something in a letter today. What are the chances?

She glanced again at the envelope and the familiar pompous handwriting.

Sharon poked her head through the door again. "Can I tidy in here? Have you had your breakfast yet?"

"No, sorry."

"Then I'll make a start with the kitchen."

"Leave the door open so we can talk. I don't feel like reading about Ben Johnson and his drug problems."

Which reminded her of something. She raised her voice slightly to be heard over the clatter of Sharon stacking the dishwasher. "Is it Merritt's you do next?"

"No, I'm back doing Michael's Tuesday afternoons. Merritt is Monday mornings. Why?"

"Just wondered." Stevie unfolded the Go! section of the paper and looked for Merritt's RE: column, which was usually in the Tuesday edition's fashion page. RE: Polka Dots was this week's pressing concern. Several paragraphs followed filled with ellipses and sentence fragments, which was intended to be stylish, she supposed, yet was somehow more symbolic of Merritt's attention span.

"Just wondered what?" Sharon said after a moment clattering around the kitchen.

"Haven't seen much of her the last little while. It seems like she's gone kind of reclusive. New boyfriend, do you think?"

"How would I know?"

"You get to snoop around."

"I do not snoop."

"You mean to tell me you don't notice things in bedrooms and bathrooms?"

"Okay, sometimes. But I'm mostly interested in making things clean and tidy, Stevie. I'm not trying to piece together clues of someone's private life."

"You're no fun."

"Why are you concerned about Merritt Parrish anyway?" Sharon shouted over the splash of water hitting the sink.

Stevie waited until Sharon turned off the tap, reflecting how odd it was to have an old high school friend become your family's cleaning lady. "Oh, I don't know." She glanced at the selection of cereals on the table. "Just…"

Sharon came through, wiping her hands on a towel. She cocked an eyebrow at Stevie. "You think she's doing drugs again."

Stevie was surprised. "How do you know about that?"

"It was the way you moved from Ben Johnson to Merritt. I'm putting two and two together."

"You do snoop!"

"People tell me things, like they do with their hairdressers. I wish they wouldn't. I got out of social work so I wouldn't have to hear about people's problems."

"So is she?"

"Doing drugs? I haven't a clue."

"You won't say, in other words."

"Something like that." Sharon turned away and ran a finger over the top of the sideboard. "Has your mother ever worked her magic on her?"

"Magic?"

"Well, she helped *me*."

"No offense, but your problem just needed a practical solution. And that's what PKT does."

"PK what?"

"Primal Katie Therapy. You know—you go in, you tell your tale of woe, and she goes: 'you think you've got problems?' and then she gives you an embellished version of her last client's predicament."

"Now, Stevie, how would you know that?"

"Okay," Stevie laughed. "I'm making it up. But for all her diplomas and letters after her name, and after retailing every therapy under the sun, her treatment boils down to this: go to school, get a job, fall in love, get married, have a baby, play nice, finish your soup—"

Some of which had been winging her own way lately. Her mother's expectations for her had always been high. Leaving a marriage seemed like a failure.

Sharon was regarding her inquisitively. "And her therapy wouldn't work on Merritt?"

"You're a social worker. You know it wouldn't. Or maybe you don't know how bad it was—Michael having to yank her out of New York and get her into treatment."

"Actually, I didn't know it was that bad."

Stevie reached for a cereal bowl. "Merritt lived here for a few years after her and Michael's parents died in that accident. She was more than a handful. "

"Odd her living here."

"It was the arrangement her parents made with mine." Stevie shrugged. "You know—if we're ever in an accident, you take the kids, blah, blah, blah. Who knew it would actually happen?"

"But they have an aunt and uncle in town."

"Somehow, I don't think the childless and immaculate Bunny Kingdon would have wanted a grubby teenager around. It's not like she challenged the custodial arrangement. Besides, the two sisters—Bunny and Merritt's mother—had some sort of estrangement, even though their husbands worked together. Anyway, I was away studying in the States when Merritt lived here. So a kind of mother-daughter relationship grew up between them, I guess. Hey—maybe that's why Merritt is so screwed up."

"Stevie...!"

"Kidding. Ma's just my old sparring partner." She smiled at Sharon. "Okay, I give her credit. Kathleen's pretty good in the mothering department. In her psychologizing way, of course. And Merritt's mother must have recognized this. Still..." She paused. "I'm not sure my mother absorbed that one fundamental tenet of dealing with teenagers—if you nag them long enough, they'll do just the opposite." Stevie gazed out the window and thought with misgiving how true that was in her case. "Anyway—"

"Are you finished with that cup?"

"Oh, I guess."

Sharon took the cup and turned to the kitchen. "By the way, speaking of Michael, he's given me notice. Well, notice of sorts."

Stevie sat upright. "But...why?"

"He really didn't say. You know Michael. He's sort of—"

"Self-contained? Private? Still waters run deep?" Stevie could feel a flush of colour rising, as it often did lately when she thought about Michael.

She gathered the collar of her bathrobe around her neck and rose from the table.

"But he must have given some idea," she insisted, stepping to the kitchen. She watched Sharon scrubbing at some encrustation on the stove. "It can't have been your work—"

"No, it wasn't my work."

"Then…?"

"He said he expected to be moving. Around the end of the year." Sharon shrugged. "It doesn't matter. I've got a waiting list of people who want me, actually."

"Moving? But where?"

"Didn't say."

"You could still clean in any new house."

"My sense was that he might be leaving Winnipeg."

"Really?" Stevie gnawed at the side of her finger. "Odd. On the phone the other day, he said he wanted to talk to me about something, or tell me something." She groaned inside, thinking of the bombshell she had kept from him for a dozen years and planned to keep forever. "I thought maybe he was going to tell me I was hopeless as a photographer," she said instead. "And that I should quit his course."

"Your photos look fine to me."

Stevie glanced at her sharply.

"Well, I do notice some things, you know."

• • •

Stevie poured Rice Krispies and milk into a bowl her mother had left out on the table. She folded the *Citizen* to the Diversions page, thinking fleetingly of her friend Leo's remark that the whole newspaper might as well be called Diversions, and cast her eyes over the People column. Names in bold type beckoned—Joan Collins, Linda Evans, Larry Hagman, Princess Diana—but the gossip proved unalluring, the type greyed and blurred. Thoughts of Michael banished even the provocative envelope so near her elbow.

What was Michael Rossiter doing?

Not for the first time she wondered what was going on in his head.

She thought back to the barbecue in Michael's yard four months earlier. She hadn't even wanted to attend. But she had run into Michael at McNally's bookstore in Osborne Village a few days earlier that warm middle of May, the harbinger of what would turn into a long hot summer—she, home from Toronto, in the process of divorcing her husband, staying with her parents while she pondered her future—and had found herself as dazed as a deer in headlamps in his presence. It had been twelve years since she saw him last.

The brave faces of their airport parting seared her memory. So, too, did the letter she wrote him from Baltimore. But he seemed to bear no ill will. She could find no excuse for not attending his party. Then, at the barbecue, feeling awkward among Michael's friends, some of them from the Winnipeg Symphony Orchestra, others fellow photographers, virtually everyone a stranger, she had overimbibed white wine and turned into—she kicked herself the next morning—a gibbering idiot.

None of the musicians scattered about Michael's lawn that evening had talked about music. Only the photographers talked about photography. She realized—and Michael later confirmed—that the orchestra members, being roughly equal in talent and ability and part of a collective that in most cases blunted any attempt at personal expression, made their hobbies their passions, almost aggressively so. Stevie dipped in and out of fierce conversations about gardening, cottage renovation, vintage motorcycles, and then learned that Michael gave lessons—no, *tutorials*, more one-on-one—in photography. She'd been surprised. She remembered Michael's bullying father, at the time owner and publisher of the *Citizen*, insisting his teenaged son spend summers in the early 70s working at the family business, as copy boy, as junior reporter, as apprentice photographer, and Michael hating it, working under sufferance, fretting to get back to his music. And now here he was *teaching* photography.

She had been in a little conversational knot, she recalled, wine glass in one hand, a chicken wing in the other, the air redolent of lilacs and barbecue smoke. Michael had been talking about some of his photographs on display at the Floating Gallery downtown. There had been another woman with them, Caitlin Somebodyorother, a bland blonde beauty, looking rather too ardently at Michael (she'd thought), and a man, a trombonist with the WSO, who had thick, fine, waist-length black hair so beautifully tended that Stevie, in her giddy state, had wondered if coiffure-cultivating wasn't his avocation. Gaping, she'd almost missed Michael's comment that he was thinking of stopping giving photography tutorials.

"Oh, no!" Stevie had squealed. She remembered it as a squeal. It certainly sounded like a squeal to her ears—girlish, high-pitched. She stared at her Rice Krispies, now a beige soup, and squirmed with mortification at the memory. "Oh, you mustn't!" She could hear herself again. "I'd love to take your course!"

Michael had regarded her with a half-smile and half-raised eyebrows. The sun beginning its descent through the trees had burnished his crop of unruly blonde hair, an aureole pierced by a ridiculous cowlick, which his passing hand had unwittingly tweezed.

"Sure," he had said with a low laugh that broke the embarrassed silence her sudden zeal had caused. "If that's what you want."

It was not what she'd wanted. Not what she'd *intended* at any rate. She knew her way around a camera. As an interior designer, Stevie used her Nikon occasionally as an *aide-mémoire* when she was space-planning, but she had never thought of her camera as anything other than a minor work tool and a vacation companion. Certainly she had never entertained the idea of a camera being anything more for her. But she could hardly have told Michael all that, could hardly have expressed a changed mind in front of him without compounding her embarrassment.

As it happened, she had brought her camera with her from Toronto to Winnipeg. And her elder brother, Robert, like her father a plastic surgeon, but long gone to the glitter that was a medical practice in the U.S., had built, then abandoned, a darkroom in the Lord basement years before during a brief teenage camera craze.

Convenient.

Well, she was at loose ends. And being near Michael again, slipping back into his life, had an irresistible allure. *God, what have I done?* she had asked herself when the buzz from the wine had worn off and Michael had started the fireworks, a quaint reminder of their childhood days when such displays attended Victoria Day, not Canada Day. Would this be happening if I'd told him what I'd done all those years ago? At McNally's he wouldn't have cheerfully invited me to anything.

Stevie lifted her head from her soggy cereal and looked through the window, down the lawn where two inky crows, like portents in a literary novel, scuffled over some scrap of food. Past the trees with their autumn tint, the Assiniboine River dappled in the morning sun. She was enjoying the photography. The assignments, the darkroom tasks, had given some shape to her days—at least they had until Michael had gone off to Europe for the summer. But now, she thought with a little fillip of joy, this evening, the tutorials, the proximity, would resume. Unless...

Why the hell was he letting Sharon go?

"Are you going to finish that?" The very person was at her elbow, jolting her from her reverie.

"No." Stevie looked down at the bowl and felt her stomach turn. "I think a piece of dry toast is about all I can stand." She rose from the table.

"There's still some banana bread left in the fridge." Sharon lifted the envelope. "I think this is addressed to you."

"I know."

"Feels funny."

"I *know*."

Sharon flicked her a glance. "Aren't you going to open it?"

Stevie stared at envelope and sighed. "I'd better get it over with, I guess." She took her unused knife and ran it under the envelope's sealed flap while Sharon loaded the tray with the remains of the morning meal. A faintly malodorous puff of air escaped through the slash and pricked Stevie's nostrils. She recoiled, her memory groping to label the familiar smell. *What was it?* The answer eluded her. She hesitated, considered putting the envelope down the garburator.

Was this a trick?

Cautiously, she pushed her thumb and forefinger into the envelope and caught the edge of the contents, two sheets of thick paper. The edges felt peculiar, crusty. As she pulled the papers from the envelope a fine grey dust followed, trickling in a thin stream to the carpet. She heard Sharon cluck.

She couldn't read either page at first. The lettering on each—gothic and official-looking—was largely obscured by splotches and speckles, grey, black, white, irregular and grainy, like paint thrown against a canvas in some abstract expressionist work.

And then it registered. The source of the peculiar odour.

"How did he get this! How did he get his hands on this!" Her hands shook as she threw one of the papers against the tablecloth. "That bastard! That miserable bastard! This one is supposed to come to me directly from the court!"

"What is it?" Sharon abandoned her task and bent down to pick up the papers, both of which had fallen to the carpet.

"My divorce certificate and our marriage certificate!"

"But what's on them?"

"What's on them?" Stevie repeated. "What's on them? I'll tell you what's on them! It's *bird*shit! They're both covered with *birdshit*!"

"Oooh." Sharon let them fall back to the floor.

"He's put them in Charlie's cage. That's what he's done. He's lined the parrot cage with them! He knows how much I loathed that disgusting bird." Stevie thrust at the air with the knife she was still holding in her other hand. It gleamed in a shaft of light. "I'll kill him. If I ever see him again, I'll kill him!"

Sharon turned away. Stevie heard a suppressed snort.

"Are you laughing? Do you find this funny?"

Sharon snorted again, more loudly this time, and turned to face Stevie, her hand covering her mouth. She nodded. Her eyes were beginning to water.

"This is not funny!"

Sharon's laughter broke through her hand. "Sure it is! It's a riot!" she spluttered after a moment, trying to control her mirth. "But don't you see, Stevie?" She gasped for air. "You're divorced. You've got what you wanted. This doesn't matter." She gestured toward the defaced document. "You're divorced now. You're...a divorcée!"

Stevie was silent a while, watching dubiously as Sharon removed a tissue from her sleeve and dabbed along her eyes. "Yes, I am, aren't I," she said at last. It was an affirmation, not a question. Her breathing grew more shallow, calmer. "I'm divorced." She repeated the words under her breath like a mantra.

"So...?" Sharon cocked her head.

Somewhere, near the pit of her stomach, a feeling of well-being, such as she hadn't felt in a long time, surged and spread through Stevie's limbs, supplanting the anger. It swirled up through her chest and face, rising to the very roots of her hair. She could sense a smile pushing at the contours of her lips.

"There. See, Stevie? It's over. La, la, how the life goes on."

"Yes, it does, doesn't it?" Michael's angelic face suddenly shimmered before her. "Yes!" She grabbed Sharon's forearms and together they twirled around the dining room table cheering and stomping. Stevie's bathrobe opened and flew around her like a dervish's skirt.

"I'm free! I'm free!"

"You're free! You're free!"

They broke apart, laughing.

"I'd still like to know how Sangster got his mitts on my divorce certificate, though." Stevie paused, catching her breath.

"Bureaucrats, probably. You've never met such boneheads. Believe me, I know. They probably mailed it to your old address."

"Or something."

"Or something."

2

The End

Kathleen Lord took the salad bowl from Stevie's hand, but kept her eyes fixed on her husband across the table. Max, however, was concentrated on stirring the salad dressing. The salad dressing did not need stirring.

"Well, anyway," she said, her bosom heaving with a sigh, "it's a sad day. That's all I can say. A sad day."

"No, Mom, it's a happy day."

"There's never been a divorce in this family."

"What? Half my cousins are divorced. Or on their way to divorce. Or should be divorced if they had any brains."

"I mean *this* family, Stevie. Your brothers and their wives. Your father and I. My parents. Your father's parents. My sisters—"

"What did you want me to do? Stay married to maintain some unbroken string of domestic bliss? Get into the *Guinness Book of World Records*?"

Kathleen attacked the undressed lettuce leaves on her plate and said nothing, her mouth being otherwise occupied. Stevie glanced out the window at the evening shadows stealing across the lawn. She had spent the day in a kind of euphoria, craving activity as an expression of her new-found bliss, her hangover vanished. She had gone for a run around Assiniboine Park. She had raked the leaves on the front lawn—a first—confounding her father, who thought GreenCare came on Thursdays. And without being prompted, as she had through much of the summer, she had prepared dinner—well, most of it—choosing as a celebratory dish her screw-the-diet favourite, veal piccatta with noodles alfredo. For dessert, she popped out to Baked Expectations and bought cheesecake. She had set the table with the good china and the fine silverware and filled a vase with the last of the mums from the garden.

"What's the occasion?" her father had asked, stepping into the kitchen as she was flouring the veal.

"You'll see."

She had stuffed Sangster's envelope with its contents into the silver drawer in the sideboard to be removed at an opportune moment. That moment came after the veal and before the salad, by which time her mother could no longer sustain a disinterested composure. Stevie made her announcement. Her parents evinced little enchantment. She didn't really care. She was celebrating for herself. She removed the envelope from the drawer. Through the last year of her marriage she had spared her parents the finer details of Sangster's belligerence, the crude suggestions scribbled on notes, the late-night phone calls, the unscheduled appearances at her office. Now that the divorce was final, now that no spiteful last-minute delay could be negotiated, she would give Kathleen and Max a tiny insight into the manners of David Sangster, Toronto developer and businessman. Her parents reacted, in the first instance, much as Sharon Bean had that morning—with perplexity.

"What your charming former son-in-law has done, beloved parents, is line his parrot cage with our marriage certificate and my divorce certificate, which he somehow obtained before I did. Want a closer look, Mom?"

Her mother, who had lifted for closer examination the glasses on a gold chain around her neck, merely wrinkled her nose and waved the offending document away.

"I'm disgusted." Her father frowned. "I didn't think he could be so petty."

"Perhaps he's just very disappointed. Lashing out." Kathleen inspected her salad fork.

"Oh, Mother, really!"

"He sounded so sincere that time he phoned here," Kathleen pressed on. "He was practically crying, you know."

"Yes, you've said. And if you say it again, I'm going to rip my head off and put it on this plate."

"I merely mention it."

"Daddy!"

Max rolled his eyes. "Kate, it's all over. Let's not go on about him, shall we? At least not for the rest of this meal."

And so her mother had managed silence for the time it took to pass the salad around the table. When she spoke, it was to sidle into a topic of related contention. They might have talked about the latest Scorsese film, or Carol Shields's novel, *Swann*, which they were both reading in paperback, or what her mother was going to wear to Saturday's opening of Galleries Portáge, the new downtown mall. They did not.

"So, then," she addressed Stevie, putting down her salad fork and reaching for her water glass, "what are you going to do?"

"In what sense?"

"Well, are you going back to Toronto?" Kathleen sipped the water. The ice tinkled.

"I don't know."

Yabu Pushelberg, the design firm she worked for, had generously given her a leave of absence while she sorted out her life. But she realized that after nine years in Toronto she had many colleagues but no true friends. The people she and David saw socially were usually his clients, sometimes hers. They had lived on a lovely street in the Beaches, at her insistence. (She resisted his entreaties to build a new, modern, monster home in some Christforsaken development he had a financial investment in.) But though the Beaches, with its cute stores and lakefront boardwalk, had the charming appearance of a community, it felt *faux* at times. Her neighbours retreated behind the doors of their character homes. She never did see a welcome wagon.

"We're happy to have you here as long as you like, honey," Max interjected, pushing his salad plate to one side.

"Thank you, Daddy." She smiled at him, then turned her head to the other end of the table. "Mother?"

"Well, of course, dear. We love having you. I just wondered, that's all. You're paying for that apartment in Toronto. All that money…"

"I know." It was she who'd moved out of the house when the marriage fell apart, not David, who suddenly became possessive about a house he'd disdained. "At least the lease is month-to-month. I'll have to decide soon, I guess. The landlord needs a month's notice and it's practically the end of this month, so…"

"And your work?"

Stevie sighed. "Almost seems like another life." She rose to collect the salad plates.

"And waste your talent?"

"I've said before—the work's really fallen off in the last year, since Black Monday hit the stock market. There are entire buildings in Toronto that have stopped construction midway. YP was *happy* to give me the leave of absence."

"You could work here, then."

"This is Winnipeg!" She opened the fridge and pulled out the cheesecake. "Hardly the centre of the universe, design-wise or otherwise."

"Has Will come up with anything?"

"Vancouver's had the same downturn." Stevie switched on the coffee maker, which she had filled earlier. She reflected on conversations she'd had with her architect brother when he visited in the summer and that she'd continued to have on the phone. Sometimes she wondered if the world was cruising toward a new Depression.

"How about residential work?"

"Ugh," Stevie said.

"You probably think this place is hideous."

"I think no such thing!" Stevie re-entered the dining room and placed the cake on the table. "This is my childhood home. It's comfortable. It's what a home should be, personal, idiosyncratic, lived-in. Not one of those sterile showcases they feature in that stack of *Western Living* magazines you've got in the living room. And anyway," Stevie continued with growing exasperation, "as you know, I'm more interested in planning commercial space, not residential."

"Then...?"

Stevie turned to the sideboard for the dessert plates. "If it means anything, I'm going to have a conversation with Nan Hughes later this week about local opportunities."

"I've hardly seen her since Kerr died and she moved into that condo," Kathleen remarked. "Is she still teaching interior design?"

"Half time." Stevie glanced at her watch and made a decision.

"Look," she said, turning back, "would you two mind if I skip dessert?"

"You don't want some of this wonderful dessert you made?"

"Ma, I *bought* this wonderful dessert. I have an appointment at Michael's."

"Back to this photography business?"

"Of course."

"I see."

"Mother, we're just friends."

"Did I say anything?"

"You don't have to."

Kathleen tugged at her earlobe and extracted one of her earrings. "And what about Leo?"

"I might see him later in the week."

"That's not what I meant, Stevie."

. . .

Autumn in the east produced leaves of such blazing and lingering red that an entire tourist industry had grown around viewing them. On the prairies, leaves turned yellow and brown and curled and died with such speed that trees could be bare and black in two weeks. No one paid to view this phenomenon, Stevie thought, standing on the stoop, fiddling with the clasp on her camera bag, though maybe advertising and promotion would pull the punters in. Gold Leaf Tours?

She briefly considered going back in the house and borrowing the keys to the Saab—the evening had turned cooler than she'd expected. But Michael's house was barely a five-minute drive away, and she didn't want to arrive early and appear too eager. Besides, cool or not, it was still lovely weather. Enjoy. It could snow at Hallowe'en. Would she still be in Winnipeg at Hallowe'en?

Ooh. Ugh. A Winnipeg winter. Perish the thought.

She reached into her camera bag and rooted around a number of canisters with black-and-white film ready to be developed at Michael's. The Nikon itself had black-and-white film with a couple of shots left. What the hell. The light was getting low, but she might as well use up the film, even if it wouldn't do justice to the autumnal colours. She took off the lens cap and stared through the lens at the slanted shafts of sunlight, hazy with dust, and the tree tops so golden the scene was almost hallucinatory. Aiming the camera westward down Wellington Crescent, she chose as her first subject the old mansion that stood between her parents' more modest home and Merritt's—a mini-mock-Georgian pile, of creamy brick with leaded windows that had been the residence of the Oblate fathers for as long as she could remember. Its chimney climbed into a sky streaked with cirrus clouds of coral and red. She framed the picture with the overhanging bow of a nearby elm and pressed the release. So close to her ear, the click of the shutter seemed almost to shatter the evening stillness. Without lowering the camera, she opened the lens one f-stop and clicked again. This time she captured a solitary jogger in black shorts, a knapsack, and a horizontally striped T-shirt who had moved into the frame, his busy limbs, she thought, a fine counterbalance to the ponderous verticals of the mansion and the trees. He would give the picture scale. Besides, he had a nice butt. She clicked a third time, but the film had come to its end. She rewound it and slipped the canister into her pocket.

It was 7:45 when Stevie turned off the Crescent and walked past Kelvin High. Darkness was closing in and the mercury street lamps began to flicker, hesitating before casting their sickly blue-white light over the cars and shrubs, and illuminating the white bands of chemical around each tree trunk, a less-than-successful act to cure the disease that was slowly killing the magnificent elms throughout the city. The air was cooling more rapidly than she had anticipated—hell, was that a rumble of thunder in the distance?—and she began to feel a chill seeping through her thin top. Perhaps she should have borrowed the car.

Oh, well, Michael can drive me home. If to home I must go.

Or maybe Leo.

What about Leo? Her mother's unwelcome question intruded. Guilt niggled at Stevie's consciousness. Well, what *about* Leo?

She had been introduced to Leo Fabian at Michael's barbecue. His arrival caused a stir for a reason she didn't quite understand. But she didn't much care. At the party, she had eyes—and ears—only for Michael. But about a week later Leo called her at home. She was so taken by surprise she couldn't find an excuse to say no to him. Picking up the phone in her parents' home to be asked out on a…on a *date,* for heaven's sake, made her feel like she was fifteen again. Her mind had raced over the faces at the party. Two *Citizen* reporters had been among Michael's guests—three, if you counted Merritt. She vaguely recalled Leo's contours—tall, solidly built, black-haired, dark-eyed. But it was his hands that stood out in her memory. It wasn't that he tended to chop the air as he talked—he did—it was that his right hand was wrapped in a bandage, apparently the result of some altercation. That had given her pause. Leo then said Michael had given him her number. "Oh," she'd responded, hurt, suddenly angry. *Michael* had given him her number. She said yes to Leo in that instant. They went to see *Bull Durham,* a decent enough date movie. Michael flew to Europe for the summer with no warning. She went out with Leo again. And so, as one hot languid day passed into another she seemed to slip into a sort of relationship with him. Really, just a friendship. She liked him. He was likeable. He was sure trying hard to impress. But…

She put the treacherous thought out of her mind and turned into Dorchester Square with its cluster of tiny shops, most of which served the leisure interests of the district's well-heeled professionals. There was a candle shop, a book store, a florist, a grocer that specialized in the gourmet fare and, lately, a new restaurant on the corner that had replaced a shabby pizza parlour, a relic of a bygone era. It had a village atmosphere in the daytime but on a Tuesday evening few people were about—only the restaurant appeared to be open for business.

Behind the shops on the east side of the street and across a lane Michael occupied what had once been the gatehouse of an estate built at the turn of the twentieth century by a grain merchant of some means. Some decades later, after the property had been subdivided, the house had been renovated and enlarged. The second storey Michael had turned into a photo studio. Stevie passed through the arched stone front gate, a legacy of its original owner. The path forked: one part curved east toward the original mansion, which had remained in spite of the subdivision of the property; the other led west to Michael's house. The heat of the past several days had given second life to the vegetation along the path, the loamy perfume mixing with the acrid aroma of burning stubble that wafted into the city from outlying farmers' fields. Stevie drew in a long breath. She was reminded of her student days when she would ride out to the university with her car pool, looping by one set of fields that had yet to give itself up to suburban development. Every September smoke from the burning stubble would drift in clouds across the highway, plunging cars into sudden twilight, obscuring vision and sending unlucky drivers into cursing fits. Stevie had found the eeriness strangely attractive. The smoke seemed an alien force blotting out the sun, a prelude to some unnatural occurrence.

And then one year something grotesque did happen: the first morning the burning fields sent hundreds of rabbits into panicked flight, hurtling across the road into oncoming traffic. Their flattened, bloody carcasses greased the highway for miles. Stevie had been repelled by the gore yet fascinated by the desperation that drove the creatures to their deaths. She shivered as much in the memory as in the cooling wind pushing through the trees that divided Michael's house from the neighbouring residence.

No light shone from the front windows. Momentarily disconcerted that Michael might have thought she wasn't coming and had left the house, Stevie made her way around the path to the back, to the rear door that opened into the kitchen. Light poured from the windows into a series of oblongs marshalled along the lawn's darkness. She climbed the short set of steps, pressed the doorbell and heard a muffled chime deep in the interior of the house. She noted from a crack of light that the inside door was not shut properly. A drowsy insect buzzed fitfully at her feet and she flicked it gently off the stoop with her toe, then focussed one eye on the thin bright vertical and waited for Michael's shadow to fill it. A portion of a chrome shelf unit dazzled, and Stevie could see the remains of food preparation on a counter. She pressed the doorbell a second time. Odd, she thought, if he had gone out surely he would have locked up and left a note on the door.

Puzzled, Stevie opened the screen door, pushed through the inside door, and stepped into the kitchen. "Michael, are you there?" she called. "Michael?" He could be upstairs in the darkroom, but the house wasn't a bunker. Sound penetrated. She had been in there developing photographs herself and heard the doorbell ring.

"Michael, oh Mikey, where are you?"

Stevie placed the camera on the counter then stopped near the open door leading into the dining room and listened intently. "Mikey, darling, love of my youth, where are you?" she said under her breath. It was then, as she peered into semi-darkness, that she felt a tiny stab of anxiety. The unlocked door, the protracted silence, something in the air, some odd indiscernible odour. Her breath began to quicken. She gripped the doorframe, frozen in indecision, unsure whether to leave or to battle her apprehension.

Then, suddenly, a light switched on somewhere in the living room beyond. Stevie skipped through the dining room with grateful relief. "Michael?" she said, bursting into the room, her spirits braced by the warm illumination of a single lamp on a piecrust table in one corner of the room. A mantle clock began to chime the hour. 8:00. Stevie glanced at its antique face and then looked up over the fireplace into a mirror that reflected the length of the room. Only her own surprised face looked back.

The last chime dissolved into silence. Stevie looked around her. Surely Michael turned the light on, she reasoned with herself. He must be playing a joke on me. He's hiding somewhere. But he's not like that; he wouldn't do that; he's not that kind of person. She called out again: "Michael!" Her voice cracked. She made herself move forward. "Oh, this is crazy," she muttered to herself, grasping one of the drapes and pulling it aside, prepared to be frightened. And then, at her feet, she saw it—a box with a cord leading to the lamp. The light was timed to come on at 8:00.

At the end of the room, from a partially opened sliding door leading to Michael's study, she noted a trickle of light seeping out onto the carpet. Some presentiment urged her forward.

"Michael?"

She hesitated by the door. Inside, in the blackness, she could see the glow of a computer screen, the cursor pulsating in an upper corner. A tiny whine came from a fan cooling the guts of the machine. Gently she pushed the panels apart, allowing the light from the living room to pour over the shelves of books, filing cabinets, plants and desk, much of it in puzzling disarray. Hadn't Sharon tidied this room?

And then she saw him.

She knew without even thinking that he was dead. His head lay in a puddle of blood on the carpet, his body twisted as if in the posture of some fitful sleep. She was suddenly aware of her racing heart, the coursing blood roaring past her ears, the ice in the air and the smell—it hadn't been imagined—of death. She grasped something cold and metallic on a table and closed her eyes against the vision, but it remained, intensified, imprinted on her retina as if in a photographic negative: a ghostly white figure crumpled on a blood red background. The image then began to dissolve into tiny dots, bubbling and fizzing, and she could feel herself about to lose consciousness. I can't pass out, she thought. I have to get to a telephone.

She willed herself to open her eyes and again confront the horror. A sob clutched at her throat. Her stomach heaved. She turned and stumbled back to the kitchen, back to the white bright kitchen and the white pristine telephone that would reconnect her to the real world. But the voice on the other end was remote, briskly asking her to repeat the address, calmly telling her to remain at the house, coolly assuring her that the police would be there very soon.

"Thank you," she said, as the police operator hung up. Her voice sounded to her ear surprisingly emotionless. With a trembling finger she punched in one more number. She spoke quickly.

"Leo, I'm at Michael's. Could you please come and get me? Now? Please?"

And then she sank to the floor.

3

Seventh Wheel

MEGO. My Eyes Glaze Over. They were the words some sour subeditor had scrawled on the very first thing Liz had written for the *Citizen* eight years ago.

She had learned quickly.

MEGO.

Bunny Kingdon was prattling on about something. Liz had lost the thread, but imaginary toothpicks supported the lids of her glazed eyes. She watched the curled ends of Bunny's girlish pageboy swing into her face as she surveyed the dinner table seeking, it appeared, some sort of agreement. She thought she heard the word "money."

Bunny has money, she thought. Bunny is a money bunny.

I've had too much to drink.

Bunny must be talking about the book she's writing. Excuse me, compiling. *Taste of Winnipeg*—a fundraiser for the orchestra. Imagine! Thinking that selling a bloody silly book of recipes from River Heights and Tuxedo matrons was ever going to put the perennially cash-strapped symphony into the black. How often did these women cook anyway? Bunny, for Christ's sake, just write the symphony a fucking cheque, you rich bitch. You money bunny.

Oops, did I say that aloud? Liz peeled her eyes off Bunny. Her eyes swam around the candle-lit table. No mouths gaped open in shock.

Thank god.

Wouldn't want to embarrass Spencer. Oh, no. Ever since the always miserable-showing Liberals had managed by some miracle to gain the balance of power in a minority Conservative government in the spring election and—hallelujah, praise the Lord—seemed poised for a revival, Spencer, the backroom boy, had decided the time was ripe for him to run for the Legislature under the Liberal banner. The opportunist. She had learned that at cocktails. Thanks for consulting me, hon. Thanks for talking about it with your wife first, sweetie pie, lover man. Just what I always wanted—to be a political spouse. Oh, yeah. My idea of fun.

She gazed through the candle's halo toward her husband, who was seated kittycorner to her, flapping his gums about something. God, look at him—he's getting so jowly. He was so lean and dark when I married him fifteen years ago. Very yummy. Now he's starting to look like some twentieth-century version of one of those prosperous burghers in a Rembrandt painting. So confident, so vigorous. So full of his own bullshit.

He caught her eye, then frowned.

Spencey's going to yell at me in the car. I'm a naughty wife. I'm a naughty wife.

I *am* a naughty wife. A very naughty wife. I'm seated at a tastefully appointed Crescentwood dinner table across from my husband.

And my lover.

Isn't it wild?

How did this happen?

How *did* it happen? Oh, right. Bunny called. Something about an informal little dinner thing before the symphony season started. Spencer Elliott was board president. Bunny was on the board. Yadda yadda. She never thought for a moment—or maybe she was only half paying attention when Bunny called—that the other guests would include the symphony's conductor and music director, Paul Richter, and his wife Else. Well, didn't she just about wet herself when she saw Paul coming up the walk, Else following with an enormous bouquet of orchids. She herself had brought nothing. Yes, I'd love another vodka, she'd said to Martin, her host, her boss at the paper, the man who had hired her to be an arts reporter. He hadn't asked.

Liz detected a nudge at her left side. A voice intoned: "More wine?"

Piss off, you oily little bugger.

She glanced at Guy out of the corner of her eye. No, she hadn't said that out loud either. Although she wished she had. And some day she would.

"Sure," she replied, groping for her glass.

"I'll get that." Guy lifted the bottle of Bordeaux. She watched his bony hand pour the liquid to the top of her glass and set it down carefully. She wouldn't be able to lift it without some wine dribbling down the side. The little shit. He did it deliberately. It wasn't his business to pour the wine in any case. He wasn't the host, he was a guest. What was he *doing* here, anyway? This was supposed to be a symphony-related do.

Odd to have seven people at a dinner party. Usually they're so couple-y. She leaned toward Guy and whispered, "Why didn't you bring Merritt?"

Guy ignored her. He was paying attention to whatever Spencer was saying. *Maybe I just thought I said that. Oh, well.*

She reached for her glass. It dribbled.

Oops. She looked around the table and stifled a giggle. No one noticed. All eyes were on Spencer. She was sure she heard the word "Jews."

Oh, no. They're talking about money and Jews in practically the same breath. I can't believe it. It's 1988, for the love of god. Not 1932.

"Spencer!" she interjected.

Her husband gave her a furious frown. "We're talking about the Kushniryk case, Liz. Are you feeling all right?"

Liz suddenly felt every eye on her. "Never better," she replied. "Go on. Sorry I interrupted. I was just...never mind."

She couldn't bear to hear about it. Spencer's firm had been retained to defend some man accused of murdering five hundred Jews in Poland or Latvia or some such place in the Second World War. A test of new legislation permitting trials in Canada of atrocities committed elsewhere. And naturally Spencer's firm took on this mighty task. How high-minded of them. Of course, Spencer wasn't personally involved. Oh, no. He wouldn't want the taint of defending some Nazi to follow him into government.

Well, let the Polish guy have it, I say. Hang him high! Then dig him up and hang him again!

Her grandfather used to say that about Louis Riel.

Liz giggled aloud.

I really have had too much to drink! I don't think like this! I'm starting to sound like an American! See, this is what will happen if evil Mulroney shoves Free Trade down our throats!

She noted everyone staring at her. She felt a slight pain in her chest. She hadn't really giggled. She had burped.

"Excuse me."

"Elizabeth," Spencer droned, as if talking to a child. "I think Bunny might like to clear. We've all been finished for some time."

"Oh!" Liz stared at her plate. She'd hardly touched a thing. "Oh, Bunny, I'm sorry. My mind...this beef is lovely. Really, it is. It's just that—"

"Have a few more bites." Bunny rose from her chair. Her tone was soothing. But Liz detected the steely charm of a chatelaine of a thousand dinner parties. "I'll just take these things away in the meantime."

"I'll help you." Else gave her napkin an elegant fold, rose from her place, and began collecting the men's plates.

Thank you, ladies, for making me feel guilty as hell.

Liz reached for her fork and watched Else glide out of the room. Even though she had to be sixty, she was truly something to behold. The frosty blonde hair. The bosoms of death. The assessing gaze. *Une femme formidable*, as Maîtresse Desilets used to say in French class. *La plume de ma tante est sur la bureau de mon oncle cha cha cha...*

"Don't mind me," she said breezily, as once again all eyes were on her. *Cha cha cha.*

"Shall we dance?"

Headline: *Guy Clark exhibits wit. World agog.* Liz straightened her shoulders. "Perhaps after dessert." She flashed him a high-wattage smile as phony as anything Hollywood could produce. *And there'll be no dessert for you, missy, if you don't finish your—*she looked down—*cold tenderloin of beef with creamy tarragon sauce.* She was sure she'd seen this in a *Gourmet* magazine at the hairdresser's recently. She contemplated the barely touched squash cup with the basil vegetable stuffing and the out-of-season asparagus on the side of her plate. She felt a more urgent need for a cigarette.

"Are you descended by any chance from Hans Richter—" she heard Guy say to Paul.

She looked up to see Paul's eyebrows ascend his forehead. Lovely eyebrows.

"—the nineteenth-century German conductor?"

"I know who he is." Liz enjoyed the wintry stare Paul directed at Guy. "And no, there's no relation. Hans Richter was Hungarian."

Liz cackled—in her head, she hoped, glancing around quickly. Oh, Guy, you moron. How did you ever become the Go! editor and arbiter of arts coverage in the city? Of course, silly me! You planted your thin lips on Martin's flabby posterior! You flattered him by consistently losing in golf and exhibiting such shameless ambition that Martin, no slouch at shameless ambition himself, raised you from junior copy editor to section editor in a twinkling. Oh, my. What fun it is working under a twenty-eight-year old, someone nearly a decade younger like you, whose interests are the stock market, hockey, and the ramblings of David Letterman in his nightly monologue. It's a treat. I can't wait to get up in the mornings.

Liz, take your knife in your right hand and scrape some beef onto your fork, and stick the whole thing in your mouth. There's a girl. You can do it. Oh, what the hell are they yakking about now?

"How did you know?" Paul's words were sudden and sharp enough to focus her muzzy attention.

"My sister told me," Guy replied, turning to Martin. "Caitlin went to the Curtis Institute with your nephew."

"What's the matter?" *Wassamadda? Was that slurred?*

It was Martin who replied. "Apparently Michael told Caitlin there was an opening for a violinist—"

So?

"I'd rather board members didn't interfere in personnel matters," Paul said, as if addressing an earlier concern.

"Well, *former* board member," Spencer interjected. "Or didn't you hear?"

"—and Guy's wondering if his sister might do, Liz," Martin supplied. She noted him studying her as she picked up a piece of asparagus with her fingers and waggled it in front of her face. Semi-firm, it reminded her of Spencer's less-than-enthusiastic penis these days. *So, I'm a little blitzed, Martin, oh eternal managing editor of the* Zit. *So fire me.* She bit off the head of the asparagus. She thought she saw Martin wince. *You big baby.* He even looks like a baby in the candlelight—a clever sort of baby, all bulging forehead, receding chin, and skin less lined than a man in his late fifties ought to be. But then he's had a pretty soft life as Mr. Bunny Kingdon. He was poor and he married rich. Bunny has money. Bunny's a money bunny.

"Oh, I doubt Michael's likely to interfere again." Guy reached for his wine glass.

"You seem very sure." Liz articulated slowly. She *had* been paying attention. Some attention at any rate.

"Well...Caitlin and Michael are very good friends. I'm sure he didn't intend to butt in. Besides, your husband says he's not on the board anymore." Guy flicked her a dismissive glance. She thought: I've never seen such a thin face on a man. It's like a whippet's. "By the way, maestro—"

Maestro—oh, puh-leeze!

"—Caitlin was first violinist with the Atlantic Symphony before it crumbled. She's living here for the time being. She's very good."

"And you would be a judge of such ability."

Liz suppressed a snicker. She glanced across the table at Paul, who had turned his great greying head toward her, the ghost of a smile on his lips. Of course it was she who, in their interludes together, told him tales of Guy the Obtuse. She smiled back at him. *Oh, not too brazenly.* She hoped. She had a wicked urge to wiggle her foot out of her shoe and run her toes up his leg. Too bad the table was glass. Well, they were eating in the conservatory. It was an *informal* supper, as Bunny had promised. *I wonder what it costs to heat this room in the winter?* Liz's eyes wandered over the plants to the sky nearing dark beyond the glass panes. *I want a conservatory.* How nice to have a conservatory. How nice to be rich. Really, really rich. Rich enough to heat a glass room through a Winnipeg winter. Her eyes returned to Paul. Wouldn't it be nice to be dancing with him in a candle-lit conservatory? *Cha cha cha.* Oh, yes.

Suddenly, she was aware of Guy's eyes boring right into her neck. She could feel hot blood rising to her face, unbidden. "What about the Guarneri del Gesu?" she blurted, hoping the question blended into the flow of conversation. Why did she let Clark get under her skin so?

"He's making a gift of it to the orchestra," Paul replied evenly, then smiled. "Didn't I read that in Saturday's paper?"

"The thing's worth a million bucks in Canadian money."

"Liz!" Spencer glared at her.

Oh, sorry, how vulgar to discuss the price of a violin.

Like she hadn't featured it in the first paragraph of the story she had written for last Saturday's paper. The whole city knew its worth.

"Anyway," Martin shrugged. "I doubt we shall see it this Saturday. I'm not sure he brought it with him from London. Bunny didn't mention seeing it, and she's been visiting next door a lot recently—this book project of hers."

"And Saturday's event would hardly be the place to introduce such a magnificent instrument." The compressed line of Paul's mouth drew her flickering attention. The last time Liz had teased him about the orchestra's engagement opening a new downtown mall, Galleries Portáge—they had been undressing at Paul's *pied-à-terre* off Central Park—he had snapped. Having to sell the orchestra's services like so much sausage. Being nothing more than window dressing, Muzak for the local philistines who thought the opening of a—god-help-us—*shopping mall* was a grand social occasion. Bravo! Liz had sat up on the bed and applauded, as if he had just brought the orchestra to the crashing finale of some mighty symphonic work. His eyes had blazed—green fire and blue fire—and, aroused, she couldn't help drawing him toward her.

She studied his face as he talked. The blue, blue eyes. Blue as sapphires. How surprised she had been the first time when he had removed his contact lenses and revealed one green iris paler than the blue. Like David Bowie's eyes, she remembered from photos in the 70s—unearthly, unnerving, yet strangely compelling; a tiny flaw among flawless features (well, she thought the broad forehead and the square, ample jaw flawless)—a suggestion of vulnerability. And like Bowie's, the result of having been struck in the eye with a stone when he was a boy. He turned his head to address Spencer, then glanced up toward the glass ceiling, exposing the powerful cords of his neck. She could hardly believe he was her father's age. His body was astonishingly athletic, and if he'd had a little nip and tuck around his face, who cared? *Cha cha cha!* Her eyes followed his glance. A streak of light crossed the glass pane. Then another.

"You're pretty loaded." Guy's murmur broke her reverie.

Liz turned her head unsteadily. "More keen observations like that, sonny," she said under her breath, "and someday you might be a journalist."

"Still bugs your ass that I'm Go! editor and you're not, doesn't it?"

Oh, screw it. I am loaded! "That job should have been—would have been—mine, but then I can't do the male-bonding thing the way you can."

"Really? I think you bond with males pretty well." He flicked a glance at Paul.

Liz's heart fluttered. *Oh, god, can he possibly know?* She said as evenly as she could: "What's that supposed to mean?"

"Oh, nothing." Guy reached for his dessert fork and began twisting it. "You never know, the opportunity might rise again."

"Opportunity for what?" Her eyes were again drawn to the ceiling, which now seemed to pulse with a dull light.

"To be Go! editor."

Liz shrugged and returned her eyes to Guy's profile, to the protruding lower lip. "I don't think I'd want it now."

"Oh, you want it."

"Anyway, maybe Axel will re-apply. I hear *Winnipeg Life* is fizzling. No October issue."

"Axel's return to the *Citizen* will be over my dead body."

Liz watched the fork go round and round in Guy's hand. *What is the little turd up to?* "Are you trying to tell me in your own weird way that you're getting a new job or something?"

"I'm just making conversation, Liz."

Like hell. "There'd be no point in my applying for your job, anyway. I don't know how to play golf."

"Then learn."

Guy looked past Liz. Bunny and Else stepped down into the room burdened with a cake tray and coffee pot. Conversation ceased. Bunny put the tray on the sideboard and glanced over Paul's head toward Liz's plate. But before Liz could grovel—she had barely eaten another thing—Bunny's attention was drawn to the glass panes above.

"Oh, look! Maybe we'll have rain after all."

"It's not lightning," Spencer said.

"There it is again."

"Perhaps it's a tow truck," Martin observed.

"Might be a police cruiser." Guy's fork slipped from his hand and hit the glass table top with a ping.

Bunny clucked. "I hope nothing's wrong. Now, who would like chocolate raspberry almond torte?"

"I would." Guy raised his hand.

Bunny regarded him—Liz smiled—like a bug that had hit her windscreen.

"Anyone else?"

But a silence had descended over the table. The sound of a siren had stolen everyone's attention.

4

Death of an Angel

Leo Fabian dropped the telephone receiver into its cradle and stared at it, surprised he'd heard the telephone at all above the whine of his power drill and the blare of the radio. While he had been thinking about Stevie—not an unusual occurrence—he hadn't expected to hear from her, much less get her call from Michael Rossiter's house.

Michael was back from Europe, apparently.

He wished Michael had stayed in Europe.

Stevie's voice was surprising, too. Breathless, urgent. "Could you please come and get me? Now? Please?"

Leo saluted the phone. "Yes, ma'am!"

He punched the radio's on/off button, neatly cutting off a local CBC weather report at the words "chance of showers," and reached for the car keys, which were supposed to be hanging from a hook by the back door, but weren't. He surveyed the crowded kitchen: the counter, the table, the workbench, the panels of oak he was turning into new cupboards, the patina of dust, the stack of unwashed dishes.

"Alvy," he addressed the golden retriever who was watching him expectantly. "Where are my...keys?"

The last word triggered an ecstatic tail-wagging. Alvy scampered down the back stairwell. Leo scrambled the other way, into the living room. He quickly scanned the coffee table, the side tables, the bookshelves, the couch, then, out of habit, snatched the remote and switched on the TV. The flickering light of the boob tube was supposed to deceive potential intruders into believing people were tucked cozily inside their homes. Wasn't there a crime wave in this city? Hadn't he written about it himself in the *Citizen*? You bet he had. Take some statistics, place them in a thin context under a provocative headline, and—bingo!—ya got trouble. Right here in River City. It was just a statistical anomaly whipped into hot air but here he was, almost guiltily, taking small precautions himself against possible intruders—replacing locks, buying appliance timers—things he would never have thought of doing ten years ago. Or even five years ago. Or last year, before he moved into the house on Sherwood Street with Ishbel.

Where the hell are those keys? He scanned the top of the TV, noting that *Death of an Angel*, a horrible piece of crap starring Bonnie Bedelia that he'd seen on an early date with Ishbel, was playing on SuperChannel.

No keys.

Think: He'd driven home from work, reheated some pizza, then driven to Beaver Lumber, then come home.

He'd worn his old leather bomber jacket to the store, the one emblazoned with an Italian flag, which he'd won at a raffle at the Italian pavilion at Folklorama one year. The air had seemed nippier.

The jacket was in the front closet.

Which—he groped in the jacket's right pocket, then through the hole in the pocket to the lining—is where the keys were last. Found 'em.

The drive to Michael Rossiter's, through the West End and across the river to Crescentwood, took less than ten minutes. Waiting impatiently behind a line of cars for the light to turn at the Maryland bridge, he glanced, as he often did at this stop, at the bleak brick face of the Misericordia Hospital, at the measly windows of the intensive care unit where his father had spent the last hours of his life, more than a quarter-century earlier. He could recall only big swinging doors that barred his entrance, but failed to muffle the chilling, sucking, bleeping noises within. He remembered struggling to reach the water fountains, then his mother being supported by his grim-faced aunts, reaching for him, her looming face wet, his fright.

Oh, fuck it. He banished the memory and concentrated on Stevie. His Stevie. No, *not* his Stevie. Elusive Stevie. Mysterious. Laughing, vivacious, suddenly silent, assessing him with her dark contemplative eyes. A little spoiled, Stevie. Prickly. A mouth on her, in several senses. He had hardly got past the mouth. What was he? Fourteen? Three months, they'd been dating. Well, hardly dating. A few movies, a few "dutch" cappuccinos, a lot of mutual commiseration, and a hug now and then. "Oh," she had said on the phone when he had called that first time, finally, after a week of screwing up his courage. There had been a world of shadings in that little word he couldn't fathom. "Oh." What *was* the matter? For three months, Stevie had parried. He would like to have thrust. She was a challenge. Leo was smitten. He had been smote. Was "smote" a word? He was a candidate for the Blue Balls Hall of Fame.

Leo turned off Dorchester Square and headed for the cul-de-sac south of Michael's home. As he braked his ancient Land Rover, he noted a police cruiser, its rotating red light casting into sharp shadow the overhanging trees and immense shrubs that formed a fence around the property. The light fell on one uniformed officer leaning into a rolled-down window.

Through his own open window, Leo could hear the crackle of the police radio. Dismay thudded against his stomach wall. Stevie's call had portended something even worse than his worst imaginings. He quickly jumped out of the Land Rover, Alvy at his heels, and started for the front gate but the officer, a woman, shouted at him to stop: "You can't go in there."

He took a deep breath. "I got a call from a friend of mine asking me to come and get her here," he shouted back.

The officer leaned back into the window and replaced the radio receiver, Leo moved toward the cruiser and repeated himself with less amplification: "I was asked to pick someone up here."

"Oh. It's you. You sure got here fast enough."

"Look, I'm only a reporter from nine to five." *Like I live this job.* "The meter's off right now. What's happened?"

"Dead body."

Stevie!

"A woman?"

"A male."

A wave of relief crashed over him. *Not Stevie.* Well, of course not Stevie, you idiot. Who would have done the phoning?

"Who, then?"

The officer shrugged. She looked like she was twenty-two, creaseless skin and pink ears under an almost punkish haircut, and pale blue eyes that regarded him coolly. "Did you say someone called you? From here?"

"I think so. Stevie Lord. Slim, dark, dark-haired."

"She's in the yard."

"Can I see her?"

"Of course you can't. And you should either have that dog on a leash or put him back in your vehicle."

Leo turned. Police officers and brick walls share a common feature: they can't be argued with.

"Detective Nickel should be here shortly," she added.

Leo thought he detected a hint of malicious glee in her voice. "Happy day," he responded. Speaking of brick walls. He had been arguing with said detective, his brother-in-law, wouldn't you know it, about Free Trade with the Yanks on Sunday at his mother's. Frank: for; Leo: against.

He opened the passenger side door and Alvy jumped in. Leo moved around the back to the driver's side, then hesitated. The officer was again leaning into the cruiser. Where was the other cop? Like Noah's menagerie, they usually travelled two by two. He looked at the Rossiter property. The gate was purely decorative, the remnant of a day when the grounds were fenced. Lilac bushes now defined its border. They didn't look completely impenetrable.

He ducked down behind the Land Rover, poked his head around the fender to note the officer's whereabouts—still yapping on the radio—then scuttled like Groucho across the patch of grass and pressed himself into the shrubbery. He paused. The wind was rising, leaves were rustling with a nice cinematic pitch. Leo squeezed his large frame into the lattice of branches, grateful for the leather jacket, and held his arm up to protect his face. Gingerly, he sidled through the yellowing foliage, endured the stabbing along his thighs, and after a moment, popped out on the other side. He peered into the gloom and strained his ears. No police life-forms in evidence. A glow of light to the west side of the house drew him across the front lawn. He hugged the corner of the house and peeked around the side. There, collapsed on an outdoor chaise, the inclined planes of her cheekbones and strong nose accentuated by a shaft of light pouring onto the grass from the open kitchen door, was Stevie. She appeared to be hugging herself, fallen into sleep. He moved quickly.

"Stevie," Leo whispered, crouching behind the chaise. "Are you okay?"

Her head turned toward him, her dark eyes searched his face as if pondering the profundity of his question. "No," she replied, finally, firmly. "No, I'm not."

He didn't know what to say next, dreaded what the answer might be. He wanted to embrace her—she seemed so small and subdued—but the only way to hold her would be to more or less climb on top of her. On his knees, the damp starting to work through his jeans, he felt a sudden and strange and madly inappropriate impulse to ask her to marry him. He was in the classic position. And she was unexpectedly vulnerable—for once.

"You must be cold," he said instead.

"Freezing."

"Take my jacket."

He slipped off the leather and tucked it around Stevie. She pulled its collar up to her chin, sighed a little sigh, and closed her eyes. Leo's mind returned to the scene: the darkened trees, the light blazing from the kitchen, the curious air of expectation. Two and two were rapidly making four.

"Is it Michael?"

He watched her eyelids shut tighter.

"Yes."

"But he's young. What? Thirty-three? He's my age—"

"Leo, he's been murdered."

And then she amended it. She opened her eyes and stared into Leo's. "It looks as though Michael's been murdered."

"Christ!" Leo stifled his mouth with his hand. He clung to the word "looks." It only *looked* like murder. Perhaps it was just an accident. He searched for confirmation in Stevie's eyes but she had shut them again. Leo thought wildly about intruders intercepted, a struggle, an accidental...an accidental what? Even though he had reported on murders and their aftermath, he had always felt detached. Murder wasn't something that happened to people you knew. It was something that happened to people in—how ironic—newspapers: sad, stupid, squalid affairs, usually; remote events that took place after drinking hours were over, in crumbling apartments, by people too crazed to realize what they had done.

The rising wind sent leaves twisting in the night air, briefly flashing gold in the kitchen light as they descended to the dark lawn. Leo glanced about. Where was that other cop? The house seemed as undisturbed and genteel as any Crescentwood home on a September evening. The indifferent sky above glowed indigo as the last feeble ray of autumn light withdrew into the night. A siren sounded faintly in the distance. Leo thought about Michael.

He wouldn't have met Stevie but for Michael. And he wouldn't have met Michael but for the schemes of Guy Clark, the Go! editor, under whose aegis Leo had briefly toiled through the thawing of Winnipeg's long winter. Once Leo had been a political reporter at the Legislature, a plum assignment. But he had involved himself, conspicuously, in trying to organize the editorial staff into a union. Management, unamused, responded with the sort of arbitrary measure the union had hoped to challenge, banishing him to the hinterland of the Go! section, the redoubt of much that was silly. Leo, who had won a National Newspaper Award in his first year for a series of articles on police corruption, had been reduced to rewriting wire service copy about Hollywood stars, answering questions in the Answers column about removal of warts, and producing featurettes on local eccentrics and their hobbies—pap, in other words. It dulled his skills and made him near furious with boredom. There were opportunities to write larger features in Go!—which was the only plus side—but Clark spurned every idea he put forward. He thought instead about his salary and swallowed his pride. One day in May, Clark commanded his presence and said, "I want a feature on angels."

Hell, Leo had thought, not some New Age shit. But he expressed his reservations more judiciously.

"I mean, Leo, the rich people in this town." Clark waved a sheet of paper in Leo's face. "The ones who write fat cheques on a regular basis to keep some of these fucking tax-supported arts groups from going down the toilet. I want to know how much they give, who they give it to, why they do it, and so on."

It wasn't the worst story idea Clark had ever doled out, but glancing at some of the names on the list Leo doubted his ability to execute a story. Christine Farquhar, Emerald Cuthbertson, Bill Noseworthy, St. Clair MacCharles, Stella Affleck: each he vaguely recognized as old Anglo money and old Anglo money valued discretion more than it valued the Georgian silver passed down from their great-grandmothers. Liz Elliott sympathized:

The angels story idea had been hurtling around Go! like a grenade without a pin, but everyone else had ducked. Lots of luck, she said, waving her cigarette: They won't talk.

And they didn't. Very politely, usually through some functionary, everyone on the list declined Leo's invitation for an interview.

Except Michael Rossiter. Even though there had been a long pause over the phone in which Leo presumed his hopes were to be dashed once more, he did agree to meet for a conversation. There had been a sort of pitying tone in Michael's voice that made him bristle, and when he said he would talk only for background, not for attribution—the faint-hearted appeal of politicians and civil servants—Leo bristled some more. But, growing frustrated with the hopeless story, he reluctantly agreed to the terms. *Attribution? Background?* Yup. Michael was, of course, one of those Rossiters, the family that had once owned the *Zit*, as the *Citizen* was unpopularly known. The brother of Merritt Parrish, fashion reporter for less than a year, who swanned into the newsroom whenever the notion crossed her mind, which didn't seem to be very often.

Better than nothing, Liz had shrugged. Michael was a photographer, played violin, and sat on the board of the WSO. He was a decent enough source, she said, of off-the-record information. But he would talk only if he thought he was doing some good, she had warned. He was Mr. Integrity.

And, in fact, at an Italian restaurant on Corydon where they met, Michael had not been at all pliable when it came to specifics about his philanthropic gestures—the nubbly, gossipy details that Guy Clark was demanding. He'd been more curious about Clark, pointing out, amused, that he—Clark—had failed to include on the list his aunt, the managing editor's wife, Marilyn Kingdon (Bunny to all), who was known to give generously to the arts—*allegedly*, that is. Of course, he couldn't really say; it was up to Aunt Bunny to talk, if she wanted. "Giving" wasn't necessarily about money, he'd added at one point. Time could be given as well. He was, for example, doing the food photography for a fundraising cookbook the Friends of the Symphony was producing for the Christmas market. That he could talk about; the publicity would aid sales. But flacking for some little project wasn't Leo's aim.

"Is it fair for society's well-being, whether it's the arts or health care or recreation, to depend on the whims of the rich?" Leo had asked on one point, frustrated, trying to provoke Michael. "Isn't charity a way for the status quo to sustain itself and salve its conscience at the same time?"

"It's all very unfair."

"Then why—?"

"Look, I agree people need justice, not charity, but sometimes acts of charity are all you can do." Michael had shrugged and stared into his coffee cup. "Wealth can be a prison of sorts."

Oh, fuck you sideways, Leo had wanted to say, but instead simply stared at the bent head, at the thick blonde hair swept back from the high forehead. It wasn't enough that Michael was rich and talented. He was good-looking, too.

"I know you don't believe me." Michael continued to study his coffee.

"I don't. But can I quote you?"

Michael looked up and laughed. "No."

"C'mon, man," Leo had said at last, "throw me a bone. I've got to go back to the *Zit* with *something*."

A guilty grin had spread over Michael's face. "Sorry, I guess I've been wasting your time."

"Well—"

"You'll have to turn it into a think piece."

"That's occurred to me."

"I know a professor at the University of Winnipeg who—"

"Donald Keating, in sociology? Doing a book on charity? I've already got a call in to him."

Michael fingered the rim of his coffee cup. "I could give you an epigraph—you know, an italicized quote before the body of the text. How about that? To make some amends."

"A bit precious for a newspaper."

"Ah, but not for the Go! section."

It was Leo's turn to laugh. "All right, what is it?"

"Well, it's sort of the root of my philosophy in this area." His expression grew serious. "It's what I believe. And I think the others on your list would probably agree, even if they haven't thought about it."

"What is it? Leo asked again.

"Matthew six, verses one through three."

"The Bible?"

"Look it up when you get back to the paper."

Leo had. In the *Citizen* library he'd found—remarkably—a red-covered copy of the New English Bible. He blew the dust off the top and turned the onion-skin pages to the Gospel of Matthew.

Be careful not to make a show of your religion before men; if you do, no reward awaits you in your Father's house in heaven. Thus, when you do some act of charity, do not announce it with a flourish of trumpets, as the hypocrites do in synagogue and in the streets to win admiration from men. I tell you this: they have their reward already. No, when you do some act of charity, do not let your left hand know what your right is doing; your good deed must be secret, and your Father who sees what is done in secret will reward you.

He stared glumly at the text. The left hand/right hand bit might do for an epigraph as Michael suggested, but otherwise it read more like a first-century editorial. He supposed he could set up some poor sap in a corporation's philanthropy department to argue for the "flourish of trumpets"—after all, corporations gave to get—then record his reaction when quoted back to the contrary no less an authority than Jesus Christ. But it wasn't a story. There was little to do but give Clark the bad news. He would pitch it as a think piece, quiz the usual tame academics, toss in some StatsCan statistics, and whisk the whole hummingbird's egg into a giant soufflé.

That week had already been a bad week, the least of which had been the futility of Clark's assignment. Tuesday, Ishbel had decided her career was much more vital than being with him, and, after two years together, without warning had left abruptly for Vancouver, kissing him carelessly, saying she would send for her things. He had been devastated. Wednesday, the spring rains had revealed a serious leak in his roof where he intended to install a skylight. And Alvarez, who had had an eye infection and had been fitted at the neck by the veterinarian Wednesday evening with what looked like a lampshade, was being as miserable as it was possible for a kindly retriever to be.

Thursday at 10:00, two days before the Victoria Day long weekend, he'd sat down across from Clark at the latter's desk in the front of the newsroom. He was late because he'd forgotten to set the alarm, normally the efficient Ishbel's chore. He was soaking because the Land Rover series IIA, which he'd spent *years* restoring, wouldn't start and he'd dashed from the house to the bus without an umbrella or even an old newspaper to cover his head. He felt sour. Pushing back his wet hair, he made his pitch to Clark, who flew into a tantrum. Leo had witnessed Clark's childish outbursts before; they were not infrequent. He had been on the receiving end of one or two himself, the last a few weeks earlier when Clark had blindly refused to release him from work to give blood to the Red Cross, which had called, as it occasionally did, for his A negative blood.

Later, after it was all over, Leo couldn't remember being enraged—losing it, as the saying went. A spurt of anger, perhaps, but perhaps he was fooling himself that it had been only a spurt. All he could remember was numbly watching Clark's cakehole flapping, the stream of words spinning into a kind of black noise. All he wanted, all he wanted in the world, was for the fucker to just shut the fuck up. Somehow—he couldn't remember willing it, but he could remember the sharp pain of bone against bone—his fist collided with Clark's mouth. Blood splattered onto the dummy copy of the day's Go! section spread out between them. There was a moment of ominous silence. Then Clark, howling, his hand over this mouth, tore out of his chair toward the men's toilet on the other side of the room. Feeling drained, Leo rose, and while thirty pairs of eyes watched in utter silence, retrieved his wet jacket from the dilapidated coat tree near the cartoonist's office at the back, and exited the newsroom for what he was sure would be the last time. He walked home, four miles in the pouring rain. He went straight to the liquor cabinet, poured himself a Scotch with his good hand, plunked down on the Morris chair he and Ishbel had restored together, and had a conversation with Alvy who, picking up his mood, plopped his lampshaded head on Leo's knee and stared at him morosely. His career was over; his mortgage payment was due (and without Ishbel's contribution); and he was probably facing an assault charge.

Three hours later, a bouquet of blood-red roses arrived with a card. "Our hero," the card read. "Love, the Go!-Go's." He knew Liz had to have been behind the gesture. She was the most fearless when confronting Guy. The other reporters in the Go! section—Ian Pears, Doug Whiteway, Alison Fussell, Karen Watkin, and Diane Fischer—were too committed to self-preservation. But, like flowers after a death in the family, they were little consolation.

The next day, two things of significance happened. Martin Kingdon phoned. Miracle of miracles, Leo wasn't fired. He would have a two-week suspension without pay. (*Okay. Not too eager now, Leo.*) He would be reassigned to city desk where he would take up the police beat, his starting point with the *Citizen* six years ago. (*Busted to private, but okay.*) And—this was completely non-negotiable—he would be required to apologize to Guy in front of the entire editorial staff. The gall surged in his throat. He hesitated, then saw the heavens open and his paycheques wing into the clouds. (*Yeah, all right. If I have to.*) You have to, Mr. Fabian, Martin assured him.

Then Michael Rossiter, of all people, telephoned. He had heard the news (how fast it had spread!), offered his sympathies, and invited him to his barbecue Monday. Where he'd met Stevie.

And now, four months later, Stevie was lying a kiss away on a chaise in Michael's yard. And Michael was dead.

Leo's mind returned to the scene. Michael certainly wasn't poor. Perhaps he had interrupted a robbery in progress, though the house, despite its Crescentwood location, didn't evince great wealth. He had an urgent desire to press Stevie for further details. He couldn't help it: Murder was music to the journalistic ear. Headlines danced in his head:

Rossiter Scion Dead at 33
Local Artist Found Dead
Life Ends in Fatal...

Fatal what? Stabbing, shooting, garrotting, poisoning? What had Stevie witnessed? He couldn't ask her.

A few streets away, the siren was rising to painful decibels. Just over the hedge, a set of brakes shrieked. Leo tensed. He had been at scenes of death before, but at a remove, on the other side of the yellow tape, fed on whatever thin gruel the cop shop's flack du jour cared to dole out. Now, he was here first, in advance of detectives and the whole scene-of-crime crowd, in advance of the rival *Examiner* and the other media (who took their cues from *Citizen* headlines anyway). Maybe this was a feature-writing opportunity. He'd have details they'd never have. And wouldn't Frank just crap himself when he read it in the paper and wonder how he got it?

Just a quick look, then out. No notebook, but memory would suffice.

He shouldn't really even be in the yard. Further penetrating a crime scene was courting trouble big time, but he remembered reading somewhere that Italians possessed an ancient habit of disobedience. And was he not Italian on his father's side?

Besides, on his English mother's side, there was this expression: In for a penny, in for a pound.

He whispered to Stevie: "You didn't see me."

Then he dashed up the back stairs of Michael's house.

5

Qwerty

Leo glanced at the body, then quickly glanced away. It was worse than he'd imagined. His own reaction surprised him. He darted down the hall to the bathroom.

"Leo!" A voice roared from somewhere toward the kitchen and shot up Leo's spine as he hugged the toilet. He wished he'd had something less colourful than pizza for dinner. He also wondered how Frank had arrived with such speed.

Coming into the house had been a stupid idea. He'd only wanted a quick peek. In and out. He didn't expect to be trapped by his brother-in-law.

"Leo!" The voice was closer this time. "I know you're in here. Come out so I can kick your ass."

Leo rose unsteadily, pulled a Kleenex from a box, and wiped at his mouth. He peered at a photograph near the sink that he hadn't noticed on his first visit in the spring. Lit by a nightlight, it was of some guy wearing a lampshade on his head and shaking hands with Howard Pawley outside the premier's office in the Legislature. "The Life of the Party," it was called. Well, at least Michael wasn't completely serious about everything. He stepped into the hall and gave Frank a shit-eating grin.

"I guess that cop figured I'd come in here."

"No."

"Oh, come on. I can't believe Stevie ratted me out."

"Stevie?"

"The woman on the chaise."

"It was the jacket covering her, you fuckwit. It's the only one I know with an Italian flag on it." Frank sniffed the air, then grimaced. "Don't you watch *Hill Street*? This is a crime scene."

"Hey! I haven't touched a thing."

"You've touched the toilet, you pussy." Frank stood with his hands on his hips, his jacket open. His paunch nearly covered his belt. "Get another Kleenex, wrap it around your finger, and then flush the toilet about five hundred times."

"How'd you get here so fast? I thought you only dropped by after forensics had done its job."

"They're busy. Some guy eviscerated his wife in the North End."

"Wow, two murders in one night. Winnipeg *is* the murder capital of Canada. I wonder how they'll play it on the front page—"

"Christ, I don't need this crap." Frank gripped his forehead. "I was in the middle of a perfectly good Blue Jays game. Now go flush the fucking toilet."

Leo obeyed.

"I can't believe you violated a crime scene." Frank was looking through the half-opened sliding doors. "I should arrest you."

"What would my sister say?"

"'Arrest him.' Anyway, I've got to get you out of here somehow. And there'd better not be a word about this in the paper."

"Let me stay. I know Michael. Knew him. Deputize me."

"This isn't a John Wayne movie."

"And I know Stevie who knew Michael—"

"Wait a minute. Aren't you here being an asshole for the *Citizen*?"

"No, Stevie called me. She found the body."

"You mean that woman outside is *the* Stevie? The one you've been dating or whatever?"

"How many women do you know named 'Stevie'?"

"Interesting."

"What?"

"I guess you don't watch *Murder She Wrote* either? Don't you know that the person who 'finds'"—Frank's fingers squiggled the air—"the body is sometimes the killer?"

"I think you watch too much television."

"Why aren't I seeing the back of you?"

"Come on, Frank. Give me a few minutes. Let me watch you do your stuff. Get into your head. Background. Detail. You know, for an investigative feature. Or features. This could be a series. Day by day of your investigation." "Death of an Angel," he thought, picking up on the title of that crappy movie. It fit, given Michael's philanthropic bent. "Besides, it's too late about contaminating the crime scene. You're contaminating it, too."

"They have my follicles on file."

"Oh, you've got some left?" Leo glanced at Frank's shiny pate.

"All right, I'm taking you out of here myself." He took a step forward.

Leo stepped back. "I'm bigger than you. And younger."

"I work out."

"Yeah? And what's that thing around your waist?"

"It's a little middle-aged spread. What's your excuse? You're looking pretty doughy, Fabian."

Leo looked down at his body. He had become a little sedentary. "I'm still bigger than you."

Frank sighed. "Fine. If I'm stuck, I can always use the evidence to arrest you on suspicion of murder."

"Fair enough." Leo joined his brother-in-law. "Though you'd have to come up with a motive."

"Let's see. This guy," he gestured through the door, "was a friend of Stevie's. A *male* friend of Stevie's. How about…a jealous rage?"

"Shut up."

"I believe I've hit a sore spot." Frank reached into the inside pocket of his jacket and pulled out a latex glove.

"Don't tell me you carry those things when you're off-duty?"

"I moonlight as a proctologist." Frank pushed his hand into the glove and reached around for a switch on the inside wall. "Okay, let's get a little light on the subject."

Leo joined him for a second look. The sharp and sickly colour was worse than monochrome. His stomach lurched. There was nothing make-believe about the sticky clotting blood puddled on the mint green carpet. And there was no mistaking the identity. Michael's lifeless white face was turned left in partial profile, his sandy hair matted with drying blood, his arms in a navy T-shirt splayed helplessly at his side. Leo's hand went to his mouth.

"Don't even think about hurling here," Frank growled, squatting to take a closer examination while Leo hovered over his shoulder. The source of the blood appeared to be under the right temple, although most of the right side of the head remained invisible, stuck to the matted carpet. Above, at the edge of the desk, Leo noted a darkened smear, as if Michael's head had hit the desk before falling to the carpet.

Frank carefully lifted the blond hair on the back of the scalp with the blunt edge of a penknife. Leo winced. The top and left side of the skull appeared to be depressed; there was almost a trough running from the crown down toward the ear with a series of darkened fissures radiating along its length.

"Very little external bleeding from this area, though," Frank mused, pocketing the knife and rising. "Something else must account for this blood. Autopsy will tell." He surveyed the room. "You've been here before. Be useful. Anything missing? Anything out of place? Anything look like a murder weapon?"

Leo followed his brother-in-law's eyes, grateful to look away. "Actually, I've only been here once."

"Oh, great. And you said you knew this guy."

"Well, I looked around."

"You snooped."

"I was at a party here in the spring. I was curious. Call it journalistic prerogative."

"I call it shitty manners."

Leo took a deep breath and surveyed the contents of the room. It was messy. He wasn't sure if it was very lived-in—unlike the other rooms he'd walked through, which were as tidy as his mother's—or if someone had messed it up. The centrepiece was the walnut desk, a great heavy Victorian piece that accommodated a computer, which was still on and humming away. Along each side, forming a U-shape with the desk at the base, was a table scattered with various books and papers, a printer, and a hinged plastic box for the computer disks, which was open. Among the paraphernalia strewn on the desk and tables were an art deco alarm clock, a fan, an ancient Olivetti manual typewriter, a telephone answering machine, a tape recorder, a small electronic Casio piano keyboard, clusters of pens and pencils set in souvenir mugs, a pencil sharpener in the shape of the Eiffel Tower, a plastic radio from the 1940s, a pair of glasses, a daytimer, and several plants. Bookshelves ranged over two walls while the third wall, opposite the door, was curtained. Between the desk and glass doors was a couch, a reading lamp, and a coffee table surmounted by a five-inch television.

"Well?"

"It's not like I took an inventory when I was here."

"Big help you are."

"All the usual stealable stuff is still here—TV, stereo, computer. But he's got a lot of expensive camera equipment upstairs. Maybe—"

"All in good time."

Frank grunted and began opening the desk drawers with his gloved hand. Leo could see a stack of writing paper, a box of envelopes, and an expensive-looking fountain pen in the centre drawer. Two of the three drawers on the right side of the desk held the usual office hardware, various computer instruction manuals and a stack of other manuals plus warranties for varied gadgets. Organized bugger. The last drawer was empty. Of the three drawers on the left side, two were full of sheet music in folders marked by the composer's name; the remaining drawer held only a few empty manila files. Frank shrugged and glanced over at the computer.

"Looks like an old model."

"Early, mid-eighties," Leo agreed, watching the cursor on the screen pulse and glow.

"I haven't figured out why people even need home computers. Your nieces are nagging me for one."

"Shell out, Frank. They can probably use it for school."

"That's their argument. But what would this guy be using one for?"

"An inventory of his ties, perhaps?"

"Screen's blank."

"And nothing in either disk drive." Leo glanced at the empty slots. "No hard drive on this baby."

Frank surveyed the room. "This guy must have had a few bucks. You'd think he could afford a more updated computer. What did he do for a living?"

"I don't think he had to make a living. His family once owned the *Citizen*, if that means anything to you."

Frank grunted.

Leo stepped toward the desk and glanced at the open disk container. There were two plastic dividers. On one a neatly typed label read "programs." It contained three disks. The other read "correspondence." It was empty.

Bet he wrote his letters with a fountain pen with perfect handwriting.

The open daytimer caught his eye. It was week-at-a-glance, only Thursday, September 29 on the right-hand page followed Wednesday, September 21 on the left.

"Frank," Leo gestured to the desktop.

Frank grunted again. "Page missing."

"No flies on you."

Leo next ran his eyes over the contents of the bookshelf. Among board games, video cassettes, stereo equipment, a microscope, and various souvenir bric-a-brac was a collection of contemporary Canadian fiction, a number of biographies of musicians, a few books of twentieth-century history, a couple of genealogical texts, several large format compilations of famous photographers, a smattering of travel literature, and a shelf of what looked to be Catholic literature, lives of saints, church history and the like. Eclectic, he thought. And, here at least, neat. Spines all aligned. Still, it was no different than his own eccentricities: his place was a chaos, but his record collection was alphabetized and perfectly aligned.

Frank was examining the typewriter. "It's just like that one at your mother's. Remember when Alison and Jennifer were little?"

When Leo's nieces were four and six, they discovered an ancient typewriter in his mother's attic and for a winter, whenever the Nickels were over for dinner, they would rush upstairs and bash away at the thing.

"I think they mostly liked the sound of the bells." Leo looked at the Olivetti, a model from the early years of the twentieth century, square and black with small circular key pads. It looked as prim, efficient and full of moral rectitude as a spinster secretary in a 1910 law office. "I'll bet it's some family heirloom," he added. "Ol' grandpappy Rossiter probably wrote blistering anti-labour editorials on it during the Winnipeg General Strike."

Frank scratched his hairless head. "So, what about family? Wife? Kids?"

"None that I know of. He has a younger sister—Merritt Parrish. She writes fashion for the paper. And there's an aunt and uncle who live next door."

"Parents?"

"Dead."

"Right, I think there was some sort of accident years ago." Leo stopped suddenly and listened. He turned his head sharply.

"What?" Frank asked.

"Someone's coming."

"Shit."

Leo's mind raced over the layout of the house as he remembered it from his exploration during his search for the toilet during the Victoria Day party. "Michael's bedroom's in the back corner. I'll go out through the window. But you'll—" He gestured to Frank's gloved hand. "—have to lift the sash. I mean, I wouldn't want to leave fingerprints."

"Then get moving."

In the bedroom, a reading lamp next to the bed was switched on, casting a warm glow across the navy duvet cover and over the hardwood floor. The rest of the room fell into shadow. Leo squinted, seeking the best-placed window. As he had noted in May, the room had once been two. A broad arch through an adjoining wall had knitted the two rooms together in an L-shape, while retaining a sense of separate functions. One part, the larger, was the bedroom proper with its own door to the bathroom. The smaller portion contained only a chair, a music stand, and a low table with a Tiffany-style lamp—or, hell, maybe it was a real Tiffany lamp. He moved toward the farthest window, felt his foot hit something, then found himself falling through the air.

"Ow, fuck," he said as the floor rose to meet him.

"Christ," Frank hissed. "Would you stop with the noise?"

"What is it?" Leo picked himself up. There was just enough light for his adjusted eyes to discern a stumpy eccentric shape on the floor. "A violin case."

"Stupid place to leave it."

"It looks empty."

"No flies on you, either."

"Michael bought a really valuable violin, Frank. Didn't you read about it in Saturday's paper? Worth a million bucks."

"No shit." They stared at the object on the floor. The case was indeed empty. In the low light, the red velvet lining appeared dark as blood. "Maybe he left the violin somewhere else in the house."

"Sure, Frank, like on the back of the toilet or the top of the microwave." A headline flashed in Leo's brainpan:

Violin theft points to murder

"And how do you know that this is *the* violin anyway?" Frank insisted. "What kind of idiot keeps a million-buck fiddle lying around the house?"

"Hell if I know, Frank. But maybe it's—y'know—a clue. Michael's lying dead down the hall. He owns a valuable violin. And, whaddaya know, here's a violin case, and no violin."

"Or maybe it's a diversion. And maybe it means bugger all. In any case, I want you out of here."

Frank moved to the window and pulled at the sash, which slid up easily. "Shit, there's a screen."

"What did you expect, Frank? This is Winnipeg, land of mosquitoes."

His brother-in-law fumbled with the plastic tabs that released the screen from its frame.

"Jesus Christ, Frank, what the hell are you doing?" A voice boomed behind both their backs.

"Would you cool it, Gerry? Keep your voice down." Frank slid the screen into the room. Leo turned. Frank's partner was as tall and morose-looking as Ichabod Crane. He surveyed Leo sourly.

"Frank, what is he doing here?"

"He's just leaving."

Leo scrambled onto the ledge and peered into the night. "I guess if I sneak across to the Kingdons'—"

"Take the long way around. If some uniform finds you, you're in deep shit. You already have a record, remember?"

"It was a youthful indiscretion, Frank. Besides it was Axel's fault."

"Whatever."

"I've heard about some of your behaviour at shift parties. I'll tell my sister."

"Remember I said I was going to kick your ass? Well, here goes."

Leo felt a shod foot firmly planted on his backside. Before he knew it, he was through the air and spiked on a bush in a rustle of dead leaves.

"And don't make such a damn racket," Frank whispered as he reaffixed the screen.

"Frank, are you out of your mind?" Leo could hear Gerry's voice raised in protest.

"Gerry, listen, there wasn't much I could—"

The window slammed shut. Leo spent a minute taking in the cool air. From his perch he looked over the trees where a slender moon was hanging low in the northern sky, threatened by slowly massing clouds. As he carefully and as noiselessly as possible disentangled himself and slithered to earth, he felt a tiny pain ripple through his lower back, the legacy of an old soccer injury and ever after a harbinger of rain. He had felt few such twinges over the dry, hot summer. He almost welcomed one now.

    Sort of.

6

In a Yellow Wood

"Can I use your phone?"
"May. May you use my phone."
What a twit. "Okay, *may* I use your phone?"
"Your reason?"
To run up bills to Beijing. "To phone the story in," Leo said to Martin. They were standing at the foot of the Kingdons' driveway. Nearby, small knots of people had gathered on the street, police cars, ambulances, and such being the usual draw. The only real diversion, however, was a uniformed officer struggling in the breeze with a spool of yellow plastic tape designed to seal off the scene of the crime.
"You don't need to do that."
"But I—"
"Is this your shift, Mr. Fabian?"
"No. But—"
"Then leave it."
"But—"
"Three buts and you're out. Now I must see to my guests."
Martin turned and waddled back up the drive. Leo stared after him. A little earlier, when he had burst onto the darkened Kingdon lawn through yet another lilac hedge, he was grateful to see the house lit up. He had been composing a lede in his mind, and was eager to get to a phone. Noting Martin's penguin silhouette at the bottom of the drive, he had breezed past the assemblage at the top with a casual "evenin' folks," surprised to see Liz Elliot (who laughed) and Guy Clark (who scowled), and headed straight for the *Citizen*'s managing editor. Small talk ensued. "Hello, Mr. Fabian, what are you doing here? Came to pick up a friend. She found Michael's body. Really, and who's that? Stevie Lord. Oh, yes, I know the family. Dr. Lord, the plastic surgeon…on the board…" Etc. Etc. Martin, who, except for the incident in May, had pretty much ignored him during the six years he had served at the *Zit*, suddenly seemed interested in his life and associations. Go figure. His white shirt front, bisected by a dark tie, glowed

blue under the mercury street lamp. He looked like someone had plugged him in, which, Leo thought, might also account for his peculiar animation. Finally, Leo slipped his request in edgewise.

No go.

Furious, Leo stamped over to Stevie who was waiting beside the Land Rover, hugging herself, his jacket draped over her shoulders.

"That asshole won't let me phone the story in," he exploded. "I'm going to look for a phone booth."

"Phone the story in?" Stevie echoed. Her voice was deadpan, her eyes two bullets.

Christ. "Sorry." He backtracked quickly. "Are you cold?"

Stevie opened the door to the passenger side. Alvy promptly thrust his head into her thigh. She stroked his sleek fur absently. "Please just take me home."

Leo walked around to the other side of the vehicle. Rain was starting to spit. He heard someone shout his name and peered through the knot of rubberneckers to see Roger Mellish, the *Citizen*'s food editor, and his lady friend—whose name slipped his mind—arm in arm, tottering up the street. Their heads were almost pressed together—well, as much as could be, given the difference in their heights—and as they approached, he could hear them, amidst giggles, doing a lazy chorus of "Found a Peanut."

"I haven't heard that song since I was seven," he said to them.

"Nor I," Roger replied, beaming, a little out of breath. "I have some memory of mother singing it to me during the Blitz. Do you know Nan?"

"Yes, we met at Michael's barbecue in the spring. Hello."

"Hello," Nan trilled. Leo thought she looked a little blotto. She was dressed in one of those shawl things middle-aged women seemed to like on cool evenings. "What's the next line, dear?" She gazed up at Roger. "Oh, I know. 'Called the doctor, called the doctor, called the doctor—'"

"Oh, Nan, stop it." Roger appeared flushed with pleasure, making his fleshy face with his white forelock look like a ripe strawberry with a lick of cream. The expression in his eyes as he surveyed the scene, however, was more grave. "What's happened here?" he asked, tugging at the collar of his turtleneck.

"Did you know," Nan interrupted thickly, "that Roger found a peanut?" She giggled.

"Nan, shush."

"Well, you did, darling."

"We've been at the Wajan." Roger sighed. "It's the new Thai restaurant around the corner. I seem to have had a mild reaction to something—the peanuts in the satay probably." Roger turned to look at the police officer roping off the area. "At any rate, what *is* going on here? Car accident?"

Leo shook his head. "It's Michael Rossiter. He's dead."

Roger's eyes widened. "Good god!" Nan, who had been crooning under her breath, "Died anyway, died anyway, died anyway last night," shuddered visibly. The words perished on her lips. "What happened?" she gasped, staring at him.

"Well, I hate to say it." And he did. "It looks like murder." He gave them an edited version of the evening's events.

"*Who* found him?" Nan asked.

"Stevie Lord. A friend of mine. She's in the car."

"Oh, my god, I know Stevie." She peered through the Land Rover's windshield. "Oh, the poor girl. Excuse me."

They watched her circle the front of the vehicle. "What does Nan do?" Leo asked, suddenly bereft of conversation.

"She teaches interior design at the university."

"Oh, then that's how she would know Stevie."

"And you say she found Michael?"

"She's been taking some photography-dark room sort of lessons with him."

"Oh, so *she* was the appointment." Roger sneezed suddenly. "I do beg your pardon." He pulled a handkerchief from his pocket and gave his nose a cursory wipe. "I'd phoned Michael from work earlier in the day saying I'd drop by this evening to pick up my reading glasses. Bunny and I were over yesterday looking at the last of the photos he did for *Taste of Winnipeg*. He said there'd likely be someone else over.

"I was sort of hoping he might be able to add the Wajan to the book," he added as an afterthought. "It's really rather good." He gave his head a shake. "Anyway, that's neither here nor there now. Goodness, this is quite…" He seemed to grope for a word. "…shocking."

"I really should get Stevie out of here."

"Nan, dear," Roger called, "let's go. Leo would like to get Stevie home." He glanced over at the police cruiser. He regarded Leo speculatively. "I guess this is your story."

"You would think. But Martin's being a real asshole," Leo gestured toward the Kingdon home and tugged at the Land Rover's door handle. "He won't even let me use his phone."

"He's an odd little man, isn't he? But maybe it has something to do with Michael being Bunny's nephew."

"Maybe," Leo allowed, sliding into the driver's seat. He actually hadn't thought of that and felt like a heel. He closed the door on the throb and glare of police lights. A couple of raindrops splattered on the windscreen, forming small craters in the thin film of dust before disintegrating and racing down the glass.

"Rain at last," he remarked, suddenly awkward.

Stevie stared ahead. "I left my camera bag in there," she said hollowly. "I'll see if they'll let me have it."

"Doesn't matter now."

"Sorry about the phone-it-in thing."

"It's what you do, isn't it? It's your job, I mean."

The journalistic cannibalism? "I suppose."

There was a silence. Leo groped around in his mind for conversation to suit the situation, but since he'd never been in such a situation, his mind was mush.

"Have you ever thought about not being a reporter?" Her voice was a tiny thing in the dark.

"Not?" Leo leapt on this. "Well, I've thought about playing forward for the Maple Leafs, but somehow I don't think it's ever going to happen." It was Axel Werner's doing that he'd ended up in journalism. Armed with a bachelor's degree in history, he'd been contemplating a career in fuck-all when Axel, who on a whim and with illegally gleaned money had bought the *Dauphin Courier*, invited him to join the staff. Of two. Him and Axel. Neither of them knowing squat about journalism, but learning quickly.

"Why?" Leo flicked the switch for the windshield wipers. "Have you ever thought of not being a designer?"

"It occurs to me. I think I ended up in interior design because my brother took architecture—"

"I thought he was a doctor."

"No, Rob's the doctor. Will is the architect. He would built these interesting models..." Her voice trailed off.

"Does this conversation have something to do with Nan Whatsername?"

"Hughes. Yes. I think I might meet with her toward the end of the week."

"To talk about jobs?"

"I guess."

"Then you are staying in Winnipeg?"

"I don't know."

They drove along in silence for a few moments. The rain was starting to tap the roof of the Land Rover. One of those sad autumn rains that nourish nothing.

"Did Michael ever *not* want to be a photographer?" he asked tentatively. He flicked her a glance, but her head was turned to the dark landscape.

"Actually, music was his first love. He went off to the Curtis Institute to study violin. I think he would have loved to have had a solo career—"

"Pretty difficult to establish."

"—but then there was all this business stuff here after his parents died. And settling Merritt. My parents became her guardian for a few years until she was eighteen."

"Why not Martin and Bunny?"

Stevie shrugged. "One of those sibling relationships that soured. Or so my mother says. Lillian had the better looks, made the better marriage—

well, on the surface—and was somehow just more...*good*. She was a Catholic convert in marriage and really took to it, apparently. Her husband's drinking made her a famous martyr in certain circles." Stevie's voice softened. "She and my mother were fast friends. Lillian was really lovely. Almost like a TV mom of those days."

Leo cast her a worried glance, then had to swerve for a cat that darted across the Crescent. "Anyway," he said, aiming away from Rossiter memory lane, "what would you be if you had to do it all over again?"

"Well, I wouldn't be Mrs. David Sangster, for one. And I'm not, by the way. My divorce papers came through today."

"Congrats...I guess."

"Congrats are fine. Anyway, I don't know what I'd do."

"You could do something related."

"Such as?"

"I dunno. Look at Roger. He was a chef. He trained at the Ritz or some big hotel in London. And worked in CP hotels around Canada. He moved into food writing."

"Why?"

"Got tired of standing."

They sped down the Crescent.

"Stop at Merritt's, would you?" Stevie said.

"Are you sure?"

"I don't want her finding out from some stranger."

Leo suspected some stranger had already been in touch, and he could guess who. He turned into the drive. Every window glowed. Imagine one person tramping around this huge house. The heating bills. The electric bills.

"What am I doing? Dropping you off? Do you want me to come in with you?"

Stevie turned to look at him. A stray beam of light from one of the street lamps illuminated her eyes. They looked bruised. Leo wanted to touch them and make the dark circles go away.

"What do you want to do?"

He looked at her and shrugged. "Be with you."

She considered him a moment, the way she did from time to time, wordlessly.

"Okay." She reached for the handle. "Have you been here before?"

"Me? Are you kidding? I'm way out of her league. I've never been able to figure out why she bothers working for the *Zit*. She must be loaded."

"You think that, do you?"

"Well, look at this house."

She gave him a wan smile. "I think you'll find that appearances can be deceiving."

7

Four Lies

Yes, she had already heard. Yes, she had had a phone call. They were almost the first words out of Merritt's mouth when she opened the door, though Stevie knew in an instant when Merritt's pale face appeared in the frame of glass that her news was not new. Something about the studied expressionlessness. The green eyes with their hard glitter. What stabbed Stevie's heart, though, was how much Merritt's eyes—not their colour, but their shape, the depth of them—reminded her of Michael's.

"But how do *you* know?" Merritt addressed Stevie as she stepped into the front hall, then glanced at Leo who came up behind. "Oh, for Christ's sake! I'm not giving you a quote."

"He's with me." Stevie turned to Leo to assure herself that he wasn't going to turn into a large coiled notepad before their very eyes. But he was distracted by the hallway's centrepiece, a large Plexiglas cube, balanced miraculously on one point, containing an artful jumble of women's shoes.

Stevie watched Merritt turn sharply into the living room. No offer to take her coat, Leo's jacket as the case was. She slipped it off and draped it over the newel post. Leo pointed at the cube, wearing an expression of cartoon puzzlement.

"It's a statement," she whispered.

"Of what?" he whispered back.

Stevie shrugged. She followed Merritt, sensing rather than seeing Leo stop short at the entrance to take in what she, too, had found startling on her first visit back in the spring. She hadn't been in the Rossiter home in more than a decade; for most of that time, too, before Merritt returned from New York, it had sat empty. Merritt had redecorated, no doubt with Michael's money. The living room and the dining room beyond were completely and utterly black: black as coal, black as night, black as death. The walls were painted with a matte finish that seemed to swallow the light radiating from a couple of art deco lamps on low black lacquer tables. The ceiling, its outline barely detectable, was black. Or, rather, it seemed a void, abetting a feeling that the corners of the room were blurring. The fireplace, mantel, and wall above opposite the entrance were covered in mirror, and Stevie could see Leo reflected in full surprise. She was reminded of her own startled self in Michael's mirror less than two hours earlier and, feeling a shimmer of panic pass through her, promptly settled onto one of a pair of black leather couches.

Opposite her, across a coffee table cluttered with art deco bric-a-brac, Merritt primped at the ends of her curls, which were damp, giving her head little intermittent shakes as though she were trying to catch an imaginary breeze. Her red hair blazed like an aura of flame. Her green silk bathrobe glowed like a field of emeralds. Hardly subtle, but certainly dramatic. Stevie was reminded of a lesson from first-year ID layout assignments: Photos framed by black card were always more forceful than white.

"How did you find out so fast?" Merritt rephrased her earlier question, drawing her legs up.

"I found him, Merritt."

"*You* found him? Dead? Oh." She glanced away, then up at Leo, who seemed to be drinking Merritt in like a man who had been without refreshment for some time.

"Have a seat, Leo." Merritt flicked a lacquered nail to a spot next to Stevie. "So, was it…horrible?"

Stevie's hackles rose, as they so often did with Merritt. As a teenager, she had babysat Merritt on a few occasions and had been so tested at every stage—TV time, bath time, bed time—that she vowed never to babysit anyone else ever again. "Yes, Merritt, it was horrible," she replied, keeping the sarcasm under control. "It was very very horrible."

"Michael was murdered," Leo interjected, seating himself.

"Well, I know that." Merritt glared at him and folded her arms across her chest. "Who'd want to murder Mr. Goody Two-Shoes anyway?"

Stevie imagined this a circumstance where she might reach across the coffee table and slap Merritt with a resounding crack—she could hear it in her mind—but she was both too numb to make the effort and too aware that Merritt had built a brittle carapace around her to keep her own demons at bay.

Leo, on the other hand, didn't seem to be finding Merritt's question rhetorical. "Well," he began, but Stevie cut him off sharply: "I'm sure the police will have some answers soon."

A silence descended. Merritt regarded her nails with a frown. Leo squirmed. Unbidden, the sight of Michael's dead body flew into Stevie's mind. Her stomach churned. Quickly she said the first thing that came into her mind: "Do you want help making arrangements?"

"Arrangements?" Merritt looked up.

"The funeral."

"Oh, that." She grimaced. "There's lots of time."

"Not really."

"We've got a few days."

"Maybe your Aunt Bunny should handle it."

"No way. I'll do it."

"Anyway," Leo interjected, "the police might want to keep—" Stevie knew what he was going to say before he said it. Autopsy. Mutilation. I'm going to be sick.

"I need to use the bathroom." Stevie leapt off the couch.

"Are you okay?" Leo frowned.

"Would you mind using the en suite upstairs?" Merritt called after her. "And get me some Valium? It should be in the cabinet."

Valium? Oh, there's *a cure.* As Stevie rushed up the stairs, an unexpected image came to her head of herself, aged fourteen, being groped by some teenage Lothario on the big bed in the Rossiter Sr. bedroom while a party given by Michael in his parents' absence rose to a noisy crescendo below. Merritt, all of ten, had crept in and begun swatting at them with her Barbie doll. That had ended that.

Just as well, Stevie thought as she stepped over clothes strewn on the bedroom floor and crashed into the bathroom. She stared into the toilet bowl, holding her stomach with one hand, covering her mouth with the other. She swallowed back the onslaught of saliva, grabbed a tissue from the vanity and wiped at the beading of perspiration along her brow. Fainting had been bad enough, more debilitating than she'd imagined. She didn't want to be sick, too.

She distracted herself by studying the interior. Thank god this little room isn't painted black. If it were, it would be like the inside of a closed...she banished the c-word before it formed in her mind. The bathroom was white, starkly so, but all the accessories carried through the downstairs theme: the towels, sloppily replaced, were black; so, too, the bathmat and the porcelain. The only relief came from the colour of some of the clothes strewn about. She glanced back through the door into the bedroom, which was—yes—black. Hard to believe Sharon Bean had been here only the day before. Then her eye landed on a splotch of powder-blue. Not a Merritt colour. She kicked at it with her toe. A pair of Y-fronts. Some bizarre trend in female undergarments only a fashion writer like Merritt would know about?

Or...?

Stevie couldn't help smiling. There was a man's T-shirt and a pair of white socks, too. She looked up and caught a glimpse of herself in the cabinet mirror. She looked like hell. Dark circles under her eyes. Summer tan vanished, it looked like. Hair awry. She turned on the tap and splashed cold water on her face, and felt a kind of relief flow through her. Her stomach settled enough for her not to worry. She dabbed at her face with a hand towel, then opened the cabinet above the sink. The shelves were lined with every over-the-counter nostrum known to woman.

But no Valium.

And why Valium?

Valium for depression.

Depression + addiction + Merritt.

Merritt had shed no tears, but Stevie knew grief lurked, with awful force. When Merritt's parents had died, alcohol had been her balm.

No tears from you either, Stevie, she thought, closing the cabinet door and noting her face's glaze with dismay.

Not yet anyway.

Stevie stepped over a puddle and reentered the bedroom, glancing at images on the TV, which seemed to be on mute. She surveyed the vanity table. Shiseido, YSL, Dior, Lancôme, Chanel. It looked like the cosmetics counter at Holt Renfrew that she had designed in Toronto. The Valium was easily found. It was the only remedy not contained in seductive packaging. She fingered the white plastic bottle cap, remembering suddenly those first shattering weeks after she'd found her husband in their bed with one of the few neighbours she might have called a friend. Valium had been pressed on her by her doctor, and she'd spent those early days in the Windsor Arms with Sangster's credit card, sitting in a fog until a tiny warning inner voice made her flush the remaining pills down the toilet.

As she picked up the bottle, a metallic glint caught her eye. Behind the pill bottle lay a cute little gold straw.

Her husband—ex-husband—had had a cute little gold straw, too.

. . .

"It was on the vanity." Stevie looked Merritt straight in the eye.

Merritt looked away.

"Water?"

"I can swallow them dry." Merritt snatched the bottle and expertly squeezed the child-proof cap.

Stevie glanced at Leo who seemed to be staring thoughtfully at Merritt's boobs. Time for him to go.

"Why don't I stay over?" she said. "Remember when I used to babysit you?"

Merritt made a noise. Her tongue was hanging out, a perch for two little yellow dots.

"Maybe I should leave," Leo said from the depths of the couch.

They both watched Merritt swallow.

"I'm not a child," she snapped.

The doorbell chimed. Merritt glanced at her. "I'll get it," Stevie sighed. She crossed the vestibule and glanced at her watch. Nearly 10:30. "Oh," she said, opening the door.

"'Oh' to you too." Frank Nickel's bald pate shone in the porch light. Behind him, a head taller, was Gerry Shorter. "I'd like to speak to Mrs. Parrish."

"I suppose this couldn't wait."

"Not really."

"Who is it?" Merritt called from the living room.

"The police." The two strode past her.

"Ah, Shorter and Nickel," Leo murmured.

"That's Nickel and Shorter, sonny." They both stared about the room.

"We're related," Leo informed Merritt.

"Happy day." She frowned at the two detectives. "Didn't one of you already phone me?"

"Me," said Frank.

"Then...?"

"Just had a few questions. My condolences, by the way."

"Thank you." Merritt smiled suddenly. She loosened the collar of her bathrobe. "Pardon my deshabille."

Stevie gagged.

"Have a seat." Merritt gestured to the couch opposite.

"Shove over, Fabian," Frank said.

Leo did as ordered. The two men sank into the leather. Leo bobbed at the other end. Shorter pulled a notepad from his pocket.

"Am I being asked for a statement? Did I get that right?"

"Kind of," Frank frowned. "We'll have something prepared later that you can sign. I just wanted to ask you some questions, you being his closest relative."

"Would you gentlemen like a drink?"

She didn't ask us if we wanted a drink, Stevie thought, plunking herself down at the other end of Merritt's couch and looking at the three men who were looking at Merritt: Larry, Curley, Moe.

"I wouldn't mind one," Leo piped up.

"Aren't you driving?" Stevie lifted her eyebrows at him.

"I suppose I am."

"And we're on duty," Frank added, clearing his throat. "Anyway—"

"When was the last time I saw my brother?" Merritt tilted her head coquettishly.

Frank scowled. "Yeah."

"Well, let me see." Merritt glanced at Shorter opening his notebook. She appeared to strain in thought. "I would say soon after Labour Day, just after he got back from Europe."

"What? He got back three weeks ago?" Stevie interjected.

"Yes. Why?"

"Never mind."

"And he was in Europe for how long?" Frank pressed.

"Most of the summer."

"Doing...?"

"I don't know. Looking at things, I guess. What do people do in Europe?"

"Shop, in your case." Stevie hadn't intended giving voice to the thought.

Merritt stuck out her tongue at her. "And Michael doesn't shop? Didn't you read Saturday's paper? Anyway," she continued, easing back into her smile, "I remember him saying he was at Glynbourne. A musical concert in England," she replied to Frank's puzzled expression. "And probably taking photographs."

"I had a postcard from Holland. Or was it Germany?" Stevie interjected. One lousy postcard.

Frank scratched at nonexistent hair. "Funny, because we found luggage tags that indicate he'd been to Washington, D.C."

"Oh?" Merritt shrugged. "I didn't know he'd been to Washington, too." She turned to Stevie. "Don't you have an aunt and uncle in Baltimore that you stayed with for a time?"

Stevie's heart fluttered. There was something sly in Merritt's expression. "Yes," she replied evenly.

"Michael studied at the Curtis Institute in Philadelphia, which isn't all that far from Washington," Merritt continued. "Perhaps he was visiting friends."

"So the last time you saw him was three weeks ago—"

"Yes, we had lunch at Le Beaujolais. It was the Friday after Labour Day."

"Amicable?"

"Yes."

There's a lie, thought Stevie.

"Why?" Merritt asked.

"Just wondered."

"My brother and I had a very fond relationship."

Whopper number two. Stevie could read skepticism in Frank's hooded eyes.

"I see," the detective said, then paused. "Did he show you the violin he bought?"

"Saturday's paper was the first I knew of it."

"He didn't mention it at your lunch?"

"No."

"I thought you had a close relationship."

"Well, we don't discuss *everything*."

"I see." Frank let silence reign for about ten seconds. "So, Mrs. Parrish, how did you spend your day today?"

"Well..." Merritt ran her hand down the lapel of her robe. "I was at the *Citizen* briefly in the morning. I had lunch with a local designer, did a little interview. Went back to the *Citizen*. Typed in a few notes." The hand took another trip down her chest. "Left about 5:00 or so and went to Jane's—it's the name of a boutique on Assiniboine Avenue," she explained for the scribbling Shorter—"for a dress fitting. Then came home."

"How long were you at this store?"

"Oh, about an hour or so. Jane's a great friend and a good source in the fashion business, so we talked a while."

"And she could corroborate?"

"Oh, absolutely." Merritt's smile tightened.

"And this evening? You came home about...when?"

"6:00. 6:30."

"And what did you do?"

"Oh, let's see—tried to find something on TV other than the stupid Olympics."

"What did you watch?"

"Some movie."

"*Death of an Angel*?" Leo interrupted.

"Yes, that was it."

"Pretty awful. Sorry, Frank."

Nickel, clearly peeved, turned back to Merritt. "You were alone?"

"Yes."

Lie three, Stevie thought. Shall we go for four?

"Why are you asking?" Merritt's finger stroked a length of gold chain around her neck.

"Just routine. Everyone your brother might have been in contact with will be asked the same questions."

This was received in silence.

"Mrs. Parrish, before we go, just one last question for the meantime." Frank stared at Merritt. "Do you know anyone who might want to kill your brother?"

Merritt's finger stopped. She tilted her head, as if in deep thought. "No," she replied. "No, I can't say I do."

Four.

Book 2

Wednesday, September 28

8

Welcome to the Word Factory

Leo awoke with the usual boner. This sometimes led to fond thoughts of Ishbel, and fond memories of—in no particular order—Lynn, Jane, Jill, Christine, Ruth I, Ruth II (Ruthie-Ann), Snjolaug (an Icelandic exchange student), and even Julie, the *Zit* court reporter who hated his guts, all the way back through the Rolodex of love to Caroline, who in grade 10 had taken her role understudying Irma La Duce in the high-school production of the same name much too much to heart, if that was the right organ. (Many benefited.) Sometimes it led to fond recollections of, respectively, the April 1972, July 1978, August 1982, and November 1983 *Penthouse* foldouts. More often lately it led to fond expectation of Stevie. But this morning it was Merritt who insinuated herself into the lizard portion of his brain.

He couldn't help noting her during her infrequent visits to the newsroom over the past year or so in some get-up or other, vivacious and aloof at the same time, like a film star doing a charity gig. But in that bathrobe! How it was that a complete asshole like Guy Clark managed to get within shouting distance was a mystery greater than the Leafs' inability to win the Stanley Cup.

Never was it truer: Life ain't fair.

He sent his thoughts to the score of the Blue Jays game, which he had heard last thing before going to bed. Shrinkage began. Stallion turned turtle. Elvis left the building. Merritt's outline and supple curves receded. But her words from last evening insinuated themselves instead. When Stevie had excused herself and gone upstairs, he had taken his chance. Well, okay, Merritt had started it by saying in a throaty sort of Marlene Dietrich voice, "So, you and Stevie?"—her green eyes glittering. He wondered if she wasn't a little stoned on something. (You'd think news of your brother's murder would be so sobering your brain couldn't process any other information.) The few times he'd seen her step into the newsroom over the summer, he had wanted to call her over and do a little interview. Subject: Stevie. Since he'd never said much more than "hello" to Merritt in the newsroom, though, he couldn't think of pretext for conversation, so he'd just let it ride. But last night, thanks to circumstance, he'd been mano a (wo)mano with Stevie's next-door (but one) neighbour, the Lord family teenaged ward, and Michael's sister—a fount of knowledge. What the hell, he'd thought. It wasn't like she needed to be handed tissue after tissue to dry her wet little grief-stricken eyes. So he asked.

About Stevie and Michael.

Amazing what you could learn in under five minutes. Much of it he'd expected. But one thing he could never have predicted. It was more than he wanted to know. And how strangely self-satisfied Merritt had been letting him know, as if it had been something she'd been dying to tell someone for years. Stevie came back downstairs. Frank and Gerry had arrived and begun doing their detective schtick. He'd barely paid attention, except when Merritt proffered a drink, which he badly could have used, only to have Stevie give him the Mothers-Against-Drunk-Driving basilisk stare.

Was he shocked?

A bit.

Was he jealous?

Kind of.

Was he hurt?

Yeah—surprisingly.

As he was leaving, Frank reminded Merritt that they'd need her to i.d. the body. She was not amused. Stevie offered to take her. Frank and Gerry left. Then he and Stevie left a moment later. The rain had stopped. Rather than take the car such a short distance, Leo had walked Stevie in silence across the dark lawn of the Oblate fathers' mansion that stood between the Rossiter and Lord residences, trying to avoid the fat drops of water falling from the old elms whose limbs swayed and creaked in the still potent wind. He'd felt like he had nothing to say to her, like leaving her at her parents' door and never calling her again. What was the point if she was so fucking besotted by the likes of Michael Rossiter?

But then, reaching the bottom of the steps, anticipating yet another of their awkward partings (Leo yearning, but not this time; Stevie backtracking), she had turned, started to take off his jacket, and suddenly asked him if he had ever seen a dead body before. Tiny beads of moisture had settled along her hair from the damp, cool air. Her eyes had glistened, staring intently at him. He had looked away, across the lawn where lately fallen leaves had gathered around the edge of a flowerbed to form a fallow wreath. He had wanted to say, "yeah, Michael Rossiter, about three hours ago." But he knew what she'd meant. He shook his head, no. He hadn't seen his father that day at the Misericordia, more than a quarter-century ago. He didn't mention that.

"I have," she said, almost fiercely, and told him about her grandfather Standish. Easter, of all days. Granddad, visiting from California, gets up from the table early—indigestion—and goes to sit in the living room. She's seven. Robert, her elder brother, is thirteen or fourteen. Her Baltimore aunt takes them into the living room. "Oh, look," she says, "your grandfather's asleep." But Robert sticks out his arm, points. His voice is changing and he booms, just booms: "No he's not! He's dead!"

And then the dam broke. Stevie thrust herself into his arms, sobbing uncontrollably. And more: For Leo couldn't help himself. Something—God knows what—had overcome Stevie. A hug turned into a groping hungry kiss. He had found himself pushing her against one of the Chinese lions that flanked the steps, and could have, wanted to, would have happily taken her right there...

Leo looked down. He was sitting at the edge of the bed, naked. Elvis had apparently not left the building. A shower was in order. Possibly a cool one.

· · ·

An hour later—shaved, showered, unbreakfasted, and unsatisfied—Leo stood at the entrance to the *Citizen* building, scratching with his fingernail at the faded remains of a once blood-red graffito sprayed onto the stained granite facing. DEATH TO MULROO, it advised. Below it another read: EAT THE RICH.

Wonder what they taste like, he thought, peeling bits of red paint from under his fingernail as he waited for Liz, who had shouted at him from down the street. He watched her lean into the wind and battle a gust of leaves, then looked up at the facade of the building. Even in the kind light of an autumn morning, the Citizen was a brooding presence on the street. No ray of sun seemed able to raise a gleam from the red brick so dulled by decades of dirt and neglect. No window twinkled because the encrusted grime had formed a grey patina that shunned reflection. The building had an air of ossification, suggesting to citizens of the late-twentieth-century world the grim rectitude of the nineteenth. Sort of ironic, Leo thought: the Citizen had been built in the new century, some time after the old Queen's death, in the garden-party years before the Great War, when an exuberant belief in the power of rational progress still nurtured human activity. Winnipeg had then reached its zenith of power and influence in the country, and the *Citizen* building, communications central, was the very expression of confident authority with its strong brick verticals and rhythmic composition of granite classical arches at street level. It had been a thoroughly modern building then, austere to Edwardian eyes. Two world wars and four generations later, it seemed ill proportioned, a clumsy massing of stone and brick, pretty damned mediocre to tell the truth, only redeemable in a period keen on architectural restoration simply because it was old.

Or such was what he'd wanted to write when he'd been assigned a series on downtown Winnipeg's architectural gems during his brief stint in the Go! section. But when he got to describing the very building in which he was writing the story, he instead did some rhapsodic bullshit that got past Guy Clark, who didn't know anything about architecture either, and which in print lay beneath the citizenry's potato peelings the next day anyway.

He could have gone on. How about the *Citizen* building as allegory of the newspaper's ownership? The *Citizen* had been a family-owned operation for most of its history until Michael Rossiter sold it to the Fleming Group, a small regional chain of newspapers, just after his father's death in 1977. The Flemings had extended the building north to accommodate new presses. Terracotta and stone embellishments had been discarded, but the facade of the addition respectfully echoed the original in its rounded arches and stripped classical detailing. Then in 1981, the *Citizen* had been sold to Toronto-based Hayward Inc., who added it to its international media empire. To accommodate even bigger and better presses, Hayward found its solution in what resembled a large garden shed tacked onto the existing structure. No windows. Brick a lousy match. One end facing a parking lot covered in what appeared to be aluminum siding.

But, unable to suck sufficient profit out of a Winnipeg newspaper in short order, Hayward had sold the paper in the summer to Harmac, owned by the moralizing, ultra-conservative, ultra-Christian Alberta businessman Harry Mack, who not only believed freedom of the press was guaranteed to those who owned one, but exercised his franchise on the editorial pages with glee. If he puts an addition on, what will it look like, Leo wondered? An outhouse? Probably didn't matter. Rumour was that property in the 'burbs was being scouted for a whole new plant.

"Should I ask you what you were doing in the lilac bushes last night?" Liz gasped, winded.

"Making my brother-in-law crazy," Leo replied. He explained the circumstances as they passed through the revolving doors into the *Citizen* lobby. "All in a night's work."

"Michael Rossiter's death will put a big hole in the arts community. Well, at least the music part." Liz jabbed the button to the elevator. "He's the one who's bailed the symphony out more than a few times in recent years."

"News to me."

"Welcome to the Winnipeg arts scene, Leo. I thought you'd figured it out when Guy assigned you that 'Angels' piece in the spring." Her eyes went up to the row of illuminated numbers above the elevator door. The *Citizen* building, which housed five hundred employees, was served by only one elevator. It seemed to be stuck on the fourth floor, their destination. "What is the matter with this damn thing?" She jabbed again at the button.

Leo glanced at her, at her hair, which was unusually asymmetrical. "Bad night?"

"Kind of."

"You look a little worse for wear." Leo scraped a wet leaf off the bottom of his shoe.

"Great. Just what a girl wants to hear."

"Should I ask?"

Liz turned and cast him a glance of such despair that he had his answer. "Come on," he said as the revolving door spit a few more people into the lobby, "we'll have to drag ourselves up the stairs. The elevator's probably out of commission again."

A winding marble staircase took them to the second floor. Two enormous oil paintings loomed, souvenirs of Rossiter days, one of Michael's grandfather, Conroy, looking wholly seized of his own importance, the other, Thomas, looking somewhat less seized of his own importance, but only just. Was it the style of these latter days, Leo wondered, or was it because the men the *Citizen*'s subsequent owners picked as publishers were such faceless corporate dweebs in need of personality transplants that no portraits of them existed?

"Merritt must have inherited her red hair from her grandfather," Leo remarked, noting the portrait as they passed. Conroy's hair was eccentrically long for a man of his generation, styled by the artist to plump nearly over the collar of his late-forties dark suit. The red coif, shot through with grey, was the first thing you noticed, that and the preposterous pose, one hand on an immense globe of the earth.

"Merritt's hair colour is out of a bottle. Very Fergie."

"You'd know."

"Trust me. I noted her roots in the washroom one day. She didn't get Michael's blonde hair. She's mouse brown. And those green eyes are contacts."

Leo glanced at the portrait of Thomas Rossiter. He was supposed to have been as charming as hell, some of the old-timers around the place said, when asked (they were rarely asked; newspapers lived for the day, not yesterday). But in the painting, he looked like he had a turnip up his ass—the features of his conventionally handsome face were frozen stiff, stern, pained.

"Painted after his death," Liz said, as if sharing his thoughts. "Or so I'm told."

They reached the second floor. The marble ended and plaster painted institutional green commenced.

"Speaking of Rossiter deaths," Leo began, his voice echoing in the narrower stairwell, "did you have to give statements last night?"

"Brief ones. 'Did you see anything?' Blah blah blah. Your brother-in-law said they'd get back to us, if need be."

"And did you? See anything, I mean?"

"Nothing that strikes me as important," Liz replied, puffing a little bit. "Spence and I drove up, parked in the driveway, and went into Kingdons'. Can't really see into Michael's yard anyway, what with those lilac bushes."

"What time?"

"About 6:45. We were the first to arrive—early, in fact. Then the Richters arrived about fifteen minutes later. Then Guy, for some reason. Somehow I don't think he was an intended guest. Bunny looked sort of cheesed off when he appeared, and then Martin disappeared for a while. Bunny probably told him to add a place setting or throw another chicken in the pot."

"Why do you think Guy wasn't invited?"

Liz's shoulders shrugged. "It was an orchestra-y thing. Guy spends most of his time trying to think up ways to antagonize the arts community. Paul thinks he's a complete idiot."

"He told you this?"

"Sort of. Anyway," Liz continued, "Guy was alone. No Merritt. Odd number at a dinner table. The lack of symmetry was very un-Bunny. I wonder if Guy and Merritt have broken up?" she added as an afterthought.

"Why were Guy and Merritt ever together in the first place?"

"Well, much as I wish Guy would fall down a sewer hole, he has a certain...intensity. Probably not bad in bed."

Leo's stomach turned. A door slammed shut somewhere below, the sound reverberating up the stairwell.

"And besides," Liz continued, "Bunny said she had originally invited Michael, but he apparently had something else on."

"He was meeting Stevie."

"Oh? Well, anyway, if Bunny had invited Michael, she probably wouldn't have invited Merritt—with or without Guy in attendance. I'm told relations are cool between Bunny and Merritt. Bunny disapproves of Merritt. But then Merritt and Michael apparently didn't get along either. What a family! Anyway, Merritt has nothing to do with the symphony, so... God, I've really got to stop smoking," she gasped, arriving ahead of him on the fourth floor landing.

Leo was a little out of breath, too. Maybe he should join a gym, as Axel had suggested. A shudder went through the building. The presses were beginning the final run of the day's edition, which meant it was 9:00.

He and Liz were, technically, late. Liz began to punch the security code buttons that allowed them through the door into the newsroom.

"Wait," he said. "I wanted to ask you about your story in Saturday's paper."

"Which one?"

"The one on the violin."

"Why?"

"I thought Michael liked to remain anonymous about his do-goodery. He made a real point of it to me last spring."

"Well, he wasn't very happy that I found out, but I pretty much nailed him on it." The door opened with a hellish grind and they stepped into the fourth-floor lobby. "It wasn't going to kill him to admit once in a while to doing a good deed."

Something in Leo's glance tipped her off. Her face fell. "Oh, no. What is it?"

"There's a violin missing from Michael's."

"Oh, Christ!"

. . .

Leo coughed, then coughed again. His desk, which abutted five others to form one battered expanse of work surface, seemed over time to have become the redoubt of the newsroom's smokers, most of them young women who waved their cigarettes like newly acquired batons of authority, nervously tapping ash to the floor as they barked into the telephones. The smoke would rise slowly, gathering around the banks of fluorescent lights in little clouds until some tongue of cold air from the ancient ventilation system licked at it. Leo imagined each time another layer of microscopic ash, winnowed from the smoke, settling onto the desks and filing cabinets, the stacks of old papers and boxes and long-forgotten flotsam that had accreted over the years on every horizontal surface without fear of removal. Wasn't this how the planet was buried? Layer upon layer of cosmic dust falling from the sky, obliterating all man's glories and vanities? Mycenae: gone. Pompeii: gone. And someday, the *Zit*: gone, too.

Or some such bullshit.

Leo waved away another stray puff of smoke and flattened out the front section of the day's paper. Two—count 'em—two murders in one night. That bumped poor old Ben Johnson down well below the fold. "A Deadly Duo" the headline read, but the North End murder got the play. And, from one point of view, why wouldn't it? Within the first two paragraphs such words as "broken," "glass," "rip," "vagina," and "intestines" stopped Leo from tearing open the miniature Oh Henry! bar he'd pulled from his desk drawer to satisfy his hunger. The murderer—

some very disaffected husband—had been caught red-handed. Literally. It was the grisly stuff of down-market tabloids. Which, oddly enough, the local down-market tabloid, the *Winnipeg Examiner*, Leo noted, unfolding it next to the *Zit*, had not played up. Instead, on its cover was a single picture, some studio portrait, of Michael Rossiter that made him look, as studio portraits do, more blondly handsome than real life. Leo remembered the night news editor at the *Examiner* was a woman.

"Death of an Angel," the *Examiner* headline exclaimed in bold red type. Fuck you backwards, Leo thought. That's my headline, goddamn it. He glanced back at the *Zit*. Big picture of shrouded corpse being carried on a stretcher from ramshackle North End house. Small picture of Michael— the same one as in the *Examiner*, bless his little limelight-avoiding heart. He passed his eyes over the sub-head:

Murder in the South End

>Winnipeg Police are searching for the killer of a 33-year-old man found dead in his Crescentwood home Tuesday evening.
>Photographer and philanthropist Michael Thomas Conroy Rossiter was discovered by...

Well, at least Stevie's name was left out. He read on. Paltry coverage. No byline. He glanced at the *Examiner*'s story. Also paltry. But paltry was the *Examiner*'s house style: more than five paragraphs might strain its readers.

And no mention of a violin in either story. He looked over at Liz, whose head was bent over the same front page kitty-corner to his desk. She caught his glance, her eyes squinting in the wreath of smoke from her cigarette, and gave him a weak smile.

"If I hadn't written that story, he might still be alive," she had moaned in the lobby.

"We don't know that," Leo had responded, wishing he'd never opened his mouth.

"He paid 550,000 pounds for the thing. Over a million Canadian."

"I remember. I could retire for life on that."

Liz had stared at him as if to say: *See?* motive. *Fault?* mine.

"How did you find out about it anyway?"

"From Belle Shulman." Liz groaned.

"Who?"

"She's a rich old ex-Winnipegger living in London. Her late husband made a fortune in ladies' underwear—

"Wearing it?"

"Making it. Anyway, she acts as sort of a hostess or liaison or smoother-over for local artists when they go to London for whatever reason. The RWB is dancing at Covent Garden next month, so I was doing a preview piece and phoned her. She's having a big party. She happened to mention—she's a real gossip—that she'd seen Michael at Sotheby's earlier in the month bidding on a Guarneri del Gesu."

"And then you phoned Michael for confirmation."

Liz nodded. "He'd intended it as an anonymous gift to the orchestra. Crap! What was he doing letting a million-dollar violin lay around the house?"

"Gloating?"

Liz frowned.

"I mean," Leo explained, "if I'd just bought a...new Ferrari, for instance, I might kind of hang around the driveway drooling over it for a while."

Liz shrugged. "I don't think Michael's the sort to do that."

"But he trained as a violinist, right? Maybe it fulfilled some dream."

Liz had stared out vacantly over the newsroom.

"What did you think of Michael anyway?" he asked suddenly.

"I don't...didn't know him that well."

"Come on. You travel in those circles."

"Not really. It's Spencer who's the greasy-pole climber. My father was a middle-manager at Great West Life. I'd rather have some other...adventures in living than go to dinner parties with boring lawyers and their boring wives."

"Still, you must have some opinion."

Liz studied him. "Why?"

Leo hesitated. "He was an old boyfriend of Stevie's," he allowed, grimacing. "From way back."

"Oh. I see."

"So...?"

"Well, he was certainly nice to look at."

"And I thought it was only men who were superficial."

Liz's expression grew serious. "I think Michael tried too hard."

"At what?"

"At being good."

"This is a bad thing?"

"It's an impossible thing."

9

Nasty, British, and Short

Leo turned from the front page and began to flip through the rest of the paper's front section, wondering as he munched on the Oh Henry! bar if he should slip down to the cafeteria to get something a little more nourishing to eat, a greasy donut and acrid coffee, for instance. But he was expecting the city editor, Ray Alcock, to bellow his name across the newsroom at any moment so he could discuss the day's assignments. He glanced up from a bus-plunge-of-the-day story (Peru, this time) and noted Alcock and his two assistants with their heads together, their lips moving intensely. Each white-shirted and balding, together they looked like a three-headed Hydra, one or another of the heads curling to look at someone in the newsroom before twisting back to the huddle. He was safe for the time being.

He thought about Stevie, but since it was a little early to phone, he turned to the sports section—Ben Johnson, Ben Johnson, Ben Johnson. Before he could read a word, a hand stuck a slip of pink paper under his nose.

"Audrey asked me to give you this."

Leo glanced at the messenger—Roger Mellish—and then at the message—from his old pal Axel Werner, former *Citizen* reporter, now editor of the struggling city magazine *Winnipeg Life.*

"What makes him think I'd be here at 8:31?" Leo wondered out loud, reading the time Audrey had printed at the top of the note in her precise hand. "I've never been on time in the whole six years I've worked here."

"Who?"

"Axel Werner."

"He seems a quite driven fellow."

"He's a fucking egomaniac, is what he is."

"I thought he was a friend of yours."

"And I say it with great fondness." Leo popped the last morsel of chocolate bar into his mouth, and made a moan of pleasure.

"Good?"

"Mmm. Want one? I have a cache in my drawer of these small ones they make for Hallowe'en."

"Well, it is a trifle early for me…" Roger appeared to deliberate. Leo watched him try to resist. It was like watching a mongoose try to resist a snake. Being a food editor and restaurant critic had its hazards, particularly if you loved the job, and judging from the extra avoirdupois hanging on his six-foot frame, Roger loved the job, at least the eating part of it. Your fate, buster, if you don't get some exercise, Leo addressed himself, observing Mellish's straining belt, and sucking in his own incipient gut. Fiftysomething, he observed too, is probably not a good age for knitwear.

"Okay." Roger plopped a pile of mail he was carrying down on Leo's desk and accepted the offering, which he opened with the fastidiousness of someone removing an oyster from its shell. Leo watched as he popped a piece in his mouth and rolled it around with a thoughtful expression. Observing him eat reminded Leo of the one time he had accepted an invitation to join Roger at a restaurant for dinner. It had been a few months after Mellish joined the *Zit* in 1986. Since he knew few people in town, various reporters were inveigled in turn to accompany him. When Leo's number came up, he'd gone, more curious over the process of reviewing restaurants than expecting a convivial evening with an oddball Brit more than fifteen years his senior. He had expected Roger would remain anonymous to the staff at La Vieille Gare, which served French food at inflated prices, but when they arrived Roger was recognized immediately and treated with extraordinary deference. Worse, Roger seemed to revel in it, behaving to the waiters with an arrogance Leo had seen only in European films. The topper was a burst of outrage triggered by a bad bottle of wine. He had guessed it was being in your element, but it had made Leo want to cringe, so he always found excuses ever after to the invitations proffered before Nan Hughes showed up on the scene. The only thing he had retrieved from the experience, besides the swell food, was the secret to restaurant reviewing without using the red flag of a notepad. Roger would place his briefcase on his lap, open it, root around for a moment as though he were looking for something, and then begin talking quietly as one would to a sleeping cat. It didn't take Leo long to realize the briefcase contained a tape recorder.

"Axel's wife has done a superb job designing the book," Roger said, dropping the candy wrapper.

"Book?" Leo's eyes strayed to a story on The Fury, the city's doomed soccer team.

"*A Taste of Winnipeg.*"

"Oh, right. That thing." Leo looked up to see a flash of annoyance in Roger's face. He had a large head but small features, which always made Leo think of creases made by a balloon artist. "Sorry."

"About what?"

"I didn't mean to sound dismissive."

Roger pushed a hand through an abundant head of hair. His white forelock, an eccentric feature, flopped back. "I didn't think you were," he drawled. "I was just thinking about the delays."

"Eve fussing." Leo laughed, referring to Axel's wife, a graphic designer. Axel had actually had to fire his wife as art director of *Winnipeg Life* after the first issue came out. She was good, but she was slow.

"Bunny says she's left town."

"Not again."

"And then there was Michael spending the summer in Europe."

"Which—what?—delayed some of the photography?"

"Somewhat." Roger selected a letter at random and began tearing at it with his thumb. "Though he'd pretty well caught up. Been working like a Trojan the last few weeks. There's still a couple of restaurants left, though. Bunny will probably have to hire someone."

"I suppose Michael had been doing the food photography gratis."

"Of course." Roger pulled a sheet of flower-embossed notepaper from the envelope. "Except for Eve, it's pretty much all volunteer labour," he continued, his eyes running over the script that Leo could see from his vantage was spidery in the extreme. "Which is part of the problem. Volunteers aren't always as dependable. Bunny had scheduled a sort of gang edit of some of the page proofs last Saturday afternoon and a number of people never showed. Oh lord," he sighed, replacing the letter in its envelope, "another old dear burning to see her family recipe for fudge in print."

"Her chances?"

"Slim, indeed." He glanced up then said under his breath, "I think Ray's slithering in this direction." Roger scooped up his pile of correspondence. "I'll leave you to him."

Leo debated whether to pick up the phone to return Axel's call and annoy Ray by keeping him waiting, but there was a humourless gleam in his eye that made him hesitate. Really, slither wasn't the right word. Alcock approached not like a snake, but like a rooster. He was Napoleonic in height, Anglo-Saxon in ancestry, and bare-knuckles in temperament. Leo's take on this was Hobbesian: he was nasty, British, and short.

"You're now on general assignment," Alcock barked, interposing himself between Leo and Julie Olsen, who quickly adjusted her chair. A sour odour wafted from him.

"What?" Leo recoiled slightly. "Why?"

"Because I say so."

"Sieg Heil."

The mapwork of tiny veins that played along Ray's nose and cheeks glowed. "Watch it, Fabian. You haven't got anyone to protect you this time."

Leo stared at him. "What the hell does that mean?"

Ray's eyes narrowed. "Michael Rossiter is dead."

"I know. I was there."

"So I understand."

Leo folded his arms across his chest. "Okay, once more from the top: What are you talking about?"

Ray turned to Julie. "Sweetheart, would you get me a coffee from downstairs?" Something from his pocket was pressed into her hand. Leo leaned forward to see Julie's angry frown. "There's a good girl."

Ray swivelled back, oblivious. Julie rose. She was a head taller than Ray and cartoon steam was coming out of her ears.

"And I'll need the change from that loonie, too, darlin'," he added without looking at her as she stomped off. "Thanks, luv."

Leo imagined a periwig instead of the comb-over. Alcock: a figure of the Enlightenment. Nope. Never. For his very first assignment at the *Citizen*, Alcock had fixed him with a humourless stare and told him to phone Buckingham Palace and ask what they thought about a Jew being appointed Lieutenant-Governor of Manitoba. Leo had countered by suggesting Ray insert something large and uncomfortable up his ass. As ever, the relationship between a reporter and an editor was antipathy, suspicion, and mutual lack of respect.

"I'm saying, Fabian, that you no longer have a guardian angel."

"I wasn't aware I ever had one. Have you found Christ now that Harry Mack owns this paper?"

Ray perched on the edge of his desk. His voice dropped. "Who the hell do you think pulled your nuts out of the fire last spring?"

"Ray, if you look hard, you'll see a question mark hovering over my head."

"Clark wanted your head on a platter after you punched him." They both glanced across the newsroom at Guy, his angry face framed in the dull haze of the room's only window. He was making a great show of ripping page after page of the Go! section, rolling them into balls, and stuffing them into an adjacent garbage can.

"Probably found a typo," Leo commented. "Anyway...?"

"Anyway, Michael interceded."

"I didn't know that."

Ray cocked an eyebrow.

"Well, I didn't!" Leo shook his head as if to reorder his brain cells. "I didn't ask him. I hardly knew the guy, for god's sake. And besides, what sort of influence would he have anyway? This rag doesn't belong to the Rossiters anymore."

"Bunny Kingdon is his mother's sister. Martin is his uncle."

"I know. But does this mean he micro-manages the horseshit that goes on in this place?"

Ray grunted. "How do you think little Miss Merritt got her job here?"

"Okay, using your influence to get your sister a job. No biggie. Besides, she worked in New York, in fashion. I mean, Jesus, you just have to look at her."

Ray grinned his canine grin, a blaze of white teeth in a blood-infused face. "But she can't put a sentence together, Fabian. The boys on the rim tear their hair out when they get her copy. Fashion isn't their strong suit."

Leo glanced toward the semi-circular desk at the front of the room. Uninterested in clothes as he was, he couldn't envision a more unfashionable collection of men and women.

"Still…" Leo was nonplussed. "How do you know this anyway?"

"I was in Martin's outer office when Clark was having his shitfit. He has what we call in Blighty a carrying voice."

"But how do you know about Michael's role?"

"Let's just say his name came up." He patted his comb-over. "All in the family, I guess. Michael using his influence with his uncle."

Leo was about to pick up on this, but Clark suddenly broke through the newsroom drone by shrieking Liz's name. Leo watched her square her shoulders and take her time lighting a fresh cigarette before rising and making her way through the sea of battered desks.

"See what I mean by a carrying voice?" Alcock pulled a penknife from his pocket and began digging dirt from his nails. "Anyway, as I was saying, you're off the police beat and on general assignment."

"Finally, after four months back on this dumb beat, there's a good story, and you take me off it."

"Not my idea."

"Whose then?"

"Martin, of course."

"Why?"

"Hell if I know."

"Fuck this. I'm going to have a word with him." Leo started to rise.

Alcock pushed him back into the chair. "Give it up. He's at St. George's playing golf with Harry Mack."

"Christian nutbar freakazoids play golf?"

"They're playing Christian nutbar freakazoid golf, I guess. Martin has some serious arse-kissing to do if he's going to get the publisher's chair he's been drooling over since Tom Rossiter popped his clogs way back when."

"Then I'll go to St. George's."

"The sign at the entrance says 'No Blacks, No Jews, No Riffraff.' I think you qualify under the final category." Alcock blew some dirt off the penknife onto the floor. "Look, how about you do the follow-up on the North End murder?"

"Psychopath eviscerates wife? Is there much more to say?"

"Oh, I don't know. You could always do the old bit with the neighbours saying, 'but he seemed so normal.'"

Leo flipped to page one. "'I always thought he was disturbed,' said Lenore Rebrinsky, his next-door-neighbour. 'He liked to weed his garden naked.'" He looked at the city editor. "Don't you read your own paper?"

Alcock shrugged. "I'm throwing you a bone, Fabian. Take it."

"I don't want it."

"Are you defying me?"

"Trying my best."

Alcock tapped the penknife against the desktop. "Christ, what does it matter? Look, keep doing what you're doing. I'll sort it out with Martin. Pretend I misheard. But you won't have a byline in the meantime."

"I don't care. It's not like I haven't seen my name in print before."

"Well, you've got about twenty minutes to get to the cop shop for the news conference."

As Leo looked up at the clock, something flew past his head, hit the wall, and clattered to the floor by Alcock's feet. Looking down, Leo noted a ballpoint pen, one of the promotional items from last fall's failed outreach to the youth market. "Pop A *Zit*," it said. At his desk, Guy Clark was snapping pencil after pencil, the tiny cracking noises rising above the newsroom hum like footfalls in a dry forest. His narrow face, a purple streak under a lock of dirty-blonde hair, leaned across a desk covered with a heavily blue-pencilled copy of the morning edition. He appeared to be hissing something at Liz, who sat in front of his desk, coolly smoking a cigarette, watching him remove each pencil from a CBC Information Radio souvenir coffee mug. The hiss grew louder as the newsroom fell to a hush, people straining to catch the essence of this latest fit.

"You spread a lie like that around and, believe me, I'll get you." Guy's words grew to a shriek.

Liz opened her mouth as if to respond, but instead a series of perfectly executed smoke rings poured forth and floated into Guy's face. She then rose and opened her mouth again, but the words, not smoke, poured forth. Unfortunately, they were drowned by the sound of one Guy coughing.

10

Connect the Dots

The plump woman patted the back of her head to judge the state of her French roll (intact), readjusted the bifocals on the bridge of her nose, then dropped her fingers to caress the keys of her Selectrix. Father Day kept leaving brochures for computers on her desk and extolling the virtues of peecees and apples or some such names, but she had dug in her heels. Computers crashed, she had heard. Typewriters did not. She would not be dictated to by some machine with a mind of its own. She was rehearsing the very speech when the two young women slipped into the outer office. The red-haired one was clearly Michael Rossiter's sister. Something about the eyes, their animation as much as their shape. But who was the other, with the dark angry eyes and the serious brow? Of course, Father Day hadn't bothered to introduce them. Oh, how she missed Father Saunders, who had retired in the spring. Such a gentleman. But these young priests...!

She had asked twice if Stevie would like a cup of coffee, but had received no response. She had tried penetrating the brain of the visitor with the same laser gaze she sometimes applied to the back of Father Day's head, but that didn't work either. Undoubtedly the magazine she had on her lap was just all too absorbing.

But Stevie wasn't remotely interested in *Winnipeg Life*. She had plucked it from a pile without thinking, the way she would in a dentist's or doctor's office, and had begun turning the pages. But the words and pictures blurred.

She had expected she would join Merritt in Father Day's office. She had found herself almost craving it—the ritual of kind words delivered by an understanding cleric. Weren't they supposed to have a handle on the big issues? But the priest had come briskly through the door at the secretary's summons, his face under the clerical collar raw and red as if windburned, his eyes inscrutable behind round glasses that turned to silver disks as they caught the morning light streaming through the church office window. The phrasing of his condolences was as economical as his movements, and after introductions in which he'd ascertained Stevie's status as a non-relative, he'd ushered Merritt back through the door to his office, and closed the door. But Stevie had had a moment to see his eyes behind the lenses as his face turned sharply from one to the other. They were small and shrewd and she had felt somehow in that moment she had been unfairly judged. It only made her feel more like a fish out of water. Candle wax, floor polish, the crucifix on the wall behind the secretary's head complete with writhing corpus. She had turned to sit in one of the chairs, found it unforgivably hard, and sorted through a pile of religious magazines until she found something secular and readable. But it was five months old, with an unpromising cover story about downtown redevelopment—*Can Galleries Portáge Save Downtown?*—and soon her mind flew to the events of the morning.

When she'd awoken, she'd found her mother perched on the edge of her bed. Which was odd.

"Mom?" She'd rubbed her eyes in the semidarkness.

"Oh, my poor Stevie!"

Then she'd remembered. The fog of sleep dissolved. "Oh!" A tiny cry lodged in her throat. She sat up. Her mother enveloped her in a hug. A memory of damp leather blunted the fragrance of her mother's Opium. She pushed Leo from her mind.

"I can't believe this has happened, my poor—"

And so it had gone. Hugging. Weeping. Counselling. This was Kathleen Lord, who had earned her therapy chops in California, no less. Her father had heard the news on CBC. He'd alerted his wife. They decided to let Stevie sleep. (*They?* Stevie imagined her father had tied her mother to her chair to keep her from barging in.) Her father left for the hospital and Kathleen, honouring her promise, had beetled over to Merritt's instead. Hugging. Counselling. No weeping. ("She has it bottled up.") Organizing—funeral, reception. Luckily Father Day phoned, so that was the church figured out. She was going to drive Merritt to St. Giles' in an hour.

"No, I'll do it," Stevie interjected.

"You should rest."

"Oh, for god's sake." Stevie swung her legs over the bed and was immediately smacked with a bout of dizziness.

"I told you."

Stevie rose tentatively and reached for her robe at the foot of the bed. Pushing her arm through the sleeve kindled the memory of another garment whose sleeve she had recently occupied. Another memory of the previous evening. She contemplated her mother, who was busy smoothing the duvet.

"Mom—"

"Mmm?"

"Have you talked with Aunt Paul lately? Or had a letter?"

"Why are you asking that?" Kathleen stopped in her tidying.

"Can you just the answer the question?"

"I haven't talked to her since last month. Her birthday. Didn't I tell you? Pauline and George have decided to sell the house in Ten Hills and get something smaller somewhere else in Baltimore—a condo."

"I guess I forgot."

Kathleen's suspicious regard worked on her like an itch. "Okay," she sighed. "Michael was apparently in Washington earlier this month."

"And so you think—?"

"Well, I don't know, do I?" Her tone was sharper than she'd intended. "And I guess I won't find out."

"If you had told him in the first place—"

"Ma, I am not having this conversation again."

"You started it."

"These are the words of a mother and therapist?"

Kathleen shook her head gently. Her eyes softened. "Sweetheart, Michael's gone and that's an end to it."

"Which 'it'?"

"All the many 'its.'" Kathleen pulled the duvet over the pillows. "By the way, there was a call from a Les Strickland for you. Doesn't he have something to do with Leo?"

"His obsessive-compulsive next-door neighbour. Probably wants me to walk Leo's dog."

Stevie had bristled a little. Alvy was a sweet dog, and, okay, so she wasn't working. But Les just presumed. And Leo had led him—somehow—to presume.

And on a day like today. She turned from her unread magazine and glanced out the church office window. Autumn leaves, crisp air. Canine enthusiasm. She relaxed: Walking Alvy might be a tonic.

The woman at the desk, alert to the movements of those waiting for Father Day, lifted her hands from the keyboard and again asked whether Stevie would like a cup of coffee. Stevie declined but she'd given the woman an opening.

"Isn't it *awful*? We were so shocked when we heard. Such a *nice* man." The persistent emphases hammered at Stevie.

"Are you a relative?" the woman continued.

Stevie stared at her. If I were a relative, wouldn't I be in there? "No," she mustered. "Just a friend."

"Oh, dear. Your *poor* thing." Cluck, cluck, cluck. "Were you a *good* friend?"

Stevie frowned. The intonation was offensive, but the woman couldn't seem to help speaking in italics.

"We grew up together. His house was just down the street."

"Oh, I see." The woman patted her bun, which looked like a small furry animal in repose. "Then you must know what an…" she paused "… *interesting* photographer he was."

"Well, actually—"

"My husband and I went to see his show last winter at the—now I can't remember the name—?"

"Floating Gallery, probably."

"In every picture, someone was wearing a lampshade on his head—"

"Oh, the *Life of the Party* series."

"—and shaking hands, and meeting politicians and well-known locals. There was even one with the bishop. It was very—" She seemed to grope for a word. "—*interesting*."

"You're an art photography fan?" Stevie stifled a yawn. *Winnipeg Life* had renewed appeal.

"Oh, dear, no. He left me an invitation to the opening. He used to come here a lot before Father Saunders retired."

"Really? For Mass?"

"No, no. During the week. Usually in the afternoons. Yes, he used to come here quite *regularly* for a time. Of course—" She leaned forward and lowered her voice. "—I don't know *why* he came here so often. Father Saunders never said." She straightened in her chair and intoned, "The relationship between priest and penitent is a *privileged* one."

And it never rains in California.

A few memories:

Michael and Merritt, dressed up and tidy, their mother Lillian ushering them into the Rossiters' big white Lincoln on Sunday mornings. Stevie on her beautiful blue Schwinn Breeze waving from her front lawn, as Lillian cautiously backed onto the Crescent.

An overheard conversation, laced with misgiving, between her parents and some neighbours. Lillian was now attending Mass every morning. "A coping strategy," her mother had explained. The expression was novel to her ten-year-old ears.

Walking alone through evening mist along the shore at the rambling Rossiter cabin in Lake-of-the-Woods. A noisy weekend party with a dozen college friends of Michael's, a September farewell to summer as the college year loomed—her first university year, Michael's third. She, feeling miserably out of place, younger than most, wondering why she was invited, oblivious to another's footfalls. Out of the veil of white, a face emerges, and like a dream, a kiss. In a moment, the barrier that was their shared childhood is broken.

And Michael, in bed with her one morning, in her first apartment on Macmillan. His back to her. She connecting his freckles with one of her

Rapidograph pens. He describing some dialectical metaphysical blather from a philosophy course, his arts elective that year. He summarized his position. She stopped cold. It was something the Pope might have said. "What did you draw?" he'd said, lifting his neck from the pillow and craning as if he could see. "Nothing, just shapes," she'd replied dully. But it had been a floor plan, for the first floor of her dream house. He forgot to turn around in the mirror later, and Stevie had scrubbed the markings off for him in the shower. A few months later, that morning in bed, that conversation, would come back to her with terrible force.

11

Winnipeg Life

"So, how's Hubris Incorporated this morning?"
"What are you doing here?"
"Hey, you called me, remember?"
"Well, I didn't mean for you to come over." Axel, on his knees on the floor, threw a file bound by elastic bands into a cardboard box.
"Fine. I'll leave." Leo surveyed the room. Twelve months and nine issues of *Winnipeg Life* later, the magazine's office in Artspace was a ghost of its former self. The walls were bare but for a framed cover of the first edition, chalk-white, here and there pocked or gouged as if someone had punched them. Leo recalled the launch party he and Ishbel had attended the previous September: food, wine, pristine walls, an enormous mock-up of volume I, issue I, lots of optimism, and Axel practically hugging himself.
"So, the rumours are true," he said.
"And you didn't call to commiserate?"
"You haven't called me. I haven't talked to you all summer. It's a two-way street, buddy-boy."
He watched Axel throw another folder into the box. Unfolded document boxes leaned against one wall, while a pyramid of bound and taped boxes stamped with *WL* anchored a corner of the irregularly shaped room. Unsold, undistributed, and otherwise unloved copies of the magazine, presumably. The only other object left in the room besides a filing cabinet was Axel's desk, which was covered with papers and the usual office detritus waiting to be packed.
"When do you have to be out of here?"
"End of the month. Which is two days away."
"So, it's really kaput, is it?"
"Not kaput. We've merely suspended publication for the time being."
"You're not seriously going to try and get it going again."
Axel carried on slamming files into the box.

"I told you a city magazine wouldn't work," Leo continued, almost enjoying his I-told-you-so moment in the sun. "Winnipeg is wholesaleville. Even the rich are cheapshits here."

"It was working fine, Leo. It's a cash-flow thing. First, the Arts Council decided to change its eligibility requirements. Then the Department of Culture was about to hand over some more funding in the spring, but the government changed hands—"

"So, big deal. You tried. You failed. Some government money got pissed away—nothing new there. Move on."

Axel pointed to the wall. "Get me one of those folded-up things, would you? And close the door."

Leo complied, noting as he had when he'd walked in that some wag had attached two question marks after the words "Winnipeg Life" on the door. Axel rose, dusted the knees of his jeans, and took the box from Leo. "It's not just government money," he said, frowning at the instructions on the side of the box. "Fuck, why do they have to make a fucking *box* complicated?"

"Here, give it to me." Leo cleared a space on the desk and began unfolding the box. "What do you mean, 'not just government money'?"

Axel glowered. "I put some of my own money in."

Leo looked up. Axel and his ability to latch onto respectable sums at the right moment was always at least half a mystery. He, however, had been instrumental in generating part of Axel's first tidy pile.

Once upon a time, at Clear Lake, where Axel's parents, Otto and Clare Werner, owned a cottage, two young men freshly out of college and avoiding employment, were drinking at the Southgate Hotel. One of them, Leo Fabian, responding to a call of nature, went into the toilet and there, while contemplating the meaning of life on a cold hard seat, heard two men come in. Thinking they were alone, the two began conversing about a drug drop, even unto exact time and coordinates. When Leo didn't return after half an hour, Axel went in to see if he had passed out. He found Leo frozen in the stall with fear and excitement, his mind roiling with possibilities.

Two days later, at 5:30 in the morning, somewhere in the Duck Mountains, Leo and Axel hurried through the forest with their knapsacks, compass and map in hand, and came upon two things. One was the dope, all nicely packaged and waiting for them like a grail in an adventure tale. The other was a naked woman picking morels. She looked just peachy in the early morning light. The naked—and unembarrassed—woman eventually became Mrs. Axel Werner. As for the dope, Leo smoked his half and gave the rest away to friends. Axel, ever the greater risk taker, and yet somehow the more canny, sold his half. With it, he made a down payment on the *Dauphin Courier*, a biweekly Eve's uncle was putting up for sale, and which Axel, on a whim, decided was just the sort of business to get into. After all, hadn't he written great essays in college? Leo, having all the skills an arts degree guaranteed in the late 70s (none) and with nothing better to do, went to work for the *Courier*. What the heck. He'd written great essays, too. How different could journalism be?

And they all lived happily ever after.

"Well, not really," Leo said out loud.

"What?"

"Nothing. I was just going over something in my mind. Anyway, some? Some of your own money?"

"I've sold one kidney and I'm functioning without a liver."

"That's a trick."

"Okay, I remortgaged the house."

Leo stared. "Doesn't the house belong to you *and* Eve?"

Axel shrugged. He moved to the file cabinet.

"Did you also sell your brain somewhere along the line? This is just a magazine." He picked up a copy from the desk. Volume I, number 6. Sixty-four pages. Full-colour. Glossy stock. Perfect bound. The thing screamed: No Expense Spared. "How did you think you were going to make this work?"

"We had a plan. We're not completely stupid." Axel yanked so hard on the file drawer, the drawer slipped its track and crashed to the floor. "Fuck!"

"Here, I'll help—"

"Leave it. I don't want you putting your glass back out. The fucking cabinet's rented anyway. Throw me that box." Axel dropped to his knees and began removing files from the drawer. "The plan was to distribute it with the *Zit*, controlled-circulation style."

"Not a bad idea."

"And we just about had it in the bag when it was suddenly scotched."

"You mean by Harry Mack? Isn't he of Scottish origin?"

"I think he left the 'enzie' or 'intosh' back in Poland. Anyway, this is before Harmac bought the *Zit*."

"Then who scotched it?"

"That asshole Guy Clark."

"But it's a business thing."

"But editorial had a say. And Clark went out of his fucking way to fuck this deal up."

Leo watched Axel slam manila files into the box. Guy always seemed preternaturally jealous of anyone who left the *Citizen* for better things. "How do you know this anyway?" he asked.

"I just know," Axel replied darkly, glaring up at him.

Leo began folding the top cover for the document box. "So, what are you going to do? I mean, now you've got this debt—"

"I'm going to resurrect this magazine, of course."

"How?"

"I'm working on it."

"Again I say 'how?'" Leo tossed him the box cover. "Appeal to the new owner? You've still got Clark blocking the way."

"Remember our plan to brick up his apartment door one night while he was sleeping?"

"Yeah?"

"Let's do it, and then run a hose from the car exhaust."

"He lives on the fifteenth floor, remember?"

"Shit."

Leo picked up the March 1988 issue again. Paul Richter, the WSO conductor, was the cover boy. How many Winnipeg readers, he wondered, really gave a crap about the orchestra's ups and downs? "Why not just go on and do something else? Forget this."

"Because."

"You are such a fucking egomaniac, Axel. You just want to rule the world, annex the Sudetenland, invade Poland—"

"Would you cut out that crap? We're not kids on Jackson Street anymore."

When they were kids on Jackson Street in Riverview and playing War, Leo and Axel invariably got stuck on the Axis side. One of the other boys' fathers had brought home a Nazi war helmet as a souvenir, and Axel usually found his eight-year-old cranium swimming in it. Axel wasn't German. He had been adopted by German-Canadians. His parentage was a mystery. Part French? Part Aboriginal? Maybe part Italian, like himself? A little Slav thrown in? All these had crossed his mind at one time or another. Axel had thick, black hair and almost olive skin. His eyes lacked a fold or two, giving him at times the oriental inscrutability of cliché. But for the eyes, the two of them had sometimes been mistaken for brothers in those early years. Leo, meanwhile, was the son of an Italian soldier who had spent most of the war on a prison farm in Devon, where he had met Leo's mother and scandalized the community by marrying her not long after V-E day.

"What I mean, Axel, is you just want to control something. You could move to Toronto and work your way up the ranks there, but—no—you'd have to accept something a little lower on the masthead."

"Shut up." Axel rose and yanked at another file drawer.

"You could have had Guy's job. You had as good a chance as Liz or Guy to be Go! editor—probably better. You know more about the arts—"

"Butt-munching was the route to that job."

"A little golf, maybe. And Guy knew how to play...and lose. And win, as it happens."

"That prick!" Axel looked at him—or stared through him—his eyes glittering strangely. He was clenching and unclenching his fists.

"No argument there." Leo backed off a little. He enjoyed riling Axel, but wondered if he'd go too far some day. When they were boys, Leo had once beaten Axel up handily over ownership of a comic book, though Axel was a year older. But in latter years, after he'd sold the *Courier* and landed in the *Zit*'s Go! section, Axel had taken to body-building with a vengeance—to prove arts guys aren't wusses, Leo figured—and it had worked. Leo, who sometimes questioned if Axel didn't harbour a secret desire for a grudge match after a quarter-century, didn't want to find out the hard way.

"Anyway, need another box? Axel?"

Axel seemed to return from some reverie. He looked with disgust around the room, and grabbed at the ponytail he'd lately affected, and which Leo hated. "Let's go to Blondie's for a burger."

"Nah. I gotta get back."

"Nose to the grindstone."

"At least I've got a job."

"You should take some risks."

"I've taken risks."

"Only because I made you."

"Like stealing a car when I was fifteen? Frank regularly brings that one up."

"Just try not to reoffend."

"Fuck you." Leo turned to go. Then he remembered his original mission. "So, why did you phone me at 8:31 in the morning?"

"Oh?—shit—I forget."

"Were you here or at home?"

"At home."

"But I'm not often at the *Zit* at 8:30 in the morning." Leo frowned. "What's up? You only ever phone me when you want something."

"That's not true." Axel squirmed. "I was just wondering—" He yanked at his ponytail and grimaced. "—I was just wondering what you were wearing to the Galleries Portáge opening Saturday."

Leo's eyebrows rose a notch. "I thought I'd wear the pink chiffon. What are you wearing?"

"Ha ha. I meant, I heard you guys had to rent tuxedos."

"That was an ugly rumour. I'm wearing my suit."

"Oh, okay. I guess I'll wear mine, too. If I can get it repaired in time. I'd thought about getting a tux."

Leo frowned. "For this you phone me at 8:30 in the morning?"
"Well, it was on my mind."
"Bullshit, it was."
"Oh, bugger off back to the *Zit*. I didn't ask you to make a special trip here."
"I was at the cop shop. It's four hundred yards from here." Leo paused. "You heard about Michael Rossiter, I suppose."
"Yeah, what a bummer." Axel turned back to the filing cabinet. "Are you covering it?"
"Sort of."
Leo expected Axel to query his ambiguous reply. Nada. Axel was bent over the third drawer down. Leo addressed the ponytail: "Did you know him very well, I mean when you were covering the arts at the *Zit*?"
"Who?"
"Michael Rossiter, you idiot."
"No, not really. Did a piece or two on his photography."
"You knew about his philanthropy..."
"Yeah, but he kept such a low profile that it never turned into a story. I think you know what I mean from personal experience."
"So...no insights."
"Nope, sorry."
"Okay." Leo turned toward the door. "Well, I guess I'll see you and Eve on Saturday."
Axel grunted. "Well, me, anyway."
"Right. Roger Mellish said Eve's a little behind laying out *Taste of Winnipeg*."
"That stupid book. They haven't even finished reading the first set of proofs she sent them. Why don't those Junior League bitches just fuck the poolboy and stop wasting everybody's time—"
"Get a grip."
"—Anyway, Eve's gone to Dauphin to stay with her parents for a while."
"Oh, oh. Does this mean your cock got out of the barnyard again?"
"You should talk."
"Hey, I'm not married. My cock's free range. Yours is cooped."
"That metaphor sucks."
"You're the arts guy. Besides, I think that's called an allusion."
Axel turned and gave him a slow, evil grin. "Made it with this Stevie person yet?"
"None of your business."
"What is it? Three months? Is she waiting to be pinned or something? Lavaliered?"

"She's had a rough time. A bad divorce and stuff."

"That's not what I hear."

Leo was suddenly alert. Axel looked alarmed. It only lasted a second, but it was perturbing. "What do you know? You've never even met her. And I haven't seen you since June."

"Hey, kidding." Leo watched Axel fiddle with a loose handle on a file drawer. "I was just trying to yank your chain, pal."

They stared at each other for a moment. Then Axel walked over and pulled the framed first edition cover off the wall. "Anyway," he said, running his finger over the layer of dust on the top frame, "I'll see you Saturday. Wear the chiffon."

"Ha ha. Fuck you."

12

An Heir

"Stop the car! Pull over!"
"What! Why?"
"I'm going to be sick."

Stevie careened through the traffic on Maryland and turned quickly onto St. Matthew's, grinding a few gears as she did so. She was unused to a stick shift and Merritt's Miata convertible was so low to the ground and visibility with the top up so poor, she felt like she was driving a kiddie car. She screeched to a halt outside a church; Merritt flung open the door and leaned over. Stevie heard retching sounds, and felt her own gorge rising. She reached around to her bag stuffed in the narrow space behind the front seat and rooted around for some Kleenex.

"Delayed reaction?" she asked, passing a wad of tissue to Merritt.

Merritt held her throat with one hand and dabbed at her mouth with the other. "Something like that," she croaked.

In fact, to Stevie, Merritt had looked remarkably composed exiting the morgue at the Health Sciences Centre. Whereas Stevie had yearned to be in on the conversation with the priest, she had no desire to share Merritt's task of identifying Michael's body. The imprint of last evening's horror would not soon fade, and to see him laid out on a slab, she was afraid, would send her tumbling to the floor once again. Merritt, however, perhaps a little paler than when she went in, had merely shrugged. "Well, it was him, all right. I don't know why *I* had to do that. I mean, you could have—"

But Stevie had cut her off with a sharp look. Merritt had taken yet another toilet break, then they had proceeded to the parking garage across from the hospital in silence. The sun, a silver disk in a silver sky most of the morning, had now pierced the clouds and bathed the hospital grounds in golden haze. After the institutional stink of the hospital, the September air was delicious—sweet and loamy. She had wished they had put the top down on the Miata before continuing. She contemplated the canvas roof now.

"Will you be okay?" she asked after some time had passed. "I can take you home first and then get my mother's car or something."

"No, it's all right," Merritt responded, flipping the sun visor down, and examining herself in the mirror. "I'll go to Leo's with you. I'd be bored at home."

"Shall we put the top down?" Stevie stuffed her bag back behind the seat with more force than she'd intended. *Bored?*

"Let's not. My hair. And it might rain." Merritt pulled a lipstick out her bag and began reapplying. She glanced over at Stevie, who was staring out at the blue sky. "Something the matter?"

"Oh, nothing."

"You can go then." She gestured at the steering wheel and replaced the lipstick in her bag.

Stevie groped for first gear and pulled away. "I gather," she began, as she tried, and failed, to make a U-turn in the street. "I gather," she repeated, as she reversed the car and set off a cacophony of grinding.

"You gather *what*? I'm not going to have any gears left, if you keep—"

"Then you drive. It's your car."

"I can't. I'm grieving."

"*And I'm not?*" Stevie, furious, ground the gear into first and the car bolted toward the stop sign.

"Sorry, Stevie. Ooooph." The car braked suddenly. "I didn't mean... Anyway, what was it you were gathering?"

"Gathering?"

"You were about to say something about...something."

Stevie turned back onto Maryland. Merritt's sulky demeanor had jolted the topic from her mind. "Oh, right." Their conversation between St. Giles and the hospital had been largely a desultory one about the funeral arrangements Merritt had made with Father Day for Friday. But now she picked up the thread. "I gather Michael had been a frequent visitor to Father Saunders, who used to be at St. Giles. He retired or something."

"Oh?"

"'Oh,' you didn't know Father Saunders had retired? Or 'oh' you didn't know about Michael?"

"I didn't know about Michael. But I'm not surprised. The Church sort of had him by the short and curlies, didn't it? I mean, deep down."

"I don't remember him going to Mass or anything when we were at university."

"Well, he had discovered sex by then, I suppose," Merritt snorted. "But still...once an altar boy always an altar boy. And of course with my mother being so pious, and Michael being so protective of her..." Her voice trailed off.

Stevie flicked her a speculative glance as she sped across Portage Avenue. "I remember the two of you getting into that big car on Sunday mornings when we were kids. I think I was sort of envious. I wanted to go with you. We never even went to church at Christmas."

"You would have been welcome to take my place. I hated it. My mother had to bribe me with new dresses. Which worked, until I passed out of the pretty-dresses phase. She wouldn't let me wear jeans to church, and I wouldn't wear anything but in those days. Well, it was an excuse. Anyway my father supported me—he never went to church, he was too busy worshipping the bottle—and that was that. I've hardly been in one since."

"Didn't you marry in church? I've forgotten the story."

"Woodsworth Building. Justice of the peace. Quick and dirty."

"Where is Mr. Parrish these days?"

"In Vancouver with his boyfriend. We still talk."

"Didn't you know he was gay when you married him?"

"Oh, sure. I guess. Hell, I was nineteen. I thought it would be sort of a laugh. Besides, I liked the idea of having a new name. 'Merritt Parrish' sounded right. I was sick of being 'Merritt Rossiter.'" She repeated the last name like it had a bad taste.

"Rossiter is a fine name," Stevie retorted, having many times dreamily inscribed it with her own. Stephanie Rossiter. Stevie Rossiter. Mrs. Stevie Rossiter.

"I just wanted to get out from under all that Rossiter-ness," Merritt continued.

"Meaning?"

"There's a stop sign there."

"I know. I see it." Stevie braked, more gently this time, and turned to her. "Meaning?"

Merritt squirmed. "I don't know. Just the responsibility, or something. Like having to live up to something. As if the Rossiters were some sort of royal family, and we all had to behave just so. My father couldn't stand it either, I know."

They drove in silence for a moment. "Michael didn't approve."

"Of what?"

"Of my marriage."

"Because your husband was gay?"

"No, because we—I—treated the vow so...carelessly, I suppose."

"Well, you did."

Stevie could feel the full gaze of Merritt scrutinizing her as she turned off Wolseley onto Sherwood Street.

"Haven't you ever wanted to do something just to thwart someone?"

Stevie glanced at her. "No," she replied.

Merritt regarded her slyly. "Oh, really? Oh, I think you have."

"Now, don't look."

"Jesus, Stevie, I doubt Leo has anything I'd want to steal."

Leaving Merritt by the back door of Leo's house, Stevie went over to a nearby oak tree, stood on tiptoe, and reached high. She grimaced, wondering as before what else might be lurking in the hollow.

"Gee." Merritt examined her manicure. "No one would ever think of looking there. Of course, under the doormat might be safer."

Stevie's felt the cool metal of the key against her fingers. "Got it."

"Do you do this often?"

"Only a couple of times. Leo's neighbour usually takes Alvy out for a run. He's semi-retired, but he had a medical appointment today." Stevie opened the screen door, then rattled the key into the lock of the second door. At that instant, the air was split by gruff barking and growling.

"Jesus! What kind of animal does he have?"

"It's a retriever. He's harmless." Stevie pushed the door open. "Aren't you, sweetheart?" Alvarez stood at the top of three steps leading into the kitchen, his dark lips curled into what looked like Queen Victoria's frown. Stevie reached out and petted the dog's golden muzzle.

"Dogs creep me out." Merritt drew back, while Stevie climbed the stairs. "Do you remember the Hughes's horrible Dalmatian? I think it was deaf or something. I was seven, and it would come bounding out and leap on me... I think it scarred me for life."

"This one would lead you to the jewels and silverware, wouldn't you, Alvy?" Stevie put her arms around Alvarez's neck. The dog's tail beat the air furiously. Then he skittered across the kitchen floor, nails clicking against the linoleum, and disappeared momentarily, returning with a beat-up teddy bear in his mouth.

"Ooh, Alvy's got a teddy," Stevie cooed as Merritt sidled into the kitchen.

"Honestly, Stevie, you'd think it was a child."

"But he's so cute." She noted Merritt gazing around with curiosity.

"I don't understand why people have big dogs. Is it cooped up here all day?"

"Like I said, Leo's neighbour helps out. Apparently Ishbel used to be able to get home during the day, if Leo couldn't."

"Ah, Ishbel."

"Did you know her?"

"A little. She's the granddaughter of—" Merritt related some long Winnipeg pedigree. "I think she worked for the NDP just to annoy her family. Her grandfather was a leading member of the Committee of One

Thousand in the 1919 strike beating back all those evil Bolshies. Probably arm in arm with my grandfather." Merritt hooted. "Anyway, she wasn't Leo's type."

"You would know this."

"I observe." Merritt ran her finger through the film of sawdust on top of an uninstalled dishwasher. "Kind of a mess, isn't it?"

Stevie watched her blow the dust off her fingers. Yes, it was a mess. Various power tools mixed with boxes and cans of food littered the counters and the kitchen table while black snakes of electric cord twisted over the floor. Lumber was stacked against one wall, which was a cross-hatch of colours, newer paint over old paint, a reminder of where the old overhead cupboards had been. A table saw stood in the middle of the room, a tomato-sauce-encrusted dinner plate and smeared wine glass pressed against the blade. Part of the dining-room floor visible from the door was covered with an old bedsheet, cans of paint stripper stacked neatly in view.

"He's doing the renovations himself," Stevie explained, though she realized he hadn't seemed to have made much progress in the three months she'd known him. She rooted in a drawer full to bursting and pulled out a plastic Safeway bag.

"I'd hire someone."

"Wouldn't want to ruin your nails."

"Well, exactly."

Stevie passed through the dining room into the living room in search of Alvy's lead. Merritt followed. The room was a hodgepodge. Some fine pieces of furniture, a cabinet, and a side table that had come from England with Leo's mother, were mingled with a dilapidated couch, a couple of mismatched chairs, and a rug whose dubious pattern seemed to be fading by the minute. These latter bits, Stevie knew, had been pulled up from the basement after Ishbel had sent for the furniture she'd considered her own. There were moments Stevie itched to pour her design talents into the room, to relieve the space of its post-Ishbel neo-bachelor excrescences. Leo had asked her advice, but she had resisted giving any.

She cast her eye over the stereo components and large television that dominated the room, over the books, magazines, newspapers, and tapes and records that lay about in precarious little piles, at the shelf of wind-up dentures, glow-in-the-dark lizards, old model train cars, mini-brix, and Pez dispensers. If she had allowed such homey disorder to invade her house in the Beaches, particularly toward the end of her marriage, Sangster would have gone into one of his rages.

"Hmm," Merritt cast her eyes about the room. "Sort of late college-dorm meets estate sale." She pointed at a lava lamp and mimed Joan Rivers gagging. "Still, it's kind of a cute house. Oh, and here's what you're looking for." She handed the lead to Stevie and regarded her with amusement. "You know what I think?"

"No, what?"

"I think he's building a nest."

"I'm sure I wouldn't know." Stevie bent and affixed the lead to Alvarez's collar. The dog was very nearly quivering with joy. "Are you coming with us?"

"Actually, I'm still feeling a bit queasy, if you don't mind. I think I'll just rest here. Where's the bathroom?"

Alvarez was delirious to be out in the soft September afternoon, snuffling noisily through the mounds of brittle leaves blown along the backyard fence, tearing around to the front of the house to poke his nose even more indiscriminately into the fetid and the fragrant, dragging Stevie along behind. He stopped finally by an elm tree on the boulevard and crouched. Stevie turned instead to look at Leo's house, plastic bag at the ready. It *was* kind of cute, she thought. Red-brown brick—more like an Ontario home. Two broad gables, a bull's eye window next to the door, a couple of coach lamps. The front window was opaque in the daylight. It shimmered with a dull reflection of lawn and trees that masked the interior of the house until Stevie readjusted her eyes and looked straight through to the dining room window on the opposite wall. There, into a square of light, a silhouette appeared, hovered for a moment, then reached down. It was Merritt lifting the telephone from the console table. Stevie had a call she wanted to make herself in privacy—Leo's place would have been ideal, she realized—but couldn't very well with Merritt present.

She glanced down the street. There was a phone booth at a strip mall on Portage Avenue, she was sure. She put her hand in the Safeway bag, quickly scooped the poop, turned the bag inside out, and tied it in a knot. Then she, Alvarez, and a warm bag headed down the street. She knew the phone number; it had been hers for a time, years ago. Oddly, it was the area code that escaped her. 401? No, that was the highway to Windsor. 410? That was it. She could bill the call to her still-active Toronto number.

• • •

"Well, you took a while."

"Alvy was enjoying himself."

"Feeling better?"

"Much." Merritt dabbed at her nose with a Kleenex.

Stevie sighed. "What are you looking at?"

Merritt had settled on the couch. She was holding a photograph up to catch the light of the window. A large brown envelope lay open beside her.

"Leo's better looking than I thought." She flicked a glance at Stevie. "Maybe lose ten pounds, work on those love handles—"

"Where did you get those?" Stevie bent to unclip Alvy's lead.

"They were sitting right here."

"You've been snooping."

"Well, it's better than twiddling my thumbs."

"Who did you phone earlier?"

"None of your business." Merritt turned to another photograph. Each was part of a series of black-and-whites Stevie had taken at Grand Beach one hot weekday in early August when Leo decided to play hooky from the *Citizen*. She had intended to devote a role of film to shadows and contrasts in the dunes along the east beach as the sun lowered but a few of the pictures were of Leo clowning by the shoreline in muscleman poses. She had made copies for him.

"Now, if only we could get him out of those cords and chinos he always wears, and those awful checked shirts. Short sleeves. Ugh." Merritt continued, returning the photo to the pile. "Maybe I should devote a future Re: column to male makeovers. We could use Leo. Do before and after. Do something with his hair. Hmm, yes. And then put him in Armani or…" Merritt quickly rattled off half a dozen names that sounded like new-style deli fare. Stevie frowned. Merritt was as speedy and crystalline as she had been the night before. She remembered, too, what she had seen on her night table.

"I don't think you'd get Leo to agree," she interjected.

"Hello, nice doggie." Alvy plunked his head on Merritt's stomach. She patted it gingerly. "Oh, I'm sure I could flatter him into it." She turned on her elbow and smirked at Stevie, regarding her speculatively. "You know, we had a little talk about you last night when you went upstairs. He asked me about you and Michael."

Stevie glanced at her reflection in an antique mirror above the couch. "And what did you tell him?"

"Everything."

"Well, I think he's figured out that Michael meant something to me in the past."

"No, Stevie, I told him everything."

Stevie looked at her sharply.

"I told him about the baby. Your baby. The one you had by Michael."

The world seemed to drop away. For Stevie, this was the second time in two days. Only this time she hovered at the chasm's edge, air cold and hard pouring into her lungs. Shivering, she managed a whisper: "My own *brothers* don't even know about that."

Merritt shrugged. "It seems so quaint—going away to have your baby."

Stevie staggered toward the nearest chair and lowered herself carefully. "How could you possibly know?"

"Oh, Stevie, really! I lived with your parents the whole time it was going on. I could hear your mother on the phone. There were letters—"

"You snooped."

"I was fifteen! And the phone bills listed Baltimore, not Providence, where you were supposed to be studying at the Rhode Island School of Design. And, anyway—"

"Does my mother know you know?"

"No!" Merritt pouted. "I assume the magic circle is just your parents, your aunt and uncle in Baltimore, you…and me."

"And now Leo."

Merritt regarded her manicure. "And now Leo," she echoed.

"What on earth possessed you to tell him that?" Stevie felt herself moving quickly from the cold of shock to the heat of anger.

Merritt glanced up at her. "Why didn't you tell Michael?"

"Answer the question!"

Merritt recoiled. She pushed Alvy's head off her lap and sat up. "I don't know. I just… I wasn't being bitchy, you know. Really. I just thought it would help if there was no bullshit between the two of you. Leo's a good guy. He'd be good for you."

"Who are you to judge who would be good for me? One two-week marriage to a homosexual, a whole string of failed, inappropriate relationships, a drug addiction. How many times have you been to Hazelden?"

"Shut up."

"Did Michael know you were using again?"

"I am not 'using.'"

"The odd recreational toot? How many bathroom visits have you had since we left this morning?"

"Shut up. At least I didn't marry a psychopath like you did."

"David wasn't a psychopath."

"Well, not *clinically*, I suppose. But he was sure a serious control-freak. You never told *him* about your child, did you?"

No, she hadn't. Even before the immaculateness of purpose that had so attracted her had devolved into obsessive perfectionism, she sensed he wouldn't have tolerated the notion. It would have been a blemish as unbearable as a stain on her dress, or a scratch on his BMW. After his career had reached some unimaginable summit, then they would have their first perfect child together. *His* first perfect child. Her child dwelt somewhere in the world, but for Stevie, who had laid eyes on her for a bare moment, she existed forever only as a subterranean ache. She looked without seeing across the coffee table's clutter at Merritt reinserting the photographs back in their sleeve.

And now Leo.

Alvy lifted his head. A keening noise arose from the back of his throat. Merritt glanced at him. "What's the matter with the dog?"

"I don't know," Stevie said, pulled back into the room. Senses a tautness in the air, she thought, patting her knee. "Come here, sweetheart."

Merritt dropped the package on the table and folded her arms across her chest. "So, anyway, why didn't you tell Michael?"

Stevie felt spent. "He was going off to the Curtis."

"He would have married you."

"You don't know that."

"Such a *good* boy."

"Good *natured*. Why are you always so spiteful about him, Merritt? When does the sibling rivalry end? He's done—did—a lot of good with who he was and what he had."

"He was another control freak, but just in a different way." Merritt thrust her chin out. "All men are control freaks."

Stevie chose to ignore this. "And besides, there were things I wanted to do in life. I was nineteen years old. I didn't want to be saddled with a child."

"Then why didn't you have an abortion?"

Stevie was silent. She looked at Merritt, who seemed to be studying her intently. Why, indeed? She had asked herself that many times in the aftermath. She could barely face the truth: that a philosophical position against abortion, which Michael had gleaned from his philosophy class, then promulgated in bed one spring morning, had decided her. That she had clung to her decision with a ferocity born of youthful zeal.

"Funny thing is," Stevie continued, avoiding Merritt's scrutiny, "Michael said he had something he wanted to tell me when he phoned me on Monday."

"Like what?"

"I don't know. But when Leo's brother-in-law mentioned Washington tags on his luggage, I thought maybe he had gone down there. Maybe he knew. Maybe someone had told him—"

"Well, it wasn't me."

Stevie lifted her eyes. "Why didn't you tell Michael? God knows, you've had enough arguments over the years. You could have thrown this at him so easily."

"What?" Merritt snapped. "And let him know he had a direct heir?"

"An *heir*? A direct *heir*? I thought you were trying to get away from this Rossiter royal family business."

Merritt shifted her weight and reached down for her purse. "A daughter, then. I meant a daughter. Jesus!"

13

Nadir

Liz dropped the cigarette end into the Styrofoam cup and considered the dying hiss as the ember hit the coffee dregs.

Sort of like my life, she thought.

Her eyes returned to the computer screen and the ten inches of meaningless drivel she'd cranked out. A puff piece about the upcoming—excuse me, *forthcoming* (god forbid she should violate one of Martin's word edicts)—opening of Galleries Portáge. The *Zit*'s huzzahs for downtown redevelopment seemed to grow in reverse proportion to its plotting to flee the downtown in favour of some ugly industrial park. The piece was about a shop in the mall that sold Inuit art—a last-minute contribution to a Friday advertorial supplement. It was the kind of crap underpaid freelancers usually did. Guy assigned it to her instead. She was being punished.

This is what I get for telling Guy to drop dead.

She glanced across the room toward Guy's desk. His chair was empty.

Perhaps he's dropped dead on the way back from lunch. What's the likelihood?

Lousy.

She looked toward the bank of windows on the south side. A natural reaction to seek the light, she thought. But someone had shut the blinds when Louis St. Laurent was prime minister and last dusted them when John F. Kennedy was winging his way to Dallas. Light existed only as a thin ghostly presence between the slats. She closed her eyes. Even that ethereal glow made her head ache a little.

Surprise! That's what happens if you drink too much.

And if you sleep on an overstuffed couch.

In the car on their way home, after the police had questioned them, after strained goodbyes were said, Spencer had been oblivious to the obvious topic of conversation. Someone they both knew—at least a little—had been murdered not a hundred yards away. Michael might even have been murdered while they were stuffing their faces with Bunny's cold tenderloin of beef, for heaven's sake. But, no, Spencer lit into her about her lack of enthusiasm for his political plans, for his wanting to serve.

"Serve, my ass," she had snapped. The booze buzz had begun to wear off. "Why even bother? The Liberals haven't won an election in this province in thirty years, and never will again. Or do you think the prime minister, if we ever have another Liberal prime minister in this country—"

"Of course we will—"

"—will call you on the phone one day and offer you a senatorship for your great sacrifice to the party in this political wilderness? You'd love that, wouldn't you? Being in Ottawa, sitting in the House of Parasites, manipulating things..."

And she'd ranted on that way, in a way she hadn't for years, reducing Spencer to chilly silence. When they pulled into their driveway, he got out of the car, slammed the door, and thrashed his way into the house. Liz had remained in the car, growing colder as the metal sucked up the interior heat, and colder still as she realized what she had done: she had never before given full voice to her antipathy to his ambitions. This was beyond snipping and snarking.

She had got out of the car eventually. She could tell from the progression of lights in the upstairs windows of their overvalued Oak Street home that Spencer had made his way to bed. She went into the house and lay down on the couch in the living room in the dark listening to the splatter of rain on the window. Like a chilly premonition, quite suddenly she felt the full weight of her unhappiness. She thought she deserved a good self-indulgent cry. Hell, her fifteen-year marriage was moribund. And Paul—

Liz opened her eyes. The near-empty noontime newsroom and all its grime and chaos rushed in. Ugh. She closed them again. In the middle of dessert, Martin had offered to investigate the commotion next door. "It's Michael," he had announced, returning a few moments later. As they looked at him expectantly, he added in a strangled voice. "He's dead. It appears he may have been...murdered."

There had been only a moment before the message hit home, but in that moment Liz had looked across the table at Paul and seen in his face not the shock she was feeling, but a kind of relief and—was she mistaken?—wonder? satisfaction? The look vanished as soon as it appeared and the dark tufted brows knitted into very proper concern, but Liz had found herself as troubled by the apparition of unconcern as she had been by the fact of murder. She had thought about it as she'd lain dry-eyed on the couch. It had been the last thing she had thought about as she'd drifted into sleep, dressed in her clothes, hugging a pillow for warmth. She had been only barely conscious of Spencer making morning noises before leaving for work. He hadn't woken her, and when she did finally stir, she felt stiff and uncomfortable—more tired than when she had fallen asleep. She was also late and had grabbed the handiest skirt and blouse, then spent precious time trying to brush out an absurd-looking wing of hair that her awkward sleep had fashioned.

She had tried again in the women's toilet to fix her hair after her scene with Guy. Perhaps she had appeared composed as she faced his invective—nicotine always helped—but she hadn't felt it. He had obviously been pissed about something when he shouted her name across the newsroom (it turned out to be an incorrect attribution in a story, which was really the night desk's fault), so she had tried to mollify him by humouring him. After all, hadn't he—she dimly recalled this—been practically palsy-walsy near the end of dinner last night? Something about changes or promotions in the newsroom? Perhaps she shouldn't have kidded him for being a seventh wheel at the party. Or suggesting, ha ha, that—okay, maybe it was a little tasteless—that he'd just dropped by the Kingdons for a nosh after giving old Michael the heave-ho.

He really was humourless. Why did she even bother? Why are women always appeasing difficult men?

Guy had fixed her with a gaze of such cold intensity, she was, for an instant, taken aback. But then he went all theatrical, snapping pencils in two like some crazy person in a bad film, and she just thought: screw you. Even the spread-that-lie-around-and-I'll-get-you threat was cornball. But then he dropped his voice and hissed at her that he knew with delicious certainty that she was fucking Richter and wouldn't that intelligence just make life all messy for a couple of ambitious men in the community. And she had felt this shock bloom like little flowerlets along her nervous system. Not so much that he knew. But that he had known all along. And that he was waiting like a spider to spring it on her. She had managed a response: Drop dead. Hardly clever. But—ah, my friends and oh, my foes—the nicotine helped.

The grind of the lobby door's security lock jolted her from her reverie. Leo bolted into the newsroom, yanked his notepad out of his jacket pocket, then, alternating hands with the pad, tugged off the jacket, which he then dumped on his desk. After a glance at city desk, manned by a decisive-as-wood assistant city editor with a Beatles haircut twenty years out of date, he headed for the library with an air of preoccupation.

Probably been at the cop shop, she thought, watching his back disappear. He was wearing, she would swear, the same checked shirt he wore when he joined the newsroom six years before. There were tablecloths in Italian restaurants of the same material. Or did he have a wardrobe of them? However gruesome Ishbel was—everyone but Leo knew she was sleeping with him to advantage her career—she at least managed to art-direct his wardrobe a little. You could always tell when Leo was between relationships. He would revert to the kinds of clothes a practical parent would buy an indifferent eight-year-old.

What a sweet cluck.

She settled her eyes back on her screen.

So clearly the relationship with this Stevie person, whom she had yet to meet, couldn't be very strong. Wasn't she an interior designer?

Liz deleted a line about Cape Dorset prints and recast it. Still crap. Her hand wandered to her purse. She groped for the cardboard of the cigarette pack.

No. I've got to ration them out. I will *ration them out.*

I wonder if Leo has any news about Michael's death.

Okay, if I have one now, then I can't have another one until, let's see, 2:30.

Or maybe he knows something about the violin.

Christ, another thing to feel shitty about. She lit the cigarette and gratefully drew the smoke into her lungs. What if Michael had been murdered for the sake of this violin? What if it had been her story that had been the catalyst? Michael would have made the Guarneri an anonymous gift to the symphony if she hadn't pursued Belle Shulman's tip, if she hadn't virtually pounced on Michael with her precious inside knowledge. Was the missing violin really the Guarneri del Gesu? She had assumed all along when she was interviewing Michael on the phone and when she was writing the story that he had had it with him in his possession. If you bought a fur coat at Eaton's wouldn't you bring it home with you? He even graciously supplied the *Zit* with a picture. But now she wondered: Can you buy an art object worth a million dollars in one country and just carry it home on a plane to another? Were there export papers? Import duties? Paperwork? Bureaucracy? Does a bonded courier deliver it later? Why hadn't she asked Michael? Hell, it had been only a nice little human-interest story at the time. Who would have thought it could become so fraught? That such details would matter?

She stubbed her half-smoked cigarette against the side of the cup, saved her half-finished story, and headed for the library. Leo would know.

She found him bent over in one of the tight aisles. One of the little metal sarcophagi drawers that held the clipping files was pulled from its bottom mooring and tipped toward the floor. She contemplated his backside for a half-second. But something drove such assessments from her head.

"Leo?"

"Oh, god."

Liz took a sharp breath. "What is it?"

Book 3

Thursday, September 29

14

The Darkroom

Thirty days hath September.
Which meant, Stevie realized, glancing at the kitchen calendar on the way to the basement, that in two days' time another month's rent for her Toronto apartment would be sucked out of her bank account.

Shall I go? Or shall I stay?

Return to opulent Toronto, scene of unhappy marriage? Or linger in Winnipeg, a thousand glorious miles away from Sangster? Toronto, where good designers could find a market? Or Winnipeg, where designers were a strange luxury? Careerwise, remaining in Winnipeg was ten steps backward. It was a city you got out of, you fled, only to sentimentalize later with ex-Winnipeggers at some party in the Annex where the pièce de resistance was a Jeanne's cake or Gunn's bagels or Old Dutch potato chips. Which you consumed while recalling the blizzard of 1966.

She had been a rising star at Yabu Pushelberg when she met David Sangster. She was a project director for Liquid, a new nightclub on Richmond, and he was one of the investors. At an early meeting they had clashed over the concept of water cascading over a glass ceiling and down the walls—his notion, which her training told her was nothing but an invitation to the gremlins of expense and technical difficulty. She saw *liquid* as metaphor, not as substance. He got his way. He was intense. She was smitten. They were married in three months, married for three years. She was right about the waterfall. The overruns were horrendous; the opening delayed; the maintenance considerable; but by then his preoccupation had moved elsewhere. She had seen the end in the beginning; if only she had done so in her marriage. Her star kept rising at YP. Holt Renfrew's cosmetics floor, the 400-seat Asian-fusion restaurant Hanoi Jane's, "E," a boutique hotel in Yorkville. For a few years she was happily preoccupied with her design career. She felt practically pampered working in such a creative shop. And the money was fabulous. Then, slowly, the economy started to drag, affecting YP and her work, but—worse—David's work, his wheeling and dealing. Almost overnight, she was the one bringing in more money.

He grew as resentful as a little boy whose sister brought home higher marks from school.

Shall I go? Or shall I stay?

I miss the work. But do I miss Toronto?

Stevie groped for the stool, then sat down to wait for her eyes to become accustomed to the dark. The first few times she'd used the old basement darkroom in the spring she'd found tiny pinholes that leaked light like stars pricking an inky sky. She's also found secreted a cache of moldy 1970s *Playboy*s, which made her wonder just how interested in photography her brother had really been. She'd thrown out the magazines and patched the holes and become cheerfully distracted from life's vicissitudes by the art of photography. At least as long as Michael was teaching it.

Now Michael was gone.

Why even bother to develop the film?

Something to do, she supposed. She had had a strangely long and deep sleep, dreamless it seemed, and unrefreshing, leaving a fogginess clinging to her that was utterly immune to coffee, very resistant to a jog in the park, and quite oblivious to her mother, whose conversation at the breakfast table had finally trickled to a stop in the face of granite indifference.

Reaction to shock?

Dully, she had picked up the *Citizen*. She had avoided Wednesday's paper. Her nerves had been too raw to face the truth in black and white. But this morning she felt herself wrapped in a thousand woolly scarves, so muffled as to deaden anything that might disturb in Thursday's paper.

The story was on page one, below the fold. The headline read: "Police seek fiddle." The story was perfunctory. There was no byline.

"And the obituary is in," her mother had remarked from her end of the table. "Third section, page twenty-seven."

Stevie folded the paper to the narrow column and read silently:

Michael Thomas Conroy Rossiter

Michael Rossiter passed away suddenly and unexpectedly on Tuesday, September 27, 1988.

Born in Winnipeg April 10, 1955, Michael was a gifted artist, volunteer and philanthropist who made many contributions to the city's cultural life.

A graduate of St. Paul's High School, he completed his undergraduate degree at the University of Manitoba school of music. In 1976, after taking first place at the Eckhardt-Gramatté Competition, he continued his studies at the Curtis Institute in Philadelphia where he graduated with a Master's Degree in violin performance. A planned solo career was never realized, however, due to matters arising from the tragic death of his parents, Thomas and Lillian Rossiter, in 1977. After returning to Winnipeg in 1981, he performed with Music Inter Alia, the Winnipeg Chamber Music Society, and Aurora Musicale while at the same time turning his talents increasingly to photography. A founding member of the Floating Gallery, his photographs have been exhibited widely at commercial and public galleries including Toronto's Jane Corkin Gallery, San Francisco's Fraenkel Gallery and the Canadian Museum of Contemporary Photography. In 1986, his photography for *Saturday Night* won a National Magazine Award. Originator of the popular M/R photography workshops, he was at one time or another a member of the board of several Winnipeg arts organizations, notably the Winnipeg Symphony Orchestra.

He is...

Stevie closed her eyes. She felt her heart constrict and a sob rise in her throat. The surface of a life reduced to a few column inches in a newspaper. The essence absent. One of a dozen obituaries that day, each life given roughly equal weight. All the same in death. She hated the democracy of it. Michael had more, did more, was more.

She took a cleansing breath and willed herself to open her eyes. The text swam. She blinked, then blinked again. The words clarified.

"'He is survived by his sister, Merritt Parrish of Winnipeg,'" she read aloud, virtually her first words of the morning. She glanced over the edge of the paper, wiped along her lids, and noted her mother studying her.

"Well, you can't blame them for being inaccurate," Kathleen said.

Stevie put the paper down. "Merritt knows, you know. She told me yesterday."

"About what, dear?"

"The baby, of course. My baby."

"Oh!" Kathleen was momentarily dumbstruck. "Your father and I didn't tell her."

"I know. Sometimes I wonder why you didn't tell Michael. The years Merritt was living here, you were in a lot of contact with him."

"I promised you I wouldn't." Kathleen smiled. "And I didn't."

"And I appreciate it."

"I guess Merritt had big ears?"

"And big eyes. She kept it to herself, though."

"I'm very surprised."

"Something about not wanting him to know he had an heir. She actually used the word 'heir.' Slipped out."

Kathleen looked out the window toward the river and frowned. "Michael was thirty-three. He had decades left to live. Why would she be worried about heirs?"

Her eyes turned back to Stevie's. An intelligence passed between them.

"But, Mom, who benefits by Michael's death? It didn't cross my mind until yesterday when she said 'heir.' Merritt benefits. Right?"

Kathleen frowned. "Not necessarily. We don't know what's in Michael's will." She reached for her coffee cup. "I presume he had one."

"But Michael wouldn't cut Merritt out, however strained their relationship was. He's the one who pulled her out of New York. He arranged treatment. He got her to Hazelden. He gave her money after she'd spent everything. And he did it before when she went off the rails."

"Why Tom Rossiter didn't set up a proper trust for his children, I'll never know," Kathleen mused, sipping her coffee. "Imagine having all that money at eighteen."

"And then having blown it all by age twenty-six."

"She resents being beholden to him."

"Well, she put herself in that position. Maybe if she had been more responsible—"

Kathleen shook her head. "It's depression, you know that. It can't be treated with reprimands—"

"I think she's using again. She claims not. Or claims it's under control."

"I wondered if she was—"

"And who's going to save her this time?"

That had put a stop to her mother's end of the conversation. Uncharacteristically silent, Kathleen had risen, adjusted her earrings, and gone off to her office. Stevie, somewhat invigorated, began to look for something else to distract herself. Novels and videos had worked most of the summer. But waiting three days to bury someone you loved was grim, she thought, peeling open the film cartridge with a can opener and cutting off the first few inches of leader. It was limbo. It was hell.

After winding the film onto a stainless steel reel, Stevie reached in the dark for the plastic surface of the developing tank. She shivered slightly. The basement was chilly. She popped the reel into the tank and turned the lid tightly. Then, with her free hand, she groped for the string that hung from an overhead lamp and yanked at it. A burst of light seared her eyelids shut and she had a retinal vision of the darkroom, cramped and jumbled with its photographic accoutrements. It reminded her too well of the ghostly vision that had flashed in her brain Tuesday when she closed her eyes to shut out the sight of Michael lying in his own blood. Her heart beat a little faster.

She opened her eyes. Her heart slowed. She poured the developing fluid into the tank, shook it to release any air bubbles, and set the timer for eight minutes. Developing film was boring. All you could do was sit and wait and every so often gently agitate the tank to make sure the chemicals moved evenly over the surface of the film. As she waited, her mind drifted to Leo.

Odd that he hadn't called her yesterday. She had expected he would. She had assumed he would. After what happened. The death. To see how she was. His kiss crept into her mind. Or at least to thank her for walking Alvy. Last evening, after an hour or two when all the phone calls seemed to be for her mother, her fingers had danced over the dial as she contemplated giving him a call. If she had called him, it would have been a first. He had always called her. He was the pursuer. He was the ardent one. She was getting over a failed marriage. She didn't want anything heavy. She didn't want him to get the wrong idea.

She was a little miffed. She recognized the feeling. Leo's attention was okay. Okay, it was better than okay. Better than no attention at all, at any rate. Hell, she deserved some attention. Surely what Merritt had told him hadn't turned him off, the pig.

She poured another liquid into the tank to arrest the film in its chemical transformation, shook it, waited forty-five seconds, poured the liquid out, then added yet another liquid to lock the images forevermore onto thin strips of emulsion. Finally, she was able to remove the reel of film from the tank and begin rinsing it in running water. Stevie looked at her watch. It would be some time before she could begin to make prints. The film had to dry first.

Shall I go or shall I stay?

The question of the morning returned as she climbed the stairs. In the kitchen, she pulled the phone book from a drawer and opened it to "H." As she ran her finger down the length of Hugheses, she considered that, no, she was not making a choice, she was merely better exploring her options.

15

What the Busboy Saw

Jason Garrity wasn't sure what he should do. He didn't know if what he had seen was important. And he wondered what his parents would say if he did decide to go to the police. They didn't seem to like cops much. He occasionally heard them refer to them as "pigs" and then snicker. They were always using such old-fashioned expressions. It was embarrassing. And what was worse, they tried to stop him watching cop shows like *Hill Street Blues* on TV. But then, when the house was robbed last year, they sure seemed glad to have the police around. "Yes, officer; no, officer," his father had said, all polite and self-righteous. What a fucking hypocrite.

Jason looked at the newspaper again. He was going to be late for afternoon classes if he didn't get a move on and he'd already had a couple of detentions for being late.

He hadn't felt like going home for lunch. His mother wasn't there anyway. She was too busy helping his father with the business. When he had been a little kid his mother had taken him every day to the bakery with her and he had played happily while the wonderful smell of bread and buns wafted over the little store. Now, of course, his parents' little hippie bakery had turned into a big-deal specialty foods supply business and they were never around. The stuff his mother left him for lunch was always weird. It was supposed to be healthy, but he hated it. Which was why he went to the 7-Eleven instead and had a hoagie and a Slurpee. He would get home before his mother and have lots of time to throw out the lunch she had made him.

That's if he didn't go to the police. That would mean having to take the bus downtown after school. Or perhaps he could just phone? But then maybe they would think he was playing a prank. He kicked at a plastic cup that rolled by in the breeze and watched as it landed in a pile of garbage that had spilled from a refuse container. If he hadn't decided to buy the newspaper, he wouldn't have had to think about any of this. He never looked at newspapers. They were just for boring old farts like his parents. And he had certainly never *bought* a newspaper before. But no one else had joined him at the store for lunch. The guy who ran the store had gotten really shitty lately when more than a couple of kids hung out. Neighbours were complaining. Apparently. So everyone had decided to cool it for a while. When Jason brought the Slurpee to the counter, the guy had really scowled at him. But while he was fumbling in his pants pocket for money, Jason had glanced at a newspaper in the stand next to the counter. He couldn't resist the word "murder" and the picture of the victim looked familiar.

"I think I'll buy this, too," he had said.

"Gee, I didn't know you kids could read."

Jason had no snappy comeback, so he ignored the guy. He looked like Hitler anyway with the cropped moustache and the strands of lank hair plastered across his forehead. Only he was even skinnier than Hitler. And stooped. And really depressing.

He had taken the paper outside, planted himself on the window ledge and between bites read the story. He knew where he had seen the victim before, on the street outside the Wajan, the restaurant he had started working in a week earlier. He was the busboy. He didn't mind the work, but it wasn't that much fun either. He had wanted to get a job at McDonald's or somewhere where there was a bunch of other kids he knew. Most of the people at the Wajan were some kind of Asian, or really old, or possibly gay. And no one in the kitchen seemed to speak English except the owner, who was too busy to have a conversation with a busboy.

His father had arranged the whole thing. His parents didn't want him to have a job at first. Homework and grades were what they were concerned about, they said. But then, when he bugged and bugged them, they decided it was okay but only under certain conditions. Like he couldn't work late. And it had to be close to home. The Wajan was opening a few blocks away and his father, who supplied the restaurant with different items, got the owner to hire his son just for the few hours over dinner each evening.

Then his parents really got into the idea of his having an after-school job. They billed it as a "cultural experience" where he would learn to "interface" with "new Canadians." They also approved of Oriental food. It was so "low-fat, high-fibre." Jason also knew that they were just as glad to have someplace to stick him after school because sometimes they didn't get home from work until seven or eight o'clock. He didn't really care. He just wanted the job to save up for a CD player. If he couldn't work at McDonald's, the Wajan was okay. Probably McDonald's didn't hire fifteen-year-olds.

He had slipped out the back entrance of the Wajan for only a couple of minutes. There had been practically no business out front and the kitchen had been so steamy and so noisy—the cook was shrieking about something and the rest of the staff had joined in—that Jason figured they'd never miss him. He had sat on the stoop facing the back lane and the high hedge that ran down its length and taken out his cigarettes. He wondered if his parents knew he was smoking. Whenever one of those stupid "Break Free" ads with those sucked-out looking kids and that hosey-looking singer came up on TV his mother would make a point of saying what good ads they were and how teenagers shouldn't smoke. Blah, blah, blah. As if he didn't know they smoked dope when they thought he was all tucked up asleep in his little bed. The hypocrites. No wonder they were concerned about the police.

He remembered the back lane had been quiet except for the dull whir of the restaurant's exhaust fan. The sun had started to set and long shadows had grown from the buildings and engulfed the hedge. None of the stores' back security lights had switched on. The lane had sunk further into darkness as he sat and dragged on the cigarette, but it was a warm, unthreatening darkness, like his bedroom when he turned out the light. He had never been afraid of the dark as a little kid. He was proud of that. He had always been independent. Sometimes he had to be. Which was why he thought maybe he should go to the police. Even if it meant his mother finding out that he hadn't eaten the lunch she had made.

On the other hand, maybe it was nothing. He tore the piece about the murder out of the newspaper, folded it into his pocket and stuffed the rest of the paper into the refuse bin. He would have a chance to think more about it during Language Arts class. After all, it was only boring Shakespeare.

It was sort of cool, he thought as he left the parking lot, that a murder had been going on, like, about a hundred metres from where he worked. It might even have been happening right while he was having a smoke. Maybe what he saw, or sort of saw, was the getaway car. It could have been.

The car must have been pressed right up against the hedge on the other side. He remembered that he had just butted his cigarette out when he heard the sound of a car starting. He looked across and saw two red lights shining through the gnarled leafless lower branches, one on either side of a white light that shone over a licence plate like a little movie marquee. On the plate were numbers and letters you couldn't easily forget. At least he couldn't forget them.

16

Antonioni

Stevie anchored one foot against the faucet and slid lower in the tub until her face floated just above the water line. She ceased all movement. Water lapping against the side of the tub ebbed. Silence enveloped the room.

Clear your mind of all thought, she thought, closing her eyes. She had taken up yoga for a time as a way of relaxing after long weeks at Yabu Pushelberg and busy Saturdays shopping and entertaining. She joined a dozen other Beaches wives Sunday afternoons at a studio above a retro candy store on Queen Street East. Then, relaxed—supposedly—they would go home and fix simple, elegant dinners for their perfect children and loving—or, in her case, philandering—hubbies.

Clear your mind, she thought again, more earnestly this time. This is what the yoga instructor had counselled.

OM.

Om-mane-pahdme-om.

She sighed. The bathwater stirred.

Why hasn't Leo called?

OMMMMMMM.

It's so unlike him.

OMMMMMMMmmmm, he was a good kisser. Her hand wandered across her thigh. The water stirred again.

No, I won't do that.

Well, maybe later.

OMMMMMMM.

Michael was a good kisser, too. David was *not* a good kisser. Not really. He might as well have been kissing himself. Perhaps he had been the whole time.

Michael.

Stevie sighed again. Only this time the sigh broke into a feeble sob. *What kind of idiot have I been?* Waiting for Michael to return from Europe, waiting to see if some spark might be rekindled, waiting in a fashion as hopeless as that of silly old Scarlett O'Hara pining after the insipid Ashley Wilkes.

Or maybe she had been more like Barbra Streisand's K-K-K-Katie in *The Way We Were*, hopelessly attracted to the blond boy, Hubble, that Robert Redford had played. At least Barbra had married him. Hubble, that is. For a time.

But now Michael was dead, and with his death had vanished such vain hopes. She felt miserably as though she were about to cry, top up the tub with her own salty tears. But she didn't. The further truth hit her: she had been a *complete* idiot. Her expectations had been utterly unfounded, her feelings for Michael had been of the purest nostalgia, born of an unhappy marriage and unsettling separation, nourished in a hot and indolent summer, rekindled by a chance encounter in a bookstore. Despite the cooling waters of the bath, she suddenly felt herself burn with a kind of humiliation.

OMMMMMM.

OMMMMMMdammit.

What on earth had she expected anyway? To pick up where they left off? And where *had* they left off?

Waving goodbye at the station.
Summer vacation.
Is taking you away.
Bye baby bye bye.

Well, waving goodbye at the airport anyway. And not summer vacation, but a summer placement with a design firm in Baltimore, where she would live with her aunt and uncle before travelling to Rhode Island in the fall. A few weeks earlier that spring, at a Camerata Vocale concert in the Pool of the Black Star, she had sensed it all falling away, the impossibility of it, she in Providence, he in Philadelphia, new lives, new friends, a veering off. He had been absorbed in the music; she, bored by Gregorian Chant, had let her eyes wander over the Legislative Building's neoclassical interior, regretting that she had already forgotten half the correct architectural nomenclature despite getting an "A" in History of Architecture I. She felt his hand slip from hers.

A little later, in Baltimore, pregnant, when she made her fateful choice and postponed RISD for a year, she wrote him, breaking it off. His reply discharged enough wounded male pride to let her harden her heart, but between the lines she read a kind of relief. He made a brief, feeble attempt at maintaining a connection, but she made no reply, other than to send a letter of condolence when his parents were killed some months later. She didn't dare fly back to Winnipeg for the funeral. She was too large with his child.

Will I see you in September?
Or lose you to…

Michael had behaved toward her in the spring only as a friend. Really. She had to admit it to herself. Even in his upstairs studio, where they had been alone together, when she had put out a vibe, there had been no reciprocity. Pictures of the blonde woman who had been at his barbecue were prominently tacked on a cork board. Caitlin Clark, he replied, when she asked who she was. Just a friend, he added, smiling. Just some promo shots.

Really?

Is she what he had wanted to talk about when he phoned her last Monday? Phoned her, mind you, three weeks after getting back from Europe. Could there have been a bigger clue to his indifference to her? Three weeks! And why wouldn't he have been indifferent? She was the one who broke it off all those years ago.

OMMMMMM.

Or was it this business Sharon Bean mentioned? Letting her go as his cleaner. Was he selling? Moving?

Well, at least she was now pretty much assured he hadn't been in Maryland digging into adoption records. Phoning her aunt while Merritt had cooled her heels—or did some lines—at Leo's house had allayed her mind on that score.

OMMMMMM.

And, speaking of Leo, why hadn't he called?
OMMMMMMMMMMMMMMMMMMMMMMMMMMMMM.
Oh, to hell with it.

The bathwater was turning tepid. Stevie opened her eyes and, squinting against the light, looked over to the clock on the vanity. The film would have dried by now and time remained to make a few prints before...before what? The day stretched out ahead.

Maybe she should call Leo.

She rose in the tub, drew the shower curtains around, and turned on the shower. Moments later, she was out of the tub, dried off, and shrouded in an old snuggly terry-towel bathrobe. It was warm and just the thing for a chilly basement. Her hair she could leave. It would dry by itself. As a teenager, she had hated her naturally wavy hair. Now she was thankful for it.

Back in the darkroom she rolled up the sleeves of her bathrobe, set up three plastic trays, poured chemicals into each, and savoured for a moment the vinegary smell that wafted throughout the room. She always felt a tingle of excitement at this point. There was something magical about photography, fixing fleeting moments on film and then forcing that film to render up its images. She was always impatient to have the finished work in her hands and often wished she didn't have to first make a contact sheet. Not that she had to. But having a sheet of negative-sized prints was a great aid in determining which pictures to enlarge, or crop, or manipulate in some way.

She switched off the main light and switched on a safe low-wattage bulb. A dull amber glow suffused the room. Sharp shadow faded into ambiguous lines and shapes as Stevie adjusted her eyes. She took the dried negatives and placed them carefully on the glass top of the contact printer. Over that she placed light-sensitive printing paper. When she closed the top and pressed a switch, a light bulb inside the box blasted the images of the negative onto the paper. With a pair of tongs she lifted the paper from the printer and slipped it into the first of the three trays. Dabbing gently with the tongs, she ensured that the paper remained immersed in the elixir. She watched as the images began slowly to separate into fields of black and white.

Twenty minutes later she had a contact sheet, damp and shiny. She switched the main light back on, reached for a magnifying glass and began to examine each of the twenty-four tiny negative-sized prints. They had been shot at intervals over the week. Whenever she had gone out she had taken her camera with her in case something presented itself as subject matter. Unfortunately her excursions had been few; most of the pictures were of the backyard, the river embankment, and assorted flora and fauna. Not exactly award-winning, she had to admit. The best ones were the final ones on the roll, those taken on Tuesday's walk down the Crescent. The setting sun had cast the trees and mansion into long shadow. Even in black and white, there was an autumnal sense—a patterning of grey shades indicating leaves changing colour, treetops dark against a hazy sky.

She pulled her magnifying glass over the contact sheet one more time, evaluating those pictures she thought might be worth enlarging. One of her mother caught in a sunhat trying to avoid the camera was good—the brim of the hat was a white ellipse with formal abstract qualities, nicely subverted however by her mother's expression of annoyance. A couple of river shots weren't too bad—glistening water, exposed tree roots, rowers with paddles erect. She looked again at the ones of the mock-Georgian mansion in deepening shadow. A detail caught her eye. She brought the contact sheet closer to the light and stared at it. She was reminded of something. Was it merely a coincidence? Probably, she thought, dismissing it from her mind. But she felt her pulse quicken, nevertheless. It was too intriguing.

There's only one way to make sure, she muttered to herself as she reached for the enlarger. A blow-up.

17

Jeopardy

Paul Richter watched the two figures retreat down the gravel drive to the black Caprice parked beside the bank of trees he had had planted years earlier as a snow barrier. The lining of the trenchcoat worn by the shorter of the officers, he noted with thin contempt, drooped below the hem at the back like an afterthought. The other one, the taller one, had been dressed impeccably, tailored blue suit, crisp white shirt, striped tie. But it had been the shorter one, Detective Frank Nickel, in rumpled corduroy, who had done all the talking, had asked all the questions, who had compelled his attention.

The men turned, each to open a car door, glancing back at him as they did so. Richter allowed a smile to cross his face, the sort of smile he used when it was absolutely necessary to importune one of the more tiresome but *reiche alte Weiber*, the old biddies, on the Friends of the WSO committee. He thought about waving, sending them off with a gesture casual and friendly; his arm even jerked in response, but he cautioned himself not to seem too nonchalant, too untroubled. I must appear to take seriously this, this murder of Michael Rossiter, *dieser Eindringling*, this interloper—this busybody. The word formed on his lips, he almost spat it out.

And it was serious. But not in the way Nickel and his partner thought. They were such predictable idiots. He really had nothing to fear from them. Not yet, anyway.

He watched the car disappear around the side of the house, down the drive toward Henderson Highway, well behind another bank of trees. His gaze shifted past Else's little greenhouse, across the lawn—kept immaculate by his excellent gardener and only now speckled with yellow leaves—toward the Red River running cold and grey, its waters headed for an Arctic shore. He shivered momentarily and turned indoors.

He ignored Siegfried and Kriemhild, the two Shitzu scrapping near his feet. High-strung, they had become particularly neurotic in the last few days, no doubt picking up on the certain tension that had seeped into the atmosphere. His eyes ran critically along the white walls that reached high to a cathedral ceiling, at his collection of paintings and drawings arranged in clusters like notes on a score. The Henk Chabot he had purchased for pennies at the end of the war; the August Macke and Franz Marc had been more recent acquisitions. There were one or two that had found their way into his collection through less than immaculate sources—he would have trouble accounting to any authority for their presence—but Nickel and his partner barely glanced at the contents of the room. Most people were undiscerning. Only occasionally, when he and Else sensed a prospective guest might be more than a little perceptive, did he violate the symmetry of his arrangements and remove a painting or sketch to a more private part of the home.

He thought of his home as a work of art. He and Else had conceived it together, planned it, sketched it, and only then brought in an architect to properly render it and bring it to life. It was to be their bastion, their retreat, their last and best home, its isolation from the city part of the charm, and they had succeeded in creating a modernist vision of glass, random stone and smooth white render. He regarded the Bösendorfer glowing richly in the sun before the window, the well-worn but still luxurious leather Confort chairs and couch, the built-in cupboards along one wall with the recesses for *objets*—antique musical instruments, Japanese masks, African figures, photographs, sundry local pieces. He looked down the few steps that led to what some vulgarian had once called a conversation "pit," toward the coffee table. He frowned. The detritus of their encounter with the two detectives irritated him: the tray with its trail of sugar granules, the biscuit crumbs on a serving plate, the cups left half-filled, coffee cooling in a scum of cream, the dark stain along the tray's linen cover where Else had spilled while pouring—so unlike her. But Nickel's questions to them seemed to follow no logical sequence, and it was during one of his inquisitorial shifts that he asked her to describe her movements late Tuesday afternoon. And she did: she had left the house in East St. Paul just after 5:30 and had driven to their condo facing Central Park, arriving about 6:00 or a little before. She and Paul had had a glass of wine and talked while he finished dressing; they left the condo about 6:40 and were at the Kingdons' by the appointed time of 7:00.

"Did anyone see you leave your house here in East St. Paul at that time?"

"No, I don't believe so," Else had replied, picking up the coffee carafe to refresh their cups. "As you can see, we're rather isolated out here."

"And no one saw you arrive at the condo."

"No. Not that I know of."

"And you left shortly around 6:40—the two of you?"

"Yes."

"Mr. Bulaong was out at the back when we came out, wasn't he darling?" She had glanced at him as she tilted the carafe.

"He's the condo superintendent," he explained to Nickel. "He was taking out garbage. That television show he's devoted to—"

"*Jeopardy*," she supplied.

"—must have finished."

"You spoke?"

"We waved," Else had said.

"He can confirm this?"

"Yes."

"Interesting," Nickel had continued, "because the Dorchester Square florist says a woman of your description, Mrs. Richter, came in to buy flowers at 6:30, just as the store was closing.

Else's hand jerked suddenly; the coffee missed the cup, spurting in a high arc over onto the tray cloth. "Oh," she cried.

"No damage done, darling," he'd soothed his wife.

"Did you buy flowers at Stems?" Nickel had continued. He had been studying them both.

"I brought orchids for Bunny, but they were from our own greenhouse," she explained, bringing the spout of the coffee pot closer to the cup, filling it. "I rarely need to buy flowers."

"I see."

Else had continued, smiling: "Orchids are my hobby."

"I'm sure there are other women who meet my wife's description."

Nickel coolly assessed Else. Watching his eyes travel down his wife's body, Richter had had to quell an urge to strike the officer. Then Nickel, to his surprise, shrugged and said: "Well, whoever it was paid cash anyway."

But he wasn't fooled by Nickel's dismissal. He had wanted to ask him what Bunny said about the flowers—presuming she had been asked—but didn't dare, didn't want to press the point lest he rekindle suspicion.

The inquiry had gone on. Nickel had learned of Rossiter's resignation. He was prepared for the inevitable questions. Yes, the resignation had come as a surprise. Yes, it had been rather abrupt.

"But, detective, I think you're rather confused. Michael tendered his resignation to the board president, Spencer Elliott. Not to me. Board changes aren't the business of the music director."

"I know. But I understand he paid you a visit the day he dropped off the letter."

"Yes, that's true."

"Did he tell you why he was resigning? He had two more years of his term, I understand."

"Actually, detective, I wasn't aware he had resigned when he visited me. I didn't get a copy of the letter until a few days later."

"Kind of odd, him not telling you."

He had shrugged. "I'm sorry. I can't explain it. Perhaps he thought it was Spencer's business, and not mine. He came to tell me about the violin he had bought—a Guarneri del Gesu—that he was donating to the orchestra."

Yes, he recalled now, looking about the living room, noting an Eva Stubbs sculpture out of place, it had been a perfectly civil conversation in that awful windowless basement office in the Centennial Concert Hall. It had nothing to do with the Guarneri. That he had learned about later, like everyone else, by reading Liz's piece in the Saturday *Citizen*. Michael's resignation from the board—which, of course, had arisen—had been a mere preface to the text of their discussion. He had mastered his shock and dismay; in fact, he had lived for years in anticipation of such a nightmare scenario, and he had been prepared. He'd proffered no explanations to Michael, no excuses. He had only enquired about Michael's plans. What did he intend to do with the information? It was something, Michael told him evenly, that he was wrestling with.

It had seemed like a threat of blackmail. Only Michael didn't appear to want anything. He certainly didn't need anything, not in the conventional sense—not money, which is what he would have expected from a blackmailer. Oh, there had been an aside about this Caitlin Clark woman, late of the Atlantic Symphony—his lover, presumably—about granting her an audition should a position in the violins arise, but this hardly seemed the price of silence. A week had gone by. The waiting began to fray the nerves. Michael had said he would get back to them. And, ironically, he had—Tuesday night, after they had returned home from Bunny's dinner party, they found a message on their answering machine. He had called, the machine intoned, at 5:20, some time after Else's true departure time.

He walked over to readjust the Stubbs sculpture, then looked about the room from the new angle, as if for the last time, letting his eye travel down the travertine flooring through a square arch to the dining room where he could glimpse the panelled glass sculpture Warren Carther had done for him that somehow managed to freeze the syncopations of music. It would have to stay with the house—it was too large and too fragile. The other art works could be sent on, if necessary. He absently plucked the string of an antique shamisen, which dominated his small collection of non-Western instruments. Nickel had been inordinately interested in the instruments, to the exclusion of his paintings and sculpture. He had had to equivocate, of course—there had been less than immaculate sources for some of these, too.

The austere twang of the shamisen had roused the dogs, who began yipping. Tiresome creatures, but Else loved them. What would they do with them? Leave them with someone. There was a handful of people in the community who were utterly utterly trustful.

But two people outside the exclusive circle knew. One was dead. And the other...

There was a whisper of silk as Else re-entered the room, breaking his reverie. She shushed the dogs, then smiled at him. "Have they gone?"

He nodded as she bent to collect the coffee cups and place them on the tray. "I wonder if we can depend on Bulaong?" she asked.

"I think we need have no fear in that quarter," he replied. Though what pressures the caretaker might ultimately succumb to, he didn't know. And soon it might not matter. "What a good thing Bunny presumed the flowers were from your greenhouse."

"I nearly corrected her, but—" She lifted the tray and looked intensely at him. "I think we must put our plans in order, Paul," she said, her voice assured, her eyes glittering.

"Don't worry, my dear." He kissed her cheek. "Everything is well in hand."

18

Déjà Vu

"Called in sick," the woman at the *Zit* switchboard said briskly.

Stevie lowered the phone. Sick? Or "sick" the way he'd been in the summer when he'd whisked her off to Grand Beach in the middle of his work week? She felt a tiny stab of guilt and worry. Perhaps that's why he hadn't called. It wasn't the baby thing after all. She lifted the phone again and dialled his home number. The answering machine clicked in after four rings, Leo's voice, backed by the banjo-picking from *The Beverly Hillbillies*, telling her in a fake Ozark tone that he was back out at the *ce*ment pond and couldn't come to the phone. Hilarious the first time, annoying the umpteenth. "Leo, pick up," she snapped after the beep, but there was only silence as the tape spooled on to a finishing beep.

Very sick? Or just out somewhere?

She tapped her nails along the kitchen counter and glanced at the microwave display. 2:12. Both parents gone. Both cars gone. Another of the joys of living at home. Why, she thought, am I worried? He's genuinely sick. That's all.

He can't pick up a phone?

Calling his neighbour Les would be a bad idea; she might provoke an anxiety attack. Worse—probably—would be calling either his mother or his sister (whom she'd met once at Polo Park shopping on a Saturday afternoon with Leo. She wasn't sure it was a coincidence). She glanced out the kitchen window. Oh, hell, she thought, and went upstairs and changed into a pair of not-completely-flattering sweatpants. She rolled up the blow-up of the photo, secured it with an elastic band and squeezed it into a fanny pack before setting off into the autumn air with her Walkman playing Tom Waits through her earphones.

Less than half an hour later she was on Leo's street, reflecting that if the month had been January, she could have merely walked across the frozen Assiniboine River from her parents' house and been at Leo's in under ten minutes. The house, sailing on a bed of fallen golden leaves, showed no sign of life. No light shone. No TV projected a shadowy dance across the window. At the front door, removing her earphones, she strained to hear perhaps the sound of one of Leo's Springsteen tapes playing. Nothing. She rang the doorbell. Nothing. The doorbell, another piece of unfinished renovation, didn't work. Sighing, she rapped her knuckles against the wood and was greeted by the sound of Alvarez's muffled bark. She waited. And waited. She tried the door. It was locked. Alvy fell silent.

She turned and walked back down the front steps, feeling strangely apprehensive, at the same time arguing with herself that apprehension was utterly unreasonable. He was *out*, for god's sake. And yet...

She studied the street up and down. But for a passing motorist, the street appeared without life. Stevie paused a moment, then stepped over the browning remnants of some flowering plants in the small garden that bordered the front of the house and pressed herself between a shrub and the bottom ledge of the picture window. The ledge was high. She grasped it, some of the flaking brown paint coming off on her hands, and stood on tiptoe, trying to peer into the living room. The room was in shadow and she had to shift her weight onto one foot to bring one hand up to shield her eyes from the reflected glare of the street. Slowly her eyes adjusted to the gloom. She could see the couch and the cluttered coffee table and then Alvy, on his haunches, looking at her, his head cocked to one side, his tongue hanging like a liver sausage. The dog lifted himself and padded to the window. As he moved forward, Stevie was alerted to a lumpy mass on the rug. Her heart crashed against her chest, her mind vented a silent scream.

It was Leo. She saw in a flash a white torso and a head, Leo's head, like a loose doll's, lolled forward toward her, empty of expression. She recoiled, slumping against the bush, which held her in prickly tentacles. "Oh god," she whispered, clutching her hand to her mouth, tears suddenly springing to her eyes. "Please, no!" Gasping for air, trying to steady herself, the vision of Michael's corpse crashing about her in waves, she edged onto the walkway, pushed through the side gate, and staggered to the tree where the key lay.

She could not steady her hand. The key, brought to the door, tapped impotently against the lock, nearly dropping from her fingers to doom in a crack between walkway and house. She forced herself to concentrate, to aim. Finally, the key found the slot and she plunged through the door, into the kitchen stairwell. Alvarez barked. She lunged for the dog and hugged it fiercely, burying her face in the fur along its neck. "Oh god, Alvy," she moaned, looking up through the chaos of the unlit kitchen, toward the grey light of the dining room and living room beyond, steeling herself, her stomach beginning to roil with apprehension. She rose unsteadily, and on shaky feet propelled herself toward the house's silent interior.

19

On Horizontal Hold

Leo had spent a lousy twenty-four hours beginning with an abrupt transformation to life lived at a square angle.

"Can't you bend up a little bit?" Liz had asked.

"Not really." Leo clutched the handle of one of the higher file drawers for support, and butted his head against the cool metal. He released a string of expletives. Every once in a while, some small movement would put his back out: twisting to reach for the soap in the shower, for instance. Or, in this case, jerking an uncooperative bottom drawer out of a cabinet in the *Zit*'s library while bending his back, not his knees, as his last physiotherapist had told him to do. "I'm going to have to lie down. Or, if you've got a gun handy, you can put me out of my misery."

"There's the couch in the back room."

"'Kay." Leo groaned. "Just sort of hover nearby, would you?" He began to shuffle forth. "Ow, shit," he addressed the floor (black and white linoleum squares).

"Put his back out," he heard Liz explain to a pair of shoes (women's).

The trek through the library and into the room that in days of yore had been the test kitchen for the food writer was horizontally Himalayan. The test-kitchen days were gone, however. Mellish did his own testing at home. The library staff was the room's only tenant now. They claimed its ill-lit recesses as their own and only their cozy coffee-break chatter could make the room convivial. Otherwise, few ventured into the musty, hollow space except the occasional reporter in need of privacy to conduct an interview.

Eventually, Leo's eyes rested on the summit, the battered brown leather cover of the couch, upon which one late night shift he had memorably and stupidly had sex with Julie Olsen, the court reporter. He hadn't been near it since. He groaned. "It's too soft."

"And the options would be?" asked his sherpa.

Leo shifted to a moan. "Let me lean on your arm while I try to manage this."

He turned slowly, then let himself tip over on his side onto the couch. The Lord's name was taken in vain and he could feel sweat begin to break out in certain nooks and crannies. A series of select manoeuvres later he was installed on the couch, staring up at the stained ceiling. A pressure cooker had probably exploded circa 1956.

"Damn, and I have some stories to write." He regarded Liz, who was frowning at him. "Busy?"

"Not terribly, why?"

"How about if I dictate and you input them into the system? Like phoning a story into the desk."

"Sure."

While Liz went back to the newsroom to fetch both their notebooks, Leo tried composing a lede in his head.

Winnipeg police are searching for clues to the killer of a 33-year-old man...

Boring.

A missing million-dollar violin may be the key to the slaying of Winnipeg photographer and philanthropist Michael Rossiter...

Better.

As it happened, violins were scarce as catgut at the news conference. The superintendent had given a long-winded bureaucratic version of a shrug when another reporter asked about possible motive. Leo, surprised that the Guarneri del Gesu received no mention, had been about to interject when a venerable journalism hall-of-fame word came to his head—*scoop*. He kept his cakehole clamped and trotted up to the homicide unit office to see if his brother-in-law was stinking up the joint with one of his cigars. He was. Frank's mouth curled with joy at the sight of Leo.

"Get the fuck out of here," he growled through the blue haze.

After trading several bons mots along this line, and before being given the bum's rush, Leo gleaned that no violin had been found propping up the toilet or otherwise misplaced in Michael's house. In other words, a violin appeared to be missing. Was it the Guarneri? Frank allowed that he was fucking trying to fucking figure that out, now get lost.

Sources close to the investigation say the violin, purchased at auction at Sotheby's earlier this month... Leo continued ruminating. Well, Frank *was* a source close to the investigation. Besides, many a good story was ruined by over-verification.

"Do you have a phone number for Sotheby's in London?" he asked Liz, who returned, pads in hand, trailing a stacking chair behind her. "What am I saying? I can't get to a phone."

"Doesn't matter, it's after 7:00 in London anyway. Is this about the Guarneri?"

"Yeah."

Liz slumped into the chair and handed over his notepad. Leo noted her expression. "Don't blame yourself."

"I do."

"It actually might not be the Guarneri," he said.

"That just means some idiot who doesn't know treasure from trash killed Michael. There's still a violin missing, right?"

"Apparently."

Leo ran his eyes over his notes and revised the lede in his head. "Missing" was purged. The result was fudgy, but what the hell. It was good enough for now.

"Pencil poised?"

"Shoot."

Leo began dictating. After four paragraphs, he paused. "But someone's got to know if he actually brought the thing with him from London to Winnipeg. If it was a gift to the symphony, maybe Richter knows."

"Doubt it."

"Why?"

Liz hesitated. "Just a feeling."

Leo frowned at her, then shrugged. "Anyway, where was I?"

"'... which was purchased at auction in London in early September,'" Liz read back to him.

"Okay." Leo continued dictating. Flipping through his notebook, he moved on to a couple of the usual break-ins and aggravated assaults for the police blotter column, then a few paragraphs about the North End murder that would later be incorporated into another reporter's backgrounder.

"And no byline," he concluded.

Liz looked up from her pad. "Why not?"

"Technically, I'm no longer the police reporter. Ray moved me to general assignment—on Martin's orders." He regarded Liz. "Is there something going on I don't know about? Are we on the verge of another beat shuffle?"

Liz frowned. "I wonder. Guy was muttering something to that effect at dinner last night, though it sounded more like shift higher up."

"Nice touch with those smoke rings this morning, by the way."

"Thanks. Earned a badge for it in Girl Guides."

"What was all that about anyway?"

"Oh, I made a sort of bad joke about his being the uninvited guest at dinner."

"Overreaction?"

"That would be an understatement."

Leo glanced at her sharply. "There's more?"

Liz's face shuttered. "Not really."

. . .

Finally, there was nothing to do but take a cab home, fetch some ice packs from the freezer, some drugs from the medicine cabinet, find a supine position, get the weight off his glass back, and tough it out for about the next thirty-six hours. Wednesday evening had been largely spent on the living room floor, half-dozing between a Blue Jays game on one channel and Olympic coverage on another. "Do not operate heavy machinery," the pill box had warned. "Do not do anything," it might better have said.

And he hadn't.

He hadn't even called Stevie.

The next morning, after about ten hours' solid bed rest with legs elevated on pillows, he could shuffle through the world at about a hundred-and-thirty-five-degree angle. Letting Alvy out for a piss, he managed to pick the Thursday edition of the *Zit* off his front steps with his toes—no mean feat—and noted that his byline-less story had not been too screwed up by copy editors. After some breakfast and a few more painkillers, he replanted himself on the floor with the phone, called the city desk and told Ray he was sick and to expect him back Friday—if anyone asked or cared.

"We don't," Ray had yawned.

"I can work on the violin angle from home and phone it in later. A sidebar, maybe?"

"Whatever."

"Thanks for the enthusiasm."

"You're welcome."

Fuck you, too, Leo thought, and briefly considered taking a PR job at Canada Post.

He called Frank for developments. Frank was unavailable. He left a message anyway and imagined a piece of paper being crumpled into a little ball. On the theory that someone in town must know whether Michael had schlepped the Guarneri del Gesu back from London himself, he rolled himself off the carpet, found pad, pencil, and phone book and then, as an afterthought, an old orchestra program he'd stuffed into a drawer when Ishbel had lived with him. He crawled back down on the floor. He thought: start with Richter—despite Liz's doubts—and then hit up a few other orchestra members. Richter was unlisted. What a surprise. He tried the concert master—mistress, whatever. His call seemed to piss her off enormously. She had already been questioned by the police, and, no, she didn't know a damn thing. A couple of other members of the violin section were equally adamant, though more polite. Clearly, Frank had already trod this path. Leo considered calling the symphony's flack, but flacks were often the last to know. Board members? Liz's husband, even? How about that blonde woman hovering around Michael at his party in May—Caitlin Clark? Formerly of some symphony or another in the Maritimes. Friend, lover, confidante? Directory assistance had a new number for a C. Clark on Roslyn Road. He got a recorded message.

Hell.

He had better luck with backgrounder material. Heinrich's, a violin maker he located in Toronto, told him Michael's Guarneri was probably *undervalued* at a million dollars. The investment climate for art objects was so superheated, with Picassos and Van Goghs going for such monstrous sums, that money went looking elsewhere, for more affordable things, if you considered a million bucks to be affordable. The art theft experts at the RCMP told him there was a trend toward stealing smaller objects, which made a violin very nearly ideal—it was light, portable, could fit in a briefcase or a suitcase, a shopping bag or a knapsack. "Normally," he told Leo, "these sorts of things are stolen by smart thieves, people with the right connections. They end up spirited into people's collections after going through several hands. The recovery rate is pretty small, I'm sorry to say."

Smart thief. Whoever stole Michael Rossiter's Guarneri—presuming it was the Guarneri—hadn't been very smart. A smart thief would have purloined the violin while its owner was elsewhere. Killing the owner to get to the violin had zero finesse.

Unless the owner caught the thief in the act.

But, as Frank had pointed out Tuesday, and Leo had seen for himself, a struggle hadn't been much in evidence.

By one o'clock, his stomach was growling. He struggled off the carpet, delighted to find his stance had ratcheted up to something closer to normal, and opened a can of beans in the kitchen. He decided he deserved a beer, and since a good afternoon nap would probably speed his recovery, he swallowed a couple more Robaxacet. He briefly considered a joint, but didn't have the energy to roll it. He settled back into his nest, adjusted the pillows and glazedly watched *Another World*, spooning the beans from the can, chasing them with the beer. Before long, he began to feel exceptionally mellow. He switched off the television, remembered to switch off the phone, and, after a few moments, had fallen into the sort of bliss that afternoon naps are made of.

He dreamed he was in a race, pacing furiously alongside Ben Johnson. Unaccountably, Alvy was running with them, too, barking and leaping joyously. It was the three of them in the lead. Leo pulled ahead of Ben. Then ahead of Alvy. And then he was on the podium, caressing, oddly enough, his National Newspaper Award, being serenaded by *Oh, Canada*, only to have the certificate ripped from his hands. Suddenly, he was in a room full of savage rodents that he realized, in dream logic, were all reporters. It was like the end of *Alice in Wonderland*: a whole pack of cards rises in the air and comes flying down at Alice and she tries to fend them off. Leo braced himself for the attack, then, in the aching torpor of dream time, became dimly aware that he was no longer in shadow land. Actual blows were raining down upon his head.

20

Wooden Nickel

"You scared the *hell* out of me!"

Foggily, through his upraised hands, he recognized his attacker. Stevie, her face red with fury, her eyes blazing, was on her knees beside him, thrashing his head with a folded copy of the *Citizen*. He stared at her, confused and sleep-befuddled for a moment, but also darkly conscious of a deeper emotion. His hand shot out. He tore the newspaper from Stevie's grasp, gripped her by the back of the neck, and pulled her toward him. She didn't immediately resist. And then she did, pulling back abruptly, her face now white, stricken.

"God, I'm sorry." Leo's words were dutiful. He wasn't sorry. He savoured the kiss. "You just looked so b..." The cliché died on his lips. She was staring at him, her chest heaving, then her face sagged, as if she were about to cry. His heart contracted.

"I thought you were...dead," she spoke raggedly.

Instantly he understood. "Oh, Stevie, I'm sorry." This time it was genuine. "Look, I put my back out. Lying on a hard surface helps." He watched her eyeing the detritus around him—the tin of beans with dirty spoon, the crumpled beer can, the crusty cereal bowl with the film of drying milk, the television remote—the light of understanding dawning in her eyes. It was not a pretty site. Nor was he a pretty sight: He passed his hand over his unshaven face, had a momentary regret for what his breath must be like, then realized he was wearing only a T-shirt and underwear, and, worse, he was straining his Stanfields. He sternly thought of the most boring story he'd ever written—a three-part exegesis on traffic-crosswalk technology.

"And then when you didn't answer the door, and Alvy was barking, and I looked through the window, and there you were on the floor, and I thought—"

"I know what you thought, and I'm sorry."

Stevie shifted off her knees. "I tried you on the phone. I kept getting Jed Clampett."

"I turned the phone off, sorry." Leo pushed himself onto his elbows.

"Don't get up if you feel better on the floor."

"Then maybe you should hand me that bathrobe."

Leo watched her expression as she silently draped the bathrobe over him. "I meant to phone you yesterday. But I got caught up at work, and then my back—"

"I thought it might have had something to do with your conversation with Merritt."

"What conversation?"

"Tuesday. When we were at her house." Stevie sat down on a chair beside him and began to stroke the dog's neck. "You talked about me."

"Oh, that." Leo squirmed under the bathrobe. "Merritt blabbed, then."

"'Manipulative' is her middle name."

"'Impulsive' is mine. I shouldn't have asked."

"Well, you did."

Leo was silent a moment. He shrugged, inasmuch as one can shrug horizontally. "Past is past."

He looked over to see her studying him. "I've been a little nuts since moving back here," she began. "Maybe you noticed. The divorce, leaving Toronto, staying in Winnipeg, living with my parents. Michael sort of fit into that old world, I guess. Nostalgia has a strange force." She faltered. "Our lives had completely diverged. He had no interest in me, I could tell. He was just being kind."

"He *is* the father of your child."

"Yes, there is that." Stevie ran her finger under Alvy's collar. "You know, when I talked to him on the phone on Monday, he said he had something important he wanted to tell me. It sounded so ominous that I thought—uh-oh—he's found out and he's furious this has been kept from him for all these years. Paranoid, I know. But then, when those luggage tags said he'd been to Washington—"

"Why is that important?"

"When I learned I was pregnant, I was in Baltimore, at a summer placement, staying with my aunt and uncle. So instead of going to Rhode Island, to design school as I'd planned, I stayed in Baltimore and had the child there. Washington and Baltimore are as close to each other as Toronto and Hamilton."

"Why didn't you tell him back then?"

"He was going off to the Curtis. I was already in Baltimore. We'd broken it off. I had ambitions. I didn't want to *force* him to marry me, or anything like that. I was too young—"

"Then why have the kid at all? If that's not too blunt."

Stevie shrugged. "God knows. I think part of it was something Michael said. He was pretty Catholic at the core, and I was dumb enough to be influenced by it. And—" she rolled her eyes "—Merritt alluded to this yesterday, but it's probably true: having the child was a way to drive my mother crazy. That was the kind of teenager I was, I'm sorry to say."

"She thought you should have—?"

"It was the mid-70s. Kathleen was in the vanguard of everything progressive in those days. She thought, in the situation, yes, I should have an abortion. She was really pissed off that I wanted to do anything as old-fashioned as stay away in some sort of shame and have a baby out of wedlock, like it was the 1950s or something. The shame for her was that I wasn't loud and proud about it. *Who needs men!? Come home, have the baby, live here! Okay, then, have an abortion!* Anyway, I made up my mind and no one could move me. What can I say? I was young, stubborn, and stupid. But I wasn't ashamed. I just didn't want Michael to know, and the only way to do that was to keep away. Well, stay where I was. In Baltimore."

Leo studied her face as she stroked the dog. "Do you think about…him? Her. The baby?"

"Her. Yes, sometimes. A little more lately, for some reason. Sometimes when I wake up, I know I've been dreaming about her."

"Did you ever see her?"

"Just for a moment. I wish I hadn't, in a way. The blue eyes. Michael's eyes."

She looked away quickly. Leo wished his eyes weren't brown.

"Somewhere out there, there's an eleven-year-old girl wandering around. My daughter." She was silent a moment. "Anyway, I'm sure she's in a good home somewhere. It was a good agency."

Leo contemplated his ceiling, his mind turning over. "Amazing Michael never found out."

"The only ones who knew were my parents and my aunt and uncle in Baltimore. The story was that I was going to get work experience for a year in Baltimore, then go to RISD."

Leo noticed a pock mark in the plaster he hadn't seen before. "So if you were able to keep this from Michael, then how does Merritt know?"

"Like I've said before, she lived with my parents for a couple of years after her parents were killed. That was the custodial arrangement. She was a little pitcher and she had big ears, I guess."

"I'm surprised she didn't blab to her brother."

"Oh, I think she had her reasons."

Leo turned from the ceiling. "What does that mean?"

Stevie made a dismissive gesture with her hand. "Doesn't matter. Anyway, look, Leo, I feel like I haven't been all that honest with you, and I'm sorry."

"Oh, hell, we're all icebergs. Ninety percent of us is below the surface."

She smiled at him for the first time. "Thanks." She reached for her fanny pack. "Shall we talk about something else?"

"Like what?"

Stevie pulled the zipper. "Like photographs, for instance. I developed a roll this morning. Want to see them?"

"Are there any with me in them?"

"No."

"Then how interesting could they be?"

Ignoring him, she pulled a manila envelope from her pack. "I didn't tell you this when we were at Merritt's Tuesday, but it was pretty obvious she had had company, even though she told your brother-in-law she'd been alone."

"Obvious how?"

"A trail of men's clothes in her bedroom."

"Eh?" Leo paused. "But does that mean some naked man was hiding in the house when we were there?"

"I doubt it. And why would he hide? Anyway, I've got a picture of him. I think. I snapped some pictures down the Crescent on the way to Michael's and this guy jogged into the frame. The pictures are black and white, but the shirt has the same stripe as the one on the floor in Merritt's bedroom." She handed the package to Leo with a shrug. "I just thought you might have some idea who it is. He doesn't look like your descriptions of this Guy Clark person, and you see Merritt at work."

Leo examined the picture, savouring it, noting the hair style of the jogger. "I'll say it's interesting," he hooted. "That's my old pal Axel Werner."

"Someone you know?"

"Well, it's not such a coincidence. Axel was just leaving the *Zit* when Merritt started, and they probably end up at the same arts events around town." He cackled. "So *that's* what he's been up to. Or who."

He gave Stevie a shorthand version of Axel's life and times. "And he's married, though god knows that's never stopped him before. Anyway, that's probably why Merritt lied to Frank." He glanced at the picture again, Axel flying along with that very familiar knapsack on his back. "Look at him. He's a total exercise nut. There's probably two dozen cans of Chef Boyardee in there to add heft."

"Or dry clothes."

"Oh, yeah, true." He wrinkled his nose. "Getting back into the old clothes would be pretty skanky."

"I wonder why he didn't take the damp ones with him?"

Leo didn't speculate. He was scrutinizing Stevie's picture more closely. "That's the old Farquhar house in the background, right? The one between Merritt's and your parents' that the Oblates use. So you've pointed the camera sort of northwest, which means he's running west."

"So?"

Leo shrugged. "Axel and Eve live near Bruce Park. He'd run east, probably over the foot bridge, and through the park, and down the Crescent to Merritt's."

"Then he probably went for a long run, and then turned back to get to Merritt's."

"Probably." Maybe Merritt likes 'em raunchy, he thought, but further speculation along these lines was interrupted by the sound of knuckles crashing against his front door. "If it's the Jehovah's Witnesses, tell them I worship Satan," he called to Stevie, who rose to answer.

"It's your brother-in-law," she whispered loudly, glancing through a trio of tiny windows in the inside door.

"Right on cue." He slipped Stevie's picture under the pillow supporting his buttocks. "Let him in."

"Well, you got style, Fabian," Frank said a moment later, surveying the scene. "You sure know how to entertain the ladies."

"I can't think of the last time you visited my happy home without Maria and kids."

"I returned your call at work. They said you were home. I was concerned."

"The hell you were."

"Okay, the fact is, I decided to drop in here on my way home to kick your ass for the violin story. You fuckwad—there's a reason why we hold back certain information, even from reporters. Especially from reporters! Sometimes there's stuff only the cops and killer know—"

"So sorry," Leo responded, uncontrite.

"—and now I've got my superiors wondering how the *Citizen* knows, and every other media outlet in town is on my back about this fucking fiddle."

"Hey, you talked about it freely to me yesterday."

"That was off the record."

"You didn't *say* off the record."

Frank glared down at him.

"So, anyway," Leo continued, "what's happening with the violin?"

"Like I'm going to tell you."

"Off the record, then. Off the fucking record. Satisfied?"

Frank struggled out of his coat and tossed it on the couch. "Doesn't matter now anyway," he growled. "The whole world knows. And why doesn't your story have a byline?"

"Internal crap at the *Zit*. Doesn't matter."

"Well, it's some protection for me, at any rate." Frank glanced woodenly at Stevie. "How are you holding up?"

"Okay, I guess."

Frank grunted and turned back to Leo. "And what the hell are you doing on the floor?"

Leo explained.

"Tough."

"I'll be better tomorrow. Are you going to tell me about the violin?"

"Not much to tell, other than that the thing did get to Winnipeg. Sotheby's says he didn't carry it with him—I guess because he was going to Washington from London and didn't want anything to happen to something that cost such a shitload of money. A courier delivered it to him on September 12, six days after he got back to Winnipeg."

"There you go: motive."

"Maybe. But—"

"He had another violin," Stevie interjected. "The one he had at the Curtis. The one he's had for years, since he was in his teens."

"Smart girl." Frank grinned.

"Oh," Leo said.

"I don't know the make," Stevie continued. "Nowhere near as valuable as a Guarneri del Gesu."

"But I thought he'd abandoned the violin."

"As a profession, yes. But he kept the instrument. For sentimental reasons, he told me. And he took it out to play from time to time."

"Could you identify the case?" Frank asked her.

Stevie thought a moment and shook her head. "I haven't seen that violin in years. I couldn't even tell you the colour of the lining. I think most violin cases look pretty much alike, unless it's an antique, or someone has gone to the trouble to decorate theirs."

"And that's the problem," Frank groused. "We have one empty case, and two missing violins. Is the missing one the million-dollar Guarneri or the other one? No one has seen the Gaurneri around here. And it seems Rossiter didn't play his ordinary violin with others often enough for anyone to remember anything about the case. At least anyone that we can find."

Stevie was studying her nails. "Try Caitlin Clark," she muttered.

"Who?"

"Tried her already," Leo said. "Doing a little investigating on my own."

"A friend of Michael's," Stevie replied, worrying a cuticle. "They were at the Curtis at the same time. They might be—might have been—lovers."

Leo glanced sharply at her. Her eyes skimmed his, but briefly.

"And?" Frank said to Leo.

"I got an answering machine." He turned back to his brother-in-law. "She lives on Roslyn Road."

Frank fished a notebook out of his suit pocket and made a note. He regarded them in grumpy silence.

"Not exactly one of your E-Z-Solve, home-in-time-for-*Wheel of Fortune* homicides, is it, Frank?" Leo said.

"No, damn it."

"Informed sources tell me professional art thieves usually have more finesse," Leo continued.

"Usually."

Leo regarded them both. Frank was running his hand over his bald pate, as if searching for the ghost of hairs past. Stevie was fidgeting with the abundance of follicles nature affords women. He wished Frank would go and she would stay.

"Seen the will?" he asked his brother-in-law.

"Not yet. Seen the pathologist's report."

"And—"

Frank opened his mouth to speak, but Stevie cut him off. "I think I'll take Alvy for a w-a-l-k." She rose abruptly. "I can live without hearing this."

She had the dog's lead and was out the door in a trice. Leo could feel cool air roll along the floor toward him.

"Just as well, I guess," Frank said.

"That bad?"

"Remember that old Olivetti? The bar at the bottom matches the head wound."

"Ouch."

"But that's not how he died. As near as can be made out, Rossiter staggered forward under the blow, then tried to grip the edge of the desk to steady himself. In doing so, he must have swiped a letter spike off the desk with his hand and then sort of rolled forward—"

"Oh crap."

"Yup. His head fell on the spike and it pierced his neck and brain."

Leo sucked in his breath.

"His death was immediate."

"Big consolation." Leo gagged inwardly. He thought a moment. "You couldn't plan for that effect, could you?"

"Nope."

"If the intent was to club Michael to death—"

"There would have been a helluva lot of mess. Blood everywhere. And on the killer, too."

Leo considered this. "You'd have to bring a change of clothes with you."

"Or take something from his closet—"

"If you were a man. Or maybe even a woman."

"—and wash yourself first."

"There's no blood in any sink or tub."

"Kind of a lucky break."

"If timing was important."

"Was it?"

Frank shrugged. "Who knows? The best estimate is that Rossiter died sometime between 6:30 and 7:15. Probably earlier than later."

"Opportunity?"

"Lots, you'd think. But we've had uniforms doing a door-to-door all day in the neighbourhood, and squat all. Seems like everyone was indoors having dinner, and everyone's dining room window in the goddamn forest of Crescentwood is obscured by trees and shrubs. Most of the shops in Dorchester Square were closed. The florist was just closing, but she wasn't too useful when I talked to her." Frank paused, staring out the window. "And the restaurant had all of two customers the whole evening—a couple with a 7:30 reservation under the name of Johnson, I figure. It was spelled phonetically J-O-N-S-U-N. I managed to yank the reservations books away from the manager—he barely spoke English and he was as tense as a ball of wire. You can imagine how many Johnsons there are in this town."

Leo savoured the moment.

"What are you grinning about?" Frank growled.

"Johnson is a sort of *nom de nosh*."

"Eh?"

"For Roger Mellish, the *Zit*'s food editor and restaurant reviewer. He was at the Wajan Tuesday with his lady friend to do a review. He doesn't want to tip off the restaurant owners, so he uses a fake name." He shrugged. "Of course, they know him. The restaurant association circulates his picture. The manager at the Wajan probably didn't want to jinx his review. No one gives a crap what the theatre reviewer in this town thinks, but the restaurant reviewer? He can make or break. If Roger liked the Wajan, then the place will be packed by the weekend."

Frank grunted.

"Besides, he lives in Savoye House, that glass thing on stilts near Wellington and Grosvenor. It's about a ten-minute walk, so maybe he and Nan—"

"Who?"

"Nan Hughes, his lady friend. Maybe they saw something or someone."

"Worth a shot, I guess." Frank fitted Stevie's pictures back into their envelope. "Can't you get off the floor? I feel like I'm talking to a corpse."

Leo propped himself on his elbows. "I have to piss anyway."

"This was stuck to your butt," Frank said when he returned a few minutes later. Leo finished knotting his bathrobe and took the photograph from Frank.

"I guess it slipped under."

Frank peered up at him. "You guess."

"Never mind, Frank. It's not important." Leo bent over and picked Stevie's photo envelope off the coffee table. He was a bit stiff, but not too bad.

"You don't seem so sick," Frank observed.

"Drugs and booze—they work just fine." Leo slipped the picture of Axel back in with the others. "I'll be back at work tomorrow."

"Remember—we never had this conversation."

"Gee, Frank, I think you've got more out of us than you've given." Leo looked out the front window. Stevie was talking to Les Strickland, who had moved over to Leo's lawn to rake it. Having a semi-retired neighbour with an obsessive-compulsive disorder was a true boon. Anxious lest all the lawns in the neighbourhood didn't match, he cut or raked every one of them himself until they did.

"I suppose you've had no luck with the missing computer disks or the torn page from the daytimer?" he asked Frank.

"Nope."

"Would you tell me if you had?"

"I'd have to think about it."

"You're a shit. I don't know why my sister married you."

"She was pregnant."

"How could I forget?" His niece, Alison, arrived seven months after the wedding. "Would you have married Maria if she hadn't been?"

"What? Pregnant? That's a lousy question."

"Try answering it."

"It was more than 'doing the right thing,' if that's what you're thinking." He kicked Leo's bare calf. "And why are you bringing this up now? It's years since."

"Hell if I know, Frank," he replied, stepping out of Frank's reach and watching Stevie break away from his neighbour and lead Alvy back to the house. He tossed the package of photos back on the coffee table. "By the way, Stevie's camera is still at Michael's house."

"Do you have your phone off?"

Frank's question made Leo turn. "I intended to snooze all afternoon, why?"

"It's ringing...or blinking." A frail red light trebled on the plastic console. "It might be for me."

"And you're the centre of the universe."

Stevie came through the front door, bringing one dog and a burst of cool air with her. Her cheeks were flushed with exertion. "Are you talking about Toronto?"

Leo laughed. The answering machine kicked in with an audible click.

"Hey!" Frank said, rising from his chair. "Someone grab that thing."

Leo turned the volume dial and pressed the rewind button. The tape made a short Chip'n'Dale shriek. They listened to the tail end of Stevie sounding slightly anxious, then Gerry Shorter with the impatience of a five-year-old at Christmas.

"Told you," Frank said, picking the phone up off the floor. His contribution to the ensuing conversation was a series of "yeahs" in varying tones.

"Some kid remembered a licence plate from a car at the scene," he whispered loudly from the side of his mouth, cupping the receiver with one hand.

"Amazing what some people can remember," Stevie commented, removing Alvy's lead.

"It's an easy one," Frank returned the receiver to its cradle. "A vanity plate—10 JETS."

"Ah!" said Leo.

Stevie frowned. "I don't get it."

"Dale Hawerchuk, Winnipeg Jets." Leo and Frank chorused.

"Who?"

"He plays centre for the Winnipeg Jets," Leo explained. "Ten is his number." He turned to Frank. "You've gotta be kidding. Dale *Hawerchuk* is a suspect?"

"Nope. "Frank pulled out his notebook and scribbled something. "Don't think so."

"But—"

Frank looked up, imperceptible pleasure crinkling the corners of his eyes. "Licence plate number 10 JETS has been traced to a woman."

"A woman? Some wacko groupie?"

"You tell me. Is Merritt Helena Parrish née Rossiter of Wellington Crescent a hockey fan?"

Book 4

Friday, September 30

21

Pissed Off

If the day outside was heavily overcast as it often was in the fall, the newsroom, hemmed by peeling walls and sooty windows, would seem by contrast to glow hot and overbright like a burning coal. If the day was also drenched with rain, and reporters stomped in with dripping coats and umbrellas, the newsroom would soon steam and smell as though the drops had burst and spurted against the hot coal. Wet wool would hang in the air with the cigarette smoke and the ancient dust. Such days made the staff as cranky as wet cats. On such days staff preferred that routine remain undisturbed.

When Leo came into the newsroom, and hung his wet jacket on a dilapidated coat tree, and threw into a wastebasket the soaking newspaper he had used as a head cover, and finally turned around to take his seat, he saw immediately there had been a great disturbance in the morning routine. Instead of reporters with their heads in the first edition, or with Styrofoam coffee cups planted on their lips, or with telephone receivers growing out of their ears, there were reporters standing in knots of two or three whispering heatedly, reporters in clusters leaning over their desks muttering intensely, and individual reporters circulating from knot to cluster like malevolent bees while telephones went unanswered, newspapers went unread, and coffee turned cold.

A few desks away, Liz was standing talking to Doug Whiteway, careful not to blow smoke into his face. She saw Leo after a moment, gestured across the room, while mouthing to him slowly: "Go to the bulletin board."

With foreboding, Leo did as instructed.

On the board, amid notices for journalism scholarships to faraway places and yellowing reminders that dress standards in the newsroom were deteriorating, was pinned a fresh pink piece of paper with a curt message.

"Beginning Monday, October 3," it read, "Guy Clark will assume duties as city editor. Ray Alcock will become columnist-at-large. Bob Pastuk will become Go! editor, *pro tem*." The notice was signed, "Martin Kingdon, managing editor."

"Crap," said Leo.

"How's your back?" Liz joined him at the board.

"Bit tender, but okay." He tapped the notice with his finger. "I'm fucked. I can't work under that asshole." He looked across the newsroom at the asshole in question. Clark was hunched over his desk in studied concentration over some section of the day's paper. A fringe of limp yellow hair hanging over his face made it impossible to read any expression. "And where's the managing asshole?" he asked.

"Rumour has it Martin came in around 7:00, pinned the notice to the board, then left. Or fled, depending on who's telling it." Liz averted her head to release a plume of smoke. "Ray apparently came in half an hour later and went apoplectic. He broke down the door to Martin's office and proceeded to urinate on his desk."

Leo raised his eyebrows. "I'm impressed."

"He'll probably be looking for job openings at the *Examiner*."

"I may be joining him. This change is okay for you, though."

"Sure. Bob's easing into retirement. He doesn't care, so life won't be complete hell. At least *pro tem*—"

"As arty-farty-Marty would put it." He looked at her. "Do you want the job?"

"Guy would block it anyway. I'm on his shit list. And he seems to have Martin wrapped around his skinny little finger."

"Roger?"

"Doubt it. Too much of a foodie. Maybe you should alert Axel, now that *Winnipeg Life* is defunct. He can come back."

"Mr. Ego's resurrecting *WL* if it's the last thing he does. Besides, he has no love for Guy. He's sure Guy killed the distribution deal he was making with the *Zit*. And…"

"And what?"

Leo hesitated. What did he know for sure? Oh, what the hell: "I think Axel and Merritt are an item."

Liz snickered. "Another love triangle."

"Another?"

"Generally, I mean. They abound."

Leo glanced at her. "Do you know if Merritt and Dale Hawerchuk were ever an item?"

"For about thirty seconds." She waved her cigarette in Guy's direction. "She must have been slumming when she picked up with him. She really does have odd taste in men. The only thing I can think Hawerchuk and Guy and Axel have in common is that they all have a certain aggressive streak. Type A's, in their way."

"Stevie thinks Merritt has RADD."

"What's that?"

"Romantic Attention Deficit Disorder."

Liz laughed. "Might explain her two-week marriage, too. Not to mention her writing style. Gushy, but with sentence fragments and lots of ellipses."

"Merritt and Guy didn't last long."

"No. But he still drools when she deigns to come into the newsroom. Which hasn't been often lately."

Leo considered one of the benefactions of death to survivors. "Ten bucks says we don't see her in this dump again."

A prompting from Audrey sent Liz scurrying to her desk to answer her telephone. Leo wandered to his and picked up a dry copy of the *Zit* to read rather than use as a rainhat. Speculation about Mulroney's imminent election call dominated the front page. The Kushniryk trial was below the fold. The Rossiter murder had fallen to page three. It was without byline, its contents little more than "investigation continuing" claptrap. One measly paragraph contained Leo's phone-in contribution—a bit about smart thieves and art theft. Damned if he hadn't had to honour his off-the-record agreement with Frank, otherwise he would have phoned in a police-have-a-new-lead-in-the-Rossiter-slaying-type story. Worse, Stevie had leapt to Merritt's defence by pulling out the running-Axel photograph. But Frank had burst her balloon by pointing out that Merritt's car had been sighted at Michael's a good hour before an ardent and sweaty Axel had jogged up Merritt's driveway.

He ran his eyes over the text again. What piss-poor coverage! Was this any way to sell newspapers? And god knows what would happen next week. "Recently Appointed City Editor's Former Squeeze Questioned in 'Angel' Slaying"? "Managing Editor's Niece Wanted for Questioning in Crescentwood Death"? Not likely. What happens if reporters become suspects? Some Journalism Ethics seminar at Red River Community College would dole out the without-fear-or-favour bullshit.

But then there was the real world.

Leo peered over the paper's edge, avoiding Julie's scornful glance, and scanned the real world and its occupants. With Guy at the helm, he was basically screwed. Who knew what crap assignments would be his? Nasty, British, and Short seemed a treat in comparison. But NB&S was gone. Leo turned his gaze toward the crescent-shaped desk around which copy editors sat like fat Buddhas, staring at their computer screens, occasionally sending a finger darting across the keyboard to lop off an offending "s" the way a frog's tongue annihilates a fly. Newsroom machinations meant nothing to them. The stage of being anxious and neurotic reporters has passed. All they had to do was hack and trim verbiage to fit it between advertisements. And then they left, carrying nothing more of the newsroom home with them than a copy of the paper, the way a butcher might carry home a nicely trimmed piece of meat. There was a bovine satisfaction to it. And the pay was better.

Or maybe he could return to Go!?

Ugh. All the lifestyle crap.

The business section?

He'd have to wear a suit.

Sports?

That happy playground had a waiting list as long as the queue for Tory patronage.

Well, he thought, I've got one more day to do what I want. Kingdon has fled. Alcock has walked. Clark is not on board yet. The assistant managing editor is in Japan on a journalism scholarship. The op-ed page team, with its Olympian view of newsroom machinations, rarely descends from the clouds. The *Zit* is in its fifth month without a publisher. And the two assistant city editors are as irresolute and fat as Tweedledee and Tweedledum, whom they resemble.

It's anarchy.

Yippee.

He quickly rooted out Dave, one of the Guys Named Dave in the newsroom, who had been assigned police stories, and wrested the Rossiter story from him. He was a beardless youth and easily vanquished.

Leo intended to begin where he had ended on Wednesday, bent double in the *Zit*'s library. He had gone to look in the vertical file for Tom Rossiter, to see how the paper had handled a previous Rossiter death, one not as spectacular as a murder, but a violent end nonetheless—a car accident. Had the *Zit* been as prissy and circumspect then? Or had the coverage been even thinner gruel, given that Tom Rossiter had been the owner and publisher when he'd snuffed it?

He zigzagged through the cluster of desks to the back of the newsroom to fetch the notebook he'd left in his jacket pocket. Mellish was sitting glassy-eyed at a computer terminal, head bent, oblivious to the passing scene. As he fished in the inside pocket of his jacket, Leo glanced over and noted that Roger had Julie's directory up on his screen. Even though he was an editor of a department of one, Roger was an editor nonetheless, and had access to reporters' computers. Still, Leo thought, he was pretty much trawling in private waters, even if the waters were those of Ms Grumpy's.

He leaned over, ignored the twinge in his back, and whispered innocently: "Did you give the Wajan a good review?"

Roger jerked up in his chair. "Jesus, Leo!"

"Sorry."

Roger switched off his terminal. "Yes," he snapped, turning to regard Leo. "It was excellent, though I think I did tell you that the other night."

Leo yanked out the notebook. "So you did."

"Indeed," Roger continued more calmly, "I thought it was good enough to go into *Taste of Winnipeg*."

"Too late, I guess."

"Apparently so. I talked to Bunny yesterday. Friesens has it scheduled for printing in three weeks, and there's pictures Michael took last Saturday that are undeveloped. He hadn't sent the film out to be processed and, of course, his house is still sealed. And my glasses are still inside," he added as an afterthought.

"What are those things on your nose?"

"I do have *two* pairs," Roger said witheringly.

En route to the library, Leo recalled a conversation he had had with Stevie at his house one Sunday in July, not many weeks after their first date, if you could call going for coffee a date. She had been helping him cut some wood sheeting for kitchen cupboards but a fuse blew with the saw and a window air conditioner running at the same time. Since he was out of fresh fuses, they'd retreated to the shade of the big elm in his backyard with glasses of iced tea. Somehow—part of the usual feints of inquiry in early-stage relationships—Leo found himself talking about his father's sudden death in the Fort Rouge railyards, crushed by a boxcar, leaving him the only kid on the block without a father, practically the only kid with a mother who worked outside the home, in the fur department at Eaton's, one of the original latchkey kids in his Riverview neighbourhood. He recalled it as a blur, a flurry of visits and casseroles and pats on his little head. He mostly remembered the toy soldiers an aunt had sent him from England. The loss of his father, he thought, had affected him less than it had his sister. He'd often wondered if that was why she'd married Frank so young, just to have the kind of masculine presence in her life that a kid brother couldn't supply. And, of course, his mother had been most affected. It was only in later years that he'd realized the extent of her struggles, and what an asshole teenager he'd been.

Like a movie segue, the conversation had slipped to Michael Rossiter, one of the signs, he realized afterwards, that Michael was on Stevie's mind. Leo had been vaguely aware that Tom Rossiter, once the publisher of the paper he worked for, had died in a car crash, but as it had happened before he worked for the *Zit*, he'd given it little thought.

Stevie said Michael had abandoned his private ambitions, his desire to be a solo artist, in the wake of his parents' death. He had completed his master of music degree in violin performance in Philadelphia, but the Rossiter financial holdings needed attention, and Merritt was getting beyond even Kathleen's resourcefulness, particularly when she turned eighteen and became a full-fledged rich brat. Even if he hadn't been able to carve out a solo career—and how difficult it was—Michael wouldn't, Stevie was sure, have returned to Winnipeg if his parents hadn't lost their lives so abruptly. He had said as much during one of their darkroom catch-up sessions. He would have toured, taught, written music; lived in New York, California, England, Italy. But a solo career demanded a monomaniacal devotion to art and an obedience to itinerancy, and he had let his attention be diverted. Well, it couldn't be helped, he had said. Shit happens. He had intended only a brief pause to sort out things, but there are no pauses in the smilingly vicious world of the arts, and the pause stretched forth like a prairie road to become his life.

"Do I detect guilt?" Leo had asked.

"It was the Christmas holidays. His parents had dropped him off at the airport. The accident happened shortly after, on their way out of the airport. If Michael had taken a taxi—"

"They'd still be alive," Leo filled in. "What happened?"

"Ice patch, I think. Or mechanical failure. I think that was the official story. My parents are pretty sure booze was involved," Stevie shrugged, looked away. "I'm not really sure. I wasn't here. I was in Baltimore."

"I thought you'd gone to school in Rhode Island?"

"I spent the Christmas holidays with my aunt and uncle in Baltimore."

She'd sounded strangely defensive on that point. Of course, now he knew why. Christmas had been the mere punctuation of a nine-month stay in the Maryland capital.

In days of yore, newspaper libraries were called morgues. It was a word Leo never found pertinent to the *Zit*'s library, which he always felt was more life-giving. As soon as he stepped over the threshold from newsroom to library, he felt he had stepped into a haven of calm and order and goodwill. The library was staffed entirely by women, most of them middle-aged, with the occasional young nun-like novice being inculcated to the arcana of bibliology.

In the mornings, the women organized history. With practised hands, a sharp ruler and a pot of glue, each took a section of the *Citizen*, cut it into column lengths, sealed the lengths together (sometimes they were as long as a man is tall) and then folded them in an almost undecipherable system of folds into little brown envelopes which were, in turn, tucked away in rows of ancient filing cabinets. Loath to disturb their liturgy, Leo went right for the cabinet marked ROB—RUT, which was at floor level. This time he carefully bent at the knee to pull out the drawer. He found the file marked Rossiter, Tom, and started shuffling through the clippings, which dated back to the late 1950s. There seemed to be nothing from late 1976-early 1977. Damn. Maybe Vera Macklin, chief librarian and fount of knowledge, had a clue.

She looked up at him as he approached the desk and released a barely perceptible sigh. "Yes, dear," she said, putting down the silver letter-opener she'd been tapping against the palm of her hand and readjusting her glasses.

"There seems to be some stuff missing from a file."

"What are you looking for?"

He told her.

"Then you'll have to try the microfilm."

Leo groaned. The microfilm machine was ancient and he hated all the scrolling you had to do.

"Here, I'll help you," she said, rising from her chair and moving purposefully to the relevant filing cabinet at the back of the room. She opened a drawer, ran practised fingers along rows of white boxes, frowned, then repeated her action.

"December 1976 and January 1977, did you say?"

"Yup."

"Odd." She drummed the cardboard box top with her nail.

"What's the matter?"

"It's not here. You haven't had those rolls out before, have you?"

"No. Don't often have to go back that many years for a story."

Leo followed Vera's eyes as they ran over the tops of filing cabinets and library tables in the vicinity of the microfilm machine. Then she lifted the grey plastic cover of the microfilm machine and glanced at the spool, disappointingly empty.

"Perhaps it's been misfiled," Leo offered.

Vera's frown grew deeper. "Well, possibly, though it's not like my girls to misfile things." She sighed. "It's got to be around here somewhere. Is it important?"

"I just wanted to see how Tom Rossiter's death was covered."

"With circumspection," Vera said dryly. Curiosity flickered in her eyes but she asked no questions. Reporters' whims were beyond her worry. "Well, then, grab a drawer and start looking."

Leo took one end of the rank of cabinets, Vera the other, and they began a chorus of banging and slamming until they met in the middle.

"Well, I'm sure I don't know." Vera said testily, her hands on her hips. "Perhaps someone in the newsroom has it, though what good it does out there—"

"Is it the only copy?"

"No."

Leo grinned at her hopefully.

"I keep a second set in an old walk-in vault in the sub-basement."

"Long way down."

"Well, it looks like I'm going to have to send it out for duplicating anyway, so I might as well go get it. It had better not be missing, too."

"Then it'll be easy to find the culprit. How many people have the combination?"

"No one. The combination's lost to time. The door's always kept open."

"Not the most secure vault in the world."

"Other than the men who bring in the barrels of trichloroethylene to clean the presses, hardly anyone goes down there any more, at least since—odd you should mention him—Tom Rossiter was alive."

"How so?"

"When I went looking for some extra storage space several years ago, I found a quite a few empty Scotch bottles lining the shelves—*quite* a few."

"Maybe they belonged to the press men."

Vera laughed. "It was single malt from some very exclusive distillery in the Highlands. I did ask at the liquor commission once, out of curiosity, and they looked it up. Had to be specially imported, and it cost nearly a hundred dollars a bottle then. Scotch was Mr. Rossiter's preferred tipple."

"Well, he wasn't a cheap drunk, then."

"No, but he could be an obnoxious drunk. Charming, when he wanted to be. But often a mean drunk. He'd have these towering rages in the newsroom about something or other." She shook her head. "Little wonder his son had no interest in this business. Mr. Rossiter would bring Michael in to do stints as copy boy or whatever, and then just tear into him if he did anything wrong. Terrible." She sighed. "Oh, well…anyway, I'll just get that microfilm."

She moved toward the door that led to one of the building's narrow interior stairwells.

"The elevator would be quicker," Leo suggested hopefully.

"I could use the exercise, dear."

Waiting, Leo stared absently through the library's dusty back window over the parking lot toward the new downtown mall. He thought about:

> …whether he should wear the same tie to the afternoon funeral and tomorrow's mall opening, or if he should spring for a new tie in the meantime
> …whether he'd ever wear a tie again if he won the lottery
> …whether Merritt was as rich as she looked
> …whether she was capable of murder
> …what she looked like naked
> …what Stevie looked like naked
> …what Merritt saw in Axel
> …what women saw in Axel generally
> …whether he'd soon be out of a job

...what he'd do instead
...what was taking Vera so long
...whether the mall would do a damn thing for downtown Winnipeg
...why there was that preposterous "á" in Galleries Portáge.
...whether he should get a new tie
...why mental conversations were circular

"Found them," an out-of-breath voice gasped, breaking into his thoughts. Vera rattled one of the white boxes. "I suppose you're going to the mall opening tomorrow night."

"It seems we're commanded to show *Zit* support for downtown redevelopment."

"Ha! Harry Mack will sell up and have us out in the sticks before you know it." Vera released the roll of microfilm from its box with a clinical snap of the hand and nimbly inserted it through the machine's nether parts.

"Amazing," Leo said.

"It just takes a little practice."

"A new machine might be better."

Vera harrumphed. "There'll be Zambonies in hell before any money's put into this department. And when you're finished with that microfilm," she commanded, "return it to me personally. Don't leave it lying around."

"Yes, ma'am."

After she returned to her desk Leo sat down to the tedious task of scrolling through microfilm. Eleven years seemed a lifetime ago. In those years the *Citizen* had gone through a major design change to conform to a contemporary standard of uncluttered appearance which, Leo suddenly realized, bore a strong relationship to the look of the accompanying advertising. But as he turned the squeaky handle of the microfilm machine and the pages rolled across the screen, he decided that he preferred the look of the old *Zit*. Its now quaint type face and narrower columns declared its serious intent. The new *Zit* looked frivolous by comparison. But old or new, Leo knew that automobile accidents, tragic and often meaningless as they were, remained the stuff of front page coverage.

He found it sooner than he expected. The accident had occurred on January 2, 1977, the story appearing in the *Zit* the next day. There was no picture. And the text was terse, just the bare bones of a police report: the time, the place, the circumstances, and the names of the victims of one of the two cars involved—Thomas and Lillian Rossiter. Accompanying the news story however, and continuing at some length on an inside page, was an obituary *cum* family history that presented Thomas and his wife in scrupulous prose as scions of a venerable old family, their deaths an irreparable loss to the community. Leo scrolled ahead to the next day's edition and found buried on an inside page a small story that added a few details to the original. The accident was attributed, as Stevie had said, to icy conditions and mechanical failure in the Rossiter car. But what Leo was unprepared for, what set his mind to wondering, was the name of the driver and the two passengers of the other vehicle.

22

A Nice Cup of Tea

Stevie stepped from the Saab, released the catch on her umbrella, and listened to the rain drum against the taut nylon. She skipped across a puddle, over Grosvenor's sodden boulevard, and onto the sidewalk, narrowly avoiding crushing a worm inching its way across the saturated cement. As she walked in the direction of Savoye House, she thought little of the sorts of things she'd planned to ask Nan Hughes; in the wake of the week's events, her career plans suddenly seemed even less urgent than they'd been all summer.

Merritt instead flitted through her mind. The afternoon before, Stevie had unthinkingly accepted an offer of a lift home from Frank Nickel and had endured a cross-examination on wheels. While polishing an effective "no-comment" strategy, she had nevertheless been reminded of the peril of being Merritt, notably in this situation: out of cash, into drugs, and—always—a turbulent relationship with her brother. She had practically leapt from the car to get away from Frank, but she had kept the front door of her parents' house open a smidgen to see what he would do. As expected, he had stopped at Merritt's. But he had had to drive away disappointed. There had been no one home.

Nor had there been the entire evening. She had walked over herself later, then phoned. Where could Merritt be on the evening before her brother's funeral? She regretted having shown that picture of Axel Werner to the detective. If Mrs. Axel Werner were no longer in residence, Merritt might conceivably be there. She had found the number in the phone book, but, again, no answer. Just another crappy answering machine.

Stevie reached Nan's apartment building, folded her umbrella, and pushed open the glass door to the tiny foyer. Water dripped from her coat. Her hand hesitated over the security buzzer. Was she really thinking of staying in Winnipeg? Her fantasy reason, she admitted to herself bleakly, had died Tuesday evening. She could go back to Toronto. But she had made an eleventh-hour call to her landlord in Toronto—it was September 30, after all—and secured her apartment for another month. Leo sailed through her mind, unbidden. Yes, he was a good kisser, my my. She pressed the buzzer next to a card in Helvetica medium script that read "Nan Hughes." After a pause an indecipherable squawk came through the intercom.

"Nan, it's Stevie Lord."

Another squawk issued forth, the lock sprang with a noisy click and Stevie, who had been leaning on the door handle, nearly fell into the lobby. Built on slender stilts over resident parking, the building contained sixteen suites on two floors with four sets of stairs, four apartments sharing a set. Sky-lit illumination over a narrow white hallway along the side of the ground floor directed her to a sign marking the second stairwell and apartments 5 to 8.

Nan stood at the doorwell of number 5, wearing a remarkable golden kimono emblazoned with a red dragon spiralling the garment from hem to neck like the serpent on depictions of the Tree of Life in the Garden of Eden.

"Did I get you at a bad time?" Stevie's voice echoed in the stairwell.

"No, no. I've no classes Fridays this term so I don't often dress until noon. I didn't think you'd mind." Nan put a hand out. "Here, let me take those wet things."

Stevie peeled off her coat and handed it over with her folded umbrella.

"Actually, I thought you might reschedule," Nan continued, grunting with effort as she pushed aside her own coats in the small closet and jammed Stevie's in. "Given that the funeral's this afternoon."

"Well, I need something else to think about."

"I'm sure you do." Nan turned and regarded her sympathetically. "You were quite fond of him, weren't you?"

"Yes."

"I seem to recall Michael coming up to see you in the lab in the Fine Arts building in your first year. Perhaps it's because I knew both your parents a little, that he stood out from all the boys wanting a look at the I.D girls." A smile flitted across Nan's face. "I remember him once having delivered—"

"Oh, god, yes, the roses. I'd nearly forgotten. Twelve dozen arriving in the middle of our last drafting class in the spring. The delivery boy staggering in—"

"Very romantic."

"I think it just made me angrier at the time. I can't remember now what the argument was about." She looked away. She knew very well what the argument had been about. Michael had teased her, saying her rebellious spirit went about as far as wanting to cover an Eames chair with terrycloth. She had bristled, but deep down it was true. Her acts of defiance to that point had been little more than the usual teenaged antics. His refusal to interest himself in the Rossiter family business, on the other hand, was a finger in his father's face every day of the week. And when he got his master's from the Curtis with his father's money, he was really going to fuck the old man by throwing it all away and going off to be a shepherd in Nevada or somewhere. He sounded half serious; worse, she seemed to have no place in this daydream. No shepherdess by his side. In her mind, she would be at Rizdee, he would be at the Curtis. Providence and Philadelphia weren't that far apart. They would meet in New York. Frequently. And then…?

It was the beginning of the end—friends since forever, lovers for a year. The roses had been overcompensation.

"Extravagant," Nan added, letting the word hang in the air a moment. Then she frowned, pushing at the sleeves of her kimono. "Less so in recent years, I think. More reserved. Rather self-contained."

"I suppose."

"Life doesn't always turn out the way we expect," Nan sighed. The comment seemed apropos of nothing, but Stevie knew what she meant: Michael had not achieved what he'd set out to do when they were undergraduates.

"Certainly, I never expected Kerr to die so young," Nan added.

"I'm sorry."

"No, no, my apologies. I don't know why I even brought it up. Anyway, don't let's go on standing here in the hallway. Go on in. Make yourself comfortable." She gestured toward the living room. "What would you prefer? Coffee or tea?"

"Oh." It wasn't a day for decisions. "Tea, I think. Something about the rain makes me want tea."

But the problem was: *where* to make herself comfortable. Stevie surveyed the living room, somewhat startled. She'd expected Nan, as a professor of interior design, to have—without question—living space signifying the great Bauhaus virtue: less is more. With every piece of furniture a paean to clean lines and uncluttered surfaces. But virtually every piece, she could tell at a glance, was period—antique. She ran a finger over a Queen Anne side chair. Gorgeous! And it wasn't just the quality. It was the quantity. The living room looked more like an auction house preparing for the weekly sale. There was a recamier in the centre of the room, but it was thick with pillows and one cardboard box that appeared to be filled with photo albums. A nearby set of armchairs similarly was covered with boxes, books, and papers, as was a small sofa pressed against a sideboard laden with china, candlesticks, and a silver tea service. Indeed, Stevie noted, there were three silver tea services in sight, one on each of three different cabinets that groaned under an assortment of knick-knacks, all of it, however, remarkably dust-free. There were a couple of hassocks, several spindly-looking side tables of no discernible use, a variety of lamps and several dozen pictures, some on the wall, some grouped on the floor, and one sitting prominently on an easel. Depicted in oils was a young woman, slim, dark, conventionally pretty, and wearing a strapless pink gown of 1950s vintage. It took Stevie a moment to realize it was a youthful Nan. The woman coming down the hall with a tray in her hands was plumpish, her hair lighter than in the picture and fashioned into a tight French roll.

"I guess you were never in our Crescent house," Nan said.

"Just at Hallowe'en, I think."

"You're surprised."

"Well—"

"Kerr was partial to antiques. Many of these things came from his family in England. So my tastes tended to be overruled."

"Bauhaus by day, Biedermeier by night."

Nan laughed. "Exactly. Anyway, let's sit down." She led the way down a passage bordered by a desk and a china cabinet to a nook in front of the floor-to-ceiling window with a loveseat, a chair, and a coffee table. "I'm sorry about this clutter. I thought after Kerr died, I'd make a clean sweep, but somehow I never got around to it in the Crescent house. And then, after my daughter moved to Vancouver—"

"Oh? School?" Stevie had a vague memory of Amanda Hughes, a sort of wan, moody child of about ten last time she saw her.

"Studying at Emily Carr. Interested in graphic design. Takes after me, I guess." Nan placed the tea tray on the low table and gestured for Stevie to sit. "Anyway, after Amanda moved, I decided to buy this condo, then ended up hauling half the furniture here. Ridiculous, I know."

"Well, they're lovely things."

"I know. But of course they don't suit Savoye House. And it's really my chance to design my own living space the way *I* want to. Still…" She cast her eyes around the confining space, her expression suggesting the task was daunting. "Roger says—" She paused, frowning. "You've met Roger Mellish?"

"Is that who you were with Tuesday evening."

Nan nodded, then bit her lip. "I'm sorry. And I do apologize for my behaviour when we ran into you. I had more wine than I should have."

Stevie shrugged.

"Anyway," Nan continued, reaching for the teapot, "Roger says I should just screw up my courage and throw all this furniture out. His idea is to call an antiques dealer, give him carte blanche, and then go to a hotel for a few days."

"Roger's not a fan of old things, I guess."

"Fan of this old thing." Nan giggled girlishly, almost splashing the tea as she poured.

"Oh, hardly old."

"Not old enough to be a widow anyway. I'll be fifty in December. See, I'm even admitting it." She handed the delicate china cup to Stevie. "But to get back—Roger's not a fan of old things. He spent his early childhood in cramped rooms in London with busy wallpaper and awful old furniture—and bombs falling in the Blitz. So he fell in love with Savoye House when he moved to Winnipeg. I've been spending time helping him get the right mid-century modern look. I should be doing it *here*, of course. But, you know, the cobbler's children go unshod. Or whatever the saying is."

"Well, it's a great building." Stevie sipped her tea, the golden liquid invitingly warm along her tongue. She settled back into the chair nearest the window, almost feeling cozy. Outside the rain-splattered window a gloom hovered over the semi-nude trees along Wellington Crescent.

"If you're thinking of buying—I don't know what your plans are—but there's one for sale. Across from Roger."

"Really?" Stevie entertained the notion. Savoye House *was* an attractive piece of architecture. And compared to Toronto's ridiculously inflated real-estate prices, probably affordable. She had money wrested from Sangster, but on work-leave from YP she had no income. The notion of housing threw her back to the usual quandary: was she going or staying? "These are two-bedroom, right?"

Nan nodded, stirring her tea, her kimono sleeve absently brushing the sugarbowl with each circulation. "I should show you around. It's ideal for one person or two. I think, after it was first built, a few families lived here. But you know as well as I do how space needs have changed. The kitchen is a bit small, too, by today's standards. Roger, being the culinary whiz he is, had his enlarged and renovated." She glanced around the room. "The construction's solid. The layout is intelligent. The balcony can barely hold a barbecue, though. And, of course, there's never enough closet space but…" she shrugged.

"How about noise?"

"Excellent. There's only four apartments per staircase, so there's no banging around in hallways and such. Otherwise, just one adjoining wall. Roger's on the other side of mine. You can hear plumbing noises because the bathrooms adjoin, but that's all right." She smiled coyly. "Roger sings at the top of his lungs in the shower and I can sometimes hear him straight through into my bedroom. But…I rather like it."

"No ensuite bathroom?"

"No, just the one."

"Well, it's certainly attractive. But I'm just not sure of what I'm doing these days."

Nan studied her a moment. "Well, I did have one suggestion for you: I can't be all that encouraging about work opportunities in the field, if you're serious about staying in Winnipeg, though I have a few leads. But I wondered if you'd thought of teaching interior design?"

"Teaching? No, I hadn't," Stevie replied slowly, startled. "Do you mean—?"

"At the school. Carol Muir, who you might remember, is having a baby around Christmas, so she's taking her leave come January. Or, perhaps, earlier. She's having a difficult pregnancy. She's forty-one and having her first."

"My teaching experience is pretty limited. The Ontario College of Art and Design invited me to give a few lectures, but—"

"Well, it's only a term position. You'd have to see the dean. But I could put in a word for you. You've got good credentials as a designer—"

"I should have brought you a resume."

"Well, you were with Yabu Pushelberg. And you're a RISD graduate. We've been saying for years around the department that we need some fresh perspective. And you've done *some* teaching, it seems."

"I'd have thought leaving the school here to go to one in the States might be a strike against me."

"Hardly. We all recognize the department is too incestuous. I think we're the only department on campus where all the instructors are graduates of the same—that is, our own—school. It's not good. I think you'll find everyone at the school today is the same as when you were there. What was your year with us? I can't remember."

"Seventy-five, seventy-six."

Nan sipped her tea thoughtfully. "You weren't dissatisfied with our program, were you? I don't mean to pry, but you might be asked in an interview."

"No," Stevie lied, draining her cup. "I just wanted a change."

"Oh, I thought it might have had something to do with Michael—"

Stevie glanced over her cup rim sharply. But Nan was reaching for a biscuit.

"—going to the Curtis Institute. Philadelphia's not all that far from Providence. I thought—"

"Actually, Nan, after Michael went to the Curtis, we weren't much in touch." Stevie realized she sounded more curt than she'd intended.

"Oh." Nan regarded Stevie with undisguised curiosity. "I see."

Stevie smiled. "Just one those of things."

"Oh dear."

There was an awkward pause.

"Well, at least you finished your year with us. Anyway, as I say, the job at the university is only a term position, and I know you're wondering what other opportunities there might be—out there, so to speak."

"There's been kind of a downturn in Toronto since Black Thursday."

"Well, you know, Winnipeg just plugs along, not as affected by—"

The telephone rang on the table near them. "Sorry," Nan said, reaching for the receiver, "I'd let the machine get it, but there's a chance it might be the school."

Stevie observed Nan's eyes widen with surprise after her initial greeting, then a kind of gravity settle over her expression as she mouthed a series of yesses of varying emotion into the mouthpiece.

"Has something happened?" Stevie asked after Nan replaced the receiver.

"That was the police." Nan frowned and pushed up her sleeve to reveal her watch. "They're coming over shortly."

"Probably want to know if you saw anything Tuesday evening—"

"But—"

"—on the way to the restaurant, most likely. Or before. Or during."

"But how did they know—?"

Stevie sighed. "Leo."

"The man you were with."

"His brother-in-law is the detective in charge of the investigation. Leo told him Roger was reviewing the Wajan. I guess they're just following leads."

Nan regarded her with mild alarm. "But I can't think of a thing. It was a perfectly ordinary day." She glanced absently around the room. "I got home from the university about 5:30. Roger telephoned at just before 6:00 to say he was going to freshen up—he walks to and from work, it was a hot day—and come get me around 7:15, which he did. And then we walked to the Wajan, which took about ten minutes." She shrugged. "Had a pleasant dinner. Roger sometimes get a bit severe with the waiters. But nothing out of the ordinary, I don't think."

She tapped her lower lip thoughtfully, then addressed Stevie apologetically: "This is an awful question, but do you have any idea exactly when Michael—?"

The word was left unsaid. She told Nan what Frank had told her and Leo—somewhere between 6:30 and 7:15, the earlier time favoured.

"Oh, well then, we were here for most of that hour. I was getting ready. I could hear Roger singing in the shower. And I don't think we even passed anyone on the street going to the restaurant."

Nan glanced down and brushed her hand along the length of her kimono. "I guess I'd better get out of this thing, if I'm going to receive the police."

"Maybe I should go."

"No, no. Stay. Finish your tea. I'll just slip on a dress."

"But—"

"I've hardly given you any help at all."

"Well, a term at the school might be interesting—"

"Come through to the kitchen." Nan rose in a swirl of silk. "If I go into the bedroom we can still hear each other."

Nan lifted the tray and guided Stevie, cup and saucer in hand, through the furniture jungle to the kitchen. "I was going to say," Nan began, placing the tray on the counter and moving down the short hall toward the back of the apartment, "that Designers Four Plus One might be looking. I understand they're minus one. They seem to be branching out into interiors for clinics and dentists' offices and the like. Have you done that sort of thing?"

"A little," Stevie responded. Working in a shop like Yabu Pushelberg had spoiled her. Having been project director for restaurants and hotels in Toronto, a dentist's waiting room seemed a little unchallenging. She glanced at the kitchen's fifties-style breakfast nook. Savoye House was attractive. But did she want to buy something if she stayed longer in Winnipeg? More than a term job, real estate would be commitment.

Nan was rattling on and Stevie didn't catch the words. "Pardon?" She raised her voice. But the reply was cut off by a sharp buzz that made Stevie's nerves jump. "Damn," Nan called from the bedroom. "Would you get that, Stevie?"

Stevie found the intercom. If the caller was Frank Nickel, he'd travelled faster than stink, which made her guess where his last stop had been.

"Mrs. Hughes?" The voice barked.

"No," Stevie groaned. "But I'll let you in anyway." She pressed a red button on the panel, then listened as the door opened on the stairwell below and soft thuds proceeded up the carpeted stairwell. She pulled the door open quickly before a hand could go to the buzzer. Frank stopped wiping rainwater from his coat to stare at her.

"Oh, for Christ's sake—you again."

"Professor Hughes was one of my teachers at university. I'm seeing her on a business matter."

"So where is she?"

"She'll be out in a moment."

"Are you going to let me in?"

Stevie stepped aside. "You got here fast."

"I was just down the street."

She watched Frank loosed the knot of his coat belt. "What did Merritt have to say?"

"The car's in the driveway. Lights are on. But Mrs. Parrish doesn't seem to be at home."

"But the funeral's—"

"Oh, she's at home all right," Frank yanked his coat off and handed the wet bundle to her. "She's just not answering her door. Or her phone. And if I have to pull her out of that funeral, I'll do it."

"You wouldn't dare."

Frank raised an eyebrow. "I don't think Mrs. Parrish's reluctance to speak with me works in her favour." He leaned toward her. "Do you?"

Nan joined them in the hall, wearing the navy-blue sheath she'd worn like a uniform every day of the year Stevie had spent in I.D. "Am I interrupting something?" she said with the authority Stevie recalled from art history lessons all those years ago.

Frank flashed his warrant card. Nan glanced at it, then, worriedly, at Stevie.

"No," Stevie replied. "Anyway, I must go. Thank you for the tea."

"Come and see me again," Nan said, helping her into her coat. "And do think about the job at the school."

"Yes, of course."

Stevie hustled down the stairwell. Soon she was outside.

"Oh hell," she thought as the cold rain drummed onto her head. "I've left my umbrella behind."

23

Fugue State

Merritt ran her forefinger down the surface of the hand mirror and then delicately dabbed the tip of her tongue. She repeated the action and then, satisfied not a single speck of the sparkling powder remained, replaced the mirror on the dressing table next to the matching brush and comb, part of a very expensive art deco vanity set that had seduced her on her recent New York visit, and which she really couldn't afford. She fingered the cool, smooth edge of the ebony and closed her eyes. Gently, she began to rock back and forth on the vanity stool, feeling the easy gallop, as the drug sought its destination. A glow suffused her limbs and then her mind surged forward onto a high radiant plateau. The pain was gone. Twice in the past week—the last time Tuesday night—she felt as though she might shatter, break into a thousand shards of glass along the dark carpeting, brittle and glistening like cold stars in airless space. But now...

What did that damn cop want anyway? She had said everything there was to say on Tuesday.

That evening, after Axel, sensing her preoccupation, had left, after the phone call, she had sat immobile, staring into the mirror over the dressing table, looking at the teeny-tiniest of lines that had appeared lately at the corners of her eyes, expecting them somehow to crack wide open and race down her body like the spreading claws of an earthquake, until she tumbled in upon herself. She had muttered a few phrases—she couldn't remember now what she said, how she sounded—and returned the phone to its cradle.

A similar phone call, the Sunday after New Year's Day 1977, had announced her parents' death. She had been home, waiting for her parents to return from driving Michael to the airport. She might have gone with them, but she begged off claiming a sore tummy, but really wanting to hang around in case the boy she met at a New Year's party called. Her physical response then, as on Tuesday, had been a kind of implosion, allayed by some accessible narcotic. At fifteen, it had been booze. At twenty-seven, the choices were more abundant. From a compact in her purse she had removed a vial, and carefully poured a small amount of powder on the slick surface of her hand mirror. Through a thin gold straw, she had applied the powder, first to one nostril and then to the other, inhaling greedily.

Today was Friday, she recalled. The funeral was in four hours. Caterers would arrive in two. She opened her eyes. The face looking back at her in the mirror seemed subtly readjusted, the skin tauter, the cheekbones higher. Or perhaps she only felt they were. No matter: she subscribed to the idea that beauty was as much psychological as it was physical. Nature had not seen fit to provide her with the absolutely perfect symmetry or utterly flawless features she once craved, that had been everywhere around her in New York when she had elbowed her way into a job with Chiang, the PR firm whose every client was fashion-related. So she had nurtured a vivacity that overcame even a hint of doubt in the observer's mind, fuelling it when she flagged with cocaine. She'd been a fixture at Limelight and The Saint and Danceteria and Palladium, all the clubs, straight, gay, whatever. She was everywhere during Fashion Week, running from one tent to another in Bryant Park, making sure Suzy Menkes was in the front row or Tori Spelling wasn't behind a column. She went to the after-parties and the after-after-parties and the after-after-after parties. How many times had she said "must have…it's all about…I'm loving…of the moment…it screams…beyond fashion"? How could you do all this without a noseful or two? The drugs were everywhere, all the time, so hard to resist. She refocused on her face in the mirror. Her eyes, she could see, had recovered some of their animation. They were her favourite feature, especially with the green contacts. Or was it her hair? She patted it gently. A feathery mass of copper waves and soft curls, she needed only to tease it with the end of a comb to return it to artful disarray.

She was glad she hadn't gone in to see Michael after all on Tuesday. Or had she? The question had been plaguing her all week. But she decided, finally, that she hadn't. She certainly remembered sitting in her car virtually camouflaged by the shrubbery in the cul-de-sac outside Michael's for what seemed like ages, unable to decide whether to pay him a visit or not. She could remember toying with the idea of telling him about her new situation and wondering if she should use it to leverage the one thing she really needed—money. She hated herself for even thinking along such lines. But she was so sick of asking for money. Every time she asked, she seemed to sprinkle more poison on her relationship with Michael. He would scrutinize her, as he scrutinized her every time they'd been together in the last eighteen months, since he'd dragged her from the flat in SoHo she'd been sharing with Diana Merlis, a fellow publicist at Chiang PR, and pushed her into rehab in Christ-forsaken Minnesota. Again. God, she had been on a real high that April day. She and Diana had been at St. Patrick's Cathedral for Andy Warhol's memorial service, which had been *fabulous*! Cast of thousands! She'd arrived back, turned the key, and there was Michael. Diana had scuttled into her bedroom. She denied it, but Merritt was sure she had been communicating with her brother.

Was she using again? his expression always seemed to say. *No, she was not fucking using again.* Well, at least she hadn't been. She had been good since leaving Hazelden and coming back to Winnipeg and working at Daddy's old rag. But Michael had gone off to Europe. (She could breathe again!) And then Guy began to freak her out. So what if it was a stinking hot July in New York?—she'd fled there for a couple of weeks. Joined up with old friends. Went to some of the old clubs. Got into some old habits.

So what? She could stop any time she wanted.

Michael had no idea what things cost. He had the material needs of a hermit. How could she possibly live on the pissant salary the *Citizen* paid? How could anybody? She thought bitterly of all the money she had lost—on friends, drugs, bad investments, mostly drugs. Damn Michael for always being the blue-eyed boy! For always doing the right thing. For being so clever and good with his share. This time, though, she had the best reason to ask for money. This time, it wasn't for her alone.

At some point she must have nodded off in the rinky-dink Miata. Surely she had. She had been to Jane's Boutique for a fitting after work and Jane, dear Jane, who could read her tension like a book, and who always had some treats for her special clients, had given her a little something to calm her down. And then it had been so warm in the car, even with the top down, that she just seemed to slip into a vivid dreaming. She was talking to Michael, imploring him, and he didn't seem to be listening. He had been as remote and preoccupied as he had seemed two weeks earlier when they'd lunched at Le Beaujolais and she'd complained about Guy. She sensed there was something he wanted to tell her but couldn't. In the dream, though, he turned his head away from her. He would *not* listen. She was screaming. There had been a cloud of noise and image, a thud and crimson, and then something whisked her out of the dream. She re-emerged into air as thick as a blanket and the shadows of dusk closing in along the cul-de-sac, frightened, wanting to gag. The great red ball of the setting sun reflected in her rearview mirror blinded her eyes.

She shook herself at the memory. A shiver, like a cold hand, ran up her back. To counter it, she studied herself again in the mirror of her vanity table and fixed on her enlarged pupils, each a black diamond in an emerald sea. Yes, her eyes were definitely her best feature. Then the nasty thought entered her head, the same one that had intruded Tuesday, after the phone call: She would have Michael's money. She would be the chief beneficiary in his will. Of course, she would.

And why hadn't that goddamn lawyer called her back?

And then she remembered what it was that had awakened her so suddenly in the car. Why hadn't she thought of it before? It had been a pounding on the pavement. The rhythm was like that of the cop banging on her door. She had opened her eyes just in time to catch a fleeting glimpse of someone bursting through the gate. She hadn't expected him, of all people, to be there, then. But it had been him, moving as though the very devil weren't far behind.

24

Shades of Mary Jo

By late afternoon, the skies were worn out of rain, and the sun, slipping through a rift in the clouds, turned oil-slicked puddles on the Crescent into rainbow mirrors. Leo hopped over one of them as he made his way to the reception, joining what seemed to be a stream of humanity eager to shake off the solemnity of the funeral Mass and the bleakness of the graveside rites and have a drink or two. The service had seemed interminable. Leo had arrived at St. Giles early, found a seat at the back, and had made himself busy scribbling down the names of various local grandees come to mourn the late Michael Rossiter. He did so on the borders of the funeral program. His notebook, safely ensconced in his inside pocket, would have flagged him as one of those thoughtless, rude, debauched reporter types—which he could be, if the need arose. He had just added the mayor's name to the list when he felt something slam into his shoulder. He looked up and noted Axel Werner's fist.

"Shove over, Fabian."

"What brings you here?" Leo's back twinged. He shuffled down the pew.

"Since when do you need an invitation to a funeral? Anyway, I knew Michael a little."

"I don't remember seeing you at his exclusive Victoria Day barbecue."

Axel grunted and pulled a copy of the Bible from the rack in front of him. "Why are you sitting way back here?"

"The better to work by." Leo held up his pen. "'At the funeral attended by the premier, the mayor, and representatives of some of Winnipeg's oldest families,'" he intoned, as if reading the news on the CBC. "Anyway, I tried calling you last night."

"I was out."

"I figured. Eve still in Dauphin?"

"I suppose." Axel opened the Bible and began flipping aimlessly. "Actually, I've been wanting to talk to you."

"What about?"

Axel looked over and eyeballed his suit. "Is that what you're wearing tomorrow to the Galleries Portáge opening?"

"Christ, not this topic again."

"Don't be such an asshole."

"You're the asshole." Leo jabbed Axel through his sweatered ribs with his elbow, then quickly jotted down another name in his pad as another nob cruised down the aisle. The gloom of the sanctuary and the gloom of the organ music were making him uneasy; he was viscerally reminded of the last funeral Mass he'd been to, a quarter-century ago at Holy Rosary—his own father's. Distractions were welcome. "So, are you going to tell me what it is?"

He looked down. The Bible on Axel's lap had fallen open at the Book of Matthew.

"Well—?"

Axel turned a page, as if he were studying the text. "I think," he said, dropping his voice to a whisper, "that I might know…who killed Michael."

Leo's pen stopped in mid-serif. "Nice bombshell, Axel. Can I ask who?"

"You can try."

"Who?"

"I can't tell you."

"What is this? The journalistic equivalent of a cocktease?"

"It's complicated." Axel reached back and stroked his ponytail.

"Then tell the police."

"I might."

"You might? You want someone to get away with murder?"

"I told you, it's complicated!"

"You know, Axel, if this was some murder mystery novel, you'd be bumped off in short order. There's always some smartass who knows something, makes a big secret of it, then is found strangled or stabbed in chapter twenty-nine." Leo doodled in his notebook. "Does whoever you think did it know that you know?"

Axel frowned. "I don't know."

"Male or female?"

"I can't say."

"A known aficionado of pricey violins?"

"Beats me."

"Is this why you called me at 8:31 in the morning?"

"Maybe."

Leo noted Stevie and her parents move up the aisle. She didn't see him. He tapped his pen impatiently against his thigh. "Does this have something to do with Merritt?" he asked.

"Merritt who?"

"Merritt Parrish, née Rossiter, only sister of the deceased and the woman you're currently fraternizing with horizontally."

Leo could feel Axel stiffen beside him. "How do you know that?" he whispered hotly.

"You thought you could keep it secret?"

"Shit!" Axel closed the Bible with a snap. "Who else knows?"

"Stevie, for one."

"And—?"

Leo shrugged noncommittally. "What's with the secretiveness anyway?"

"I'm married."

Leo hooted. "Like that's stopped you before."

"Okay, it's partly Merritt."

"Really?"

"She wants it that way."

"You're telling me—" Leo began, then lowered his voice as a frail elderly couple shuffled into the pew in front of them. "—you're telling me that Merritt doesn't want her brother's killer found?"

"I told you—it's complicated."

"I'm beginning to believe you." Not, Leo thought grimly.

Axel growled under his breath. "She's really hot, Leo."

"And really rich?"

Axel's fist landed on Leo's shoulder, harder this time. Fortunately the suit padding cushioned the blow. "Fuck you, Fabian."

A grey head swivelled and a rheumy eye regarded them balefully.

"We're in church, you asshole," Leo said under his breath, kicking him in the shin. "Watch your goddamn language."

They had sat the rest of the service in silence. Leo's attention wandered, as it usually did anytime whenever he was in a church, which was rare. Mostly he wondered why Axel had chosen to tantalize him with knowing who Michael's killer might—*might*—be. Only the homily focused his mind. Father Day had not been oblique about the snatching of a life in its prime and he had waxed vehement on the subject of restitution. Pretty illiberal for a late-twentieth-century Christian, Leo reflected, scribbling away on back of his program, but, hell, it made good copy.

The gathering graveside afterwards was brief but intensely grim. People, Leo included, seemed unhappily surprised to be standing in virtual mud, unable to hear the priest, and shivering in the damp air. Stepping through the door into Merritt's house, however, he began to feel his spirits lighten. Part of it was the promise of spirits, he considered, slipping off his coat, noting the mayor in the living room sipping a scotch and ogling Merritt's now-entirely-appropriate funereal decor.

Couldn't be a better time to have a black rug, he thought, handing the coat to some flunky, looking behind at his own trail of muck merging into the trails of others. He turned into the living room. A fair crowd, and a choice one. Drop the big Kahuna on this address and the minority government would be more minor still, he thought, watching the mayor begin a smiley schmooze of the finance minister. Clearly, this was going to be a working funeral for more than just Leo. He patted his chest, feeling the bulge of his notebook. There was one person in particular he wanted to talk to.

"Guy Clark as city editor?" he said to Martin Kingdon, who waddled past him. What he'd read on the microfilm that morning still played in his head. "Your memo surprised the hell out of some of us."

"He'll do a fine job," Kingdon hissed over his shoulder and disappeared into a knot of men, all of them six inches taller.

The hell he will. Leo grabbed a drink off a tray. He noted Axel pointedly ignoring him, pretending to look at an art deco sculpture on the mantle, as if he'd never seen it before in his life. He went in search of Stevie and espied her in the dining room, talking with a hefty woman who was unfamiliar to him. Stevie was dressed in a black sheath, which just seemed to set off her dark hair and dark eyes. Her hair was up. She looked like one of the women in Robert Palmer's "Addicted to Love" video. I'm a sick man, he thought: I'm getting horny at a funeral.

She turned and smiled at him, which made it worse. "This is Sharon Bean," she said by way of introduction. "We went to school together. Sharon owns a cleaning company."

"A cleaning company of one, actually."

"Sharon was Michael's cleaner," Stevie added.

"Oh?" Leo turned his attention from Stevie's charming profile to look at Sharon. She looked like she might do windows, too, and carry her own ladder.

"I was last there on Tuesday." Sharon lowered her eyes. "I still can't believe it."

"Have you—?" Leo began, but Stevie interrupted him. "I'll just leave you two," she said. "There's someone I should talk to."

"Wait," he said, watching her give Sharon a little hug, and wishing it were him. "Will I see you—?"

"Come for dinner."

Leo groaned. "Hell, I have to go back to the *Zit*."

"Oh." She looked disappointed. "Well, anyway..."

"Talk later?"

"I'm going to be here for a while. To keep an eye on Merritt."

"I know someone else in the room who can do that."

"Ah," Stevie smiled knowingly and disappeared behind someone's back.

"So you're the famous Leo Fabian," Sharon said.

"You read my stuff?"

"Hell, no. Stevie's mother has dropped your name. I clean for the Lords, too."

Leo felt his face begin to heat up. He didn't realize he was conversation fodder for cleaner and client. "And are reports favourable?"

"Discretion is the watchword of the cleaning business," she laughed.

"And here I thought it was bleach." He took a sip, studying her over the rim of his glass. "I was about to ask you a minute ago—have you talked to the police?"

"No, why? Should I?"

"When were you at Michael's?"

"In the afternoon. Between about 2:00 and 5:00."

"You might have been the last one to see him alive, you know." He paused. "Well, second-last."

"Third-last, actually. When I was leaving that man—" She gestured toward the living room and craned her neck. "—well, he was here a minute ago. Michael's uncle, Mr. Kingdon. He was coming up the path."

"When was this?"

"A little after 5:00."

More than an hour before time of death, Leo thought. He frowned.

"Something the matter?"

"Oh, nothing." But Leo's brain roiled with questions. "Back door or front door?" he asked.

"If you mean which way Mr. Kingdon was going, then back door. I left by the back door and passed him by the side of the house."

"And you left the door unlocked?"

"Michael was home."

"The whole time?"

"He wasn't when I got there. I let myself in with my key. He arrived about twenty minutes later." She raised an eyebrow. "I'm not sure I should be telling you this."

"That discretion thing? He *is* dead, you know." Leo was blunt.

"More that reporter thing."

"Call it background. You know the concept?"

Sharon flashed a set of even teeth. "I have a master's degree in social work."

"Shoot me now," Leo said, flushing.

"Maybe later. What do you want to know?"

"Everything."

"If you think cleaning ladies spend all their time snooping, you'd be wrong."

"But you must notice things. The violin, for instance—"

"I've dusted a black case in that dressing room off Michael's bedroom once a week for the past three years. It's never moved. I've never seen it open. Michael never mentioned it to me. If that Guarneri I've been reading about has been in that house in the last few weeks, then I didn't see it."

Leo admired her efficient reply and thought she would be hard to live with. "Were you in that room he uses as an office?"

"I clean everywhere but his upstairs studio."

"Did you note a daybook, a diary?"

"Yes, it sits on his desk."

"And—?"

"Was it open? Yes. Did I read it? No."

"Your eyes didn't sort of pass over any jottings?"

She shook her head. "Leo, one of the reasons I dumped social work was because I *didn't* want to know about people's private lives."

Leo sighed. "Computer disks?" he asked feebly. "Were there any on the desk?"

Sharon glanced up at the ceiling in thought. "There were some in a smoked glass—well, smoked plastic—box. I remember because they were multicoloured, and I could see them through the glass when I was dusting."

"Well, that's something. Having a computer with no hard drive and no disks was odd." He stepped out of the way to let someone pass. The place was becoming very crowded. "Hope the fire chief's not at this reception," he remarked. "I wonder why she didn't have it in the church hall or something."

"I think Merritt likes to show off her decor."

Leo raised in eyebrow.

"I clean for Merritt, too."

He laughed. "Does your card say 'By Appointment to the River Heights Bourgeoisie'?"

"I sometimes slum in the West End."

"I don't need a cleaning lady."

"That's not what I hear."

"That's not very discreet."

"You're not my client."

"True." Leo downed the last of his Scotch. He could feel the liquor moving through his veins. It was pure pleasure. "So," he said, tapping his fingers against the glass, "was there *anything* remarkable about your Tuesday at Michael's?"

"Not really," she replied, shrugging.

"Was he in the house the whole time you were?"

"In his studio upstairs for part of it, and then he went out to mail something. He was gone about forty minutes or so."

"Has Canada Post removed *another* neighbourhood mailbox?"

"I think he walked down to the post office on Corydon."

Leo glanced over Sharon's shoulder. An elderly man with a flushed, wrinkled face above a clerical collar was holding a glass of amber liquid in each hand.

"Don't let your right hand know what your left is doing, Father," he called.

The priest held up both glasses and toasted Leo. "I think Our Lord might make an exception in his case," he said, beaming, then turned back to his own conversation.

"Father Saunders," Sharon lowered her voice. "I thought he might take the service. The new priest doesn't have his warmth."

"You know him?"

"I go to St. Giles too. Father Saunders retired in the spring."

"Too?"

"Michael was a regular."

"My father was lapsed RC," Leo said, wondering why that had sprung into his head. "My mother's lapsed Anglican. I think I'm lapsed agnostic."

"I think I might become lapsed if we have too much more of depressing Father Day."

Leo didn't respond. He suddenly thought of something that Sharon could do for him—and it wasn't mop his floors.

He explained.

She regarded him skeptically. "I'm not sure. It doesn't seem right. And it might not be good for Stevie."

"Let me worry about that."

Sharon was silent a moment, then she regarded him slyly. "I do have an opening for anyone who wants a cleaning lady."

"You drive a hard bargain."

"I'm a businesswoman. Here, I'll give you my card." Sharon opened her purse. "And I'm not being opportunistic," she added, rifling through its contents. "Stevie's told me about the state of your place—"

"It's not that bad."

"—and Michael was letting me go soon anyway—and, I might add, it had nothing to do with my work."

"Why then?"

She handed him a card. *Bean Cleans*, the embossed type declared in aggressive red. "Heaven only knows," she said. "The man was a mystery."

Caitlin Clark was easy to pick out of a crowd. As Leo recalled from Michael's party in the spring, she bore an uncanny resemblance to her brother, which should have been a fate worse than psoriasis, but, thanks to some genie of the genes, wasn't. Guy's chin was weak. Hers was heart-shaped. His hair was a thatch of dull straw. Hers was a cap of honey gold. She was the same height as Guy, which made her becomingly tall for a woman, but forced him into the unforgiving category of short men. When he was lost in thought, Guy thrust his lips forward like a petulant child. When Caitlin was lost in thought—as she appeared to be when Leo touched her sleeve—her lips pressed together in a little moue, which made her look darned kissable, if you could forget who she was related to.

She had been in a conversational knot with three other people, one of whom, a reedy fellow with volumes of kempt hair down to his waist, he recognized vaguely from Michael's barbecue as an orchestra member. She had seemed happy enough to be drawn away when Leo introduced himself.

"You're the one who punched my brother," she remarked in Leo's ear as he wedged into the crowd to look for a quiet spot.

"Oh, shit."

"Don't worry. I don't think it's something he doesn't deserve from time to time."

Startled, Leo turned to look at her. There was a flush along her fine cheekbones.

"He knew where I was, and he didn't bother to call me," she continued.

She had flown to San Francisco the week before, he learned as they made their way through the kitchen to a back sun porch—to see old friends, play at a couple of recitals, and audition for the San Francisco Symphony. She only learned of Michael's death from a copy of the *Citizen* the flight attendant had handed to her on the flight from Vancouver that morning. She'd barely had enough time to change and get to the church.

"So I'm still in shock," she said, stepping down onto the stone floor. The room was chilly, the furniture wrought iron, and every cushion black. It was about as uninviting a room as any could be on a damp fall day, which was probably why everyone else was shunning it. Leo pulled out a chair for Caitlin and noted her flinch as the back of her thighs hit cold vinyl. Her black suit had a short skirt.

"It was lousy of Guy not to let you know earlier," he responded, taking a chair opposite, glad of wool trousers.

"I'll give him hell later."

"I'd like to see that."

She smiled wanly. Leo started to say something, then noticed her eyes. Deep blue, with a touch of mischief. He blanked, then started over. "He's just been made city editor—"

"What a surprise."

Leo started. "You're not? Surprised, I mean."

"No."

"He's only twenty-eight."

Caitlin shrugged, then tapped his hand with her finger. "Anyway," she said, "what did you want to talk to me about?"

Leo, recovering from the erotic jolt of her touch, blurted: "Your parents."

"They're dead."

"I know."

Caitlin's eyebrows rose. "Why are you interested in my parents?"

Damned good question, he thought, looking into her lovely but puzzled face. "Symmetry?" he replied, feeling slightly ridiculous. "Your parents. Michael's parents. Killed in the same car accident. Guy and Merritt. You and Michael—"

"There never was a me and Michael." Caitlin cut him off. "We were just good friends."

"Sorry, I didn't mean—"

"Are you suggesting I'm next?"

"Beg pardon?"

"Symmetry—your word. Michael's gone. So, by your logic, I'm next?"

Leo stared at her. "God, no." He told her about his morning's work scrolling through *Zit* microfilms. The Rossiters, he'd learned, had taken Michael to Winnipeg Airport to catch a Toronto flight with a connection to Philadelphia. Sometime later they left, but their car jumped the meridian curb on the airport approach and hit an oncoming car, driven by none other than Caitlin's father. The Rossiters and Caitlin's mother, who was in the back seat of the Clark car, were killed instantly. Caitlin's father, who had been driving, died two days later of massive injuries. And Caitlin, who had been in the passenger seat, en route to catch a later Toronto-bound flight, escaped—thanks in part to a seat belt—with minor injuries. The accident was attributed to icy conditions and mechanical failure in the Rossiter vehicle and later affirmed by investigation.

The play the *Zit* gave the Rossiters hadn't surprised him. After all, Tom Rossiter had been the publisher of the paper. And the relative indifference shown the Clarks hadn't surprised him either. They were nobodies by comparison. But a certain irregularity among the facts and figures sent his bullshit detector into high alert.

"Look," he said, "is this painful to talk about?"

"You could have picked a better day."

Leo looked down at the table, then back up at her. "How about tomorrow?"

Caitlin shrugged. "It's okay. Actually it's interesting that a journalist is asking questions about this. Nobody did then. What is it you found troubling?"

"There were several hours between Michael's flight and yours. That means the Rossiters must have stayed in the airport long after he'd flown out."

"Exactly."

"And given what I know about Thomas Rossiter's alcoholism—"

"He stayed at the airport drinking. He was blind drunk, well over the speed limit, and, therefore, criminally negligent. He, in effect, murdered my parents and his own wife. Have I gotten to the point?" She regarded him with her remarkable eyes. Her voice held no bitterness.

"Quicker than I expected," he replied, startled. "And yet—"

"Nothing was done about it? Guy and I called it Chappaquiddick North." She smiled.

"Cover-up?"

"Yes."

"Wow." This was more than Leo had expected. "And you didn't try to—?"

"I believed what was told me at the time, what you read in the paper."

"Then how—?"

"Michael figured it out pretty fast. And then his uncle, your boss—"

"Martin?"

"—as much as told him he'd made certain arrangements to protect his father. Apparently, the police had encountered a drunken Thomas Rossiter in the past and been instructed to get in touch with Kingdon should anything happen. Which they did. I assume, and Michael assumed, that a certain friendship existed between Kingdon and someone well-placed in the police."

What a surprise, Leo thought. The old story of elites moving quickly to protect their reputations safe in the assurance that few—including journalists—had either the will or the opportunity to question received wisdom. He said, "I take it from your tone Michael wasn't all that grateful to Martin."

Caitlin ran her hand down a crescent of blonde hair. "Michael was...confused, troubled. He felt guilty. He and his father had had a terrific argument at the airport. He was pretty wild in our first year at the Curtis. He had some heavy thing going with a German girl who was there, like me, on a scholarship, and he was drinking a lot." She paused in her stroking. "Anyway, one night, after he'd had a few, he told me what he knew about our parents' deaths."

"Shocking."

"Yes."

"Then why—"

"Didn't anything happen? He wanted to pursue it, call for a new investigation, even though it was his own father and involved his own uncle. But I asked him not to. It's that simple. I didn't want my life turned upside down. I was still having nightmares. And—I know it's a cliché—but nothing was going to bring my parents back."

"And Guy?"

"What about him?"

"Did you tell him?"

Caitlin sighed. "Finally, I did. He was a teenage newspaper reader, which must be pretty rare. And he'd started to piece parts of it together. When I was back here during school breaks—my grandmother took care of Guy—he would pester me with questions: didn't I think this was weird, and so on."

"And how did he take it?"

"Mostly he was angry at me for not telling him, and for stopping Michael. It was sort of the beginning of our estrangement."

"I wonder why he didn't do something about it—your brother, I mean."

"He was very young."

"I mean later. It's not too late, even now, to call for a new investigation."

Caitlin turned to look at a flurry of leaves that a gust of wind had blown against the glass walls of the sunporch. She hugged the jacket of her suit closer, shivering. "Well, maybe the passage of time has worked for him, too. Anyway, we don't talk about it anymore—when we talk, that is. And I have no more interest now than I did all those years ago in revisiting this. I don't really want to *be* in Winnipeg." She paused. "It's a place of death for me, really."

"Then why are you here?"

"Part of it was Michael's doing. When the Atlantic Symphony collapsed last spring, he suggested coming back to Winnipeg. He thought he might be able to use his influence with the WSO. Which doesn't seem to have worked out, since he spent most of the summer in Europe. And Guy was here, and my grandmother was in a nursing home here. Although she died last month—"

"I'm sorry."

Caitlin shrugged. "And now Michael's gone. There are few attachments for me here now. You see, we were air force brats. I was born in England. Guy was born in West Germany. We lived in half a dozen places in Canada before moving here, where my mother's mother lived. I really only spent my undergraduate years here. And I *hated* the winters."

"But it's a *dry* cold." Leo whined.

Caitlin laughed. "Print it on a licence plate. I'll take the San Francisco fog."

Leo shrugged. "Guy seems to have gotten used to it."

"He's done well here."

"Very well."

Caitlin regarded him slyly. "I know where your little journalistic mind is going. You're thinking Guy's used what he knows about Martin Kingdon and the Rossiters for some advantage."

"No," he lied.

"He's still my brother," she responded evenly.

Leo could see that she didn't believe him. "Well, you'll allow that he's risen far, fast."

"I'll allow that he's a little obsessed with the Rossiters."

"I think the thing with Merritt is over."

"Really? I hadn't heard." Caitlin abruptly turned her face to stare out across the lawn and the coils of wet leaves. "Just as well," she added. The sun porch was getting darker with the darkening day. Before many weeks were out there would be no light at five o'clock in the afternoon. But on this gloomy afternoon, the last day of September, there was sufficient light to sharpen the contours of Caitlin's face and define a set in her jaw. And then, as suddenly as she had averted her gaze, she turned back to him.

"Are you intending to open up this can of worms?"

"In the paper?" Leo paused. He thought about the gatekeepers: Martin, who surely had stripped the clipping file and removed the microfilm roll; Guy, who would, on Monday, be his immediate superior. "I haven't a clue," he replied.

Caitlin shrugged. "Well, I'm getting a little chilly out here." She began to rise from the chair.

This time it was Leo's turn to touch her hand. "Wait," he said, again feeling a spark, "you don't have any idea who might want to murder Michael?"

She sat back down. Her eyes searched his. "Who? No. But—"

"But?"

"Well, I know something about the why."

"Meaning?"

"The story I read in the paper—your story, I presume—is wrong."

"How so?" said Leo, affronted.

"It was full of speculation about a stolen Guarneri del Gesu. I guess I should go to the police."

Leo stared at her, puzzled. "Why?"

"Simple." In the light coming from the kitchen, Leo could see flecks of green glowing in the depths of blue. God, she was cool hot. How could Michael have resisted? He barely heard her say: "*I* have the Gaurneri."

25

Bumpf

Liz ground her cigarette into the ashtray with a fierce satisfaction, which she usually did when she'd completed a story. She scrolled the words up and down the computer screen a few times to check for spelling and punctuation errors, detected none, and then hit the send button. Across the room, copy editors waited with machetes.

They can hack it to bits, she thought; it's nothing but crap anyway. The *Citizen* was putting out yet another advertorial supplement to mark the gala opening of Galleries Portáge—there seemed to be one every day—and she'd got stuck at the last minute filling in some of the spaces between the ads with her deathless prose. She'd been assigned a piece on what the local elite would be wearing to the opening—*of a shopping mall, for chrissake.* It's the kind of thing Merritt Parrish should have sunk her pointed teeth into, but since she was on bereavement leave, Guy had assigned the stupid thing to her. Deliberately, she presumed. Just to irritate her. She'd ended up phoning old sorority sisters and the wives of Spencer's cronies and wives of symphony board members—people she thought might comment after much begging, the topic being so asinine. But, as it happened, no one needed to be begged to discuss her gown or her jewellery. How happy people seemed to be to talk about themselves and their possessions! How thrilled to see their names in print, not realizing that in print their bright telephone chatter would look foolish and frivolous.

Even a week ago she would have judged the assignment the nadir of her career but this gloomy Friday afternoon, she found she was just as glad to have something innocuous to do. Her mind was occupied elsewhere. Since Tuesday night, she and Spencer had spoken only as necessity required. They had taken last night's dinner separately and each had contrived not to be in the same part of the house for rest of the evening. Of course, she had moved to the guest bedroom. Even though it was Spencer who had precipitated the argument by failing to notify her of his election plans, it was she who was made to feel blameworthy for challenging him. The atmosphere at home very nearly crackled with tension. They had avoided confrontation for so long—she could barely remember the last time they had argued—that they had no resources for managing it. Now they were on the other side of the wall from indifference into uncharted territory of acrimony and recrimination. She wondered whether she should move to a hotel for a while so she could think.

She wondered, too, if she would find the sympathy she craved from Paul. Since Tuesday, he had been remote, disengaging himself from any lengthy phone conversation at the symphony, pleading work as his excuse. In the beginning she had expected nothing enduring to come of her affair with him. She had entered into it casually, with a kind of devil-may-care attitude—a strong signal, though unacknowledged, that she was again tempting the fate of her marriage. But, more recently, she had discovered sprouting within herself the dangerous but not wholly unwelcome feelings of caring deeply for Paul. Meanwhile, his ardour seemed suddenly to be cooling. Perhaps, she thought, he had sensed her feelings and sought to ease his way out of anything that might slip from his control. Yet she couldn't imagine him not confronting her, not telling her that it was over, unless, like hers, his manoeuvres in love contradicted his manoeuvres in work. She could easily enough confront Guy Clark if she had to, yet how easily she had let her relationship with her husband fester.

And Clark. How had he learned of her affair with Paul? She had confided in no one. Did Paul blab to someone? It hardly seemed likely. But then she thought back to the murderous glance Else had dispatched at the Kingdons' dinner. Did she know? She and Paul had been married for so long, yet she assumed Paul had been unfaithful many times in the past. He seemed so unruffled, so practised and charming. So *European*. Perhaps Else condoned his liaisons. Liz had no idea. Paul always deflected any discussion of his wife, describing his time with her, Liz, as precious and secluded—romantic talk whose charm persuaded her even while she recognized it as nonsense. At least Paul did not bore her with banal justifications that Else did not understand him, or satisfy him. But even if Else was aware of his infidelity, how would it ever get to Guy's ears? The only other person who had probably guessed at her relationship with Paul was the caretaker at Paul's downtown apartment. But Paul had assured her he was unfailingly discreet. It was worth his while to be.

She couldn't believe Guy would pass along his knowledge to Spencer. He had nothing to gain, unless he was so perverse as to find satisfaction in her humiliation. Her marriage would likely end as a result. Did it matter anymore? Liz sighed. Her head was beginning to spin. She seemed to have thought of nothing else in the last two days.

She looked over the top of her computer terminal and glanced around the newsroom. Everywhere, reporters were hunkered down in front of their terminals, racing to meet the Friday deadlines for the early Saturday edition.

Here and there a few other reporters circled the room like hungry buzzards waiting for the first available terminal to open up. In recent months, terminals had had a habit of disappearing in the night, allegedly for repairs but in reality for the growing needs of the advertising department. None had returned. With supplies meagre, demand had raged. Arguments flared over possession, on occasion just short of battle. Friday afternoons were worst. Liz realized her reverie in front of a blank screen would be interpreted as pure selfishness. Feeling a pair of eyes on her back, she rose, smiled at the familiar face, and travelled around to the other side of the bay of desks and sat down at her own. There was still a small pile of mail retrieved from the box earlier in the afternoon but left unopened in the rush to complete stories before deadline. Judging from the logo, an artfully entwined "G" and "P," Galleries Portáge bumpf was enclosed in at least some of the envelopes. Liz tossed them in a nearby bin. She had been saturated with the topic of Galleries Portáge. If there was anything newsworthy in the envelopes—which she doubted—it was too late now. Other envelopes contained a variety of announcements and communiqués from various arts groups, many with "For Immediate Release" typed urgently at the top. They were usually days late and inconsequential. Anything truly urgent was communicated over the telephone. Liz opened the envelopes anyway, but quickly added their contents to the garbage.

The final envelope in the pile was large, brown, and thicker than most to cross her desk. It had also been addressed by hand, which gave Liz pause. Hand-addressed envelopes often contained the work of complainants or cranks or people possessed by the news value of their dubious artistic accomplishments. Sometimes they contained complimentary letters, but not often. People were rarely compelled to express their pleasure over something written in a newspaper.

She tore the top from the envelope and tugged at a file folder contained within. A paperclip pinning a letter to the file cover came away in her hand. The folder was jammed in. She yanked harder. Finally, it shot out of the envelope and, as it did so, part of its contents slipped from the bottom and she caught a glimpse of writing in a foreign language.

She straightened the file with a sharp tap on her knee and then looked at the cover letter. "Dear Liz," it began. The letter was two pages, typed. She turned to the last sheet to look at the signature. A flutter of surprise came over her as she read the name: Michael Rossiter.

Quickly, she flipped through the contents of the file. It made no immediate sense. There were photocopies of what appeared to be old documents and affidavits, a lengthy transcript, and one aged grainy photograph, a reproduction, the subject of which filled her with disquiet. She turned back to the letter.

"Dear Liz," she read again. "I think the enclosed material will shock you. It shocked me when I came across it this summer. But the evidence it contains is, I think, irrefutable. I thought about ignoring it, but then I decided I couldn't. I can't let another injustice go unpunished. However, for private reasons I can't follow through. So I'm sending it to you with the expectation that you can give it the treatment it deserves. I realize I may be placing a burden on you, but from our past associations I know you to be thorough, fair-minded, and unafraid of a challenge. And it is, in press parlance, a 'good story.' (I guess there's one drop of family ink in my veins.) Let me explain…"

Liz continued to read. As she did, the sounds of the newsroom—the click of the keyboards, the whir of the computers, the jangling telephones and barking reporters—slipped into oblivion. In the dreadful silence, she was aware only of her heart crashing in her chest, her breath quickening and gasping as her eyes passed over the words again, and then again. Grotesque images raced through her mind, the black and white clichés of the cinematographer's art, for what she had read she had never experienced, never could experience. But the images were sufficient. She felt weak and sickened. "Oh, Michael, you're wrong, you're wrong," she whispered to herself. "I can't be fair-minded, or thorough, or anything with this. I can't do it. I can't do what you ask."

She closed the cover of the file with great weariness. She didn't need to look at the documentation. Only a deranged mind would make a false accusation of such enormity, and Michael, she knew, wasn't crazy.

Across the bank of desks a concerned voice inquired: "Are you all right?"

"Fine," she replied. "Just a bit cold in here."

She opened a bottom drawer in her desk and bent over to tuck the file into a stack of forgotten papers. She hesitated, running her thumb along the blunt edge of the manila tag. A frisson of panic gripped her. What would she do? She couldn't leave it in the drawer with the hope that it would slip from her memory the way so many other papers had. And she couldn't suppress her memory. She couldn't imagine going about her business with the knowledge that this thing was pulsating in her desk drawer like some malevolent animal. It had to be uncaged. Yes, goddamn it, it was a good story. Horribly good, frighteningly good. Properly handled it would make someone's career.

But not hers.

She rustled some papers with the pretence of searching for something, then quietly returned the file to her lap. Everyone was concentrated on his or her end-of-shift task. She looked across the room at Guy, who was sitting in profile, frowning at something on his screen. She made up her mind. Behind her was a series of small rooms, one of which was used by the *Zit*'s cartoonist, who, typically, finished his work by noon and headed for the bar. It contained one of the few typewriters left in the building, an old Remington, occasionally used by reporters who wished to type a message, or sneak the time to write a personal letter. Liz slipped into the room with the file and partially closed the door to signal a desire for privacy. She sat at the typewriter, contemplated its ancient keys for a moment, then pulled the letter from the file and started to type with determination. Twenty minutes later she had produced a new version, leaving out her name, and Michael's name and address, but retaining all the pertinent information. She put the facsimile letter into the file, and then returned to her desk where she stuffed the original in her overstuffed file drawer. At some point soon, she knew, Guy would leave his desk to fetch coffee or go to the toilet. She would have her opportunity.

As predicted, a few moments later Guy rose from his seat, put on his sports coat—a formality pompously enacted every time he left his desk—and exited the room. Liz then made her way with studied nonchalance toward the front, hugging the file lest she drop it and scatter its contents to the room. No one paid attention to her. She was just part of the traffic. She dropped the file on Guy's desk. No one noticed. Everyone in Guy's vicinity had, over time, turned their desks to angles that allowed them vistas other than Guy's head. Bob Pastuk, who sat nearest, kept his back to the newsroom. He didn't even seem to hear the tiny rustle of paper, or if he did, he didn't seem to care.

She returned to her desk, her heart pounding, wondering whether she had followed the right course. Had she been cowardly in turning Michael's information into an anonymous accusation? Should she have confessed the source but begged off the story, stating conflict of interest? Or would Guy have forced her to do the story anyway? That would have been untenable. No, she thought, this way the story would get out but she would be left with whatever peace she could find. On Monday, Guy would be the city editor and he would assign it to one of the city reporters. If he thought he could get a story ready for Saturday's paper, he would have to give it to someone else. She was leaving. She hurried to grab her coat before Guy returned to his seat. But before she left the newsroom, she made one quick telephone call from the privacy of the deserted receptionist's desk.

26

A Cool Reception

Stevie stood at the door listening to Merritt retch. She regarded the cracker she'd had in her hand when she'd gone up the stairs after Merritt bolted from the reception, felt herself turning a little green, and tossed it in the wastebasket beside the vanity. On the other side of the bathroom door, the sound of someone disgorging her guts continued, followed by a toilet's flush, then a tap's shriek. Water surged into a basin.

Too much booze. Too much agitation. Merritt had behaved like it was opening night at a club, not closing time for her brother. Her greetings were metallically bright, her laughter hollowly coquettish. She kept tossing that mane of red hair back with the idiot abandon of a B-list actress. And she was in and out of the first-floor powder room like someone with a bladder problem. Doing lines, no doubt. Stevie had felt like tying Merritt's hands behind her back.

And then, abruptly, with the house largely emptied of mourners, Merritt's face had lost its colour and she had raced upstairs. Since no one else had seemed inclined to go see what was the matter, not even this Axel person who had been hovering awkwardly about, she'd done her female nurturing duty, and followed Merritt. She'd been about to say the time-honoured "are you all right?" but the vomiting had answered that question.

Splashing sounds penetrated the bedroom. Stevie felt herself almost yearning for the shock of cold water along her own face, a balm after you'd purged all the sourness inside.

Suddenly, the penny dropped.

The door opened. Merritt tottered out, her face drawn, her mascara smudged—a ghost face under a red fright wig.

It wasn't booze and drugs and agitation.

"You're pregnant."

Merritt staggered past her, leaving a train of sourness in air, and plunked down on the vanity stool. "Give the lady a cigar," she said, turning to the mirror and picking up a Kleenex.

"How far along?"

"Seven weeks."

"You've been to a doctor?"

"Of course I've been to a doctor." Merritt dabbed at her eyes. "I was there on Tuesday."

"Tuesday?" Stevie echoed.

"Yes, Tuesday. Oh, happy day." Merritt tossed the Kleenex into the wastebasket. Her hand went to a vial on the vanity.

"What are you taking?"

"Just something to relax me. It's been a shitty week."

"Is that wise? You're having a baby."

"I'm having an abortion." Merritt responded flatly. She shook a couple of pills onto her hand. "I can ingest whatever I damn well feel like."

Stevie watched her in the vanity mirror put the pills on her tongue and swallow them dry. She wondered how Merritt managed to be so lucid given what she put in her mouth and up her nose. Practice, probably.

"Does the father know?" she asked as Merritt opened a jar of face pads.

"Should he?" Merritt began methodically rubbing away the streaks of mascara. With each stroke, her face seemed to diminish. Her eyes started to look small and naked. "Well…?"

Stevie shrugged.

"You didn't exactly tell the father of *your* baby, did you?" Merritt continued, glancing at Stevie in the glass.

"Different circumstances."

Merritt made a raspberry.

"Well, I presume it's not Dale Hawerchuk's," Stevie snapped.

"Not unless sperm can cross town. Anyway, I haven't seen him in ages."

"Then why do you have his team and number on your licence plate?"

"I got it when vanity licences first came out." Merritt leaned into the mirror. "I thought it would be a laugh. But Dale freaked out. He wanted it for *his* car." She snorted. "We broke up over that. He even offered to buy it off me. Now I just keep it to piss him off."

Merritt turned and looked at Stevie. "Why are you bringing up my licence plate of all things?"

Stevie hesitated. Clearly, Nickel had had no success bringing it up either. "It just sort of jumped out at me earlier," she lied. "Anyway, you could have the baby."

"Like you did? No thanks."

"I mean, keep it. You're twenty-seven. I was nineteen. World of difference."

"I've made up my mind. I don't want it now."

"Now?"

Merritt's hand hesitated over the clutter on her vanity. "I thought at first, maybe. I even thought Michael might approve, for once. You know—me doing something responsible. And he could help out, you know—financially. But now—"

The chime of the doorbell cut her off.

"Oh, hell, who could that be?"

"Someone downstairs will get it. You've still got guests, you know."

"I'll get to them," Merritt responded impatiently. Her face hung like a pale moon in the mirror. "Just let me reapply."

Stevie sat down on the edge of the bed. She pulled at the edge of the coverlet. Were the sheets black? Yes, they were. And silk, too.

"Besides," Merritt continued, oblivious, "if I had the baby, I'd probably have to have some sort of sick relationship with the father—*who must never find out*," she added glaring at Stevie through the glass. "He's a total creep."

"Well, the creep's been making goo-goo eyes at you all afternoon."

"Who?"

"Axel."

Merritt gasped. "How do you know about him?"

"They should just put a sign on the highway outside the city that says: Welcome to Winnipeg, The World's Biggest Small Town."

"Shit! We're trying to keep it quiet."

"Because he's married? I'm told he wouldn't win a faithful-husband contest."

"No, because of Michael—"

"Why do you make him out as this ogre of disapproval—"

"Because he is—was. He would never say anything. He would just *exude* disapproval. You haven't been around for the last ten years. He'd gotten very sanctimonious. And anyway," Merritt moved her head from side to side, taking in her profile. "Axel's not the father. Guy Clark is."

"Good god."

Stevie's ear pricked. She rose from the bed and went to the door.

"What is it?"

"I thought I heard someone in the hall."

"River Heights homes are always creaking and moaning. It's the shifting soil. You know that!"

Stevie poked her head down the hall toward the window that overlooked the front yard. Only voices funnelling up the stairwell claimed her attention. "But I thought you broke up with Guy Clark in the spring," she said, pushing the door partly closed with her foot.

"I did."

"Then…?"

Merritt slumped on the vanity stool. "I don't know what the hell happened. I don't even know why I went out with him in the first place, really. He was just sort of persistent. And, like, he's my boss. This working for a living sucks, by the way—"

"Welcome to the real world." Stevie sat again on the bed.

"—and then I tried to ease out of it, and he really didn't accept it. He sort of kept calling, or he'd show up at Safeway when I was shopping or—"

"You mean, he was stalking you?"

"Kind of, I guess."

"You *guess*?"

"So, anyway, I thought 'okay, maybe if we just talk it through.' I mean, at work he'd been civil to me, at least to that point. So one evening—it was just after the long weekend in August, after I'd got back from New York—I got a call, and it was him begging me to see him. His grandmother had just died—she'd apparently raised him—and he was crying and carrying on, and so I went over to his apartment and..." She glanced at Stevie. "How stupid am I?"

"You're up there."

"That's not the worst. Afterward, after we, you know, *did it*...I still told him what I'd intended to: that it was totally over, and to please stop calling, and—" Merritt's voice faltered.

"And...?"

"He went nuts. Yelling, swearing, smashing the wineglasses against the wall of his apartment. I tried to get out, but he grabbed me, and threw me down, and I thought he was going to—" Merritt paused, put a hand up to her face.

Cold fingers tore at Stevie's insides. She said nothing, waited.

"—anyway, a neighbour came pounding on the door. He sort of snapped out of it."

Stevie breathed a sigh. "Thank god. Did you go to the police?"

"Oh, please. And tell them what? Nothing really happened—well, except that I now have this little souvenir." Merritt touched her stomach. "And Guy behaves like a total bastard to me at work.

"I did tell Michael, though," she continued after a moment. "Well, I gave him an edited version when he got back from Europe. Thought maybe he could do the big-brother thing. He could always make Uncle Martin squirm for some reason, and so I thought pressure might be applied down the chain of command, or he could read Guy the riot act, or something." She sighed. "Guess it didn't work. Guy's still behaving like a bastard. When I go in. Anyway, it's over."

"What?"

"The job. I didn't want to work at the stupid *Zit* in the first place, but Michael insisted. Thought it would be therapeutic. Now I don't have to work there at all. Or anywhere."

"Why?"

"Oh, Stevie, figure it out. By the way, would you like to drive me to Johns Mayhew tomorrow morning?"

"The law firm?"

Merritt smiled. She appeared recovered. The makeup helped. "It's reading-of-the-will time."

Stevie had spent a lifetime resisting her own mother's psychologizing. She knew the basics: that Merritt had missed something in her childhood with an alcoholic father and a distant, ineffectual mother; that she had nevertheless been traumatized by her parents' sudden death, that, despite appearances, she was depressed; that she was self-hating; that she didn't understand her own hell; that the substance abuse was linked to all of the above. But there were moments when she thought what Merritt had needed as a child was to have been spanked long and hard—yes it was wrong, but at least it was a form of attention. She'd been a spoiled brat at nine, a spoiled brat at fourteen, and she was still a goddamned spoiled brat. She was about to say as much when the crash of someone's knuckles against the door sent her flying off the mattress instead.

Axel burst into the room, his eyes taut, his mouth a severe line, his dark complexion darker still with blood. He rattled Stevie with a killing glance and then barked at Merritt, "The police are here and they want to talk to you."

"Shit!" Merritt responded to the mirror. "Why do they keep bothering me? Well, tell them I'll be down in five." She whipped her head around. "What's got into you?" she asked Axel, who was standing smouldering on the wall-to-wall.

"Nothing!" Axel stomped out of the room.

Merritt frowned.

"You know, I think he might have been listening." Stevie grimaced, glancing back at the door, which she realized she hadn't closed fully. The creaking in the hall hadn't been the house shifting.

"Oh, Christ. Are you sure? All that stuff about Guy. He hates Guy. I wonder if he heard the pregnant bit. Double shit!"

"You haven't told him, I suppose."

"Well, *duh*, no. It's just you and my gynecologist." Merritt quickly began applying eye-liner. "I sort of thought about telling Axel. But the timing wouldn't work."

"What? You mean tell him he's the father? You're a monster."

"Oh, shut up. I said I *sort of* thought about it. I'm not crazy. I like Axel a lot. I don't want to jeopardize it."

"He's got a wife."

Merritt made a dismissive gesture with a lipstick. "You know he told me he fell in love with me watching me put on lipstick in the Concert Hall lobby after *Romeo et Juliet* last spring at the opera. Isn't that sweet?"

Stevie, a member of the league of betrayed wives, bit her tongue.

"He stopped to tie his shoe and split his suit jacket right up the seam." Merritt smiled. "Now if I could just get him to cut off that awful ponytail. What do you think?"

"I think I'm going to go downstairs."

"'Kay."

"And Merritt," Stevie said, rising, "this time with the police, try telling the truth, the whole truth, and nothing but the truth."

"So help me God? This is like twelve-step crap."

"You might need Him."

Fifteen minutes later, Merritt descended the staircase, tapped the Plexiglas cube of shoes she'd collected in New York as if for luck, and made her entrance in the living room. A few mourners who had loitered long enough to give her their condolences scuttled out, leaving Merritt alone with Frank Nickel and his partner but for Axel, who was seated on a chair, arms folded across his chest, casting malevolent looks at everyone, and Leo and Stevie, who were propping up a wall.

"And now," she addressed Frank before he could open his mouth, "the whole truth, and nothing but the truth." She glanced at Stevie, who rolled her eyes. "Axel was here, with me, all of Tuesday evening—well, until about 9:00."

Frank smiled. Merritt smiled back harder. The Rossiters had not scrimped on orthodontia.

"I see," said Frank. "From what time would this be?"

"From about 6:00," Merritt replied, taking a chair next to Axel.

"From *about* 6:00," Frank echoed.

"Yes."

"Mr. Werner joined you here about 6:00, after you'd been to Jane's Boutique."

"Yes. 6:10. 6:15. Around there."

"I see," Frank said again. He looked at his partner. "Gerry?"

Gerry stared at him.

"You're on."

As Frank sank into the buttery couch, Shorter rummaged in his suit coat, pulled out a notebook and in a bland official tone, read: "Tuesday evening at approximately 7:10, a car bearing the licence plate 10JETS was seen leaving the cul-de-sac adjacent to the property of Michael Rossiter. The licence plate was checked and found to be registered in the name of Merritt Helena Rossiter Parrish."

He snapped the page of his notebook loudly, startling everyone but Frank, who extended his arm nonchalantly along the back of the couch. Much of the confidence seemed to drain from Merritt's face. She flicked Stevie a hateful glance.

Frank opened his mouth to continue, but Axel interrupted. "Impossible. We were together all evening. Whoever claims to have seen this licence is either blind, mistaken, or malicious."

Frank lifted an eyebrow and turned his gaze on Merritt, who was squeezing the leather arm of her chair into a pucker. "Well?" he said.

"She doesn't have to answer your questions, Frank," Axel interjected hotly. "She has a right to legal counsel, you know."

Frank held up his hands. "You're way ahead of me, buddy. I'm not making any accusations. I'm just asking some questions based on new information."

"She still doesn't have to answer them."

"Stop it, Axel," Merritt said weakly. "Yes, it's true. I was parked outside my brother's on Tuesday." Her eyes glistened. "But I didn't go in. You have to believe that. I just sat in the car."

"But you *intended* to visit him."

"I...I wanted to talk to him about something."

"What?"

"It's not important."

Frank grunted. "So you just sat. For how long?"

"I don't know. I sort of fell asleep. I dreamt—"

"What time did you arrive, then?"

Merritt hesitated. She glanced helplessly at Stevie.

"A little after 6:30, I think, maybe," she replied.

"Then your car was parked there for some thirty to forty minutes."

"I guess."

"With you in it the whole time."

"Yes."

"Did anyone see you?"

Merritt shifted uneasily on the leather. "I don't know. I was sort of out of it."

"Then did you see anyone?"

Merritt was silent.

"Because, it's the right time and the right place." Frank's mouth was a grim line. "Honestly, Merritt Helena Rossiter Parrish, it doesn't look good, you having an unaccounted-for half an hour twenty yards from your murdered—and let's not kid ourselves—wealthy brother."

"Hey!" Axel shouted.

"You have a contribution to make?"

Axel retreated. Frank shifted his gaze back to Merritt, who was twisting an emerald ring on her hand.

"Okay, I did see someone."

"Who?"

Merritt bit her lips.

"Who?" Frank repeated more insistently.

Merritt released a heavy sigh. "Axel."

Axel's head swivelled. He stared at Merritt, his face flushed, pulsating with anger. "It's a lie!"

"I saw you, Axel." She pouted. "You came running out of the south gate. Sorry."

Axel opened his mouth to protest, but Frank cut him off. "You were seen running east down Wellington around 7:30. I think we're talking vicinity—"

"Oh, come on. I often run down Wellington Crescent. And, besides, I hardly know Michael. Why would I—"

"Yours was the last number he called. His phone's got one of those last-number-dialled buttons. I got your answering machine."

Axel blustered. "Well, he didn't leave me a message. I don't why he would have been calling me."

"And yet you were at his house Tuesday evening."

"I wasn't *at* his house."

"You were *in* his yard."

Stevie could see Axel's jaw muscles working overtime.

"All right," he spat. "I've been looking for investors. I'm trying to restart my magazine. I thought Michael would be a likely backer."

"Thought? So you were unsuccessful."

"I'd written to him. I tried a formal appeal with business plan and all that."

"You didn't tell me any of this," Merritt interjected hotly.

Axel ignored her. "Anyway, he left me a message at home Tuesday. I guess because the phone's out at *WL*. He said he couldn't. Something about making some changes in his life, whatever that means."

"Were you disappointed? Angry?"

"Disappointed," Axel replied evenly. "But angry? Not angry enough to kill someone, if that's what you're trying to get at."

"Then what brought you to Rossiter's house? Someone construct a jogger's path through his yard?"

"I thought I'd take another shot at it. Make a personal appeal. It was a whim."

"Oh, a *whim*."

"Look," Axel responded with new anger. "Merritt wasn't home when I came by. Michael's house isn't that far away, running. I took a chance he might be in."

"And was he? In?"

"I don't know. I didn't try to find out."

"Why not?"

"I changed my mind."

"I thought that was a woman's prerogative."

Axel gave Frank a level gaze. "I changed my mind because of something I saw."

"And what was that?"

Axel flicked a glance at Leo. "I don't know if I should say," he drawled. "I wouldn't want to be bumped off in chapter twenty-nine."

Book 5

Saturday, October 1

27

Fish

Leo knew better than to question his luck—at least when it first presented itself. He'd slept late, crawled downstairs to make some coffee, fetched the *Citizen* and the *Globe and Mail* from the front step, let Alvarez out and in, then crawled back upstairs to bed. "Police seek new clues in Rossiter slaying," was the headline over his page three story.

Well, they will be, once they read this story, he'd thought with a certain glee, imagining Frank opening his paper and blurting some sort of expletive-deleted expression in front of Maria and the girls. After all, when he'd gone into the *Zit* late the previous afternoon to file an update on the Rossiter investigation, he was the only one who knew the Guarneri was safe and sound in the hands of bona fide violinist and friend of the deceased, Caitlin Clark. He half-expected Frank to phone as he breezed through the rest of the *Zit* then ploughed through the *Globe*. But the air was cool in the bedroom—largely because the plastic covering over the hole in the roof intended to be a skylight had leaks—and the dog was warm, and so he'd found himself falling back into slumberland. He'd awoken some time later from a dream to the sound of someone shouting his name below—Stevie, he'd recognized through a fog.

"Up here," he'd croaked.

"Are you alone?"

Am I *alone*? Jesus! "Yes. Just me."

Just me.

A dog.

And—he glanced under the covers—a bone.

Stevie had burst into the room, her dark hair in voluptuous disarray, carrying the fragrance of an autumn morning. Her face bore an expression Leo had not seen before and could not fathom as she began unbuttoning her coat.

And then she began unbuttoning her blouse. Leo emitted some sort of gurgling noise—he couldn't remember what it was now—and jabbed his foot urgently under the covers at Alvarez's stomach. The dog turned his majestic golden head toward him, regarded him with surprise and sadness, then hopped off the bed.

"I think," Stevie said, flinging the last of her things onto a chair, "you know what to do."

Afterward, Leo spent maybe twenty-five seconds questioning his luck. Delayed grief fuck? He'd heard of those. Charity fuck? Sports fuck? Comfort fuck? Love-you-mean-it fuck? Marry-me fuck?

Oh, what the fuck.

She'd been at Johns Mayhew, the lawyers, with Merritt, he drew from her after they'd dozed a little and reawakened.

"And?" he murmured.

She was turned away from him. He held her, running his hand over the flesh of her stomach, marvelling at its softness.

"The Winnipeg Foundation gets most of it. Earmarked for arts programs."

"One way to make sure your left hand doesn't know what your right is doing, I suppose."

"What?"

"Never mind. What else?"

"Well, there's me." Leo felt as much as heard her sigh. "I got all the camera and darkroom equipment."

"And this is...good?"

Stevie was silent a while. "I'm not really that interested in photography, Leo," she said at last. "Besides, I have my brother's things." She turned toward him. Leo felt her breath along his neck and her next words seemed to hum along his skin: "I'm sorry."

"For what?"

"I think you know."

Leo kissed her forehead. He was in a mood to forgive Pol Pot that unpleasantness in Cambodia. "You're worth waiting for."

She leaned her head back on the pillow to look at him. She smiled shyly. Leo felt himself begin to blush. "Anyway," he said quickly before the conversation turned into an awkward mushfest, "who else got what?"

"For some reason, Caitlin Clark and that brother of hers that you dislike each got about a third of a million."

"What! Guy got that much money? Uh-oh."

Leo thought back to Frank's interview with Axel the evening prior. What had kept Axel from going into Michael's house Tuesday was the sight of Guy Clark coming out.

Frank had leapt on this like it was a hot dinner in a cold climate. "What time?"

"A few minutes after 7:00. I looked at my watch before going into the yard. There was still light."

"You talked?"

"No."

"Did he see you?"

"No, I don't think so. I was in shadow, under a tree. He was standing on the back step and the light was on."

"What was he doing?"

Axel had shrugged. "Nothing. He just stood there a few moments, not moving. Then he walked down the steps and disappeared around the house. I think he was heading over to the Kingdons'."

"Was he carrying anything?"

"A briefcase."

"So then why didn't you continue with your plans to visit Rossiter?"

Axel had shifted uncomfortably in his chair. "I don't know, really. There was something weird about Guy, about the expression on his face. Maybe it was the porch light exaggerating it, but it seemed macabre. I just wanted to get away."

"Do you have any reason to dislike Guy Clark?" Frank had asked abruptly.

Axel had been unprepared. His face flushed. "No," he exploded as Frank regarded him stonily. "You think I'm making this up?"

Frank had shrugged, then asked coolly: "So what's the expression that creeped you out?"

Axel's eyes had sought the back corners of the black room. "Rapture," he replied after a moment. "I think I'd describe it as rapture."

Recalling the conversation afterwards, Leo had thought Axel had been doing the dance of the bullshit artist that comes from too much feature writing. Rapture, my ass. But now, with Stevie's revelation, it didn't seem so preposterous.

"But I don't understand," Stevie said, drawing him back from his reverie, "why the Clarks would be beneficiaries at all, and neither does Merritt. And the lawyer was no help. Caitlin knew Michael from the Curtis but—"

Leo explained. The accident. The other victims.

Stevie listened with growing disbelief. "Restitution?"

"Atoning for the sins of the father." Or some such Biblical guff, he thought. "Caitlin might find the gesture inappropriate."

"And Guy?"

"Oh, he'll eat it up. But could he have known he was in Michael's will?"

"There was no will," Stevie said.

"But—"

"It wasn't a will as such." Stevie drew away from him. "The lawyer called it an *inter vivos* trust," she explained, turning on her back, looking up at the plastic on the ceiling that was flapping gently in the wind. "In effect, Michael was preparing to give away all his money. While he was alive."

Leo blinked twice. "But that's nuts." He thought warmly of his own tiny savings, his lovely RRSPs, his sweet little CSBs, that endearing stock portfolio he had started with a broker he knew. Who could part from such things?

"He was going to keep some of it, surely."

"Even the house was to be sold, and the money folded in."

"And then what? Beg on the streets?"

Stevie turned to look at him. "I have no goddamn idea," she replied with some vehemence.

"But didn't he tell the lawyer?"

Stevie shook her head. "Apparently his intent was to tell everyone his plans at a later point."

"You're angry."

"Yes. I don't know why, really. When we were first dating, I once asked him what he wanted to be when he grew up—"

"Concert violinist, I thought."

"He said 'shepherd.'"

Leo snorted.

"It wasn't funny at the time. It just told me he wasn't thinking about us—about me and him. He had some sort of extravagant vision of himself, alone, overseeing a bunch of stupid sheep—humanity at large, I suppose. I'm starting to sympathize with Merritt. His managing her life."

"But to the good, surely." Odd to be defending Michael, but—what the heck—Michael's intercession had saved his job. "I mean, at least in Merritt's case. Doing a turn at the *Zit* has probably been good for her."

The glance Stevie shot him suggested otherwise. "I doubt she'll be there much longer."

"Ah! I was beginning to wonder if Merritt got cut out."

"She's in. But the money's not free and clear. Michael set up a trust. She'll have a generous income, but someone else will be managing it. The lawyer at Johns Mayhew is the trustee. In fact, she doesn't get the first payment until she rejoins a drug rehab program. Back to Hazelden, or wherever." A smile flitted across Stevie's face. "She threw a fit over that one."

"She's not that bad, is she?"

Stevie's smile turned to a frown. "She's on the slippery slope. Didn't she seem sort of stoned to you at the reception yesterday?"

Leo felt an urge to reach out and trace her face with his finger. "And that's it?"

She glanced at him. "No. The trust includes one other person."

Let it be me, he thought fleetingly.

"A child."

Leo nearly swallowed his own tongue. "*Your* child? He knew?"

"No."

"Then what child?"

"*His* child."

"Another child? But—"

"He has a son who lives with his mother in Holland. Or West Germany. I'm not sure which. He's about ten."

"Did you know about this other kid?"

"Michael didn't even know."

"Oh, not again. Michael sure spread himself around. Talk about—what's the word?—*fecund*." He shifted to avoid a blow to the gut.

"The boy sought him out. That's why Michael suddenly went to Europe and stayed there so long."

"So who's the mother?"

"Someone Michael was with at the Curtis. That's all I know." Stevie smiled at him glumly, then looked away. "Are you going to fix that hole in your ceiling?"

"Eventually," he replied, drawing closer to her, suddenly indifferent to ceilings and wills. "I think you've had a kind of shock this morning."

Much later, after Stevie had left for home, Leo padded downstairs and began to root through the refrigerator. Unbreakfasted, ravenous, he had offered to make something for them to eat in bed, but she had wanted only coffee, having inhaled its aroma when she'd first come into the house.

"The lawyer gave us water," she'd said, leaning over the far edge of the bed.

"How do you take your coffee? I forget. Sorry."

"Oh!" she had exclaimed.

"What?"

"I'm just looking at your story." Her voice was muffled. She lifted the paper where Leo had left it folded at page three. "So Caitlin Clark had the Guarneri the whole time. Well, that puts a different spin on things."

"Your coffee?"

She had smiled at him. "I like my herrings red and I like my coffee black."

"There's still a missing violin, though," he'd cautioned, exiting the bedroom.

"But would anyone kill someone for the sake of an ordinary violin?" she had shouted after him.

Good question, he thought now, staring blankly at the refrigerator's contents. Maybe somewhere in the city there's one hopping mad thief with a murder on his conscience. He lifted the lid of a plastic tub and sniffed tentatively at its contents. Or, more likely, the violin theft was always a diversion. He dumped the spaghetti into a casserole and put it in the microwave. *Cui bono*? Merritt. Caitlin. Guy. Maybe Axel, the hound. Some psychopath at the Winnipeg Foundation? He watched the casserole, spot-lit, spin slowly on the glass tray. But Michael hadn't made a will. He'd set up a trust. No death was needed to transfer the wealth. If the beneficiaries had only waited a while…

Of course, who knew about Michael's arrangements with his lawyer, anyway? And why, in the name of Daddy Warbucks, was someone as young, intelligent, educated, and accomplished as Michael Rossiter giving away all his money? The very stuff the world sought with such greedy passion. He pulled the casserole from the oven and gave the contents a desultory stir. Massive nervous breakdown? Awesome blackmail scheme? He took a deep breath. Is this wonderful spaghetti sauce or what?

Stomach growling, he returned the casserole to the oven for a few final spins. Maybe Michael decided, in some crisis of conscience, to make a break with the world by breaking with the kind of life he was leading. Non-violently, that is. The French Foreign Legion. *Does it still exist? A desert island? Are there any left on his crowded planet?* Leo recalled his interview in the spring with Michael for Guy's aborted feature about Winnipeg's angels. Michael had done a money-doesn't-buy-happiness riff on him. "Wealth can be a prison of sorts." Oh yeah? Send me to that slammer, he'd thought then as he did now, a blizzard of useless Lotto 6/49 tickets swirling in his head. Michael had referred to the Gospels. Matthew 6:1-3. He recalled the first line: *"Be careful not to make a show of your religion before men."*

The microwave dinged. Leo ignored it. He felt a quickening of his pulse. He glanced up at the clock above the sink. It was not quite three o'clock. He found the phonebook in the hall. It was the first Saturday in October, one of the last remaining Saturdays in the year with the promise of snowless weather and what's his name, the priest, would probably have weddings stacked like aircraft over O'Hare. But it was worth a shot. As he dialled St. Giles, he felt a surge of excitement. It seemed like such an obvious route of enquiry he didn't know why he hadn't explored it earlier. Perhaps because the church was something he had happily eliminated from his life before he was twelve years old, he had forgotten what a power it could be in the lives of others, even contemporaries who he assumed shared his own skepticism.

He was surprised when Father Day himself picked up the phone. There was no staff on Saturdays, he said, sounding distinctly distracted. Leo would be quick. He explained his concern. Father Day said he knew little. He was too new to St. Giles. But he had heard from Father Saunders—Leo recalled the retired priest from Merritt's reception—that Michael had sought spiritual advice for a period of time. Yes, possibly re-examining his life. Yes, "crisis of conscience" might be a suitable description. But Leo would have to ask Father Saunders. The sessions had ended some time ago, and while Michael had continued to come to St. Giles for Mass, he and Father Day had not had any illuminating conversations. However, he understood that Michael had taken his quest—Leo thought he detected a slight edge of cynicism behind the word—elsewhere. He suggested Leo pursue his enquiries there and gave him a name and an address. Directory assistance would have the phone number. Then he rang off. He was sorry, he said wearily. A wedding party was awaiting his presence.

Leo had quickly written down the details, but then he stared at it for a while, sinking slowly into a kitchen chair. The implication was so startling, so peculiar, that he couldn't take it in at first. But however strange and unexpected it was, it made sense of recent events in Michael's life; perhaps, too, he thought, it would make sense of his death. With growing excitement, he phoned directory assistance, got the phone number, and was gratified to be connected once again with the correct person. He had been expecting a dour tone and great circumspection but instead the man on the phone seemed to burble with goodwill. Come and visit us, he insisted. So Leo made an appointment for the very next day, in the early afternoon.

Then he made a restaurant reservation for the evening.

And then he ate.

A few hours later, lying on the bed, dressed in his suit trousers, half-listening to the first splatter of rain slap against the plastic over the skylight, he wondered what Stevie would make of this new information. Or if he should even tell her. The thought of her made him start. He switched on the bedside lamp and looked at his watch. If he didn't soon leave for her house, they would be late for the Galleries Portáge opening. He leapt off the bed, put on his suit jacket, gave himself a check in the mirror and raced downstairs. He was looking forward to the evening in a way he hadn't thought possible earlier in the day, before Stevie had come.

He was slipping into his trenchcoat in the downstairs gloom when suddenly a burst of light turned the windows incandescent and a clap of thunder beat the air so ferociously he had to catch his breath. Alvarez, who had followed him downstairs, scuttled under a nearby table. The fresh penetrating odour of ozone filled his nostrils as he opened the back door. Lightning and thunder continued to attend a torrent of hard rain but it seemed farther away, at a safer distance. Leo stepped into the yard, collar up, only to be alarmed by another sound, this one yawning and terrible. He looked up and saw through the brightening sky a black shape hurtling toward him. He jerked back. The lightning had cleaved a dead limb of the old oak tree and it crashed to earth right at his feet. Like an afterthought, the key that he always kept hidden in the tree trunk followed. It jingled onto the stone path and caught one feeble ray of the setting sun.

28

Vanity Fair

*W*innipeg's *business and community leaders were out in full force for an exclusive preview opening Saturday evening of Galleries Portáge, the multi-million-dollar, government-subsidized mega-project intended to revitalize...*

Leo peered past the orchestra, awkwardly jammed into a sunken courtyard below, sawing its way through some piece he didn't recognize—Mahler?—to Doug Whiteway, one of the Go! lackies, who was scribbling in a pad. It was the kind of crapola story he'd be stuck with next week when he went on general assignment. Guy would grind him down with fluff stories and evening and weekend shifts until he quit in predictable disgust. If Guy didn't find some excuse to axe him in the interim, that is.

And this time, he thought grimly, watching Whiteway tap a kilted gentleman on the back, there was no angel to mysteriously intercede.

Well, let's see, if he *were* writing this up—and sometimes he couldn't help doing ledes in his head—he'd be excising the "exclusive" bit in no time. Better not to let the unwashed who were paying for this sucker through their taxes know they were being excluded from the champágne opening. Which meant "government-subsidized" would have to go, too. And he would probably end up substituting a more hopeful "expected" for the more cautious "intended." After all, ripping out part of the heart of Portage Avenue and building a shopping mall in its place had been sold to the public as a saviour of the decayed downtown.

How easily self-censoring came in the journalism game.

Oh, what the hell, some persnickety, turnip-up-his-ass copy editor would change it anyway.

And speaking of saviours, wasn't that Harry Mack, the new owner of the *Zit*, Whiteway was interviewing? He recognized the face from photographs. Sleek, silver-haired, and opulent, like some of those grain-fed televangelists that stank up the airwaves late at night. What he hadn't known was that the Christer wore a kilt. This was ominous. The Rossiters had had an agenda when they owned the paper—the glories of the Liberal party—but they spent money like drunken sailors. Brock Hayward, the Bay Street vampire who bought the *Zit* before Leo came on board, cared only about money, and attacked the payroll and capital expenditures with a rusty scythe. Now, with Mack, who took the *Zit* off Hayward's hands when no one would buy it, it looked like agenda *plus* cost-cutting.

Not to libel the Scots, of course.

He could imagine what Mack was saying to Whiteway: "an estimable addition to the downtown fabric…will undoubtedly reinvigorate Winnipeg's core…blah blah blah."

Everyone at the *Zit* knew Mack's henchmen were busy scouting property on the fringes of the city. The plan was to abandon the downtown like so many rats fleeing a sinking ship and build a new plant in the fortress suburbs where most of the readers lived anyway.

Leo watched Mack grow squinty-eyed with delight in his own company while Whiteway vigorously recorded every pearl to drop from his lips. Where was Martin? Why wasn't he dancing attendance? Or Guy? Meanwhile, to Leo's right, the coiffed, gowned, and suited, plastic champagne flutes in hand, rode up one gleaming silver escalator, and to his left, they rode down again. Humanity flowed like a river past immaculate fig trees, past the lottery booth, past the spindly clock tower, past the orchestra, past the butcher's, the baker's, the candlestick maker's, and the House of Sunglasses/Cookies/Chintz/Cheese, through pools of soft light and around pools of gurgling water. And then they flowed by it all over again, because there was really no final destination, no magnificent sea into which one could be subsumed.

Hundreds of card-carrying members of Winnipeg's booboisie, lured by free nosh and booze and with nothing better to do with their time, found themselves trapped, wandering aimlessly around a downtown shopping mall Saturday evening.

The occasion was a riffraff-verboten preview opening of Galleries Portáge, the multi-million-dollar, government-subsidized mega-project without a snowball's chance in hell of revitalizing…

Well, there are the ledes of your dreams. And then there's reality. Besides, a good lede shouldn't exceed twenty-five words—Axel had presented this as gospel when they were at the *Dauphin Courier*; he had read it somewhere—and that lede bordered on logorrhea. Maybe if "lured by free nosh and booze" was deleted. Leo began to count it out in his head. Then he spotted Stevie. She was wearing a dress that seemed to worship every curve of her body. Ledes flew from his head.

"What took you so long?"

"What were you thinking so hard about?"

"Ladies first."

"Men designed this building. Not enough stalls in the women's washroom. Your turn."

"I was thinking about the Scottish clearances of the nineteenth century." Stevie frowned.

"Doesn't matter. What do you think of Galleries Portáge so far?"

Stevie's eyes raked the space, then settled on his. "I'm having this overpowering sense of déjà vu."

"Funny. So am I. Champagne?"

An anorexic twentysomething in a spandex body suit flitted by with a tray of drinks. She was one of several dozen gussied up in harvest colours and fake leaves to look like some sort of autumn sprite, which was odd because in the mall it was endless summer. They must have hired the entire corps of the Royal Winnipeg Ballet, too, for this schmoozefest, Leo thought, snatching a couple of glasses off the tray, while the young woman pliéd absently.

"Blecch!" Stevie grimaced, sipping hers. "I've sucked on tastier pennies."

They turned to gaze down over the courtyard, at the busy orchestra and the teeming crowd.

"Wow," Leo deadpanned as another sprite floated by with appetizers. "Does life get any better than this?"

He grabbed a couple of shrimp from the tray and looked at Stevie inquiringly. She shook her head. "I spy Surface and Psyche in the conga line for the escalator," she remarked.

"Huh?"

"My parents. It's my brother Will's joke. My father fixes people's exteriors and my mother fixes their interiors."

Leo glanced down through the cross-bars of the clock tower. Stevie's father he liked. He was quiet, with a slightly amused turn to his mouth. Stevie's mother, however, was something else altogether. From their brief encounters, he had the sense she was weighing him in some balance, like a pile of bananas, and found him wanting—unripe, perhaps, or poor value for the weight. The grocery analogy always came to mind when he thought about this. Once, not long after meeting her for the first time, he caught a glimpse of her at Grant Park Safeway (she didn't see him) bearing down on her cart as though she were driving a tank through enemy territory. When he'd called to pick up Stevie not an hour ago, she had sat him down while Stevie was upstairs getting ready and said, "I understand you're sleeping with my daughter."

Leo's throat had seized.

"Well, good. It's about time. I was beginning to think there was something wrong with you."

"It wasn't me," Leo had managed to squeak.

"I know," she'd clucked, patting his knee maternally, and turned to a discussion of Manitoba leading the nation in crime-rate increase, which had been on the front page of the *Examiner* that morning. "Call us Killerpeg," the headline read. Her argument: Tory government. His counterargument: meaningless statistical anomaly. Or maybe it was Ben Johnson's fault.

"What's it like having a mother who's a psychologist?" he asked Stevie, biting into the shrimp, watching the Lords step onto the escalator.

"Psychedelic."

"As in 'mind-expanding'?"

"As in 'bizarre.' No Dr. Spock for me. I remember coming home early from school in grade six and often finding the living room full of naked people shrieking their heads off. It was her primal-scream period. I've told you my mother's American. They met when my father was doing his residency in San Francisco. My father says being American is half the explanation of her."

"Was your mother naked, too?"

"I think I blocked that part."

"Freaky."

"It didn't seem that odd, really. I was just annoyed because I couldn't get my homework done. The noise carried upstairs. Finally, one day my father came home unexpectedly early. What's the orchestra playing? It sounds so familiar."

"I think it's Mozart's Mall Concerto. What did your father do?"

"Put his foot down. My mother went shopping for an office the next—"

A sudden movement diverted them. The clock tower, all Tinkertoy spindles and whirligigs, seemed to shudder as gears and wheels began to click and twirl, triggering a set of bells. The clock chimed cheesily. 8:00. Below, Richter, his baton in the air, jerked his head up. His eyes blazed with a kind of fury as he beheld the clock mindlessly tolling the hour.

"Holy crap," Leo said, "if looks could kill, this clock would be a mass of uncoiled springs."

"Doing Muzak for a mall opening is likely killing *him*."

"The price is right, probably. The WSO isn't swimming in moolah. Sources say," he added, thinking of Liz. And where was Liz? He'd sidled past Spencer earlier, but he was arm-in-arm with a woman not his wife—mostly likely his mother, given her age, unless he was moonlighting for an escort service.

"They should scrap this *Taste of Winnipeg* book and do *Maestro Richter's Workout'n'Weight Loss* book instead," he added, noting Richter's arms thrashing the air.

"May be one of the reasons why symphony conductors are so long lived," Stevie said. "Von Karajan and George Solti are still conducting and they're in their eighties."

"You're smart."

"She saw it on *Sixty Minutes*." Stevie's father joined them.

"Thanks a lot, Daddy."

"It's a good aerobic workout."

"Anyway, Richter is older than he looks." She leaned toward Leo and said out of the side of her mouth, "He's had a little work, you know. So has his wife."

"Stevie!" Dr. Lord frowned. "What I say about my patients isn't supposed to leave the house."

"Oh, really, Daddy. No one can hide the fact they've had a facelift."

"But some people think they can. And that's the way they want it. Richter is a very private person. Besides," he added, dropping his voice as the orchestra finished the piece, "for him, it was only a little work around the eyes."

"Oh, yes, his eyes," Stevie said. "Like Bowie's—one blue, one green. Didn't you tell me that?" She addressed her father.

"Really?" Leo turned to look. "Hard to tell from here."

"I think he wears contacts anyway."

"It's called heterochromia of the iris," Dr. Lord explained. "It can be an indicator for certain genetic disorders or syndromes—"

"Isn't that Caitlin Clark down there?" Stevie interrupted, pointing over the railing.

Leo followed her eyes toward a blonde woman wearing a rose-coloured dress talking to a man whose back was to them. "I think so, yes."

"Would you excuse me, then?" She handed Leo her glass. "There's something I want to ask her."

Stevie edged her way between her father and Leo and headed toward the down escalator.

"So, is he sick—Richter, I mean?" Leo asked Dr. Lord, keeping one eye on Stevie.

"No. He could have a propensity to deafness, if it's the syndrome I'm thinking of. But it's pretty rare, and I don't think there's any indication he has a hearing problem."

"Beethoven was deaf and wrote music."

"But I don't think he had to conduct an orchestra. Oddly enough, I passed someone earlier here with an indicator for the same syndrome."

"Who?"

Dr. Lord shrugged. "Never seen him before." He looked over Leo's shoulder. "You'll have to excuse me, too. My wife is signalling to me. How's your back, by the way?" he added, turning.

"Much better, thanks," Leo called after him as Beethoven's Galleria Symphony swelled up from below. *Nice of you to ask. I'm not kidding.*

Leo handed both glasses to a passing sprite, then, noting Stevie and Caitlin had disappeared down the first-floor gauntlet of shops, decided to wander down the second-floor equivalent.

The occasion was a riffraff-verboten preview opening of Galleries Portáge...

he continued, composing copy in his head as he passed various members of Cabinet, city hall, the business community—and their wives, of course.

...the multi-million-dollar, government-subsidized mega-project without a snowball's chance in hell of revitalizing the downtown.

"Twenty years ago, Main Street was razed to build the Centennial Concert Hall with the promise of urban renewal," said some critic I'd find if I was really doing this story, "and Main Street is still a wasteland. Why would anyone think a mere building would reverse decades of decline?"

Invited guests vacuuming canapés down their gullets Saturday night and guzzling great quantities of Canadian champagne were generally pleased, however, with the bland mega-square-foot structure that seals off three blocks of Portage Avenue like a bunker.

"It's spectacular," said one sozzled suburbanite who will probably never darken the place again...

Leo grazed his way down the toyland Main Street, past the gallery of twinkling shops, accepting the finger-food offerings of various pixies, imps, and fairies, refusing the so-called champagne, nosing in doorways at the piles of goods he wasn't interested in buying, and pausing to exchange scornful remarks with various and sundry—mostly *Zit* colleagues—whose expressions morphed from that vaguely stupefied look creatures get in enclosed spaces to an ironic detachment when they realized they *were* vaguely stupefied creatures in an enclosed space.

Symptoms of *Mall*aise? Or, perhaps, Mal de Mall?

The average copy editor's boredom was measured in punning headlines. Leo had done a stint once, filling in for someone on leave.

Having a Mall, Wish You Were Here

Fear and Malling in Winnipeg

The Mall that Ate Downtown

And so on.

Leo yawned. *Where had Stevie got to?*

He spied Axel leaning against a balustrade that appeared to overlook another courtyard. Or, rather, he spied a familiar ponytail trailing down the back of a very loud suit jacket.

"What the hell is this?" he said, fingering the fabric, noting the obnoxious blend of colours.

Axel spun around, and smacked Leo's hand away. "It's Manitoba tartan."

"You've got to be kidding."

"It's called irony, Leo."

"Really? You're too subtle for me. It looks more like you went rummaging through some Shriner's closet. I know—you've spent so much time on the Nautilus, you don't fit into anything else."

"Fuck off."

Leo snickered. "Enjoying all this?" He glanced down over the balustrade at another water feature.

"In a postmodern kind of way," Axel replied.

"Which means what exactly?"

"Well, if you don't know, I'm not going to tell you."

"What are you being such an asshole about?"

Axel glared. "Well, gee, let me think. Lots of stuff, but in your case maybe it's because my oldest friend thinks I'm a murderer."

"I didn't say that. When did I say that?"

"I didn't say 'say.' I said 'thinks.'"

"You're a mind reader suddenly?"

"I didn't appreciate that remark in the church."

"About Merritt and the money? Get over yourself."

Axel continued to glower. Leo regarded him for a moment. What a sulky bastard. "Well, maybe I've hit bone then," he said hotly. "You doth protesting too much and all that crap."

"Shut up."

"You've always done stupid impulsive things, Axel. You were the one who said, 'hey, why don't you steal that car?'"

"You could have said 'no thanks.'"

"You were the one gung-ho to pick up that dope that time."

"*You* told *me*. You were the one sitting on the shitter at Clear Lake and overheard those dealers."

"You bought a newspaper on a whim. I still don't know where you got the money. The dope wasn't worth that much."

"Well, you worked for me."

"You quit the *Zit* to bankrupt yourself starting some stupid magazine. And you're the one so determined to start it again. So it's not completely beyond the call of reason that you might have bonked Rossiter on the head because he wouldn't hand you some loot—"

"Well, I didn't."

"—and then try to pin it on Guy."

"That prick deserves it. He fucked up *WL*'s future, and he…never mind."

"What?"

"Nothing."

Leo snatched a baby quiche from a passing sprite, and gave a passing thought to its calorie content. "Are you here with Merritt?"

"Sort of," Axel replied irritably.

"Where is she?"

"She just went downstairs."

Suddenly, the fountain, which had been burbling politely below them, sent a huge plume of water high into the air. It surged past Leo's face to almost lap the glass canopy reflecting darkly another storey above their heads. The crowd on two floors, as if observing a miracle, groaned with pleasure.

"Which reminds me," Leo said, feeling a waft of damp air as the column of water crashed back down to the pool, "I finally did the deed with Stevie."

"Congrats. I was beginning to think she was a lesbian. I mean, that name—"

"It's Stephanie, for chrissake. I've told you. Stephanie was too sucky. She's been calling herself Stevie since she was four."

"All right, already. I forgot." Axel turned and looked sourly over the scene below. "Isn't that her over there—beside this pond, or whatever it's supposed to be." He pointed. "Who's the blonde she's with?"

"Caitlin Clark."

"Oh, that's her. Merritt is really pissed about this will or trust or whatever it is of Michael's. Why would he give money to a scumbag like Guy Clark and his sister, of all people?"

"It's a long story."

"You know?"

"Some of it."

"Well, tell me. Merritt hasn't a clue."

But Leo was alerted to activity below. Merritt was visible elbowing her way through the gridlock around the miraculous fountain toward Stevie and Caitlin. Even from on high he could see a look of concentrated fury on her face.

"Uh-oh," he said, transfixed.

"What?"

"Merritt." Leo pointed toward the moving figure in the green dress. Stevie and Caitlin had seen her too. Stevie seemed to lean backward as if impelled by a force of nature.

"Oh, Jesus," Axel said.

Neither of them moved.

"I can't hear a thing," Leo said, leaning over, watching the furious opening and closing of Merritt's mouth while Caitlin backed away from her.

"Fucking noisy water."

"Looks like we might have a major hair-pull here," Leo said, not undelighted. The argument continued. The crowd slowly edged away. "Hey, this is better than Krystle and Alexis. Where's the volume control?"

"Fuck off, Fabian." Axel stared anxiously at the scene. "I'd better get down there."

"Don't hurry," Leo said with gleeful insincerity, watching the Manitoba tartan race toward the stairs.

Too late. Caitlin had backed toward the pool under the relentless onslaught. The result was as inevitable as Mulroney's re-election. You could run it in slo-mo like a hockey replay. Caitlin pitched backward, appeared to recover her balance, then teetered anew at the edge of the pool, arms flailing. Seeing her advantage, Merritt thrust both hands against Caitlin's shoulders. Caitlin's daintily shod feet seemed to lift off the tile like it was a banana skin, and she flew backward just as the fountain once again began its preposterous ejaculation. This time there were two crashes of water.

New lede, thought Leo.

The preview opening of Galleries Portáge Saturday evening was marked by a skirmish between two women that ended in near-drowning in one of the mall's ponds.

Okay, the "near-drowning" was a little over the top.

29

The Famous Chapter Twenty-Nine

Guy Clark sat rigid in his chair glowering at the few lines of type running across the top of his computer screen. The characters burned garish and neon-bright, the cursor throbbed at the end of the last word typed, impatient and demanding. Rage flared suddenly and he jabbed the justify button hard, cursing as the words reordered themselves into paragraphs along the left side of the screen. His exertions had yielded barely four inches of copy.

He had once overheard a couple of reporters in the library sniggering that his byline file contained only six stories while their files were stuffed, and how ridiculous that he, Guy, was an editor when he had hardly ever *written* a goddamn news story, much less a feature. Rage had flared then, too, and the rejoinder had been on his lips: if you guys are so fucking brilliant, how come I'm an editor and you're just a couple of dumb beat reporters? But he had kept his control. Knowledge of other people—their opinions, their ambitions, their weaknesses—was always useful in the long run. Even the avails of library gossip. He recognized the voices, knew the reporters. Now that he was city editor, they would sidle up to him, try to humour him, appease him, entice him into certain kinds of stories, or try to avoid certain assignments or shifts, whining, cajoling, arguing. He would reward or punish as he saw fit.

The fact was, advancement in a newsroom had little to do with ability or talent or education—those were the givens and those he had. No, to advance you needed to be able to seize opportunities. It was a matter of the useful application of knowledge. That was it, he thought with a surge of self-congratulation that swept away his earlier anger: the useful application of knowledge.

How useful, for instance, had been his knowledge about Kingdon. He remembered well the day Caitlin told him their parents had not died haplessly as the result of some road condition or mechanical failure in a car, but that they had been killed—yes, killed as surely as if they had been shot with a gun—by a rich drunk, a stupid, over-privileged, rich drunk, and that that truth had been manipulated and obscured until it was turned on its head, the victims banished to oblivion, the killer exalted as a fallen hero. He had been teenaged then but still young enough to believe that what poured from newspapers or radio or television was not only true but truth itself. That notion had gone out the window in that moment. He began to study newspapers, to examine the ways they handled information, to read between the lines, alert to their biases, their presumptions. He enrolled in journalism at Red River Community College. Though that snob Martin tended to discount community college diplomas, Guy had been able to impress him as pugnacious and ravenous for the fray of daily newspapering. How Martin—who had achieved his position simply by marrying well and who favoured reporters with university degrees—loved to surround himself at the higher levels with ambitious proles. And he had played it to the hilt, rising with extraordinary speed, first to the desk, then to the editorship of the Go! section, which gave him access to editorial conferences and a warmer relationship with the man who was destined, whether he knew it or not, to be his benefactor. Martin liked him, or at least was amused by him—it didn't matter which—and began to take him into his confidence, master condescending to pupil. But lately, Martin had seemed to cool toward him. Oh, yes, there had been problems—high staff turnover in Go!, reporters going over his head and whining to Martin about unfair treatment, complaints from the arts community perennially unsatisfied with the coverage of their narcissistic busywork—but none of it was of any consequence. He wasn't challenged in his job, he explained to Martin one day. And he wasn't. Go!, with its horoscopes and recycled Hollywood gossip and recipes and reviews of fruitcake dance groups, was marginal to the life of the *Citizen.* He wanted something meatier, where his abilities might truly be tested. Something like city desk. Martin had dismissed the notion.

Poor Martin. Of course, it was well known he had long been the aggrieved bridesmaid, never the bride, when it came to the publisher's chair. Tom Rossiter had advanced Martin's career when he married his wife's sister, but that career had stalled in the wake of Tom's death. He was pushing sixty. With the last publisher retired with Hayward's sale of the *Citizen*, his number had come up again, and it was the last time it would. The Mack purchase in the summer had laid the groundwork. A zealous right-wing Christian Albertan—a frightening combination, but what the fuck—Harry Mack demanded the publishers of his newspapers be impeccable. Harmac investigated backgrounds thoroughly and held upper management to a standard that would make the Pope tremble. So Guy had told Martin the story of his life that day in the sanctuary of Martin's office, the oddly bare office that suggested only a temporary encampment en route to the rooms of dark wood and old leather in a more secluded part of the building. He told Martin precisely why he had become interested in newspapers. And Martin had become most accommodating. Closets rarely contained one skeleton, after all. And he had only had to suggest that they did. Mack, of course, would never tolerate corruption at the highest level of his organization. They were the purest of the pure. Harry Mack and his big-Texas-haired wife Blanche made Quakers seemed debauched. Or at least they liked to present themselves as such.

Yes, he had made a useful application of knowledge that day. And now there was something else that would be useful. Some material had appeared on his desk Friday as if by magic. At first he had been dubious about the truth of its contents. The information was so astonishing as to be almost absurd and he wondered if some bastard in the newsroom weren't playing a complex trick on him. But all the papers, though they were photocopies, bore the unmistakable signs of authority: insignia, stamps, numbers, signatures. As a trick it would have been too elaborate for the meagre minds of the newsroom slugs.

His first thought had been: Scoop! Saturday edition! But then he reconsidered. He needed to be absolutely sure. The paper's lawyers would probably have to vet it. There wasn't enough time. And, besides, the story could screw up the Galleries Portáge opening. Since the *Citizen* had thrown its weight behind this downtown renewal bullshit, that wouldn't be a wise move. Guy let his fingers dance along the computer keys. No, Monday would be fine. Better, even. He would write the story himself over the weekend and present it as a *fait accompli* on the first day of his assumption of city desk. It would start his stewardship with a story that would turn the city on its ear. He would show the whole newsroom what a good story was, and how to handle it. And once that was done...

He swivelled in his chair. One bank of fluorescent lights illuminated his desk, but the rest of the newsroom was in shadow. The remaining desks, the computer terminals, the piles of old newspapers, books and other detritus of the business lay soft and amorphous like slumbering animals in a darkened forest. Only the glow of one distant computer screen, carelessly left on, broke the shapeless gloom. Its thin light seemed to agitate the dust around it into a sympathetic phosphorescence, giving definition to a Styrofoam coffee cup, a glass ashtray precariously balanced on a stack of white papers, a dog-eared dictionary. The only sound was the faint whine of the fans cooling the computer system.

On these rare Saturday evenings when he came to work, when the newsroom was devoid of people, when it was quiet and dark, and he was sitting in his corner looking outward across the plain of empty desks, he felt almost at peace. There was no need for the Monday-to-Friday vigilance. Nothing in the environment could thwart him or contradict him. There were no other editors plotting his humiliation, no reporters frowning and gossiping, no superiors expecting his obeisance. The room was his. He could do what he liked.

Well, not quite, he thought and snorted out loud, the sound strangely amplified. He was indulging a fantasy of power a little bit. The room was empty, after all. But soon, starting Monday, he would move to that desk right over there, the one at the top of the room that all other desks faced like sunflowers bent towards the sun. He would have much more authority. He would be able to shape events in ways he couldn't before. A kind of glee seemed to run through him, almost like the irrepressible glee he'd felt as a child when Christmas approached, those long-ago Christmases when his parents were still alive. He would be good. He would use this new power beneficently. Now that he had reached this stage he could. Before, there were always others continually, *continually* undermining him. But on Monday...

He turned back to his screen and the moment of pleasure dissolved. The four inches of copy stared back at him. He muttered another curse. This story should just write itself. That's what he told his staff. Of course stories just wrote themselves! How could they not if they were good stories? But the morons he had inherited when he was appointed Go! editor always seemed to bristle when he offered such wisdom. Most of them thought of themselves not as reporters, but as writers, real writers distinguishable from the mere hacks in the paper's other departments. But he had news for them: they were hacks, too; only they had more column inches in which to display their putrid prose—prose that he always had to repair and rework, of course, and with no thanks. Liz was the worst offender, forever contradicting him. Axel had been bad, too, but he was gone. He had taken great pleasure in fucking up his controlled-circ plans with the *Citizen*.

Hadn't Liz been surprised when he had said he knew about her affair with Richter? It had started with a simple observation. One day he had noted her walking to her car, then veer off suddenly toward the condos facing Central Park where the Richters kept an in-town apartment. There had been something furtive about her as she'd rounded the corner, the quick glancings around, that had piqued his curiosity. He had heard that her marriage was strained. All it took was a little detective work, a friendly and remunerative conversation with the condo superintendent. And the way she looked at Richter at the Kingdons' dinner party. Was everyone else stupid? Was he the only one with any perception? Wouldn't it be interesting if her husband found out, just when he was planning to run for political office? It wouldn't look good, a messy separation in the middle of a campaign.

He had enjoyed dangling the Go! editorship in front of her at the party. She had wanted the position once. But he had beat her to it. Now he had to admit that in some ways he was sorry she hadn't been named in his place in Friday's announcement. Even if she was always challenging him, she at least had more brains than that idiot Pastuk who had replaced him. Maybe he should lean on Martin to give her the position permanently. With what he knew about her now, perhaps he could continue to exercise some control in the Go! department. On the other hand, those insinuations of hers about his activities Tuesday night before arriving at Kingdon's...

He thought back to that night. He had left the *Citizen* diligently late, but a little early for his appointment with Michael. Debating whether to drive home first, drop off his briefcase and change, he passed Merritt's Miata parked on Assiniboine Avenue outside Jane's Boutique. He'd parked a discreet distance away, and then, when she came out of Jane's, he followed her. The crazy bitch spent half an hour driving all over the place, down Wellington to Assiniboine Park, then back along Corydon. When she turned onto Stafford he figured she was going to her brother's. Was it to be a meeting with the *two* of them?

He didn't know what the meeting was supposed to be about anyway. Michael hadn't said, but it had the effect of a royal command. Besides, he was curious. He had glimpsed Michael only once, when he allowed himself to be lured by a very persistent publicist into accepting an invitation to an opening of some weird photographs at the Floating Gallery. Michael was supposed to be Mr. Nice Guy. Hell, he *looked* like Mr. Nice Guy. Merritt, however, dripped acid about her brother when they'd been together. Michael Rossiter was controlling, judgmental, and miserly—ego masquerading as altruism. Among other things.

He parked on the north side of Michael's property, grabbed his case, and quickly got out of the car. Since she had turned the street before, she would be parked on the south.

God, he was obsessed with her. Watching her cross the newsroom sometimes, he wanted to jerk off under his desk. He could hardly believe she had gone out with him in the first place. He had to get rid of her. Get her fired. He couldn't stand it much longer. That episode in his apartment...

Was *that* what it was supposed to be about? Was Michael doing some protective big-brother routine?

But he didn't see her in the yard. Shadows stretched across the lawn. The house was still: No figures in the windows, no lights switching on against the early evening. There had been only the sound of a few car doors slamming on the street, and some sort of to-ing and fro-ing next door at Kingdons'. He almost turned and walked away. But then he decided, hell, he was here. He wasn't going to take any shit from Michael Rossiter...

Guy looked at his watch. He needed to make an appearance at the mall opening, make sure to praise the Lord and pass the hors d'oeuvres with Harry Mack and his lieutenants. The Mack empire seemed bent on media acquisition. He needed to be remembered. He didn't want to spend the rest of his life in this burg in the middle of nowhere. And model-thin Julie Olsen would be there, too. After work Friday, he had gone to Pantages bar.

Julie had been there. Funny, she had never paid him any attention before. Funny, she should find him interesting on the very day of his big promotion. Oh well, one of the perks of the job. And it helped him keep his mind off Merritt for a few hours. He hadn't got back to his own apartment until late afternoon, and then only to change before going to the *Citizen* to get a start on his big story before hopping over to the mall. She hadn't been anxious for him to go. And he was looking forward to spending another night with her. This night. Tonight.

The phone had been ringing when he turned the key to his apartment. The caller insisted on talking with him.

Begged, actually.

Fuck you, he had wanted to say. But he liked the idea of himself as compassionate, as gracious, willing to hear an argument. He said he was just on his way to the *Citizen*. Meet me in the newsroom, he said.

Guy ran his fingers over the keyboard like it was a piano. Gibberish burned onto the screen. He frowned. Glanced at his watch. Cocked an ear toward the door to the newsroom.

Had she chickened out…?

Michael hadn't answered the bell to his door, but it had been open anyway, so he walked in. He called out, but there was no reply. He should have known there was something wrong. The open door. The silence. He had walked around, looking into different rooms, admiring the stuff, repeatedly calling Michael's name to disguise the unwarranted intrusion when he had caught a glimpse of something human through a sliding panel. He had poked his head in and there, glistening red in the dwindling light seeping through windows opposite, was a patch of blood. Michael's face was in it.

It had been a shock. He could admit it to himself now. He had never seen a dead body before. He hadn't felt nauseous or physically revolted, but he had felt for a moment a loss of strength, a wobble in the knees. Of course, they didn't let him see his father after the accident, or even his mother in the hospital—her injuries had been too severe. He had begged to see her but his grandmother wouldn't let him. He was too young, she said. And then his mother had died. After he cried over that, he never cried again…

He had turned from the sight of Michael Rossiter's fallen body toward the desk to look for a phone. It was an automatic response. Then he noted an open appointment book, with his name clearly inked in. A kind of paranoia swept over him at that moment. Might the cops make something of the accidental connection between his family and the Rossiters? Accuse him of exacting some sort of delayed revenge? Or would Merritt say Michael had intended to read him the riot act?

They had argued. There had been a fight.

He thought only long enough to tear the page away from the coil binding without leaving a print. Now there was no proof Michael had been expecting his visit. Merritt wasn't around. Clearly she had not parked. She had driven on. Why get involved? And just in case anyone had seen him in the neighbourhood, he would hop over to the Kingdons'. Martin would give him an alibi. No question.

He had retraced his steps through the house. He hadn't touched anything, didn't touch anything, and there would be no footprints. The weather had been too hot and dry for that.

But when he got outside and gulped the fresh air, an almost giddy feeling of happiness surged from somewhere deep inside, surprising him. Sick, maybe—he thought that now, almost guiltily—but in that moment he found Rossiter's death weirdly satisfying. The son of the man who had killed his parents had himself been killed. A rough symmetry. Crude justice, but justice nonetheless.

Into this reverie, the insistent burr of an electronic doorlock barely penetrated. Some mechanical function of the subconscious duly noted the sound and sent a delayed message to the cerebral cortex, but by the time Guy paid attention, the sound had died and silence had again closed in. He turned to look. Probably one of the sports reporters in to file a late story. Sports had its own room down the hall, in the opposite direction from the newsroom. Or it was one of the cleaners, although cleaners didn't usually work on Saturdays. Or perhaps security, or what passed for security—one skinny Filipino with a flashlight.

He tapped out a few more words and thought again of Merritt. He couldn't help himself. He was sure she was seeing someone else. She wasn't the kind of woman who was long without a man. But who? Hell, she'd been with Dale-fucking-Hawerchuk briefly, and hadn't there been some record producer when she'd lived in New York? And some nightclub owner? Visions of Merritt and anyone else made him pigsick with jealousy. Even if she talked to some other guy in the newsroom, he could feel a cold rage begin to wash along his nerves. The intensity of his feelings for her dismayed him; he would feel his self-control begin to slip its mooring.

God, she was hot. Even her druggie history was alluring. But there was this other attraction—the link between their families. He had been fascinated by her ignorance of the connection. She presumed he knew all about her parents, and she never asked about his. Not ever. In the end, their affair had been brief. It had taken some work to get her attention in the first place. Being Go! editor helped—she had to talk to him; he was her boss, even if Martin had basically foisted her on him in the first place. He dared himself to ask her out, just to see if she would. She'd looked faintly amused, but condescended to say yes. Okay, basically, she had just been playing with him. And he had enjoyed playing. There was no reason it couldn't go on. But then she ended it. On a whim. By then he was lost, besotted. Her action stunned him. Made him furious. It was hard to keep decorum in the newsroom but after work...

He would run into her in a grocery store and she would look so surprised. He would show up at the same clubs and bars. He phoned again and again, but she never picked up. He got tired of talking into her answering machine. Finally he got her to agree to meet him. His grandmother had only just died. He had never felt so low, and Caitlin had her own grief to contend with. He had to admit he had got a little weird with Merritt that day in his apartment. He'd done a bad thing. But afterwards, for a time, the obsession seemed to fade. She didn't show up for work for a long time. He covered for her, told Martin she was viewing the fall fashions or spring fashions or whatever in Dallas or Paris or Milan or somewhere. And then in late August she turned up again in the newsroom and treated him with all the disdain that seemed to be in her blood, but still flipping that long, red, actressy hair in his face.

So absorbed was he that he didn't hear at first the faint rustle of clothing or the short quick intake of air behind him. When he did, it was much too late. The hands were already around his throat, crushing him with a surprisingly strong, steady grasp, the unexpected odour of warm rubber assailing his nostrils as he instinctively threw open his mouth to fight for air. Foolishly he reached up to try and tear apart the alien pair of hands but his fingers, damp with sudden sweat, fumbled along a slippery surface. Gloves. The thought ripped through his fevered mind as he tried to struggle out of the chair, gagging and gasping. But the full weight of this other grunting creature was forcing his head down, down toward the keyboard of his computer while with waning strength he fought to retain his position, to clutch some part of his chair, the desk, anything to achieve the leverage that would allow him to throw off his assailant. But everything, papers, books, pencils, flew out of reach. He could feel himself shooting backward down a long tunnel. The blood roared in his ears. The computer screen shrank to a microdot before his fading eyes. And then, suddenly, his head was right against the cool thick glass of the screen and the brightest whitest diamond flashed in his brain.

30

Design is Everywhere

"I remember," Stevie said to Nan Hughes, "the very first words you wrote on the blackboard in first year."
"'Design is Everywhere.'"
"That's it."
"I still write it on the board every year."
"It was sort of a revelation to me at the time," Stevie continued, looking across the sunken courtyard, past the musicians who were returning to their seats to start another set, toward Tickles 'n Giggles, a store that sold overpriced children's wear on the other side. Waiting for Leo to get her coat, she had been mentally evaluating the design of Galleries Portáge.

How visually exciting are the spaces?
How interesting is the sequencing of space?
How original is the design?
How visually literate was the architect?
How honest are the material choices?
How careful was the construction?

To each she had ticked off "not very."
Nan, her shoulders wrapped in a shawl, had joined her. "Doing a crit?" she had asked.
"Can't help it."
Nan, too, let her eyes travel over the interior surfaces. "Too bad they didn't hire a local architect," she sighed. "The designers are from Baltimore. I guess they don't know any better."
"I've an aunt and uncle in Baltimore," Stevie responded, apropos of nothing. But she had been reminded of her own self-exile in the Maryland capital, which made her think of her conversation with Caitlin Clark about Michael's son before Caitlin had taken her unscheduled plunge in the water feature. Which made her think about Michael. Which made her ask Nan about her interview with the police the day before.

"Not much I could tell them," Nan had responded, shrugging.

"Well at least we know now the Guarneri wasn't the motive."

"Yes, I read it in today's paper. Perhaps, sadly, it was just some random act of violence after all."

Which had made Stevie think of Nan's introductory epigram in first year interior design. "At the time," she said, "it made me consider the interconnectedness of life, all the circumstances that seems like chance, but suggests design. Heavy stuff for the teenaged mind."

"I think Kerr used to teach something along those lines in his philosophy courses—somebody or other's proof for the existence of God based on the notion that the great complexity of creation could only be explained by the existence of some cosmic designer—God, in other words. Design, in effect, *is* everywhere."

"Including Michael's murder."

"I believe Kerr referred to this—in capital letters—as the Problem of Evil."

"I wasn't going that far." Stevie folded her arms over her chest. "I was just thinking that there *is* a motive for Michael's death and that someone planned it. It was designed."

Nan glanced at her watch.

"Had enough?" Stevie asked.

"Of our philosophical discussion?"

"No. Of the mall."

"Oh, I think so. I only came out of curiosity. Roger had the invitation. No one at the school got one. They probably sensed we wouldn't be wild about it."

"Where is Roger?"

"He thinks something in one of the appetizers is off. Have you noticed how few toilets they've incorporated into the design? And poor signage, too. Where's Leo?"

"In the same place, probably. He's supposed to be getting my coat, but he's taking a long time."

"Have you thought any more about our conversation yesterday?"

"About joining the department. A little." She flicked a glance at Nan. "I guess I should make up my mind soon, shouldn't I?"

Nan nodded. "Come over and talk again if you like. I think I have your umbrella, by the way."

Stevie thought back to the morning. She had been so fed up when she'd left Johns Mayhew, she barely knew what she was doing. Only when she had deposited a fulminating Merritt at her house and driven instead to Leo's rather than immediately face her mother with evidence of Michael's obtuseness did she realize what she had to have, what she needed, and what she needed to give.

Well, it had been a while. And Leo was—why did this surprise her?—good. Goody, goody, good. Pyrotechnics, shooting stars, thunderbolts, steamy passages from Jackie Collins novels—that sort of good.

Here was a reason to stay in Winnipeg.

"How about if I let you know early next week?" she said to Nan.

"You're looking very flushed suddenly, dear."

Stevie started. "Am I? Oh. Warm in here."

Nan gathered her shawl about her and raised an eyebrow. "You're much too young for the change. Anyway, I think I'll go and loiter around the men's. If I can find it. Oh, and here's Leo. Have you been to the washroom?" she asked him.

Leo looked like an offended five-year-old. "No, I—"

"Never mind," Nan interrupted airily and disappeared into the milling crowd.

"Was there a line-up at the coat check?" Stevie asked.

"Not bad. But I was looking around for Axel." Leo held up her coat. "I wanted to talk to him about something."

"What?" Stevie turned and put an arm in one sleeve.

"He was wondering why the Clarks got bequests in Michael's will or whatever-it-is. Or does Merritt know now? I haven't seen either of them since the swim-athon. Did Caitlin tell her, if she could get a word in edgeways?"

"Caitlin didn't even know." Stevie turned and began to button up. "The lawyer hadn't called her yet. So she had two poolside surprises."

"Is she okay?"

"Caitlin? She's fine. Her dress isn't. Hopefully, she didn't swallow any of the water."

With the onlookers standing around useless as stones, Stevie had taken a dripping Caitlin to the washroom and emptied the paper towel dispenser trying to dry her off, which didn't endear either of them to the rest of the women in the toilet with wet hands. She then took some of Caitlin's soggy money and appealed to a salesclerk in a Bathtique store to sell her an enormous beach towel, even though officially the shops weren't open to trade during the gala opening. Caitlin had remained surprisingly composed after the attack, despite the humiliation of a public dunking. Stevie thought at first news of Michael's gift was working as an emollient, but while they waited for a taxi, a towel-wrapped and teeth-chattering Caitlin said she was more numbed by it all than anything. Guy will be delighted, she allowed, rolling her eyes. Have you talked with your brother recently? Stevie had probed, wondering if Caitlin knew Guy was under some suspicion. No, she'd replied sharply. And, she added, anger surfacing for a single instant, "the little shit was supposed to meet me here and hasn't shown up."

"So, did you find Axel?" Stevie asked as Leo pushed the door open for her.

"No," he replied as they stepped outside onto the mall's rear plaza, which abutted the *Citizen*'s back parking lot. "Maybe he took Merritt home before she turned the event into a wacky pool party."

A wind had arisen in the time they'd been in the mall, drying the pavement so that water remained only in places where poor workmanship and the whims of nature had left depressions.

"What was it you wanted to ask Caitlin about in the first place?" Leo asked, hopping over a puddle, feeling in his jacket pocket for his car keys.

"About Michael's son," Stevie replied, going around, rather than over. She put a hand over her eyes. Bits of wind-blown newsprint, binder twine, and dead leaves were whipping around her.

"What would she know about it?"

"They were at the Curtis together, remember?"

Leo stopped suddenly. "Would you mind if we went up to the newsroom for a few minutes?"

"Sure, let's just get out of this wind." She rubbed a dirt particle from her eye.

"This way." Leo gestured to what in the faint light looked like a black hole cut into the centre of the *Citizen*'s backside. "What did you learn?"

"The mother was from some ultra-conservative German family. She insisted on studying in the States. Probably so she could have some fun. And she did, according to Caitlin. So when *it* happened, the family came and got her and locked her up in a tower. Where she could let down her hair no more."

"Name?" Leo pushed open what looked to Stevie like something out of the days of ice-wagons and street cars, a crudely constructed wooden door with chipped green paint that had set within it yet a smaller door. It was this one they stepped through.

"Dankmar, I think," Stevie replied, hiking her skirt, sensing her pantyhose shredding on the chipped wooden frame.

She found herself in a storage room illuminated by a single lightbulb. In the shadows were battered blackened newsboxes, squat and ponderous, crowded like tombstones in a midnight cemetery. Her nostrils filled suddenly with the odour of dust and something chemical.

"It's ink," Leo responded to her bout of sniffing. "And anxiety."

They moved down a short passage toward an interior door, then stepped from the gloom into the front lobby's blaze of light. The torch-shaped wall sconces and the vaguely Egyptian design of the lobby reminded Stevie of a mausoleum. Past the revolving door to the street, it was pitch. Their footsteps echoed hollowly on the marble floor.

"The kid goes by his mother's name," Stevie continued, noting the skirl of the ancient elevator as Leo pressed the button.

"But if this Dankmar woman was such a party girl, how do we know Michael was even the father?"

Stevie watched the red indicator light over the elevator flash 4, then 3, then 2.

"Well, I guess Michael was satisfied that he was," she replied.

"Mmm."

The elevator thumped to a halt and she stepped in. "I've never been in the *Citizen* newsroom before."

"Well, you're in for a treat." Leo pressed 4. "Believe me."

Stevie sniffed the air in the confined space. A new, but familiar, scent assaulted her nostrils. A perfume. She couldn't place it. "So why did you want to come up here?" she asked, flicking a glance at Leo.

"I want to check one of the files for background. I have an interview tomorrow."

"On a Sunday?"

"A reporter's work is never done."

Stevie frowned. "Something to do with Michael?"

The door opened. Leo ushered her out into a tiny lobby space with a plate glass door opposite. "Sort of. Yes." He gave her a funny look.

"What?"

"I'm going out to the country." She watched him press a sequence of buttons on the door lock. "I'm going to visit a monastery."

"A monastery? But—"

Her words drowned in the lock's noisy rasp. Leo pushed the door open.

"But—"

Her words were drowned again. Only this time, they were drowned in the din of a bone-chilling sequence of screams. Stevie knew where she had smelled that perfume before.

31

Déjà Vu All Over Again

Leo watched Axel, his arm like a plaid bear's around Merritt's overpadded shoulders, half-dragging her through the library door to the staff lounge beyond. It crossed his mind to wonder why the library lights were on, but he was so glad to have Merritt and her shrieking piehole out of the newsroom that he let the thought fade to black. What's with women and this screaming thing? Do they learn it from the movies, or is it natural? Yes, Guy was dead. But, as he and Axel were frantically calling the police and trying to get a message to Martin at Galleries Portáge, Merritt kept erupting into these bizarre ululations. Finally, Axel grabbed her and crushed her to him so hard his white shirt was imprinted with a transfer of her made-up face.

She's grooving on this, he thought. It's the Joy of Histrionics.

Leo was proud of Stevie—she was made of sterner stuff, or different stuff, at least. But he was worried, too. Merritt's screams, so sharp once he and Stevie had dashed into the newsroom, Axel's unreadable face when he turned to them, the half-shadowed room, some strangely familiar but unpleasant tang in the atmosphere, had frozen her like a small animal on a night highway. She'd known without being told. It was all he could do to make her sit. He had practically had to fold her onto the nearest spot, a step on the corkscrew staircase that ran up to the composing room on the fifth floor. She was there now, facing away from him and the body at the front of the newsroom, half hidden behind the iron fretwork.

The room was garish, sickly green under the fluorescent lights. He'd swept his arm over the whole bank of switches when he'd realized, slower than Stevie, what was going on. He took a deep breath and dashed toward Guy's desk.

"He's dead," Axel had intoned.

Leo stared at him.

"Well, don't look at me." A scowl crossed Axel's face.

"Better than looking at him. Marginally."

"What are you doing up here anyway?"

"More to the point, what are *you* doing up here?"

"Merritt was going to clean out her desk. She's quitting."

Before Leo could open his mouth again, Merritt had opened hers. Axel carted Merritt off. Then he and Axel hit the phones. Now he was going to see for himself. Twice in one week I'm doing meet'n'greet with the unexpectedly deceased, he thought.

This is not healthy.

The sight of Guy lifeless, however, had none of the sudden shock he'd felt when Frank had raised the lights on Michael's corpse. If anything, Guy appeared to be slumbering like some narcoleptic office worker who couldn't help his head falling to his computer keyboard. His eyes were even closed. Michael's eyes had been open, staring. That had been the worst. Had Guy died with his eyes closed? Could you if you were being strangled? Or had the killer closed the lids?

What sick delicacy.

It was clearly a strangling. It didn't take a close examination to see the bruising on either side of the neck above the shirt collar. And there was bruising, too, along the forehead just below the hairline. He glanced at the blank computer screen. Had his head been smashed against the thick glass?

And what had he been doing here? Why hadn't he been at Galleries Portáge? Clearly, he'd been dressed for it. His usual fucking little preppy tweed jacket wasn't hugging the back of his chair. The jacket of an expensive-looking blue business suit was. Guy's shirt was blazing white; the tie, what Leo could see of it, striped and understated. What had the devious little shit been up to in the newsroom? The only thing on his desktop was the Saturday Go! section with some angry blue-pencilling around misspelled words, the blue pencil itself, and a coffee mug, clean, with *Pop A Zit!* on the side. Leo itched to open the desk drawers, but thought better of it. He bent down to run his eyes over the desk's surface to see if a trail of disturbed dust would indicate the removal of something telling, but, of course, Guy's desk was clean as a whistle. Where other newsroom denizens let their desks become encrusted with grime, Guy, the little tightass, would regularly trot over the men's washroom and come back with a soapy paper towel to wipe down his surfaces.

And the computer was switched off. Had it been all evening? He didn't dare touch it to see if it were still warm. Had Guy been working at something? Had the killer switched off the machine with the same sort of peculiar care that led him—or her?—to close the dead man's lids?

When they began phoning, Leo had glanced at Axel's powerful hands a moment too long when he lifted the receiver. Axel caught the look, understood, glared at him. He put his hand over the cup of the phone and snapped: "Fuck you. Don't even think it."

But Leo thought it.

He walked over to a computer terminal that had been left switched on. He had an idea: try to access Guy's computer and see if he had been editing or writing anything that would explain why he would forego sucking-up possibilities at Galleries Portáge for work. He typed in his own access code, RLF322. His parents may have anglicized their last name from Fabiani to Fabian, but that didn't stop them saddling him with the horrible moniker Raffaele Leonardo. The number 322 was for an apartment on River Avenue he'd lived in when he'd started at the *Zit*. He waited while the computer whirred and clicked. Stevie suddenly appeared at his side, taking one of the half-broken swivel chairs.

"Are you okay?" he asked, noting she kept her coat wrapped tightly around her.

"No."

"Do you want to sit with Merritt and Axel while I wait for the police?"

"I'd rather be with you."

Leo wanted to lick every inch of her body. But it wasn't the time or place.

"What are you doing?"

"Trying to see what Guy might have been up to." He tapped in a command.

"I have something to tell you."

He took his eyes off the screen. "Oh, god, what now? You're always telling me stuff. I never have anything to tell you. Apparently, I'm an open book."

"Merritt is carrying Guy's baby."

Leo couldn't suppress the gagging noise that rose from his throat. "How do you know?" he said.

"She told me yesterday, at the reception."

"When you two were upstairs?"

Stevie nodded.

Leo glanced back at the screen. He frowned. "Does Axel know?"

"Somehow I think he does."

"Shit!"

"What?"

"Oh, it's as I suspected. I'm denied access to Guy's desk."

Stevie turned her head just enough to see the screen. "What are you trying to do?"

"Everyone's got an access code to the computer system, and they're supposed to be secret."

"But they're not."

"Not really. I know the code of the woman who sits next to me. But there's not much point snooping because what most reporters have in their computers is boring. I tried an old code from a short stint I did on the night rim I did a few years ago but—" He read the words on the screen to her. "'Access denied.'

"You see, the higher up the food chain you go in this place the more access you have. A reporter can only access his own desk. A copy editor can access his own plus that of everyone equal to, and below, his station. A section head like Guy could access all that plus the other section heads—"

"Then—?"

"I need Kingdon."

He folded his arms and looked across the room at Guy's body slumped over his computer keyboard. More than anything he looked absurd, his death slumber a mockery of the indolence he often accused others of displaying. Who killed him?

Who?
What?
Where?
When?
Why?

And sometimes how?

He couldn't face the notion of Axel being involved.

"Perhaps this is like *Murder on the Orient Express*," he said, thinking aloud. "The whole newsroom did it!" He affected a clown's frown. "But, then, why didn't they ask me to join in?"

Stevie stared at him.

"Gallows humour."

Who, what, and where were givens. Guy Clark was murdered in the *Citizen* newsroom.

Why? Beats me.

And sometimes how. Strangulation. Easy. How did anyone know Guy was here? Good question. But how did whoever get in? The door had a coded lock. But staff, ex-staff, spouses, ex-spouses, lovers, ex-lovers, children, friends and neighbours all knew the combination. Even various nutbars, who for one reason or another liked to wander up to the newsroom at odd hours, knew it. Hell, the whole world was only six degrees of separation from knowing the combination to the *Zit*'s newsroom.

"What's the combination on the lock of the door we came through?" he asked Stevie.

"Don't *you* know? You opened it."

"Indulge me."

She frowned, thought about it. "One, three, five, two, four."

"See, even you know it."

"Hard not to notice. The sequence is so obvious."

"Although I suppose Guy could have *let* whoever in."

They lapsed into silence. Leo glanced again over the top of his computer at the slumberer and considered that since the shock had worn off and he wasn't exactly overwhelmed with grief at Guy's passing he ought to be working on the story. Hell, it was front-page stuff, a jesusly novelty: NEWSROOM SLAYING. But whose front page would it grace—or besmirch, as the case may be? The fucking *Examiner* had beat them to the punch with a new Sunday edition, and the news of ructions at the *Zit* would soon be crackling through the *Examiner*'s police squawkbox. For the *Zit*, on Monday, it would probably be five inches on page three—the journalistic equivalent of a discreet gentlemanly cough. And one of the members of League of Daves would probably do the reporting.

As if following his logic, a phone rang on a desk across the room. Then another.

"Here we go," he said to no one in particular. "Word's out."

The phones were reinforced by a grinding buzz like that of a giant insect.

"Martin, at last," Leo rose. Another phone rang, this one next to him. His hand hesitated over the receiver.

"Leave it," Martin snapped, rounding the corner.

Yet another phone began ringing two feet away. Kingdon ducked into the telephone operator's booth and with a kind of controlled franticness ran his eyes over the switchboard. Finally, he yanked at something and the ringing stopped. Face red from exertion, he stepped from the booth. His eyes darted to the far corner of the room.

"Are you quite sure Mr. Clark is—"

No, Martin, he's trying out a new yoga position.

No, Martin, he's tapping out a story with his nose.

No, Martin, he meditating according to the principles of Guru Conrad Black.

"Yes, Martin, he's dead. There's no doubt."

"I see."

Leo watched as Martin's eyes were drawn again toward the spectacle of a dead body in his newsroom. He seemed suddenly confounded by indecision, rubbing his hands and rising on the balls of his feet as though about to speed off somewhere, though not to the sanctuary of the management offices where Guy's body lay uncomfortably close. Finally Martin moved to a chair near Leo and sat tentatively on its edge. It was the first time Leo had seen him sit down in the newsroom.

"And you phoned the police?" he said in a vacant tone.

No, Martin, Stevie and I have been too busy making love on this desk.

No, Martin, Stevie and I decided to phone all our friends in Australia.

No, Martin, Stevie and I are completely stupid and don't know how to behave in a crisis.

"Yes, Martin, of course."

"Ah."

"Do you have access to Guy's desk?"

Martin's puzzled face looked up at him.

"His computer. Can you access it?"

"Oh? Yes..."

"Then call it up."

"I don't think—"

"Oh, for Christ's sake, Martin. Guy might have been writing something. It might be a fucking clue."

Martin hesitated. He pulled a handkerchief from somewhere past his dress coat and began mopping at a line of perspiration along his forehead.

"Take off your coat and stay awhile," Leo said.

Martin did as instructed, wheeled over to the computer terminal and then, collecting himself, began to tap on the keys, one plump hand covering the other so as not to reveal his sign-on code, as if anyone gave a shit.

The immediate result was disappointing. There were only a few entries in Guy's desk, each encoded with the time of day the story was last handled. There were no entries at all for Saturday.

"Try the Go! desk or the city desk." Leo leaned into the computer screen. "Maybe he finished his story and sent it elsewhere."

But there were no stories in the directories with Guy Clark's initials on them to indicate their origin. Nor were there any in half a dozen other directories that seemed possible destinations. Finally, Leo suggested calling up the "kill" file, the repository of all the old, used, or unwanted stories generated like so much garbage in an abundant society, but fully accessible only to senior editors. A simple press of the "kill" button on the far right side of the keyboard did not destroy a story so much as consign it to a computer limbo, where it was allowed to linger for a few hours (in case someone contemplated resurrection) before it forever vanished from the system.

With no one having worked at the *Citizen* all day Saturday, the kill file should have been empty. But it wasn't. With excitement rising, Leo watched the initials GXC flash on the screen next to a line of shorthand information, the title and length of story, and time of consignment. He had been correct. Guy had been writing something after all.

"Bigstuff," he muttered, reading out the story's slug. What a fucking ego. No clue to the contents. And the contents were few. The length of story was indicated at 3.8 inches, barely more than a few sentences. Still, he thought, impatiently leaning over Martin and typing in instructions himself, it might be a lead, more than enough to suggest the nature of Guy's story. But when he entered the command, the computer flashed "audit trail closed."

"Shit! Why can't we call up the story?"

"Because, Mr. Fabian, that's the nature of the kill file. The point of it is to get rid of the refuse. We can't keep everything forever. The computer system would clog."

Leo groaned. "But, Martin, the killed story stays in the system for a few hours—"

"One hour."

"—and could be retrieved in an emergency."

"True. But I don't know how."

Or you won't tell me, you fat little twerp. "Then someone else must know. Alcock! Alcock must know. Where's a phone book?"

"That man is *persona non grata*. He fouled my desk."

"Urine's supposed to be good for walnut."

"Well, Mr. Fabian," Martin drawled. "You've got five minutes before it vanishes. Look at the time. The story was killed at 9:06. It's now 10:01."

A minute later Leo had Alcock on the phone. It took another two minutes to calm his rage. The former city editor was pickled yet lucid, not unlike a typical afternoon in the newsroom. "Just shut the fuck up, Ray, and give me the codes."

"Mr. Alcock," Martin picked up an extension. "Give him the goddamn codes. Now!"

The squawking stopped. Leo typed in the sequence as directed. The computer whirled through its motions, and then the story flashed complete onto the screen.

They stared at the green glow. Leo felt like he had been punched. All the air went out of him. "Shit!" He slammed the phone back on the hook, cutting Alcock off in mid-expletive. "It's gibberish."

On the screen was exactly 3.8 inches of assorted letters and numbers in a nonsensical stream.

"Oh, well," Martin said airily. Leo stared at him. Martin looked relieved!

"Maybe it's the result of his head hitting the keyboard," Stevie suggested.

Martin seemed to take in her presence for the first time.

"Stevie Lord, a friend of mine. Stevie, Martin Kingdon, ME of this place." Leo gestured one to the other. *And no, Martin, she isn't someone you hired, then completely forgot about.*

"How do you do?" Martin intoned, rising.

And neither is this a tea party.

"You must excuse me. I have something to attend to in my office."

Leo watched him take a wide berth through the sea of desks. Without thinking, Leo darted after Kingdon and caught him just before he could disappear into his inner sanctum.

"Martin," he said in a low voice, blocking the way. "I know why you wanted me off the story."

"And why would that be?"

"You thought that I would dig too deep." He paused. "Do you remember Chappaquiddick?"

Martin regarded him stonily.

"You know, Mary-Jo Kopechne. Ted Kennedy. Car accident. Ted's friends do a nice little cover-up."

"And your point, Mr. Fabian?"

Leo took a deep breath. "Guy knew you'd organized all the falsification in Tom Rossiter's death. He knew because his sister had told him, and she knew because Michael had told her. Ten years ago, you thought you could curry favour with your nephew, Tom Rossiter's son and heir, by covering up what was, in fact, manslaughter. Four people dead, one injured. But it didn't work. Michael despised his father, and disdained you for being so venal."

Martin pushed him out of the way. "I could have you *fired*, Mr. Fabian."

"You could."

"I *should* have fired you last spring."

"An angel interceded."

"Ah, you know. And I thought my nephew preferred circumspection in his acts of kindness."

"I had another source."

"In any case, your intercessor is dead." Martin sank into the shadows of his office.

"And two of the people who know about your shenanigans are dead," Leo called after him.

Martin's face reappeared out of the gloom. "Are you blackmailing me, Mr. Fabian? Angling to be city editor, perhaps, now that we seem to be without one?"

"No, Martin. I don't work that way."

Kingdon grunted. "When the police arrive, you can tell them where I am."

The door missed Leo's face by an inch.

The newsroom seemed suddenly claustrophobic. Leaving Stevie to her own thoughts, he wandered to the back and stared blankly for what had to be the hundredth time in his so-called career at an ancient wall display of miniature front pages gathered under the rubric, World's Hundred Best Newspapers.

Smart move, Fabian. Now you'll be at the top of the shit list until pigs have wings. Your byline and the front page—or any page—shall be strangers one unto another. Yea, and forevermore.

His eyes focussed on the mini-*Osservatore Romano*, then passed from the mini-*Times of India* to the mini-*Citizen* of 1950s vintage. Maybe it had been one of the hundred best earlier in the century. But then Michael Rossiter had sold it. Later, a flock of Bay Street buzzards bought it. After they'd finished eviscerating it, they sold it to a Calgary Christer, who would probably wring the last penny out of it by shrinking the news hole, downsizing the staff, and inflating the advertising. And pussies like Martin Kingdon would be there to aid and abet.

A great crashing noise broke into his reverie. When Leo turned to look, he saw Frank Nickel beating his fist impatiently against the glass of the newsroom door.

He scowled as Leo pushed the door open. "You again."

"It seems I have a nose for news, Frank."

"Who's the unlucky stiff?"

Leo permitted himself a facetious smile. Frank growled.

"I hate to tell you this, Frank. But it's someone probably in your top ten suspects list for a certain other murder."

"Who?"

"Guy Clark."

"Shit!"

Leo pointed Stevie to the doorway at the opposite end of the library that led to the unofficial staff lounge. "I'll be with you in a sec," he said.

Frank had more or less ordered them out of the newsroom. Leo had helpfully alerted his brother-in-law to the aborted "bigstuff" story, presented Guy's remarkably tidy desktop with a Vanna-style flourish, and was about to pull out one of the desk drawers for a look-see when Frank karate-chopped his forearm. A coincident distant banging on the lobby door was a signal the forensics had come to take holiday snaps and grub around, so all superfluous living characters—Leo and Stevie—got the boot. Leo neglected to tell Frank that Martin was in his private office, perhaps quaking.

He disappeared into the forest of green filing cabinets in the library, pulled out a drawer marked "T," which, thank god, was at eye level, and began fingering quickly through the envelopes of old clippings organized under subject.

No "Trappist." Damn.

"Religious orders"? "Roman Catholic Church"? He looked down the tight tidy row of coffin-like drawers. No wonder they used to call newspaper libraries morgues.

"Religious orders, Roman Catholic Church"?—too broad.

"Our Lady of the Assumption"?

"Our"?

"Lady"?

"Assumption, Our Lady of"?

Where was Vera when you needed her?

He rounded a corner to find the "A"files and nearly tripped over a floor-level file drawer that some idiot hadn't bothered to close. Grabbing the handle of a higher file drawer to right himself, his eyes fell on the door that opened on one of the building's interior stairwells. You could exit the library that way; the stairs would take you down four flights to the musty back room Stevie and he had passed through earlier. But you couldn't enter the library (and therefore the newsroom) by coming *up* the stairs. He had tried it once. The door was always locked on the stairwell side. Leo glanced up at the library's bank of fluorescent lights. He wondered again: Had they been left on since...yesterday? Or...? Is this the way the killer left? Through the door, down the stairs, out the back?

He pulled out the "A" drawer and began to rummage. It would have to be someone familiar with the eccentricities of *Zit* HQ, he mused.

About five hundred people.

Well, that narrows it to a Pakistani village.

Still, four hundred were home, probably watching television. Fewer than a hundred—from editorial—were grazing at Galleries Portáge.

That narrows it to a Saskatchewan village.

And 9:06. Where was everyone at 9:06? Everyone was everywhere at 9:06. Who could account for individual movements at a mall? All he could remember was Paul Richter murdering a clock with his eyes at precisely 8:00. And the Krystle Carrington/Alexis Colby memorial slugfest about half an hour later.

Leo found "Assumption, Our Lady of." It was like Guy Clark's byline file: thin as Melba toast. He opened it quickly. Looked like a couple of lifestyle features (monks have lifestyles?) plus a couple of newsy-looking pieces. He slipped the file into his inside pocket and walked toward the back. Removing files from the building was forbidden, but what the hell, worse crimes had been committed at the *Zit*. One of them recently.

Still, whoever it was had taken a fair chance. There were other people out on streets, in parking lots. Or looking out of windows, as Axel was doing now in the back room, his hand clasped behind his back, staring out at the black sky.

"Were the lights on in the library when you two came in?"

Neither Axel or Merritt answered. Axel's only movement extended to the pushing of a wedding ring around and around his third finger with his thumb, an unconscious stroking that seemed to mesmerize Merritt, who monopolized the centre of the battered couch, her legs tucked under her, worrying a bright lacquered nail.

"Axel?" He addressed the ponytail.

"What?" Axel's voice snapped.

"Lights. Library. On or not on when you came in?"

There was a hesitation. "On," he said finally.

"You're sure."

"Yes, I'm sure. There was the bank of lights on over the front of the newsroom, and the library lights. Also on."

Leo looked around the room, at the couch where he had had his monumentally stupid tryst with Julie Olsen, where he'd lain with a sore back three days before. Once, too, there had been a talented writer who after lunch every day turned the battered couch to the window and fell into untroubled sleep. Finally, his snores reached the wrong ears and he was sacked, although afternoon naps were the least of his sins.

Leo glanced at Stevie, lost in thought, plucking at some loose stuffing poking from the arm of her chair. He returned his eyes to Axel's back, to the expanse of Manitoba tartan. Ironic, my ass. The jacket was probably his father's. The fucker was so maxed out on his credit cards he couldn't buy something new.

He sighed. He'd known Axel forever. It was Axel who'd got him to the hospital when he'd hit a tree on the monkey trails in Assiniboine Park on his three-speed after drinking a quart of Southern Comfort. It was Leo who calmed a raving Axel lost in the middle of the frozen prairie at three o'clock of a January morning after doing 'shrooms by pointing out that all they had to do was follow their own ski trails back through the freshly fallen snow. It was Axel who kept him from climbing the water tower on Kenaston Boulevard when he was tripping. And Axel who convinced him to buy a motorcycle (so he could borrow it; then watch it slide into the Red). And Axel who made him play drums in his (very) short-lived punk band, Axel and the Rods. Leo still had the T-shirt.

"So tell me," he said. "Where were you at 9:06 this evening?"

Book 6

Sunday, October 2

32

Bees

Manitoba: Horizontality Beckons You. Leo flashed by the sign on the Trans Canada—the handiwork of the advertising firm that had produced the paper's failed Pop A Zit campaign. Only political connections could be keeping them in business, he thought, turning his eyes to the (admittedly horizontal) landscape. The weather had recast itself once again. As far as his city eyes could tell, the periodic rain of the past several days had left little trace on the countryside other than to remove the pall of dust from harvesting or clear the haze of burning stubble. Late-morning sun beat the shorn grain fields into gold, flamed the willows canary yellow, and reddened his face and the arm he rested on the open window of the Land Rover. Breathing in the sweet air, he imagined he was in Australia where summer was just arriving. But when he looked up, winter's approach was all too evident. The incandescent blue of summer was gone. The sky was pearly, whitening. Clouds raked northwards with frail fingers. A black chevron of geese crossed high and—this was the discouraging bit—south. And, to lend journalistic authority, the car radio reported the first frost.

Traffic was light. Everyone had to be at church. Or sleeping in. Or milking cows. Or whatever the hell it was people did in rural Manitoba on Sunday mornings. Sleeping in with Stevie would have been his Sunday-morning choice. He would have postponed this trip to Our Lady of the Assumption before you could say two Hail Marys and an Our Father, but Stevie, understandably (he supposed), had found Saturday evening more vivid than just a trip to the mall.

Of course, it hadn't helped that he and Axel had come to blows, of a sort. Axel had responded to Leo's 9:06 question by flying off the handle and punctuating his critique of Leo's "unfounded suspicions" by socking Leo in the stomach, which Leo unthinkingly returned. Further punches might have been exchanged, but Merritt apparently decided shrieking would once again have an effect. Which it did.

Where had Axel been at 9:06? The answer, so far, was *none of your fucking business, Leo.*

He sucked in his stomach. It hurt. What with his back still a bit tender from Wednesday's injury, it had not been a good week for his midsection. Axel, he presumed, was in less discomfort. Leo's fist had felt like it was hitting a wall. All those ab crunches Axel had been doing had had their effect. What hurt more was being hit by your oldest friend. He almost wished Stevie hadn't filled him in on the gloomy details of Merritt's pregnancy on the ride home. He would have preferred to think of Axel as just wildly pissed off with him for hefty teasing than actually feeling trapped by an awful truth and lashing out.

Oh, to hell with it.

Leo stepped on the accelerator. Maybe getting out of the corrupt old city into the pristine countryside was the tonic. All those earnest hard-working folk growing healthful canola and going to the Protestant church of their choice on Sundays.

He flashed by a Rural Crime Watch Area sign.

Or maybe not.

He was almost disappointed when his journey ended. After he'd driven an hour straight over flat terrain, the road had veered beckoningly toward a line of smoky hills and began to meander, rising lazily on ancient glacial mounds, dropping softly into sheltered valleys. He eased up on the accelerator and savoured the peaceful seclusion, the relaxed human scale of the unhorizontal landscape. A few fat cows dotted patchwork fields; the sun glinted off the metal roofs of distant silos; gravel byways wound past groves of trees toward comfortable-looking farm houses. He almost missed the sign. He made one wrong turn, fooled by an old telephone post high on a hill that stood against the sky for all the world like a crucifix. Then, further along the main road, he saw the rough brown plaque with the word *monastère* burnt into the wood and then, in the middle distance, the monastery itself, a large two-storey box of sandy-coloured brick, as utilitarian looking as a modern high school.

He parked near a cluster of fir trees and hauled himself out of the car, stretching after the long ride, taking the kink out of his back. Though the monastery was also a working farm, there was no evidence of habitation. He travelled up the gravel road connecting the monastery grounds to the main highway and admired the neat fields, the carefully tended flower beds with their borders of whitewashed stones, and the sturdy white barns, but he wondered if some mysterious race had created this tiny perfect civilization and then abandoned it. The breeze carried the only evidence of animal life—the tweedle-dum of a jay.

Across the gravel lot, he noted a sign designating part of one of the low white buildings as the information booth. Were they recruiting? But the commercial element of the monastic enterprise hit Leo with force when he stepped over the threshold into a dark, cramped room and inhaled the peculiar suffocating odour of church annexes, a mixture of wax and cleaning fluids and old books, remembered from his childhood. There was a glass display booth and a cash register and shelf upon cluttered shelf of plaster statuary, candles, rosaries, and other keepsakes, most of it cheap and garish, and of course, rows of jars of Trappist honey and Trappist cheese. Leo found himself so depressed by the tackiness of it all that he didn't hear footsteps coming down the hall. He flinched when he turned and saw through the shadows an apparition, a pale young man, short and thin, with a knobby skull visible through the bristles of black short-cropped hair. The eyes behind the hornrims glittered with curiosity. Leo stared at him for a moment longer than was comfortable, then said, "I have an appointment with the novice master, with Father James Hart."

"Of course. Yes. We have been waiting for you. Follow me, please."

Halting syntax and the trace of an accent suggested that English was not his first language. But before Leo could add anything, he found himself hurrying through the door and down a path behind the young man at a speed unseemly for a monk. He slowed down enough to hold the door open for Leo and then led him at a more reverential pace through the main building.

Like the exterior, the interior was utilitarian. The halls, with their off-white walls and grey terrazzo flooring, were clean and smart but they weren't dissimilar to those of contemporary office buildings in any urban centre. Boring, Leo thought. But what did he expect? Medieval French masonry in the middle of the prairies? He reflected as he was shown into a small dark room with a very ornate table that the *Zit* feature stories on the Trappists were poor preparation for reality. Such phrases as "strict and austere observance of the Benedictine rule," "a communal life of prayer and retreat," "exclusively contemplative life" seemed psychologically deceptive. They suggested something idealized and rhapsodic in the best romantic tradition. Instead, what he had seen so far seemed much more ordinary—a factory farm with a gift shop. Had Michael himself actually been attracted to this?

After a moment he was joined by his host, who came quietly into the room on slippered feet and carefully closed the door. Father James looked to be in his mid-forties. He was tall, over six feet, and heavy-set in his white robe and black scapular, with big hands that enveloped Leo's in a powerful handshake. In proportion to his body, however, his head was small, and its shape was like that of a perfect tonsured egg, cheeks and chin all silkily plump. His eyes, which seemed to wander as if they couldn't focus, were disconcerting. Though the room was in shadow, his grey-blue irises captured a ray of light from the room's only window, and reflected it glassily.

They sat at the far end of the table nearest the window. It framed a view of hills and trees of such picture-postcard intensity that Leo couldn't help remarking that its beauty seemed almost contrived. He regretted saying so as soon as it slipped from his mouth and then, with shock added to embarrassment, he realized suddenly that Father James was blind. The wandering eyes were sightless eyes; the hills and trees existed only to the ear and the hand and the intake of breath. He apologized, but Father James was not offended. He laughed openly and agreed that it was likely true; as memory served, there was something almost artificial about the view from the window. The autumn weather engaged them in small talk for a few moments and then, after an awkward pause, Father James said, "Father Abbot gave me news of the tragedy yesterday, only a few moments before you telephoned, as it happened. I'm afraid we're slow to get the newspapers here. And then only Father Abbot is privy to them. I take it you were a friend of Michael's?"

"Well, more of an acquaintance." Barely. "Were you told that I write for the *Citizen?*"

"Yes." A small frown creased his forehead. "But I'm not sure—"

"I'm looking mostly for background." A classic journalistic line if ever there was one.

"Well—"

"I won't quote you by name." Classic line number two. "I just want to understand the person that Michael was. And this—" He gestured vaguely around the room. "—was obviously going to be an important step in his life."

"Yes, it was."

"Then—?"

"I hope I can trust you to be careful of our privacy."

"Of course." Number three.

Leo tugged at the coil of notebook in his shirt pocket. The man was blind. But his hearing was probably acute.

"If you don't mind, I'll jot down a few notes."

"Well—"

"Just for my own reference." Number four. "As I said, you won't be quoted."

Father James's frown straightened. He nodded in assent.

"I think," Leo continued after a moment to collect his thoughts, "it will come as a complete surprise to people who knew Michael that he was going to do…this." He lifted his arms to indicate the universe of the monastery, forgetting for the moment that such a gesture would go unnoted. "Hardly anyone seems to have been aware that he was planning to make such a—" He groped for the word. "—drastic change in his life."

Father James clasped his hands on the tabletop and looked across at Leo, his eyes in motion as though seeking something on which to alight. It had an odd assessing effect. Leo felt exposed in a way he wouldn't have thought possible with a sightless person.

"You use the word 'drastic,'" Father James replied. "Perhaps it does seem drastic. But Michael's been on his way here for some time."

"You mean he had been thinking about taking this step for some time."

The monk nodded. "So it's not as abrupt as it might appear. Although I wonder a little at Michael not talking with friends and family about it. He was looking forward to joining us and I would have expected him to share his feelings, his joy."

"Maybe he never got the chance. Or he changed his mind. It's not the usual career path these days."

"Admittedly."

"Then what the hell was he up to? Oh, sorry."

Father James smiled broadly. "We're human. Hell, damn, shit. There, feel better?"

Leo smiled. "A bit."

"Father Abbot can't hear us. And anyway, he can curse a blue streak when he's provoked. Atones for it later. As do we all. Of course you won't print that."

Leo lifted his pen guiltily. "Of course not."

"What Michael was doing here," the monk continued, "was seeking God."

Oh, Him, Leo wanted to say. He wondered if he had the imagination for this. His own religious education flashed before him like a fifteen-second commercial. His father, nominally Roman Catholic, dying when Leo is seven. His mother, nominally Church of England in the old country, having joined the United Church in Winnipeg, making him go to Sunday school. Leo rebelling at age eleven arguing—typical for a kid his age—that the stories about Christ have about as much substance as Santa Claus and the Easter bunny. Does Mom pack him off to that awful church-basement Sunday school anyway? No, she buys his argument, or at least pretends to, then stops going herself.

"Seeking God," Leo echoed flatly.

"Yes, indeed. That's what we do here. Seeking God is our business."

"You're sure not what I was expecting."

"And what were you expecting?"

"Oh, someone a little...dour. Pious, perhaps."

"You're accusing me of impiety?"

"Well...I..." Then he noted Father James's smile. "No," he laughed. "But somehow you don't seem to me to be typical."

"Now who among us is typical?"

"Well, from what I've read, the typical Trappist monastery isn't exactly the United Nations. Most have rural backgrounds, lots still come from Europe like—and I'm guessing here—the fellow who met me at the gatehouse. Most join when they're quite young, and, if you don't mind my saying, without a heck of a lot of post-secondary education. It's not a profile Michael Rossiter fits. And somehow I suspect you don't either."

Father James stroked his chin. "Well, I did come from Europe. That meets one of your criteria."

"But—"

"I was born in Ireland, but my family emigrated to the States after the war, when I was very young, to a place outside Boston. I had the typical Irish Catholic childhood, and my mother would have been thrilled if I'd shown any inclination to the priesthood, but I didn't. During the Vietnam War I moved up here. I lived in Vancouver and the last thing I did before I came here was complete a master's degree in psychology at the University of British Columbia."

"That seems a big leap."

"From Gestalt Prayer to Jesus Prayer in a single bound."

"Damascus experience?"

"Not quite. I exaggerate."

"But your Catholic upbringing was the groundwork. It helped."

"Didn't hurt."

"Then there are some similarities between you and Michael. He was educated and accomplished. So what would bring two talented modern guys to a place such as this, a small isolated community cut off from the world."

"As I said earlier, seeking God."

Leo groaned inwardly. "Is it really that simple?"

Father James nodded and added in an Irish brogue, "Yes, my son, it is that simple."

Leo laughed and made a few doodles in his notepad. "Did the two of you discuss his past at all?"

"Yes."

"Can I throw out a few half-baked notions?"

"I'm all ears." He smiled. "You have to be when you're blind."

Leo glanced up from his pad. "How about: he was running away from something? Or felt really guilty about something and wanted to atone, big time. Or wanted to feel purposeful rather than purposeless. Or thought the whole bloody world was just too much and wanted some fresh air."

"Things I might have said if I'd stayed in psychology," Father James responded. "Although I would have piled on the jargon, of course." He paused, closing his eyes and lifting his head to catch on his eyelids the warmth of the sun, which had begun to penetrate deeper into the room. "Look, if you think about it your way, you've reduced a life to a series of actions and reactions. I know what lay in Michael's past. Someone of his age who makes a decision like this has a 'past.' I had a 'past,' too. But I can assure you he was not running from anything, nor was I. He was coming *to* something—"

"But what he was coming to is a kind of circumscribed life, a life of silences and penances and permissions. It's like stepping from the twentieth century into the twelfth and to me that seems like denial, an avoidance of the world." He paused. "Sorry. Am I going too far?"

"Don't apologize. Michael and I had these very same sorts of talks. There were things he had to wrestle with."

"Does this mean you're giving credence to psychology after all?"

"Sounds like it, doesn't it? Look, we do make assessments. There are men who come here who we can tell fairly soon would not be suited to this sort of life."

"But was Michael really suited? It's not just that he had different talents, he was—" Leo wanted to say, a normal person. "—he was fairly social, outgoing. He seemed to like people. He liked women." He paused. "There's a child." He wanted to say child*ren*. "Did you know that?"

"Yes."

"And that's no problem?"

"No. You see, for a Trappist everything is altered at the gate of enclosure and it's altered forever. What happened in the past is of little consequence."

Maybe here in Trappistville, Leo thought. In the real world, the past had great power to intrude. He tried to imagine Michael Rossiter dressed in the uniform of a monk, waking up long before dawn, working in the fields, spending long hours in prayer or meditation, enduring an austere diet, the silences, the loneliness, the lack of sex.

"You can leave if you want, right?" Leo put the finishing touches on a World War I bi-plane in his notebook. "The decision to stay isn't final."

"Oh, no. During postulancy, either side may reject the other."

"And how long does that last?"

"Six months."

"Do you think he would have made it? Maybe all this was just a romantic impulse on his part." Although saying that, he thought about Michael relinquishing all that moolah, which seemed pretty damned final.

Father James gestured toward the room's interior. "Would you mind getting me a glass of water?"

"Sure." Leo swivelled his head around. The room had begun to feel warm. The sun, having travelled farther into the western sky, cast its rays deeper into the room, illuminating a large crucifix and a tapestry rendering of the monastery in a flat Grandma Moses style. At the end of the room, near the door, he saw what he hadn't noted before, a small counter and set of taps. He rose and located a couple of glasses.

"Michael was a seeker," Father James continued as Leo ran the water into the sink to chill it, "and I believe his search was sincere. Yes, I think he would have made it. Yes, he was educated and talented. But sometimes those things we call talents or abilities can be crosses. I think Michael was prevented from coming to Christ by his great possessions."

"I don't think he lived the high life, Father," Leo said over his shoulder.

"No, I mean his talents, his abilities, the musical, artistic side. These are great possessions."

"But you see these things as a burden. I'd say they made him the human being he was. By choosing to come here, he had to deny all kinds of stuff about himself."

"It's God who chooses."

Leo filled the glasses. "And are you sure that God had chosen Michael?"

"That I can't say for sure. I'm not party to another man's relationship to God. You see, that relationship here—one man to God—is primordial. The life here in the monastery is meant to enable a life of prayer and union with God. You make a break when you come here. It has to be God and God alone."

What lay unspoken between them like a shadow was Michael's unexpected death. Taking Father James's reasoning, Michael had not been chosen for a religious life after all. He had either been called away—and in a violent fashion—by the all-wise God of no-last-name or some great evil had intervened. Neither was an acceptable explanation. Michael's murder was not an occasion of beneficence or of malice. It had design, but the designer wasn't supernatural.

He set the glass of water before Father James in a pool of light cast by the sun. The monk's hand found the mark readily.

"I can see shapes if there is sufficient contrast between light and dark," he said without prompting. "But I've learned to depend more on other senses."

"This then is relatively recent."

"Relatively," he echoed. The monk's eyes, with their unresponsive pupils, seemed aimed at the middle of Leo's head, a vague shape among other varied vague shapes in the room. "It happened a couple of years ago. I had a severe reaction to a wasp sting and the result was damage to the optic nerve."

"Yikes."

"It's rare, though not unheard of."

"You keep bees here, don't you? And sell Trappist honey?"

"We've just started honey production again. The brother who had been in charge had been very ill. And I was never involved with the apiary in the past. No, this happened in one of the barns. I disturbed an angry wasp. I never knew I had an allergy. However," he added without irony, as though the explanation were obvious, "it was God's will."

Leo felt like kicking something. To hell with God's will. If Father James had gone into that barn a minute earlier or a minute later he might never have encountered the insect. It was no more God's will that Father James be blinded than it was God's will that Michael Rossiter be murdered by a blow to the head. Both events hinged on a series of circumstances that could at some point have been altered. God, whoever he was, didn't live in events such as these. He gave Father James an edited version: "I have trouble finding a divine purpose in tragedy."

"Perhaps I've phrased it too simply. I don't believe God's the author of my disability, but I believe it's His will that I find meaning within the changes it brought to my life."

"But what about Michael's death, his murder? How can we find meaning in this?"

"You're asking me to answer the most troubling question in all the world: reconciling the presence of evil in the world with the nature of God."

"Is this a tactful way of avoiding the question?"

Father James laughed. "Perhaps," he said. "But I look for meaning within the context of my faith in Jesus Christ. I'm not sure what I can do for you. I'm a seeker, too. My position here doesn't provide me with all the answers."

"But still, you think there might be some meaning in all of this."

"I think everything, ultimately, serves God's purpose."

Leo disagreed in spades but decided not to press it. He took a swallow of his neglected water. It was well water, a far cry from the chlorinated stuff that percolated through the city's arteries. This was how water was supposed to taste—cold and sweet. He put down the glass and looked at Father James, feeling as he did that an unbreachable gulf separated them, which it did, in a way. He decided on a more practical line of questioning.

"When was the last time you saw Michael?"

"Late May. He was here for a few days on a retreat."

It must have been a week or so after the Victoria Day holiday when he'd first met Stevie. Had Michael already set his mind on this momentous change in his life at that point? Had he been thinking about Our Lady of the Assumption while they stood around his yard and his house eating his food and drinking his liquor? He asked Father James the same questions in abbreviated form.

"He wrote Father Abbot a letter shortly afterwards asking permission to join our community in August. Normally there is an observership period where someone is integrated into the life of the community for a week to a month before postulancy, but Michael had already shown us he was ready during earlier retreats. We were looking forward to his arrival."

"And yet he didn't arrive in August."

Father James swallowed the last of his water. "A letter came shortly after the first one saying he was going to postpone his arrival."

"There was no sense, then, that he had changed his mind."

"No. He made clear that his decision to join us was firm. He would come in the fall."

And then Michael had gone off to Europe.

Leo tapped his pen against the side of his notebook. "And was that letter the last you heard from him?"

"No. A letter arrived Friday reconfirming his intention to join us. I gather he had spent longer in Europe than he had intended."

Leo thought with rising excitement back to his conversation with Sharon Bean. She had mentioned Michael going off to mail something on the day of his death. He thought, too, of the missing computer disks.

"Was it typewritten?"

Father James smiled. "I couldn't tell you. It was read to me."

"Of course. Sorry."

"Look, this has been a terrible tragedy. I was wondering if you might like to take a look around. It may help you understand Michael's decision."

Leo didn't think it would help at all, but what the hell.

"Sure," he said, rising from his chair. "Can I give you any help?"

"When we get outside I'll take your arm."

Later, as he drove back down the gravel road that led to the main highway, reminding himself that he had to make one stop in Charleswood, Leo considered that he might have come a little closer to understanding Michael's decision to join a religious community. Walking around the monastery grounds had helped. Would he have felt the same if the sky had been dark with rain or the landscape deadened by snow? Probably not. But on a day of high sun, fragile clouds, and air scented with hay and honey, he thought being in nature might be a fair exchange for the sacrifice of career and money and the other givens of modern life. Within this pattern of golden fields, working to the rhythms set by sun and soil, was the life that so many seek—community, good work, peace.

Or some such bullshit, he mused, composing parts of the story he intended to write when he returned to the city.

God, Not Mammon
Murder victim sought monastic life

It was a terrible irony, he thought, that Michael had been killed just when he had been about to die to the world anyway. Those who gained by his death would have soon gained by his retreat to the monastery. Similarly, anyone who felt loss would have shortly experienced that loss. Except, perhaps, for one person. Did someone have reason to fear Michael's retreat into silence, someone who knew of his plans?

33

Keys

It was well past noon before Liz crawled from bed. She had slept fitfully, dreaming violent dreams from which she would emerge in a sweat to fight for air, gasping, her mouth parched, her nostrils clogged by the desiccating atmosphere of a room sealed against nature. Something alien about the hardness of the bed, the clatter of carts in the hallway, the pattern of dark and light would alert her muddled brain that she wasn't in her own home, in her own bed. A sickening spasm of regret would follow. Then she would again sink into troubled sleep.

At 11:00 she awoke fully for the final time—tired, her head throbbing from hangover, unable to coax sleep's return. Drapes slung untidily across the ribbon window were poor filter to painful sunlight. To her ragged vision, the orange material seemed to bulge and glow as malevolently as a jack o'lantern while the rest of the room simmered in shadow, the shapes of the fake wood bureau, desk and table against the opposing wall blending into one horrible chocolate mass.

She had gone down to the hotel bar late in the evening, seeking an antidote to her restlessness, the long afternoon walk having done nothing to relieve her distress. She had had dinner in her room and then switched on the TV, but *Hockey Night in Canada* bored her silly, and the alternative programs—idiot American sitcoms—were worse. She eyed the instructions for ordering one of the adult movies through the cable, but watching a bunch of strangers mindlessly rutting held no enchantment. Perhaps with a lover—and a scoop of irony—it might have. But the lover was absent. So was the irony. She had turned back to her novel finally, but she had come to repent her choice. She had thrown *Anna Karenina* hurriedly into her bag when she left the house Friday evening thinking that a big fat read would be just the escape she needed. Had it been that long since she first read it? How could she have forgotten that it was the story of a woman who abandons her pompous husband for a passionate liaison with another man? Everything that she sought to push from her mind kept crowding back again and again as she turned the pages.

She had been seated at the bar only a few moments when a man dressed casually in jeans and a striped golf shirt took the adjoining stool. From a glimpse in the mirror behind the array of bottles she judged he was a little younger than she. He appeared to be in his early thirties, handsome enough, with a lean hawkish face, and a sleek hairline receding from a widow's peak. His intentions couldn't have been clearer and she found herself appraising the possibilities for diversion. In this particular idiot American sitcom, this was the bar scene where the weekend cowboy tried to pick up the lonely and lovely lady. She was not far wrong, as it turned out. She let him buy her a drink and he told her he was in town at a locksmiths' convention. He was a locksmith; well, in the security business really, he explained with the kind of false modesty meant to suggest reserves of influence and power. But she preferred the word "locksmith" with its suggestion of medieval craftsmanship. As she continued on to the next vodka she began to find the craft strangely interesting, quizzing him on everything from technological advances to the rising paranoia of homeowners. It was one way of deflecting the conversation from anything too personal and he seemed to enjoy the attention. It was so easy to slip into the reporter thing, to appear interested. She guessed he had a wife who was superbly bored by his line of work. That he had a wife was not in question, although he didn't say so and she didn't ask. But the white line on his tanned ring finger couldn't be disguised.

Talking with a stranger, however inane the conversation, has a certain therapeutic effect. And the conversation, as she continued to a third vodka and a fourth, did become more inane, at least as much of it as she could remember now, sitting in bed wondering if she should call room service for an antacid but opting instead for a cigarette. Somehow they had slipped from the practical side of his business into a boozy Freudian subtext of keys and locks. The implications of the jokes—locksmiths had a million of them—and the stories—another million—were clear and soon there were the brief but meaningful silences and the lowered voices. She had noted two things earlier, before her head had begun to swim: one was that he was drinking less than she; the other was that the room was full of men, locksmiths presumably, and that some of them appeared to be inordinately interested in the activity at the bar. The mirror told her so. This all seemed quite hilarious at the time. Years had passed since she had been in a pickup situation and she found herself enjoying it and, in an ironic way, enjoying the apparent belief that he was scoring. Finally, foolish in his security, he excused himself to go to the men's room. When he was out of sight, she picked her purse casually off the bar and made for the elevator as steadily as she could.

Before he got off his stool he had asked her name. "Anna," she had replied in a smoky voice she had developed for the part. "What's yours?"

She couldn't remember now what it was. Bob or Rob or Ron or Don—some generic male name. She felt a little sorry for him now. It wasn't until she had rolled into bed that she realized she had stuck him with the bar tab.

She wondered if she should go down to the hotel restaurant for breakfast. She really didn't want to run into him having a late breakfast—she picked her watch off the side table—or a late lunch, rather. The thought of food was off-putting in any case. Her hangover wasn't severe, just sufficiently unpleasant to deny her an appetite for eggs Benedict, say, or even French toast. The more urgent need was for something to drink. She phoned room service, ordered orange juice and tea, and then flopped back into the pillow, turned on the bed lamp and picked up her book. She read a few lines, failed to absorb their meaning, and put the book down.

She wasn't sure if this impromptu retreat was accomplishing what she'd hoped it might. She had been barely aware of her intentions when she left Paul Richter's apartment Friday evening. She just knew she had to get away somewhere and the idea of escaping into a hotel grew as she drove home. She threw a few things into a bag, returned to the car and then, about to drive away, got out and went back into the house to leave a note for Spencer. "I've gone to a hotel for a few days," she scribbled hurriedly. "I need time to *think*." She underlined the last word twice and then added as an afterthought: "You'll have to take your mother to the mall opening. I won't be there." Typically, even in the middle of this crisis, she was arranging the social niceties of his life. In her mind, the afterthought sounded withering and dismissive, but, in fact, Spencer had to be reminded to pay attention to his mother as he had to be reminded to pay attention to anything not directly relevant to his precious career. He would probably interpret it as a simple directive, she thought. He needed someone on his arm at the gala and he would have been pissed off to have to go alone, a man in his position. She was even introducing a public relations advantage he probably wouldn't have thought of otherwise: the sight of the aspiring political candidate taking his dear, sweet mother to an important social event while his wife—what excuse would he give?—was "feeling a little under the weather."

For some reason this note, written in haste, played on her mind. Why had she even mentioned a hotel? Was some part of her mind hoping that he would try to contact her? There were a hundred hotels in the city but surely he would have the sense to know she wouldn't take a room in some flophouse out on the highway. But at the registration desk of the Winnipeg Inn, she had obscured the trail by giving neither her name nor her maiden name to the clerk, but her mother's maiden name, and paid in cash.

She looked around her room, at the indifferent furniture, the monstrously huge television set, at the Group of Seven reproductions on the wall opposite, the bedspread with its broad orange stripes, vibrant even in the semi-darkness—all of it so banal compared to the home she had once so carefully decorated. Had she taken an irrevocable step coming here? "A few days" she had written on the note; in other words, the weekend. But the weekend would be over in a few hours. Would she be home then? Or would she stay on and go to work from the hotel? She had to return home at some point, if just for the sake of a change of clothes. Should she start looking for an apartment? Go and stay with a friend? Stay put?

Saturday, on a long aimless walk across the Provencher bridge and around St. Boniface, she had started to compose in her mind a list of pros and cons, her mind going back and forth like a cerebral tennis match. She didn't love Spencer, or at least she was no longer *in* love with him—that was the main consideration. One too-large River Heights home was about all they shared these days, and only inertia seemed to be keeping them together. On the other hand, maybe there was some hope. Perhaps if they had a child. She was thirty-seven, Spencer forty-one. It wasn't too late, tick, tick, tick. They should have had one earlier. They had *planned* to have one earlier. But then no child arrived, and neither of them seemed to have the courage to explore the reasons why. Spencer's climb up the corporate ladder became more urgent, his political involvements more intense, his workload more tyrannical. She left her pretty but dull job editing a literary journal at the University of Manitoba for a greater engagement with life at the *Citizen*. At home apathy took root.

On the other hand—could one have three hands?—it was probably too late. Spencer was absorbed in his career and if she wasn't exactly absorbed in hers, enough remained to keep it interesting. At least she wasn't beholden, as her mother's generation had been, to a husband for the sake of bed and board. Her job at the *Citizen* paid decently. There was some opportunity for advancement. And now that Guy Clark was moving to city desk, one of life's more hellish aspects was removed. Perhaps she should seek the Go! editorship after all.

Shit, why had Guy Clark popped into her head? In a way, it was he who had precipitated this crisis. How did he know anything about her private life? She was sure she had been careful. But that didn't matter now. The question was whether he would really divulge what he knew, or just continue to torture her with it. And why did she care anyway? This wasn't the nineteenth century, for god's sake. Society wasn't going to excoriate her and drive her to such despair that she would throw herself under a train!

But if Spencer did find out, the marriage really would be in trouble. His pride wouldn't tolerate being—that funny word—a cuckold. Why was there no equivalent word for a woman betrayed by her husband? And why had she allowed herself to entertain the word *betrayal*? It was a cutting, accusing word and it frightened her a little. Yes, it was a betrayal, at least of those vows taken so long ago and in a frame of mind that never anticipated it would be tested. But somehow the marriage had become one of such indifference, that the real betrayal was more *their* betrayal, hers and Spencer's, of the pledge to love and honour.

She reached for the ashtray and extinguished her cigarette. Her mouth felt thick and furry. There were water glasses in the bathroom, but even the thought of cool water splashing in the sink couldn't tempt her from bed. Besides, she thought, she wouldn't be able to stop herself draining glass after glass and that would only leave her with a stomach cramped and bloated. No, room service would arrive any moment. Then she would be forced to rise. She felt a sudden ache for sweet sugary orange juice and hot sweet tea.

She reached for another cigarette but then, disgusted for the thousandth time with her addiction, tossed the packet across the bed. It had occurred to her in this weekend of reflection, in her search for some kind of key to the meaning of life—well, her life anyway—that she was addicted to unhappiness. She sought it out, savoured it, wallowed in it, and then, when it looked as though she could finally achieve the equanimity she envied in those around her, she would snatch at something that would bring her down. The affair with Paul hadn't been the first, though it had been the longest and the only one with someone who lived in the city. Once, some years back, not long after she had started work at the *Citizen*, she had gone to interview a cellist, a guest artist with the symphony, in his hotel room. He was French, very attractive. Eventually he suggested they complete the interview in bed. After that, they kept up for months a passionate and hopeless telephone affair, he in some hotel room or concert hall somewhere in North America or Europe, she from the *Citizen* surreptitiously using billing numbers from the paper's other departments. Finally, the relationship, such as it was, petered out from its own impossibility, and from a high, Liz had sunk into depression. Spencer, as usual, had been oblivious to her mood. Sometimes she wished he had found out and then there would have been the crisis she both dreaded and anticipated. A couple of times she had taken the chance of using the home phone and when Spencer queried her about these long distance calls to St. Louis or Houston she had wanted to scream, "I was talking to my lover, you idiot!" But instead she excused them as calls related to arts stories she had been working on.

There had been a few others. But each liaison, for different reasons, had been as precarious and futile as that first one. Finally, there was Paul. She felt her stomach flutter as her mind fixed suddenly on the last time they had made love. It had been on a Wednesday, ten days earlier. They had met, as usual, at his apartment and, as usual, after work. She could always excuse early evening absences to Spencer by saying she had to work late on a story, not that he was often home himself at dinner time. Paul was there to greet her. Orchestra rehearsals always ended promptly at three-thirty, and if he had no other business, he would be at the apartment preparing something light to eat, opening a bottle of wine, or readying some other surprise. These *cinq-à-sept* idylls in the antique iron bed of the condo's tiny bedroom were oases of happiness for her. Paul was a lover imaginative and attentive beyond any she had ever had, certainly beyond Spencer, whose puppy-like enthusiasm of their early marriage had dwindled over the years into something perfunctory and distracted, as though having sex with her was either convenient or obligatory. She never thought of Paul as old, though he was, as the saying went, old enough to be her father. But her widowed father, retired to British Columbia and a life of sedentary gloom, had flesh that never questioned the law of gravity. Paul battled it. His work was a swimmer's regimen, propelled arms onstage, proscribed diet off, his leisure time a discipline of exercise, most of it taken outdoors. But the outcome, the lean strong physique, was not the attraction. It was, rather, the interior man, the one behind the cultivated mask of pride that had drawn her to him. She felt sometimes like a pupil, he the teacher with accumulated wisdom and the weight of years lightly borne. Cocooned in his arms that Wednesday, she had suddenly realized that not only had she fallen in love with him, but that for the first time she was experiencing love itself, in its purest, most indestructible form. She had started to laugh and cry at the same time and, silently, he had held her more tightly until like a baby she had fallen into sleep.

A terrible groan reached her ears and she realized with a start that the sound had come from her own throat. Of course, she had doomed herself once again to misery. Between that evening and the evening at the Kingdons' she had lived in the giddy expectation of upheaval; that he would announce that he had left his wife and would she share his life? And yes, she would. But at the Kingdons' he had been unapproachable. Even for the few moments when his wife and her husband had been out of the room, he had behaved as though they were mere acquaintances. She knew now why. The explanation had arrived with Michael Rossiter's package.

A soft rap sounded on the door and she was shaken from her thoughts. She dragged herself from the bed, put on her bathrobe, and opened the door to a gangly pimpled youth in a uniform bearing a tray with the orange juice and tea.

"On the table by the window will be fine," she said to him.

He did as she asked and then without permission proceeded to open the drapes. The sunlight blasted Liz's eyes and her head pounded.

"I wish you hadn't done that," she muttered, drawing the back of her hand against her eyes.

"Sorry," he drawled, then added officiously: "It's after twelve o'clock. Reception wants to know if you're staying another day. Twelve is normally check-out time."

Liz felt suddenly like slapping him and took it as a mark of how far she was hurtling from her own youth that she now found people this young to be almost unbearable.

"Yes," she snapped. "I will be staying another day. Would you tell reception? Thank you so much."

She held the door wide so he couldn't mistake her desire to be rid of him immediately.

"You're welcome," he responded airily.

She slammed the door and her head throbbed once again. The orange juice was fresh-squeezed but it was thick with unstrained pulp and warm as blood. She felt vaguely nauseated drinking it, and its benefit was illusory anyway. Her thirst was not slaked. Only the sugar in the juice contributed to a lessening of fatigue.

She poured a cup of tea and took it to the window. Her eyes adjusted to the light and she looked southeast over the city past the Red River, glinting in the sun, toward the streets she had walked the day before. Then, as now, she had tried to push from her thoughts the other Paul, the Paul whose awful secret had poisoned her heart. She would try to invoke the man of ten days ago who could charm her thoroughly, who had resurrected feelings long dormant, even the man who could amuse her at a dinner party by slaying the egregious Guy Clark with a cutting word or two. But the other Paul Richter, the doppelgänger twin within, could not be denied. He had battered his way into her consciousness. And each time, she had shivered, as she shivered now in the heat of the sun pouring through her window. What she had read in that file, and what he did not deny Friday at his apartment, had terminated their affair as surely as the schemes of a clinging wife. His hands, his beautiful, slim, strong, sensitive hands, which brought order from the orchestra's chaos, which brought ecstasy from her willing body, had once beat the life from a man. His eyes, which had looked into hers with tenderness, had once fixed on another's death-panicked eyes until they became staring and lifeless. And there was more, much more.

Her teacup rattled in its saucer. She had started to shake, a sob clutched her throat. This is why I'm here. The thought tore at her. This is why I'm in this hotel. It isn't because of Spencer. Brooding on their marriage had the comfort of the known quantity. Separation, divorce, perhaps reconciliation—she could deal with these things. But not murder gone unpunished. And not committed by someone she loved.

She didn't know what to do. When Paul asked her coldly Friday what she intended to do with the information, she had lied. She had said she didn't know, that for the meantime she had locked the file in her desk drawer. She had felt suddenly frightened of telling him the truth, that the file was in another's possession, and it wasn't until a few moments later that she realized why. She had been slow, stupidly slow, in making the connection, but when she did, she felt the full force of it. Heart pounding, she had had to clutch the side of the piano in Paul's studio to steady herself. The last person in possession of this information had been murdered. And yet, as this thought seized her mind, she wondered at its possibility. It wasn't that her lover was capable of murder. She knew he was. It was the timing. The timing was wrong. But she asked anyway, as nervelessly as she could, chilled by the possible answer. She had to know, to hear not just his words, but to read his face, his gestures.

"Did you," she asked, staring at him, her breath slowed to a whisper, "kill Michael Rossiter?"

His response had been brutal in its simplicity. Silently, he had walked to the door and shown her out, his expression forbidding. But the door did not slam behind her as she expected it to. He must have lingered for a moment watching her back as she walked down the hall toward the elevator. Only then, as she rounded the corner did she hear the soft shush of the door slowly brushing the thick carpet and the barely audible click of the lock. There was a delicacy in it that she chose to interpret as regret, or sadness. And she wondered then, as she wondered now, looking out across the river, if she had done the right thing by placing the damning information in Guy's custody. By doing so, she had virtually guaranteed Paul's ruin.

But as she had several times in the last hours when she permitted herself to dwell on this, she could feel herself soften. After all, she rationalized, the murder had taken place long ago. Perhaps under the circumstances it had been, if not excusable, then at least understandable. Perhaps the years had punished him sufficiently. Surely there had been times when he had been racked by guilt. And wouldn't the revelation disrupt too many lives? There would be too much past raked over the coals. All she need do was dress, get over to the paper, and retrieve the file. It had been so late in the afternoon when she placed it amid the other papers on Guy's desk. It was likely he never picked it up, or, if he had, paid no attention to it, or not understood it. He was such an idiot. There would be only a skeleton staff early Sunday afternoon at the *Citizen*. No one questioned you if you looked through another's desk. Few had working locks. It was just presumed you were looking for a pen or one of the elusive dictionaries.

But then, once she had it in hand, what would she do with it? Destroy it? Destroying the evidence would not destroy the truth. She imagined that truth with a spectral power to intrude upon her life, to come swooping down at awkward moments with all its attendant guilt and horror, the way the magnified sins of childhood could suddenly violate one's hard-earned adult serenity. Could she live with that? She didn't know, had no idea. She wondered if she was living in a moral vacuum. How could she doubt that what she had done was correct? She could only admonish herself for lack of courage in following the story herself. But between the mind and heart lay a minefield of doubt.

She took a last sip of tea, a cheap commercial blend that had brewed so intensely between hotel kitchen and her room its astringency left her mouth dehydrated. In the bathroom, she swallowed several glassfuls of water and immediately regretted it. The chlorinated taste was vile and she felt swollen. With the only hope of refreshment lying in a long hot shower, she tugged the curtain and adjusted the taps. Perhaps, she thought, removing her bathrobe and stepping into the gratifying warmth of the streaming water, happiness was only an animal response, to food, to warmth, to sex. Human beings could never be truly happy because their needs were so much more complex.

Nearly an hour later, Liz stood in the newsstand tucked in a corner of the hotel lobby. Feeling marginally better, and sure it was too late to encounter BobRobRonDon, she had decided to eat in the restaurant. *Anna Karenina*, even in paperback, was a poor dining partner—too bulky to manoeuvre with knife and fork—so she opted instead for a magazine to accompany the tedious task of dining alone. But which magazine? she wondered, surveying the racks. So many magazines, so few worth reading. Lacking an avocation, she found nothing compelling in the innumerable publications on model cars, knitting, or bodybuilding; the newsmagazines were uniformly insipid, the American ones jingoistic. Business magazines abounded but she could never really understand the cultish interest in people who really did little more than buy cheap and sell dear. Neither could she understand the interest in the squalid lives of Hollywood celebrities. She had already read the *New Yorker*, *Harper's* and *Atlantic*—the only magazines she admired. That left the women's magazines. The soft-headed, vaguely pornographic chatter of *Cosmopolitan* was tempting but finally she closed her eyes, waved her hands over the section, and pulled out a *Chatelaine*. At least, she thought, there might be some story ideas she could pinch.

A heavily made-up woman of uncertain age was minding the counter. She had been humming noisily since Liz had arrived in her shop and it was only when she went to pay that she realized the woman was accompanying a transistor radio with sound so thin it was barely audible. As Liz fished in her purse for some money, the song faded to an end but the woman continued to hum the refrain absentmindedly in a high quivering voice, quickly losing the melody, and almost drowning the signature tones heralding the CBC hourly newscast. She took Liz's money without comment and handed back change. Liz turned to go but then her ears pricked. She thought she heard a familiar name in the newscast.

"Could you turn that up for a moment?" she asked.

"Sure, honey." The woman fumbled with the radio. There was a squawk and then the sound of someone speaking in French. "Sorry, I've turned the wrong thing. Can't understand this gibberish. Now let's see—"

She peered at the radio, pushed one of the tiny buttons on the side, and the original broadcast was restored. She turned the volume.

"That help?"

But the newscaster had turned to an Ottawa story—the election call. Canadians were to go to the polls November 21.

"No, oh well, that's all right. I just thought I heard the name of someone I work with at the *Citizen*."

"You work at the *Citizen*?"

Something in the tone of the woman's voice brought a chill of premonition to Liz. "Yes," she replied haltingly. "Why? Has something happened?"

The woman regarded her with a mixture of concern and curiosity.

"Well, I hope it's not a friend of yours, but there was someone murdered there last night—"

"What!" Liz groaned. She had heard correctly.

"—a real common name," the woman continued, her eyes fixed on Liz's. "Clark. I remember now. Somebody Clark. Are you okay, honey? It's someone you know, isn't it? That's terrible. I hope you weren't close."

"No, we weren't close." To her own ears her voice sounded disembodied. She seemed to be speaking from a well of horror and disbelief. "We weren't close at all."

She had to get to a telephone. She felt the urgent need to talk to someone, to find out more. Perhaps it was just some strange coincidence. But her racing heart told her that it wasn't. There was no coincidence in this.

"Dear, don't forget your magazine."

But Liz heard nothing. On unsteady legs, she half walked, half ran across the lobby. Her mind didn't even acknowledge the man with the hawkish face and the receding hairline stepping out of the elevator as she stepped in.

34

Island Episode

Stevie lifted her eyes from the menu. She'd had tons of terribly trendy Thai in Toronto, and would have settled for Sunday dinner at Skinner's Hotdogs after a cozy autumn drive down the River Road or something like that, but Leo had insisted on the Wajan. Had, in fact, made a reservation. Which—if one had to be here at all—was wise. Nan had said she and Roger Mellish had been the only ones in the place Tuesday evening. Now it had the elbow room of a sardine tin. "Power of the press," Leo had remarked after they'd been shoehorned into their seats. He had unfurled the review clipped from Saturday's *Zit* and was comparing it to the menu.

"Satay—yum," he said. His hand ran down the clipping. "It reminds me of what I ate every day of my life until I was twelve."

"Which was?"

"Peanut butter sandwiches."

"Me, too!"

Leo took her hand absently and kissed it. "We'll always have Jiffy."

He returned to his studies. Stevie glanced around the restaurant's interior. When she had started with YP in Toronto, she had been part of a small team designing a bistro on Avenue Road, so of-the-moment that a year later, when she went there for dinner with David, she found it depressingly brittle. It looked the same fate for the Wajan. Keep it simple, honour the ethnic roots of the cuisine, be understated. But this was a giddy hybrid of twentieth-century styles. She ran her hand over the surface of the table. It was metal, gunboat grey, complete with rivets, and cold to the touch. The chairs, black and lacquered, had the sinuous curves of art nouveau while the geometric patterns around a tiny bar, mid-room, suggested art deco. The color scheme was sombre; the eye was drawn to a large mural that wrapped three sides of the room—a frenzy of lines and planes, blacks and whites with splashes of blood red in a style vaguely futurist. She gave the Wajan a year. Then someone would put in a new pizza take-out.

But for now the fashion lemmings were galvanized. From her vantage point facing the door, she noted a stream of disappointed folks who hadn't thought to make a reservation being turned away. She began to wonder how they were going to squeeze in Leo's friend.

She had been at Leo's in the afternoon, ransacking the house looking for Alvy's lead, wondering why Leo couldn't have taken the dog with him to the goddamn monastery. They were both males, weren't they? Surely they could both have got past whatever device turned females into piles of ash. The phone rang. Thinking it was Leo for her, she lifted the receiver, said, "How's their cheese?" and was greeted with heavy breathing. Somehow, it didn't seem like Leo's idea of a joke, and if it was, it would be the last time he saw her naked. She was about to slam the phone down, when a strangulated woman's voice asked, "Is that Stevie?"

It turned out to be Leo's colleague Liz Elliot. Of course, she wanted to speak to Leo, and she was so insistent and anxious and oddly secretive all at once, Stevie found herself, after telling her that Leo was gone for the afternoon, extending an invitation to join them at the Wajan, which seemed to be the next assured Leo-opportunity.

Now, sitting in the restaurant, she wished she hadn't. Or hoped that Liz had changed her mind. Stevie was still trying to wrap her head around all this monastery crap. She didn't feel like entertaining the problems of a third party.

"Drink?" Leo asked, interrupting her thoughts. A waiter hovered.

"Maybe I'll try this Thai limeade."

"Make it two."

"Is that Liz?" Stevie noted a tall, dark-haired woman in large sunglasses scanning the room, then elbowing past an exasperated-looking maitre d'.

"Hold on a sec," Leo said to the waiter. He turned and gestured to Liz. "Drink?"

"Vodka tonic," she replied in a dull, flat voice, removing her sunglasses. Stevie noted in the restaurant's pall the dark-rimmed eyes, the white mask of her face.

"I hope I'm not intruding." She regarded Stevie tentatively.

"Hell, no," Leo replied instead, reaching for a chair that had become vacant at the next table. "Have a seat." He introduced the two women, then frowned at Liz. "You okay?"

"Not really."

Leo flicked Stevie a puzzled glance. "Missed you at the mall last night," he addressed Liz as she removed her coat and sat down.

"How was it?"

"More fun than a barrel of monkeys."

"Was Paul there?"

"Richter? Yup, sawing the air like it was cordwood. Why?"

Stevie watched Liz fold her sunglasses into a case, then into her bag. She recognized the ache in the gravity of her gestures. There had been a time in her own life—not that long ago—when motion, too, had seemed unendurable.

"Anyway," Leo continued, oblivious, "the real capper came at the end of the evening."

Liz looked up. "I heard."

The waiter returned with their drinks. "Are you ready to order?" he asked, after settling them on the table. Stevie glanced at the others—Leo scratching his head, Liz worrying the plastic corner of the menu—then at the waiter. He looked like a bright kid. "I think the Roger Mellish special for three."

The waiter sighed. "The lunch choices or the dinner?"

"Oh, right," Leo interjected. "He always does a lunch one day and a dinner another when he's reviewing."

"The dinner," Stevie replied.

Liz reached into her bag and pulled out a pack of cigarettes.

"I'm afraid there's a no-smoking policy," the waiter intoned, scribbling their order.

"Damn." Liz stuffed the cigarettes back into her bag. Her face crumpled as if cigarette-denial was the last straw. An uncomfortable silence ensued. Stevie was suddenly conscious of the drone and clatter of the other diners.

"Do you want to go somewhere more private?" she asked.

Liz shook her head. She took a sharp breath. "I think," she said, looking at neither of them, but somewhere into the dimmer reaches of the underlit restaurant, "I may have been responsible for Guy's death."

"Wow," said Leo. "I wondered who'd be the first to take credit."

Liz smiled weakly.

"Sorry," Leo said, taking note of Stevie's raised eyebrow. "But, seriously, are you—?"

"No, no. I didn't...I didn't *do* it. But—"

"But what?"

Liz sighed deeply, and stirred the ice in her vodka with her straw. "I got a package in the mail at work on Friday." She looked up and held their eyes for a moment. "From Michael."

"He'd been making good use of the post office," Leo remarked.

"Mine was a large envelope, really. Like the kind we get at the *Zit* when someone is doing a big promotion. But it was addressed by hand, which made me wonder—"

"Hand-addressed always being the first sign of nutbar correspondence," Leo explained to Stevie.

"Anyway, I opened it." She stopped, closed her eyes. "Inside was an ordinary manila envelope," she continued, speaking through her fingers. "And inside that were photocopies of old documents and copies of photographs. I didn't know what it was at first, but then I found a long letter from Michael explaining them, as well as explaining why he sent them to me. The package also contained excerpts from a trial…"

She opened her eyes. The table, like the other tables in the room, was lit by a single halogen spot and in it her eyes were moist, suddenly red-rimmed.

"… a trial that took place about a year after the war ended. In Germany." She sighed deeply. "A war crimes trial."

Stevie started. "Does this have something to do with that Kushniryk trial that's been in the paper?"

"No." Liz shook her head.

"That's to do with crimes in Latvia," Leo explained.

"This is something else." Liz sipped her vodka. "Something that took place near Holland."

"Holland?" Stevie echoed.

"The East Frisian Islands. In the North Sea."

"That where Michael sent me the postcard from." In her mind's eye, Stevie could see a picture of a lighthouse with a riot of flowers in the foreground.

"I think the island is called Borkum. I haven't been near a map. I spent the weekend at a hotel."

Leo looked at her askance. "Honeymoon over?"

"You might say."

"What about this island?" Stevie interjected.

"Sorry," Liz continued. "Anyway, the summer before the war ended, some Americans crash landed their plane on this island. All of them survived—there were seven of them—but they were forced to surrender to German soldiers."

She stopped and again closed her eyes. "You know, I've spent all weekend trying to keep this out of my head. I only read the abstract of the trial once—it was an English translation—but the details are burned into my mind. When I think of it now, I see it as though it were a film loop going round and round, these doomed Americans, travelling that little island…" She broke off.

"You see," she continued after a moment, opening her eyes, "their plane had crashed on the north side of the island, but the routine apparently was to take the prisoners a few miles to the south side so they could be transported to mainland Germany. And so—" Liz's voice broke. Her eyes sparkled with tears.

"Take your time," Stevie said.

"Okay, give me a second." She stared at her glass as if it held some truth. "First of all, the prisoners were taken to be processed at some sea fortress that the Germans maintained on the island. I guess it was some routine procedure. There was a six-man guard detail assigned there to take them to the southern port. Apparently it would have been easiest and quickest to transport them by truck, or some vehicle. But it was decided instead to have them march the distance, and not by a direct route, either, but by a long meandering route through the main part of the only town on the island. This six-man guard detail was led by a seventh, a young officer named Karl Staudt. He could speak English and it seems he led the initial interrogation of the prisoners."

Liz lifted the glass and sipped deeply.

"So they set out," she continued. "The prisoners were told to keep their hands above their heads at all times. And the guards were told not to protect their prisoners from any attacks by civilians."

Leo and Stevie groaned in unison.

"Yes, it's a critical detail." Liz grimaced. "You see, the Germans had been told the Allied bombings of their cities were acts of terror, criminal acts, and, according to the abstract and to Michael's letter, the Nazis encouraged reprisals against any Allied prisoners of war who came into their hands—"

"Even though it was against the Geneva Convention or such like, right?" Leo supplied.

Liz nodded. "That's why the long route to the port was chosen. The authorities of the town had already begun inciting the local civilians when the soldiers began—" She groped for the expression. "—began their awful trek."

"Oh, my god," Stevie murmured.

"They started off along the beach," Liz continued. "You can imagine how exhausted these Americans already were. They had been through an airplane crash, through capture, and through interrogation. But when they fell out of step, or when their arms began to fall from their heads, the German soldiers battered them with their rifle butts."

Stevie felt a shiver go up her back.

"Then came their first ordeal. Some conscripted labourers working on the beach had formed two lines—a gauntlet, in effect—and beat the prisoners. The German guards didn't join in this, but they tolerated it.

"That changed when the procession moved into town. A crowd had already gathered. There were screams for blood and some of the civilians began attacking the prisoners. It was in the midst of this that Staudt, who had been leading the prisoners, lost his control. There was one American, a small man apparently, whose name…"

Liz faltered. Her hand went again to her mouth.

"I'll never get his name out of my head," she spoke through her fingers. "Albert Bird. A short sad name. A flier's name. Little Albert Bird. His pants kept slipping from his waist. And when he lowered his hands to fix them, he was hit. Then, in town, amid this hysteria, he collapsed, or he tripped on his pants, or he was pushed. But he went down and Staudt went crazy. He beat him about the head with his rifle until…oh, god." Liz's hands went to her face "…until he was a bloody pulp, shouting all the while that his father and mother, his relatives, had been killed in Hamburg when the city was bombed and that he was their avenger. Finally, while the crowd looked on, he shot Albert Bird, killing him."

"Jesus!"

"Wait, Leo, there's more. The six remaining prisoners were marched around the town and they endured endless beatings and humiliation. They came very close to the port. In fact, they nearly reached it, and autopsies on the bodies afterwards suggested they would have survived the torment, and possibly even the war. But they didn't. Staudt and the other German soldiers shot them. Murdered them. And then, of all things, they buried the seven in the local Lutheran cemetery."

Liz paused and drained the last of her drink. "I could use another." She signalled to the waiter and tapped her glass.

"Anyway," she continued, "about two years later, after the war had ended, and Germany was occupied, an investigation was made into the events, and a trial was held in West Germany, somewhere—I've forgotten. Murder and assault were the charges made but the perpetration of war crimes was the nub of the accusation. There were several civilians on trial, those who had either assaulted the prisoners or incited the assault. They were found guilty and received a variety of jail terms. But all the members of the guard detail were found guilty of murder and subsequently hanged. However, one person escaped justice, the officer in charge—Staudt. He had slipped out of occupied Germany before the case was ever brought to trial."

The waiter interrupted them with Liz's drink, a tall glass that glistened and sweated in the circle of light. Another waiter settled a food-laden tray against the rim of the table. Liz leaned her head back and took a deep swallow of vodka. A slight flush came to her pale cheeks. She glanced at the impassive waiter, then took a deep breath.

"It turns out that Karl Staudt lives right here in the city."

35

Rendezvous

Liz barely noticed the waiter fussing about the table, placing a heated plate in front of her, setting down the platters and bowls of food. So little had she eaten all day, she was beyond hunger. The vodka lay heavy on her stomach; the food, beautiful and clever as it looked, smelled almost revolting. As she waited, her mind flew to her meeting with Paul Friday evening.

His manner on the telephone had been formal, so unlike the endearments of other phone conversations, that she had walked to his apartment through the gathering gloom of day's end with a gnawing sense of dread. In the front lobby of the building, she had nearly changed her mind and made a hasty exit, but for some reason she had turned her head at that moment and looked into the face of the caretaker whose tiny office opened out toward the elevators. His perennially cheerful expression had given her heart. He was like the faithful pet whose simple presence alone restores tranquillity and she returned his wave as one might pat a dog, as a ritual connection to the normal and the familiar.

On the phone, she had said she needed to speak to him urgently, but when Paul opened the door to her, surrounded by the strains of recorded music—and thank god it wasn't Wagner—she sensed that he knew precisely why. Normal concern or curiosity was absent in his expression. Instead, the deeply etched frown lines had pulled his mouth into a look of bitter disapproval. His eyes quickly assessed her own and she saw in the hall mirror as she removed her coat that hers betrayed her despair. Her courage began to drain at that moment.

"As I said on the phone, I'm pressed for time." Paul followed her into his living room. His voice was cold. "Else will be arriving shortly. We have a social engagement."

"I've tried to reach you a couple of times in the last two days to talk—"

"And I've been very busy with rehearsals. But you haven't come here this evening to admonish me for failing to return your phone calls, have you?"

No, she thought. And in that moment she wondered what she had come for. To hear from his own lips that his whole adult life was a lie? To hear him deny Michael's evidence? To receive, gratefully, some other story that would absolve this crime? Her actions in that last hour or so had been driven by raw emotion. Now she wondered if she had made an intelligent choice by coming to see him.

"I needed to see you because I've had some—" She faltered. "—some disturbing news." How lame the description sounded. "Well, more than just disturbing…Paul."

What she was going to say next sounded absurdly like something from an old film and she attempted a laugh. But it was more a cough that sounded from her throat.

"But then Paul Richter isn't your real name, is it?"

He had moved to the black leather couch that dominated the room and motioned for her to sit down.

"I've used it long enough to make it real," he replied neutrally. "It's who I am now, and have been for forty years. That other person, Karl Staudt—I'm sure you know the name—died in the war."

It was blunt. And she was glad of it. She hadn't known how she would have handled denial.

"My knowing this doesn't seem to disturb you," she continued, sitting tentatively on the edge of the matching chair opposite him.

"Disturb me? Of course, it disturbs me. But I'm neither surprised nor shocked. I suppose I've known in the back of my mind that a moment might come when someone would challenge my identity. But," he added with distaste, looking away from her, "as it happens, this is not the moment. This is only the aftermath."

"Michael Rossiter, you mean."

"Yes. He came to my office last week. He'd been in Europe. He'd found out. By chance, I gather. But trust him to be thorough."

"You didn't deny it."

"How could I? He'd gone to some length to get the documentation, and I've never been prepared to go through the kind of circus that idiot Kushniryk is going through, standing up in court, pretending—"

"Then why didn't he—?"

"What? Go to the authorities? He told me he had to think about what he was going to do. He said he was going away again. Or something. Anyway, he intimated to me in our meeting that handing it to the press might be the way to deal with it."

"Blackmail?"

"Hardly. Rossiter needed nothing from me."

"He could have gone to the police."

"He could have. But perhaps there's something of his family's newspaper legacy in him." He added archly, "A good story, as it were?"

"And this is why you were so distant Tuesday at Martin and Bunny's."

Paul shrugged. "I thought perhaps you might be one of the reporters he would get in touch with. After all, he knew nothing about our...relationship. I doubted Rossiter would give the story to the squalid *Examiner*."

"And Tuesday, you weren't sure if I already knew."

"At first. But by the time we had sat down to dinner, I realized you couldn't know. Your manner was too...sociable. If you had known, I assumed you would look, and probably feel, as you do now." He paused and looked at her clinically, his eyes unwavering below the tufted eyebrows. "How *do* you feel?"

The question had disconcerted her. Then she understood it was somehow calculated to deflect the course of the conversation onto more familiar ground—her psychological state, an area she realized with a burst of anguish she had shared with him much too often, and without reciprocity. He had always been daddy. Now she felt she was being manipulated. But habit was strong and she answered in terms she knew he would find agreeable: "I just feel numb, Paul. I feel completely out of my depth. I don't know what to do."

"Why should you do anything?"

"Because...because you're someone else, someone with another name, with this...this *past* attached to it."

"And you want to do what? Expose me? Like a good intrepid little journalist?"

"Paul, please don't do this. What I want is to understand." Her voice constricted. "Your life is a lie, isn't it? A horrible lie."

"That would be overdramatizing, Liz. Part of my life is an invention, I don't deny it. But it was a necessary invention. The rest of my life, the great part of my life, is as public as that of anyone in my position."

"That's not quite true. You've never been the social animal some of the WSO's past music directors have been. You've rarely done interviews or gotten involved in public events unless there was some direct link with the orchestra. Yet you've never been so reclusive that curiosity would be sharpened. You've taken a risk just being an orchestra conductor. But at the same time you've tried to minimize that risk. You've been very careful."

"Liz, when I was a boy I wanted nothing more in the world than to be what I am now. The war interrupted my musical education. Nothing, nothing!—including that incident on that stupid little island—was going to stop me reaching my goals. I took a risk escaping occupied Germany. I took a risk entering England. Think of my eyes! I had to keep one covered with bandages, pretending I had an injury. I dyed my hair. Every day for the first year I feared recognition, arrest. There were items about the Esslingen trial in the papers. I read them. But then, as time went on, the fears lessened. My English was nearly flawless. I had a new identity and no one questioned it. But, yes, I've had to be careful over the years. Of course I have."

"But that incident, as you call it, is not a minor event. It's coloured your whole life. It has to have done. I remember asking you when I first interviewed you about American engagements and you brushed the question off. You said there was sufficient work elsewhere. But now I know why you don't conduct in the U.S., the single richest classical music market in the world. You might be on a list. Or someone might make a connection. You're just lucky the Americans so completely ignore this country.

"And," she continued, pieces of the puzzle rapidly falling into place for her, "it's always been a wonder that you've stayed so long in this city. You're so good at what you do, everybody says so. Much too good for a city as small and isolated as this. Most accomplished people only stay here briefly. They want brighter lights, better opportunities. The natural destination for someone like you has always been some large American centre."

Paul regarded her gravely. He gave an ambiguous grunt and then said, "I'm not displeased with my career."

Liz didn't believe it. Something in his eyes, some small regret told her so. Suddenly he seemed diminished to her, disappointed, older.

"Do others know about you?" she asked quietly.

He shrugged. "Perhaps one or two suspect, but they are members of a community who would rather let the past go undisturbed."

"And Else? Does she know?"

"Of course she knows. She knows everything."

His emphasis on the final word alerted her to something else. "Including...?"

He looked at her with exasperation. "I'm trying to tell you, Liz, that there are no secrets between Else and me."

"Including us, I suppose."

"Are you surprised? You never once asked."

It was true. She hadn't. She had just assumed that their relationship was as precious to him as it was to her; that their time together was privileged; that, perhaps—and this was a fantasy, admittedly—both their lives would be altered in some profound way—each would leave his spouse, they would marry, perhaps have a child. It was not too late for either. But now she knew what she was: someone's mistress. At the Kingdons', she thought she had been enjoying the stimulation of intrigue when all the while Else had known precisely the reason for her mood. She felt herself burning with humiliation.

"...understood that the arrangements were for Spencer's sake," Paul was saying. "We've always met here, at the same time."

"And I was just part of your schedule?"

"No, Liz. You're interpreting this badly. I do care for you. But Else and I are bound together in an unusual way. She knows my past. But I know hers, or, rather, I know her family's. But I shouldn't even have told you that. Do you see how I trust you?"

Was she wrong, or was there an element of special pleading in his voice?

"In other words," she said, "your marriage is based on mutual blackmail."

"Not at all." He paused as if to gather his thoughts. "You were right earlier, when you said that island episode had coloured my life. What it has coloured is my relationships with other people. I can never afford to be completely candid, completely free, with anyone. With Else I can be. There's a level of understanding and trust that few others can appreciate. Ironically, our marriage is, in other respects, 'open.' So, you see, now that you know, there's no reason we can't continue as we've been doing."

Liz froze. His proposal that she sweep what she knew under the carpet was obscene.

"I can't do that!" she cried. "You committed a horrible crime. You're a war criminal—two of the most odious words of the twentieth century! You asked me how I felt earlier. I don't feel numb. I'm horrified. I'm appalled. I can't believe you could have done what you did."

"It was war, Liz. War. Millions were killed. I was a soldier of the Reich. What do you think I was supposed to do? What do you think English and Canadian and American soldiers were doing? I don't accept this term, 'war criminal.'"

"You're listed as such with the United Nations War Crimes Commission and with some other registry—"

"The Central Registry of War Crimes and Security Subjects."

"Thank you," she continued coldly. "The men you were with were all tried and hanged as war criminals."

"'War criminals' ran concentration camps. They were SS. I was not."

Liz rose from her chair. Its confines, its proximity to Richter suddenly seemed odious to her.

"The uniform doesn't matter. And it doesn't matter whether it was the six million, or seven. Jews or Americans. What you did has been called by minds older and wiser than mine a war crime. You engineered the murder of seven American airmen in the most sadistic and public manner. You, particularly..."

She could feel her head swimming with the memory of the words she had read, of Karl Staudt brutally pummelling poor Albert Bird in the face and she closed her eyes. A second later she opened them to see Paul, his features emblazoned with rage, rise from the couch.

"They murdered my father, my sister, my aunts, my whole family!" he shouted, coming toward her. "American airmen. English airmen. Do you think this episode was not an act of revenge on the part of the Allies?"

"But those men, those seven, weren't the ones who killed your family. They were innocent—"

"Innocent!" He grabbed the back of her neck with one powerful hand and pushed her head forward so that her eyes could not avoid his. "What would a woman of your generation know of any of these things? You can't have any idea of what it was like, what we were feeling, what we had to go through."

Frightened, yet unwilling to believe he would harm her, Liz pushed at his arm.

"They were prisoners of war," she said. "You were trained soldiers. There are conventions, norms—I don't know what exactly—about how such people are to be handled. I do know you don't kill your prisoners."

She broke free of his hand and took a step back. "Don't you have any remorse?" She could hear in her voice an appeal for something she could understand.

But Paul's rage seemed to evaporate as quickly as it had appeared. He turned away. "No," he said dismissively, "I don't have any remorse. It was war. I was young. They were the enemy."

So this was it then, Liz thought. Somehow if he had expressed regret, given a sign of repentance, even a hint at the guilt that must surely attend such a crime, she would have understood. She would have been able to forgive him, defend him perhaps, if it came to that. Now she felt fevered, as though bacilli implanted in her at some point had suddenly bloomed along her veins. She heard herself say, "On Tuesday, at the Kingdons', when Martin came into the room and announced the Michael was dead, the most peculiar expression crossed your face. You didn't looked shocked."

"Death doesn't shock me, Liz. Remember, darling, I've been though a war."

The endearment, delivered with disdain, pricked her like a shard of ice, cold and sharp.

"But to clarify," he continued, oblivious to her pain, "if you need clarification, I thought that since he was dead, his knowledge of my past would die with him. I thought perhaps any evidence he had—papers, pictures, transcripts—would be incomprehensible to the police; that they would just dismiss them as part of some hobby activity. That was naive, of course. But then when the police mentioned nothing to me during questioning at the Kingdons' and then again at my house the next morning...well, anyway, let's just say it was a feeling of relief that came over me at dinner. And, of course, surprise.

"Now let me ask you a question." He moved over to the stereo and pressed a button. The music stopped instantly and a hollow sound rushed to fill Liz's ears. He looked at her steadily and asked, his voice suddenly loud and reverberating in the still of the room so cushioned from outside noise: "Since you have this file in your possession, what do you intend to do with it?"

It was then that she had lied. Some small fear had snatched at her brain, tying her tongue.

"It's locked in my desk drawer at work," she had said. "I...I don't know what I'm going to do with it."

"You realize of course that it will ruin my career, my reputation. I may be deported, charged, forced to face trial. Is that what you want?"

Then, as now, sitting with Leo and Stevie in the restaurant among all the chattering Crescentwood diners, she didn't know what she wanted. It was all too late anyway. She had given over possession of the damning evidence to another person. Then it had struck her, finally: Paul was capable of lying on a grand scale. He had murdered. He, more than anyone as far as she knew, had something to gain by Michael Rossiter's death. Maybe, somehow, he had gone earlier to his house, before the dinner party, struck Michael a killing blow, and gathered up what he could find—computer disks, whatnot—not realizing that a copy had already been mailed to her. But, no, it didn't make sense. There were alibis. That look on his face had been surprise, wonder. Not satisfaction.

Oh, surely.

Still she had asked. She had had to.

"Did you kill Michael Rossiter?"

And those were the last words she had spoken to him. They were probably the last words she would ever speak to him.

36

Hide in Plain Sight

A busboy, obviously young, obviously inexperienced, and just as obviously concerned to prove himself adept, misjudged the balance of a heaped tray of dishes he had been carrying shoulder-high from a vacated table. From his vantage point Leo could see in the dangerous tilt of the tray the accident before it happened and when it did, when the tray fell to the floor in an explosive cascade of forks and plates and water glasses, he didn't jump in his seat as the others did. He simply asked, "Why the hell didn't you go to the police?"

Liz had given them a precis of her encounter with Richter. Now she turned from the spectacle of broken crockery to meet his puzzled eyes.

"Because…" she began, then looked away. "Because I've been having an affair with him."

Leo and Stevie greeted this in silence, Stevie because an affair had killed her marriage and she had a low opinion of such recreation; Leo because a new wrinkle had been added to the front-page story that was already percolating in his brain.

"You sure know how to pick 'em," Leo said lamely, purging such observations as *wow, you've been fucking some Nazi!*

Liz said nothing, toyed with some white rice with a chopstick. She couldn't get it to her mouth.

"He killed Michael." The realization, the enormity of it, stunned Stevie.

"We don't know that for sure," Leo responded.

"He must have gone to Michael's before that dinner party."

"I asked him," Liz said. "I asked him if he'd killed Michael."

"You *asked* him?" Stevie regarded Leo's colleague with a mixture of horror and distaste. "He denied it, of course."

"Actually, he didn't answer."

"The wonder," Leo muttered, watching the kid, returned with a brush and pan, bend to sweep the broken crockery, "is that Richter's been able to hide his identity all these years."

"Not such a wonder," Stevie snapped. "If a former secretary-general of the United Nations like Kurt Waldheim can do it, then some symphony conductor in Manitoba can do it, too."

Leo's mind roiled. Front page. Query *Saturday Night*. No. A book! Screen rights! Money! Opportunity! Screw you, *Zit*! Never to have to work under the likes of the Guy Clarks of the world ever again!

A bubble burst. He had been reminded of something. "When you came in, Liz, you said you thought you were responsible for Guy's death."

"I put Michael's package to me on Guy's desk."

"Christ."

"I couldn't deal with it, Leo. I guess you could say it was a complex conflict of interest that Michael could never have anticipated when he sent me the stuff. I couldn't personally expose someone...well, someone I believed I had fallen in love with. But I couldn't just toss the file away, either. It's too..." she faltered. "I mean those men on that island... So I kept Michael's letter to me—I locked it in my drawer at work, and I typed a new, anonymous one, attached it to the inside of the file, and put it on Guy's desk. I figured Guy—of all people, can you believe this!—was my best hope. He was moving cityside Monday, could take the story with him and assign it to someone in that section, and I would be left completely out of it. So I waited until he left his desk for a few moments, went over and laid it on top of some other things."

"There was nothing on Guy's desk last night." Leo unintentionally bit into a chili in the gai pad kaprow.

"You were there?"

"We went up to the paper after the concert," he gasped, reaching for the limeade. "But Axel and Merritt were there ahead of us. They found him."

Liz appeared to absorb this. "Had he been dead long?"

"Unlike with Michael, Guy's time of death is pretty precise." Between cooling sips, he gave Liz a condensed version of the evening's events.

"Then Paul couldn't have—" Liz began.

"Why not?" Stevie forked chicken off a skewer. "The orchestra had lots of breaks, and it's only two minutes across a dark parking lot."

"But the newsroom has a security door."

"Leo says half the city knows the combination."

Leo watched Liz push a pink and oily shrimp around and around her plate with her chopsticks. "How," he asked, "would he have known Guy was in the newsroom on a Saturday evening? How would *anyone* have known?"

"The meeting had to have been arranged," Stevie supplied.

They ate in silence for a few moments. Leo itched to pull out his notebook, still snug in his pants pocket with jottings from his monastery visit.

"Wait a minute," he said. "How did Michael get the goods on Richter in the first place?"

"Chance, according to his cover letter," Liz replied. "For some reason, he'd taken a couple of the symphony programs from last season to Europe with him, and he was showing them to a German woman he knew, or met, or something. The woman recognized Paul immediately. Even after all these years."

Leo and Stevie stared at each other, each with the same thought: What's her name Dankmar, the mother of Michael's son. The woman who recognized Richter was probably the Dankmar woman's mother, or her grandmother, or some member of her family.

"Paul said he'd been a child in the war," Liz continued. "His parents were killed in the bombing of Hamburg. He said he'd been raised by an old aunt." She shrugged. "All lies, probably. If only I'd checked."

"But what reason would you have had to be suspicious?" Leo argued. "Being orphaned in the war isn't unusual."

"Besides," Stevie added, "with his looks, it's easy to believe he was a child in the early 1940s, not a young officer."

"In journalism, you take things on faith, then end up repeating old lies." Liz smiled at them glumly. "Would I be correct in thinking there was no file found?"

Leo shook his head. "Guy's desktop was clean as a whistle, but then, he's neurotically tidy. Frank took a quick look through the drawers while I was with him, but there wasn't anything that looked unusual."

"It's something you might miss. It was thick, but otherwise it was just a plain ordinary brown manila folder."

"Full of photocopied stuff, was it?"

Liz nodded. "Michael must have done a lot of research. Berlin. A place called Ludwigsburg, where there's a central office investigating war crimes. Washington—"

"Washington?" Stevie's head snapped.

"That's where the photocopy of the trial transcript seems to have come from. Or part of it."

Liz flicked her a puzzled glance. "Is it important?"

Stevie shrugged, oddly relieved and wounded that Michael's mission in Washington had been unconnected to their own personal history.

"I wonder where the file is now?" Leo mused, "He probably wouldn't have carried it back with him to Galleries Portáge. People would remember him holding a big fat file. I suppose he could have gone down to the parking level and stuck it in the trunk of his car."

Liz shook her head. "He would have walked. He and Else have a condo on Central Park."

"Threw it in the trash then."

"There's the big drums in the newsroom and the library."

"Or outside."

"Possibly."

"I don't remember any bins between the mall and the paper the route we took," Stevie remarked.

"There might be a city-owned one at the *Zit*'s front entrance." Leo strained to recall details of a streetscape he passed by a dozen times a week. "Or on Portage Avenue. Depends on how he exited the building." He thought about the *Zit* library lights being on. But would Richter have known about the interior maze of the Citizen building? Was that the kind of stuff Liz and he talked about?

"Or maybe Guy hid it somewhere? He must have realized what kind of a ticking time bomb it was."

"I should drive over to the *Zit*," Liz said with sudden urgency. "Maybe it's still there in some bin. And Michael's original letter is locked in my desk drawer. If I give it all to the police, they won't think I'm a crazy person pointing to one of the city's most prominent citizens."

Leo regarded her gravely. "There are three people who have had their hand on that file, Liz. Two of them are dead."

Liz stared at him a moment, then looked away. "He had his opportunity."

Leo looked to Stevie. "We'll go with you."

"It's okay. There's staff there Sunday evening."

"Listen, I'm phoning Frank, and then we'll join you at the *Zit*." Leo signalled the waiter, then glanced toward the maitre d's pulpit.

"You won't be able to make yourself heard anyway, even if they let you use it," Stevie remarked.

Leo's eye went to a fleck of satay at the corner of Stevie's mouth. "I know where there's a phone."

"Where?"

"Down the street."

Stevie started. "At Michael's?"

"I thought we might pick up your camera."

"But—"

"I have a key." Leo fished in his jeans' pocket. His stop-off at Sharon Bean's had been fruitful.

"But how—?"

"Never mind." He turned to Liz. "Let's bill this meal to the *Zit*. We're on a story."

37

Mnemonics

Leo watched as Liz in her black trenchcoat crossed the street and melted into the shadows on the other side, black on grey. He almost thought her vanished, but then she stepped into a shaft of hazy sunlight in a lane between two buildings, casting her own deep shadow onto the street. The door of a car parked at the curb not ten steps ahead of her opened at that instant, a tall figure stepped out and darted in her direction. Leo's pulse raced. But it was a skinny kid in a baseball jacket, racing to demonstrate his gallantry to a girl on the passenger side who'd already opened her own door.

"He's probably fled the country," Stevie remarked as Liz reached her own car and gave them a reassuring wave.

"Richter?" Leo turned to study her face. The fleck of satay still clung endearingly. He bent and kissed her, his tongue reaching out to swipe at the peanutty crust. "But why kill, then flee? Better to just flee."

Stevie fingered the corner of her mouth and frowned. "What was that for?"

"I lost my head." The satay fleck was still evident. "Anyway, we'd better hurry."

He took her hand and tugged her along.

"I don't really need the camera that badly, Leo," Stevie said, resisting.

"But I need to make the call."

"There's a phone booth across the street. Look." She pointed.

"C'mon."

"What are you up to? You didn't get the key from—was it Sharon?—anticipating the need to use Michael's phone."

Leo let go of her hand. "Okay, I confess. I thought we could go over the same ground as Tuesday. I was thinking 'feature.' I didn't know about Richter. I never expected Guy to—"

"I feel like I'm being used."

"You're not. I just want to make the story authentic, real…we can go back to the car if you want."

Stevie studied his face for a moment, trying to interpret his sincerity. He was not bad at the puppy-dog look. "All right," she said slowly. "Although I'd rather go away and forget the past week ever happened."

"I know. I'm sorry. I just have to do this. It's what I do."

Leo took her hand again and they walked in silence for a few moments around the corner and up the street. The neighbourhood, Stevie noted, didn't look quite as it had earlier in the week. The trees had been robbed by wind and rain of half their foliage, and the result, drying in rekindled October sun, crackled beneath their feet. The air was hazy and mellow, but with just a sting of coolness. In its mix of perfumes she thought she could detect the aroma of burning hay creeping once more into the city from outlying farms, and her mind, charged by the visceral power of smell, was seized by the memory of Tuesday night. Oh, screw me for agreeing to go along with this, she thought, feeling more and more reluctant. With photographic clarity she saw herself again on these streets, the trees before her more abundantly cloaked, a wind rising, the sky darkening.

Leo felt a pressure run along Stevie's fingers. "It'll be okay," he said. They passed through the stone gate. "What are you thinking about?" he prompted.

"Rabbits."

"Rabbits?"

She told him.

New lede:

It was rabbits that gave Stevie Lord her first premonition of Michael's death. More than a decade earlier, on her way to university one morning, Waverley Avenue had turned into a carpet of blood, fur and viscera from rabbits fleeing the burning stubble in an adjacent farmer's field. It was that aroma, which blankets Winnipeg every fall like a shroud, that acted on her like a powerful mnemonic...

Mnemonic's too literary.

...as a powerful reminder—

Stevie's hand gripped his harder. "I'd come along the path here and was just about to turn into Michael's house," he heard her say. "I guess it had been so many years since I had been back in the city in September that the odour was all the more bizarre, and it seemed particularly strong that evening with the wind rising. Then I noticed that there were no lights on in the front of the house—like there's no lights on now—and I thought, well, this is odd. It looked like no one was home."

They continued down the path, more quickly now, turning the corner toward the back door. The sky didn't seem to Stevie as dark as it had been the evening she had last trod the path—she and Leo were earlier than she had been that evening—but the sun had already begun to sink behind the thorny crown of trees on the west side of the yard, flaming the red brick of the house, superimposing a feverish web of shadowy lines against the staid horizontals.

Leo found the scene divertingly malevolent. Just the stuff he needed. He pulled his notebook from his jeans, a pen from his jacket, and began scribbling.

"How can you see?" Stevie asked.

"Don't worry. I can usually read my chicken scratches."

Stevie hugged herself, seeing the scene as she had Tuesday night, a dark massing broken by bands of warm yellow light that poured forth onto the lawn. Then, she'd felt relieved the lights were on. It had meant Michael was at home. Now the windows were blank, lifeless. She shivered.

Leo shifted the pen and pad to one hand and fished deeper in his jeans pocket.

"What's that?"

A ray of sunlight caught the metallic finish of the key in his hand.

"Maybe we shouldn't."

"It'll be all right."

"Aren't we violating some law?"

"Probably." Leo began steering her toward the porch. "Was the inside door open on Tuesday?"

Stevie sighed. "A crack." She eyed the door. It was all coming back, damn it. She felt the railing, as she had that night. It was cool and damp. She could almost see the porch light gleaming. She pushed back against Leo as they climbed the steps. Her heart was beginning to thump. Leo gently nudged her forward.

"And then what? You knocked?"

"Doorbell. That's when I noticed the inside door was open. I could see into the kitchen. There was this buzzing noise."

"Buzzing noise?" Leo pulled at the screen door as Stevie stepped aside, and fit the key into the lock.

"It was a wasp, one of those yellowjackets that seem to come out of nowhere in the late summer or early fall. It was sort of flopping around near my feet. Fitfully."

"Did I tell you Father Hart was blind?" Leo grunted. The key was a bit sticky.

"No."

The key turned. Leo pushed the door open and reached around with his hand to find a light switch. "He was stung by a wasp. Seems he was severely allergic."

He turned. The porch light made a halo of Stevie's head. "C'mon, it's safe."

He switched on the kitchen light. The room blazed up like a candelabra.

Stevie stalled. She couldn't make herself go over the threshold. She stared down, the way Alice did when she was about to address her footwear. "I thought it was stunned or drowsy," she said stupidly.

"What was?"

"The wasp. Maybe it had stung someone."

Leo stared at her. What she had said seemed to work on him like a yeast. He gripped her arms and pulled her over the threshold into the kitchen.

"What?" She struggled a bit.

He gripped her harder. Stared at her. Suddenly, his tongue darted onto her face. He licked her, just above the lip.

"Leo!" Stevie recoiled. She stared back at him, wide-eyed. He wore the most peculiar expression on his face. His breathing had turned heavy. "Oh, no," she cried, misinterpreting. "Not here. No way. Oh, Leo, this is sick. Let me go." She wriggled harder in his grasp.

Wait a minute! Wait a minute!" He continued gazing at her wild-eyed. "Allergy," he muttered.

"What is the matter? You're frightening me, Leo."

"Allergy," he muttered again, gripping her harder. His tongue darted out to lick her again.

"Stop doing that! Why are you doing that?"

"You've got satay on your lip." His tone was wondering. He seemed to be staring through her. "Satay. Don't you see?"

"See what?"

"He's not allergic to peanuts." The truth hit him like a knock to the head. There was a burst of pain, and then a flood of well-being as shock gave way to the peculiar pleasure of knowing.

"Who's not?"

"Mellish. The next morning at work he ate an entire chocolate bar right in front me. Stevie, the fucking thing was *full* of peanuts!"

Stevie stared at him, uncomprehending. And then she, too, felt a sudden rush. "He was sneezing. And wasn't he wearing a turtleneck? As if to cover—"

"He's been wearing a turtleneck all week."

"I pushed it with my toe through the space between the stoop and the house."

"What?"

"The wasp."

Leo released her. She sped back out the door and down the steps and began rummaging through the hollow space under the stoop. Just enough natural light remained to silver the outlines of shapes, including a papery ball, a wasps' nest, clinging to the underside of the wood. She thrust her hands into the accumulation of dead leaves, turning them aside, and then, there it was, protected from rain and sun by vegetation and the stoop's overhang, the tiny perfect carcass of the insect, its body ringed with black and yellow stripes. Leo looked over the railing into the palm of Stevie's hand, illuminated by the light falling from the kitchen, and wondered that something so small could be so powerful and so important. Its venom could blind one man. Or it could make another swell and itch.

Stevie frowned at her possession. "It could be another one."

"And it isn't exactly evidence. But it doesn't matter anyway."

"But why, Leo? What would be the motive?"

"I don't know." Leo looked back into the kitchen. He could see Stevie's camera case on the counter. His eyes searched for the phone. There it was, on the wall.

"Surely," Stevie was saying, "Nan would have noticed the scratching and stuff *before*—"

"Liz! She's gone to the *Citizen*."

"He wouldn't know she knows."

Leo bit his lip. "He usually sits at the same bank of desks."

"We could have it all wrong."

"I've got a bad feeling, Stevie."

"There'll be police around. You said."

"*Zit* staffers won't have much trouble getting access."

"He'd have to be crazy—"

"Then he is crazy." Leo bolted back through the kitchen door and grabbed the telephone. He held the receiver to his ear, his fingers quickly punched the newsroom's number. But there was something odd about the phone.

"Shit!" He slammed the receiver back into the receptacle. "They're not answering."

38

I Walk Alone

Roger Mellish had driven past the *Citizen* several times Sunday morning and Sunday afternoon. Each time, parked in front, in the no-parking zone, had been several blue and white police cars as well as the sort of dark unmarked sedans whose very anonymity marked them as official. When he went past the first time he couldn't refrain from smiling. There was a certain excitement to being the real object of inquiry, being so close to those inquiring, yet so removed from their speculations. But by the third and fourth drive past, with the police vehicles still in attendance, he had started to get a little annoyed. He needed to retrieve the file, had to retrieve it, certainly before the library staff returned Monday morning, but best before 9:00 Sunday evening when the night news editors began their shift. A visit to the newsroom in the afternoon of a non-working day by the food editor might be thought unusual but not remarkable to the few staff in attendance in those hours. But to suddenly arrive at 10:00 or 11:00 Sunday night would be considered most peculiar.

He could avoid appearing in the newsroom proper by taking the longer route to the library—left down the hall, not right to the newsroom, then go around through the back room. But the more he delayed, the greater the likelihood that others would be using the library. His other option was to go up to the newsroom while the police were in the building—as an employee he had every right—but there was too much risk involved. Who knew where the police were loitering? Or how many there were? Would they search his briefcase? Ask questions? He was, he supposed, on the list of suspects. He had been near Michael's Tuesday night. He had been at the Galleries Portáge opening. But far down, far far down. After all, what motive could they ascribe to him? What evidence did they have? Even if they found the file, they would never be able to link its contents to him.

But then that wasn't the point, was it? He didn't want them to find the file, couldn't let them find the file. It wasn't for his sake. It was for Paul's sake. And Else's. Everything he had done had been for their sake.

By late afternoon his window of opportunity seemed to be closing and he felt anxiety bite for the first time. With one heavy fist he hit the steering wheel and cursed Guy Clark for his arrogance and cursed whoever it was that had found his body. He, Roger Allen Mellish, was the one who was supposed to have discovered Guy dead. He was going to go up to the newsroom early Sunday morning, retrieve the file from its hiding place, shred its contents, and then call the police in a tasteful show of shock and grief. His story would have been that he went to work on his day off to use the computer to write an entry on the Wajan for Bunny Kingdon's *Taste of Winnipeg* book. He had even contacted the restaurant Saturday to get the chef's cooperation. Given the nature of his review, he was only too glad to help. The only risk to this plan, a slim one, he had thought, had been if the inept and lazy security guard had done his job for once and thoroughly checked the building. But, instead, someone else had found the body, thus giving the police a head start.

At 6:30 he stopped for a quick supper at the McDonald's on Portage Avenue near Sherbrook, a restaurant he would never have deigned to visit in any other circumstances. But a management indifferent to his opinion of their internationally sanctioned mediocrity and a clientele absorbed either in courtship rituals or in unruly children guaranteed his anonymity. As the hamburger meat slid precariously on its slick of poisonous-looking sauce and bits of lettuce dropped into a Styrofoam container, he told himself that he had nothing to worry about. Even if the police wished to make a wholesale search of the newsroom, he was sure Kingdon would go to some lengths to stop it, or at least delay it. Besides, the library wasn't the likely first place to look.

He finished the hamburger, the grease sticks posing as french fries, and a chalky-tasting milkshake. As always, food, even insipid food, was a comfort. He felt a kind of postprandial torpor sneak up on him and he closed his eyes, just for the moment, and the clatter and chemical smells of the restaurant faded. His sleep the previous night had been less than adequate. Out of shallow depths he had surfaced again and again into consciousness, playing and replaying in his mind a cherished scene where he would tell Paul what he had done. He saw himself drive out to the house on the river north of the city, the house he visited so rarely—and wisely so, of course—and there, perhaps in the living room with its grand piano, or out on the terrace if it were still warm, he would reveal everything—well, everything but Else's cooperation, how she had agreed to make that phone call to Guy. Wouldn't Paul think him clever? And be so grateful? And finally extend the truly warm welcome that, so far, had always seemed somehow elusive.

Well, he wouldn't tell *everything*. Maybe it would be unwise to reveal Else's cooperation, how she had agreed to make that phone call to Guy. Or how she had phoned him very early Wednesday morning to, in effect, thank him. Yes, it had been a form of thanks. She and Paul had planned an informal visit on Michael before dinner at the Kingdons', but had decided against it when they'd glimpsed him, Roger, slip through Rossiter's north gate.

He opened his eyes, momentarily startled by the restaurant's childish colours and bright lights. He needed to tell Paul quite soon. He had hinted of retiring from the symphony, of leaving, going somewhere where the winters weren't so long and bitter.

And then, of course, he had lately had this terrible obsessive urge just to talk about what he had done, to anyone. He had almost confided in Nan on their drive home. She had been uncharacteristically silent, and he, admittedly exhilarated, had chattered away. How odd, a murder in a newsroom, he had said, for the news trickled through those remaining at the mall after Martin had been summoned, over the PA system, no less. Oh well, nobody much cared for Guy, he had said. And so on. It was a little frightening now how close he had come to confessing.

He rose, left the restaurant, and went to the car. His step was buoyant now, his anxiety gone. The air was soft. He looked across the parking lot to see the cold twilight sky slashed by a trail of jet exhaust in the setting sun as crimson as a new wound. The waning light reminded him that time pressed but still he felt assured that before the hour had passed, he would have successfully retrieved the damning file and be rid of it, and with none the wiser.

And, as luck had it, when he drove past the *Citizen* once more, no police cars or other official-looking cars monopolized the no-parking zone. The building sat in gloomy solitude. Only a smudge of light from a few of the dusty windows suggested any human habitation, while the street, true to a Sunday evening, was empty of people. He parked one street over, got out of the car, briefcase in hand, and made his way toward the *Citizen* building. Feeling confident, he started to whistle, an indiscernible little tune—unlike Paul, he had no ear for music—but one which seemed to come to him out of his childhood. And then he remembered. It was *I'll Walk Alone,* a wistful ditty played frequently toward the end of the war. Even if he had been too young to know or understand the words, still, the tune had been oddly heartening in those confusing days after his mother died and he had been lost, an orphan, in the London rubble, before being shipped north to live in the country near Gripthorpe with hateful old cousin Bernice. Not that his courage needed bolstering now. What he was about to do was only a bit of tidying, really—the last act in a stratagem that had already threatened to come apart once. How fortunate that he had logged into Guy Clark's computer desk Friday evening and read his little reminder to himself with all those pompous asterisks. Although the wording had been brief, and barely articulate, it was enough to tell him that Clark had received a copy of Michael's information. The covering letter, unaddressed, undated, in draft form, that he had glimpsed on Michael Rossiter's computer Monday while he had waited for Michael to come back from Bunny's, had been completed and mailed after all. If Bunny hadn't asked Michael to help her carry a box of old books to the garage before their meeting, he wouldn't have had time to let curiosity overwhelm him, wouldn't have started him trawling through the menu on the floppy disk. He read a few letters slugged MONAS1, MONAS2, etc. Michael was joining a religious community. And soon. It was too bizarre. Then he'd read one slugged RICHTE.

His world changed in an instant.

Of course, one could only do with Guy Clark what one had done with Michael. After the first, a second termination hadn't been difficult at all, though he'd had to use his hands, the way he'd intended with Michael. He couldn't have risked blood on his suit and returned to the mall. The rubber gloves had been a good idea, made it seem less personal somehow; rather like wringing the chickens' necks on Bernice's farm. He'd planned a gloveless ritual for Michael, but walking behind him on his way to the study that evening, Michael had somehow seemed bigger, heftier—younger. Not like that sitting duck, Clark. The advantage was lost with a man as tall as you. So he'd lifted the typewriter as Michael bent over his desk, to stun him, only he'd never expected the luck of Michael's head falling on a letter spike.

He turned the corner and brought his whistling in under his breath. Across the street and just ahead of him a woman, almost lost in the shadows, was hurrying alongside the great arched windows of the Citizen Building. At first he thought nothing of it, but then he recognized the stride. It was Liz Elliott. He wasn't disconcerted. Nothing was going to go wrong. But he was puzzled. Go! staff, except when they were reviewing arts events, rarely worked nights and never Sunday night. He stepped into the darkened doorwell of one of the abandoned stores across from the *Citizen* and waited. There was no sense in joining her at the elevator. He would give her time to get to the fourth floor on her own. Most likely, he thought, she had some work she had to catch up on.

After a few moments, he resumed walking up the street, keeping as close as possible to the buildings' shadows without seeming conspicuous, although why he was being so surreptitious he wasn't sure—the boyish thrills probably. The only people who passed him were a couple of sullen teenagers all in black who failed to give him so much as a glance. Once opposite the *Citizen*'s entrance, he crossed the street and quickly pushed his way through the revolving doors into the lobby. As always, the high, narrow chamber provoked disquiet. Perhaps it was the torch lights high on the walls, dimly illuminating the dark marble, or perhaps it was the stencilled designs like those on a pagan tomb, but it was the only physical space from which he sought immediate release. It was why he rarely used the elevator—he couldn't bear to wait for it. And it was why, despite the poundage born of middle age and fine food, there remained some spring in his legs—climbing three flights of stairs several times a day helped.

Still, when he reached the fourth floor, he was panting. The past five days had been stressful, and even now, when everything was drawing to a fine conclusion, tension lingered, though he preferred to view it as excitement. Through the frosted glass on the door opening to the tiny elevator vestibule, no shadows showed and no sound came. He opened the door, stepped into the vestibule, and pressed himself against the farthest reach of glass wall that divided the vestibule from the fourth floor lobby. From there it was possible to see if anyone was occupying one of the rear desks in the newsroom. There was no one.

He pressed the sequence of buttons that unlocked the door. As always, the lock yielded with a sickening grind, and he gritted his teeth as he had done only twenty-four hours previously. Then he had been in a hurry, his nerves razor-sharp, wanting nothing to go wrong. Now, he had time. Not a lot of time. But enough. He turned left, in the direction opposite the newsroom, and made his way down the hall, past the closed door to the sports department, and into the back room. He had chosen soft shoes. He wouldn't be heard and none of the bored few in the newsroom would think anything other than that one of the sports reporters had arrived for one of their odd shifts.

He reached the rear door into the library and stopped. He had heard something—the faint but distinctive rumble of a file cabinet drawer closing. Curious, he stood by the door and strained his ears, waiting to hear footsteps fade as whoever it was returned to the newsroom by the main door. Then he heard another drawer open. Then, after a few seconds, he heard it close again. Then another open. And close. And yet another. And still another. All at regular intervals. Someone, he was sure, was making a concerted search through the file cabinets.

Had figured out the hiding place.

His heart lurched. He could hear the blood rush past his ears, felt a tautness overtake his limbs. He moved carefully, noiselessly, into the first, and smaller, of the two connected rooms, around the photo file cabinets and toward the dividing wall. Judging by the direction of the sounds that the interloper was busied with the row of cabinets against the back wall, he moved quickly into the room, to the shelter of one of the thick poster-encrusted columns. In that moment, he recognized the back of the head leaning into the file drawer, the short, glossy dark hair, the one hand held high with the ever-present cigarette. He closed his eyes and cursed inwardly. He could feel beads of sweat gathering at his brow; his hands closed in on themselves until they were tight angry balls of flesh.

What was she doing?

And then it came to him. On Friday, that look on her face. As white as a sheet. She had had something in her hands, hadn't she? Even though he couldn't see. Then she had disappeared into one of the back rooms. He had thought little of it at the time. But now he knew that Michael hadn't sent his miserable gleanings off to Guy Clark alone. He had sent a set to Liz, too.

No! That couldn't be!

Otherwise why would she be searching the library? There was just the one set of papers, somehow passed from Liz to Guy. A wave of cold panic washed over him.

She knew! She knew everything!

And then he knew what he had to do. He edged away from the column toward the door leading to the newsroom and, slowly, ensuring the hinges remained unstressed, pushed the door until it was not quite shut. Then he looked over at the top of Vera's desk. There it was, neatly placed among the effects of the *Citizen*'s meticulous librarian—the silver letter opener Vera had received from her staff after twenty-five years of service.

39

Concatenation

Liz could barely remember driving from Dorchester Square to the *Citizen*. The greater part of her mind had brimmed with other thoughts—despairing thoughts about life's absurdities, about chance, about how the private and paltry decisions of anonymous individuals were powerful enough to set in motion a whole train of events culminating in tragedy. And how that tragedy could lock you in an awful embrace. If Michael's son hadn't felt compelled to seek his father, Michael would never have visited Germany, would never have pulled from his luggage those symphony programs that included photographs of the maestro, would never have shown it to someone who could link a face to an event after all these years. But then this string of beads had started with Michael's meeting the German girl in Philadelphia, just as her own intersecting loop had found its origin in her deciding one day in second year to study not at a carrel at creaky old Elizabeth Dafoe Library where English majors studied, but in shiny new Robson Hall, where law students studied. In the next carrel had been Spencer Elliott, in his final year of law. They had fallen in love, married, grown apart; she had taken a job at a newspaper, met Michael Rossiter, met Paul Richter. What might have happened if she had sat in another part of study hall that day?

And then it all intersected with one larger, world-shattering event that had deflected millions upon millions of lives. Paul Richter would never have been on that East Frisian Island if there had been no war to put him there. But then perhaps there would have been no war if one individual hadn't risen to power in Germany. But yet that rise to power was predicated on a whole host of other events, other decisions. As she parked the car and stepped onto the street, the bizarre notion had come to her that she would not be going to the *Citizen* on a Sunday evening in autumn of a year late in the century to look for this oppressive file if Archduke Ferdinand had never gone and got himself assassinated. Liz shivered, although the evening was not chilly. In a dreamlike, disturbing way, she felt like her very movements along the pavement next to the grey, gloomy *Citizen* building had been somehow preordained. She felt other eyes watching her. She had become a figure in a film loop, forever and again condemned to walk the same path for some unseen audience. But what she was walking towards, she didn't know.

Riding the elevator to the fourth floor, she'd tried to shake off these morbid thoughts. She'd determined not to think of Paul. She wouldn't think of anyone or anything. She would concentrate on retrieving Michael's cover letter. It was what a journalist was supposed to do—stick to the task at hand and never mind the context or the consequences.

When she had turned into the newsroom, there had been few people about. Alcock, apparently unaware he'd been fired, had been standing at the telex machine, frowning fiercely at something while a couple of young reporters, mirroring his frown with their own, had remained glued to their computer screens. No one had paid any attention to her as she made her way to her desk, pulled her keys from her purse, and bent over to unlock the drawer. As she did so, she glanced across the room at Guy's desk. How unremarkable it looked, how clean, how tidy, how ordinary, how *Guy*! Was it all a dream?

She had yanked at the overstuffed WSO file in her overstuffed drawer and extracted Michael's letter. She stared at it, unseeing. The type seemed a blur. Burn it—the thought flickered in her mind, then died. She looked toward the library. Photocopy it, put the copy back in the file. Just in case. *Just in case what*? She wouldn't let her mind dwell there.

On her way to the library, she had glanced into the trash bins dotted around the newsroom. Each was virtually empty. Likely, they'd been cleared early Saturday morning after the night news staff had left.

In the library, waiting for the photocopier to warm up, she had checked the wastebaskets. Empty. She had run her eyes over the forest of filing cabinets and the yards of shelving, the stacks of books, the various cardboard boxes of god-knows-what, the microfiche and microfilm machines, the desks, cupboards, chairs, plants—all of it in so small a space it was a wonder Vera was able to maintain order. Something Leo had said, something about the lights in the library being left on taunted her. Would Guy have waved all the file's damning material in Paul's face, had it open for him to see, and to seize? Or—and surely this was more like Guy—would he have concealed it, or at least the bulk of it, somewhere?

Or had Paul hidden it somewhere? No, that didn't make sense. How would he retrieve it?

The file wasn't in Guy's desk, Leo had said. And he wouldn't have slipped it in one of the reporter's desks. (And let someone else get the credit?) He might have taken it home. Or...? The library was ideal, a midden, a haystack. Was it possible? Or was she inventing all this to put off going to the police? The photocopier's indicator light declared readiness.

She had seated herself on the edge of Vera's desk, pulled a lighter and a cigarette from a package in her purse, lit it, and assessed the situation more closely, thinking that perhaps finding the file—if indeed it was to be found—perhaps wouldn't be so difficult. You could eliminate certain areas easily—shelves (too open), clippings file cabinet (drawers too narrow), desks (locked). The cupboard below the photocopier had drawn her eye. But a quick investigation revealed nothing but tidy stacks of photocopy paper. The other machines in the room offered no hiding places. That really left only the big cabinets for the photo files and the vertical files—although, granted, there were banks of them. On the other hand, Vera did put colour tags on the files to code them. *The* file would have no tag.

What one would Guy have picked? The farthest one? It was half buried against the back wall, nearest the back-stairs door. This is nuts, she'd thought to herself, pocketing the lighter and walking over. I'm procrastinating like mad. Give up and get over to the cop shop.

She opened a drawer, half-expecting her first try would yield up the thing, and when it didn't she'd been mildly disappointed, as though her 6/49 ticket had failed to win. A second drawer and then a third had been similarly devoid of anything save the usual blue, yellow, pink, and green files. Finally, she had knelt on the linoleum and opened the bottom drawer. Nothing.

She had started again on the next cabinet, proceeding down the drawers one by one, feeling as she did so that she really was losing it. It was a long shot. And she was probably dead wrong. The file wasn't here. But she found herself anyway leaning on the top drawer of a third set of cabinets, trying—shudder—to think like Guy.

It was then that she thought she heard something, a soft footfall, a rustle of clothes resisting movement. Please don't use the copier, she thought, prepared to dart out and snatch the letter from where she'd left it under the lid. But there was no other sound.

She turned to the next set of cabinets, and repeated her movements, again with no luck. She was about to open the bottom drawer when she noticed something about the construction of the filing cabinet that had escaped her conscious mind before. Between the bottom drawer and the bottom of the cabinet itself was a height of about four inches. If the bottom drawer was removed completely, a dead space just deep enough to hide a thick file would be available. Then the drawer could be replaced, covering over the space, revealing nothing if it was rolled out in the normal fashion. Rarely did anyone pull a file door out completely. It was a reasonably clever hiding place, in the short term. It was worth a try.

She pulled out the bottom drawer. There wasn't much room to manoeuvre and the drawer was surprisingly heavy. With a grunt she was able to hoist the drawer off its rollers and begin the task of dragging it out.

But she stopped midway, for suddenly she felt the presence of someone looming beside her, heard the sound of laboured breathing, smelled a distinctly masculine odour of sweat combined with something more visceral—fear. Out of the corner of her eye she saw the bottom of a pant leg and a shoe, a soft brown oxford, laced in a fastidious double-knot, a patina of dust along the outer sole. She froze. The edge of the file drawer dug into her toes. A familiar voice hissed in her ear:

"What are you looking for, Liz?"

But before she could speak, she felt the presence lean over and press to the side of her neck the cold, sharp point of a knife.

40

Missing

"This," growled Leo, clutching the wheel of the Land Rover with both fists, weaving through traffic on Sherbrook, "is a town of Sunday drivers Sunday driving on fucking Sunday. Get out of my way, you old fart," he bellowed to the Crown Victoria in front of them.

Stevie pressed her feet to imaginary brakes. "This isn't how I want to die." Her teeth sieved the words.

"You won't."

From Michael's, they had raced to the phone booth, but no one in the *Zit* newsroom responded, which was itself worrying. It was drive or die trying. Stevie preferred the former, at a pace perhaps five kilometres over the speed limit, but no more.

"Are you sure about Mellish?" she gasped, as Leo rounded the corner onto Ellice on what seemed like two wheels.

"Call it a journalistic hunch."

The University of Winnipeg blurred as they hurtled past.

"But why?" she insisted, in part to keep her mind off Leo's driving.

"Beats me."

In a moment, he had turned again and brought the Land Rover to a shrieking halt in front of the *Citizen* building.

"Hurry," he said, leaping out. A pale waif in a miniskirt stepped from the revolving doors onto the pavement. It was Julie Olsen, his smokeaholic deskmate. What was a court reporter doing at work on a Sunday? She glared at him, as she had been doing for the past three years. Stevie came up behind him. Great goddamn timing, he thought.

"You haven't seen Mellish come in, have you?"

Her face in the *Citizen*'s entrance light was sallow and mournful. Leo predicted a long career in newspapers.

"Nope." She raised an eyebrow, as if surprised he had even spoken to her.

"How long have you been here?"

"Since 4:00."

"And you've been in the newsroom until now?"

"Like, yeah." Julie's brow furrowed in mild annoyance. "Is there a problem?"

"Any cops around?"

"Here?"

"Yes. There was a murder upstairs last night, you know."

"I know. What's the matter with you? There was a cop here when I came to work. They've gone as far as I know."

"Have you seen Liz?"

"I saw her walk through the newsroom. At least I think I did. I was busy on a story so I didn't pay a whole lot of attention." She regarded him solemnly, then frowned at Stevie. "I'm on my way to pick up Chinese, by the way. Do you want anything?"

But Leo was already pushing his way through the door.

"No, thanks," Stevie replied for him.

Rounding the corner into the newsroom, after racing up the stairs and hammering at the entry-code buttons, he was struck by how perfectly normal everything appeared. It was just another slack Sunday evening with a few listless reporters lost in the paper heaps and the sea of desks.

"Why don't you fucking morons answer your phones?" he shouted to Alcock between gasps for breath, quickly surveying the newsroom for Liz's presence.

"They haven't rung!"

Leo had a flash of Martin unplugging switches the night before. "Go into Audrey's booth. The goddamn switch for incoming calls is probably still off."

Leo tore past into library, Stevie in his wake.

The library was soundless. But there was the lingering odour of cigarette smoke.

"Liz?" he called. "Liz!"

Stevie pointed to a desk by the photocopier. "There's the purse she was carrying in the restaurant."

"Liz!" Leo called again, this time more urgently. He stepped quickly up the aisle into the second room of the library and looked out into the back room where they'd been barely twenty-four hours earlier. There was no response. He returned to Stevie. "Maybe she's in the women's can."

"I'll check."

Leo began a fast search through the forest of filing cabinets, going up and down the narrow aisles, looking for what, he wasn't sure. Liz's dead body? If she hadn't responded to his calls, she couldn't be nearby. But something was wrong. What was it? The purse! Don't women drag their purses with them everywhere? Particularly to the toilet?

And then, on the floor, next to one of the back filing cabinets, he noted a cigarette end. It hadn't been stubbed out; it had been left to burn down to the filter tip. A brown streak on the linoleum was the souvenir. He picked it up and felt the end. There was a touch of warmth against his fingertip. A lingering odour, acrid and putrefying, assailed his nostrils. He couldn't imagine Liz leaving a cigarette to burn on the floor. She wasn't that careless. Well, except in her private life.

He looked at the door to the back stairwell and turned the knob. On an impulse he stepped through. The door closed softly behind him. He strained his ears. All the tiny squeaks and groans of the old building seemed to find a dull amplification in the muffled rush of rising air in the narrow shaft. The only distinct sound he heard as he made his way down to the third floor was that of Alcock shouting his name somewhere in the library, but it seemed remote, as though from a dream memory. He wondered if he should turn back and alert Stevie, but the downward direction of the stairs somehow gripped him, compelled him to follow gravity's course. Liz had to have come this way. There was no other explanation for the abandoned purse and her absence from the newsroom. And there was no other exit from the fourth floor.

He tried the door to the third floor. It was locked, as was the door to the second floor. When he reached the first floor, he hesitated. Because the back staircase was a fire exit, the door, he was sure, would open, and open into the dim back storage room with its jumble of newsboxes. A vision of Liz, laid out like a corpse among them, rose unbidden to his mind and for the first time he felt a ripple of fear. He turned the knob and stepped onto the concrete surface of the room, the scrape of his shoes sounding unnaturally loud. But there was no other sound and an examination of the room yielded nothing. Even through the shadows, he could see the clutter afforded no space for someone to hide, or leave a body, and he felt a moment of relief.

But had she left by the back door? Or turned the other way and gone through the front lobby? Surely he and Stevie would have encountered her. And there was still the matter of the purse. He looked at the second of two doors set into the wall. Like the one from which he had exited, like so many doors in the *Citizen* warren, it was completely anonymous, windowless, heavy, grey-painted, giving no clue to outsiders what lay on the other side. He knew where it went, of course—to the subterranean precincts of the building, a whole other world, warm-blooded, pulsating, the air brewing with barely recognizable smells. Here was the source of so many of the building's recognizable characters, gruff men in blue uniforms, the Morlocks who occasionally ascended to the newsroom to complete obscure tasks among the decadent Eloi.

This time Leo put his hand to the knob. Am I nuts? Why would Liz go into the basement? But if she were *taken* there...?

The knob turned. His heart skipped a beat. Shouldn't it be locked on the weekend when no one was around? Or was the *Citizen* building's fortress exterior and tortuous interior considered insurance enough against any intruder?

As soon as he swung open the door, a draft of warm fetid air hit him in the face, a pungent mixture of grease and ink and sweat. There were two basements, he recalled, one on top of the other, although the separation of functions was obscure. It had been so long since his last visit he'd forgotten the heavy old wood stairs. And there was more light than he remembered. Along the stairwell and passage of the first of the two basements, the walls, layered with glossy paint, shone luridly blue-white under the fluorescent lamps. In his mind the place was always dark.

He paused in the passage and considered his options. His earlier visit had been cursory. What he had seen had suggested to him a space as honeycombed and confusing as the building above-ground. In diminished incandescent light off to his left, titanic spools of newsprint lay like slumbering beasts. To the right, a series of small workshops. Beyond them, around a corner, the passage trailed off into darkness.

It was then that Leo, his senses grown more acute, thought he heard voices drifting upwards from the staircase. While the basement seemed silent, deep in the background a muffled pounding, steady and relentless, throbbed like a great heart. Disturbing at first, it soon felt strangely comforting. Now the sudden intrusion of a human element acted as an alarm and he could feel himself tensing. He strained again to hear, but this time no sound was distinguishable. Had he imagined it?

He gripped the banister and descended the final set of stairs carefully lest the wooden slats creak and betray his presence. The sub-basement was gloomier than the one above, the lighting more intermittent, the ceiling lower, the passage in front of him narrower. The incessant throbbing of the building was less intense here, but the smell of oil and chemical was sharper. Leo was uncomfortably aware of his own rising apprehension. The voices had not been his imagination. From off to his right there came the low vibrato of a male voice, its owner and the words undistinguishable. By contrast, the higher pitch of a female voice seemed to penetrate the thick rough-hewn walls. The words were similarly indistinct but in the tone held a quality of suppressed panic. There was no doubt the voice belonged to Liz. He felt now the full assault of fear, a clutching at his gut followed by a rush of adrenaline so strong that his heart suddenly pounded furiously against his chest. He knew what he had to do. Flight was out of the question.

41

Family Matters

At first Liz had been too startled to be frightened. It had flashed through her mind that a poor joke was being played on her, but after she had twisted her neck away from the knife point, and looked at the meaty hand holding the handle, then looked along the leather-swathed arm into Roger Mellish's eyes and saw in them the strange and blazing hostility, felt its penetration, her limbs seemed to grow numb. Crouched on the linoleum, anchored by the heavy file, virtually trapped, she had had to fight back the wave of panic that had surged through her. To his whispered question about what she was doing she had tried to affect indifference. But her reply had come out as a mumble and when he demanded she repeat herself, the word "nothing" sounded to her ears as guilty and foolish as a child's lie. He had made her close the drawer then and directed her, silently, knife flashing (although part of her mind realized it was Vera's letter opener) to remove a different bottom drawer farther along the set of cabinets near the back stairs door. Her deduction had been correct. The file had lain in dust along the floor below. But she had had no time for self-congratulation. Mellish had snatched the file and pushed her toward the backstairs door. Her mind had roiled with other things: should she run? shout? But then it had been too late and she was on the other side of the door.

For a moment on the landing Mellish had seemed to hesitate, his hot breath pouring onto her neck in moist blasts. When she arched her back in an involuntary shudder, the point of the letter opener had slipped between her shoulderblades in an unnecessary reminder.

"Why were you looking for this in the library?" he had asked in a low voice.

The question had caught her off guard.

"I wasn't."

"Liz!"

"It was a hunch," she replied when she had gained control of her voice. "I heard about Guy on the radio. I thought maybe the file would still be—"

"But that doesn't explain the library, Liz."

"I asked...Alcock if anything had been found with Guy's body. He said no, and the newsroom seemed a poor choice to hide a file—all those locked desks—so I thought maybe the library—"

"Why did you assume this file would be in the building at all?"

"The news reports had said police suspected a link between Michael Rossiter's murder and Guy's. That meant it had to be one of only a handful of people and all of them would be at Galleries Portáge. Someone couldn't carry a file that size back with them into the mall without being noticed. Either that or Guy had hidden it to protect himself. That's why I assumed it was here, at the paper."

She had thought her pounding heart would burst from her chest. She had not talked to Alcock. The newscast she had heard had made no such claims. Only a whim had suggested the file might still be at the *Citizen*, not ash in a fireplace. But he seemed to have believed her.

"You weren't at the mall opening, were you?" he had asked.

"No."

"Why not?"

She'd hesitated.

"Why not?!"

"I checked into a hotel. I just needed to be away from my husband for a while."

"I see." He had paused and then said in a suspicious tone: "There've been news reports on all day."

Believing herself caught in the lie, she had held her breath in dreaded anticipation. But Mellish continued in a different vein: "Then why did you just come here now, in the evening? Have you discussed this with anyone else? Have you talked to the police?"

Now, forcibly pushed in a vault in the sub-basement, a starkly lit narrow chamber with a ceiling just low enough to contort her neck, she wondered if she had given the best answer. She had tried to remember from novels and movies and news features what one was best advised to do in a situation such as hers. Play for time, she had thought. If she had told him the truth, that Leo knew, that soon—she prayed—someone would notice her unattended purse and her long absence and alert the police, then he might panic. His laboured breathing, his strained voice, had told her he was not as calm as he tried to appear. So she had lied, had told him she had stayed in bed all day and had heard no newscast until the supper hour. This had apparently satisfied him. But now, with her only hope lying in someone finding her absence from the newsroom significant and beginning a search, she thought: would they think to come this far? All the way to the building's dungeon?

When Mellish had forced her from the landing down the back stairs her still-hopeful mind had raced over the possibilities for flight. But there had been always the knife point to keep her disciplined. "You can scream all you want," he had said. But, of course, screaming would have done nothing. Except for the fourth floor, the building was virtually empty and the stairwell was a sink into which all sound poured and none released. There had been a moment in the backroom of the first floor. The door had jerked back on a faulty pneumatic hinge as she stepped through and for the briefest span she was out of Mellish's reach. With an animal's urgency, she had darted toward the door that led into the front lobby, but Mellish had been quicker, grasping her shoulder painfully, digging his fingers into her flesh while his other hand pressed the tip of the knife against her back. The swiftness and strength in a man of his girth had surprised her and it had been then that she had begun to lose hope.

On the way down the basement stairs, as he peeled off his leather jacket, she had asked him the obvious questions: Why is this file important? What does it have to do with you? But he had only grunted and refused to reply. She had tried to bargain with him then. Let me go, take the file, and we'll forget all about this. But it had been a pointless and desperate act on her part, born of the fright, and he had remained curiously silent. There had been only his rough breathing, the echo of their footfalls, and then, as they reached the second of the two basements, something new, the distinctly rank and sweet odour of sweat, of the sort that accompanies sudden terror, cutting through air already redolent with its own peculiar pungency. Now it seemed to fill the vault, and Liz could see the stains blooming along Mellish's shirt. His hands, oily with perspiration, methodically rotated the handle of the letter opener. His eyes had lost their earlier rancour and were instead opaque and in-turned. Was this the way he behaved with his previous victims? If so, it made him seem even more dangerous, almost demented, so short-fused that the wrong word or wrong gesture would set him off. Or did something else lie behind his agitation? It occurred to her then that he might be claustrophobic, or phobic in some other way. But danger lay in that as well. He would be mad to get out.

He waved the knife at her. "Move farther back," he ordered, dropping his jacket and the file on the concrete beside him.

She did as she was told, taking a few steps backward until she could feel the cool wall against her shoulderblades. The vault was about ten feet deep, with a tier of shelves on each of the side walls and a meagre centre aisle. She had been in it once before, years earlier, with Vera, in search of a particular microfiche. Certain little-used or rare library items were stored in the vault, but she could tell from a quick glance that things had changed. Where she stood at the back, a few microfiche filing cabinets remained, but the shelves, which she'd remembered as having contained stationery items, now seemed cluttered with bits of machinery, items that spilled over from the shelves visible just beyond Mellish's shoulders. None of them looked serviceable as a weapon.

"I want you to find a piece of paper," Mellish said. His voice was tight, his breathing still hard.

Perplexed, Liz looked vaguely around the shelves. "Why do you need a piece of paper?"

"It's you who needs a piece of paper, my love. You have a suicide note to write."

A cry almost escaped her lips. His intent was clear. She battled to maintain a semblance of calm before replying. "Why would I be committing suicide?"

"I don't know, do I? You'll have to think of something. You're the talented Go! writer. You've been feeling depressed. No. I have a better idea. You'll confess to Guy Clark's murder and now you're feeling remorseful."

"They'll never believe it, Roger." It was the first time she had said his name. Somehow it seemed important to re-establish their bond as colleagues. "I don't think many women are strong enough to strangle a man."

"They'll believe it. You look capable enough and they're desperate for a solution. Besides, you weren't at the mall. You were in a hotel. Hotels don't keep track of their guests' every movement. What kind of alibi could you possibly get?"

Liz thought quickly. "I met someone. He would vouch for me."

"A man? You really *are* having marital problems, aren't you?" His eyes narrowed suddenly. "What's his name then?"

"Vronsky. Steve Vronsky." It was the first name that came to her mind but she regretted it as soon as it slipped from her mouth. It sounded ludicrous to her ear.

Mellish, however, failed to catch the allusion to Anna Karenina's lover. He shrugged impatiently and said, "It doesn't matter. I'll bet there's a Mrs. Vronsky somewhere who would be very unhappy if she knew what her husband was up to."

She wanted to laugh. In other circumstances she would have laughed. But she felt the vault growing warmer with her warmth and the vision came to her suddenly of the door to this tomb slamming with deathly finality. How long would the air last? And then she remembered something Vera had said casually on her previous visit: "We never close this door. It has a combination lock and the combination was lost years and years ago. So be careful if you're ever down here on your own." The memory struck her with terrible force. Even if it were determined she was inside, would there be enough time to bore through the steel and stone before the air ran out? She shivered despite the vault's heat. She had to keep him talking. Time was her single ally. Shaking a little, feeling now a chill like those that accompany fevers, she said, "What about motive, Roger? What reason would I have to murder Guy?"

"You hated him!" The irritable tone of his voice suggested her question was completely unreasonable.

"Okay, everyone disliked him, Roger. But that's hardly enough."

"Shut up and find some paper."

Liz bent down and began to grope around the shelves nearest her. She guessed pieces of paper might be binding the packets of microfiche, but that would be her last resort. In the meantime, she would stall by a painstaking search through the debris on the shelves, which, as luck had it, appeared genuinely to contain no paper.

"Hurry up!" Mellish said.

"Then you look at your end."

"No!" he shouted. And then more softly, as if trying to get himself under control: "No. I don't care for confined spaces. And besides, I don't want to leave fingerprints. Just in case."

She had been right. His agitation had more than one source. How could she use this? She thought: I must appear to sympathize, to care. She said, "Have you always been claustrophobic? I've always been a bit acrophobic myself." She hoped she had the word right. Acrophobic? Heights? She rattled on: "Ever since I was a child I've been uncomfortable with heights. When did confined spaces start to bother you?"

To her surprise, he answered straight away. "Since a bomb landed on the shelter I'd taken refuge in. I was a child and I was buried alive. I had to be dug out." He gave her a sickly grin. "So you can see that I'm rather sensitive to places likes this."

"It must have been dreadful for you," Liz murmured, still methodically turning things over on the shelves. "This was in England, I suppose?"

"Of course it was in England! Do you think bombs dropped out of the sky here?"

"I'm sorry, Roger. Sometimes I forget you're English. Your accent isn't that strong."

"I worked hard to get rid of it. I hated England. I couldn't wait to get out. I had nothing but unhappiness there. Now stop stalling! Look in that bloody file cabinet at the back. There's got to be some paper in there."

Liz pretended to fiddle with one of the drawers as though it were locked, or stuck. "Your mother died in the war, did she?"

"She died in the same bomb shelter I was buried in."

"And your father?"

"I didn't know my father."

"Did you have no other family?"

"For fuck's sake, forget about my family. I want you to open the top drawer of that cabinet and show me what's inside."

She did as she was told. The drawer contained bundles of microfiches, twenty or thirty fiches to a bundle, each covered with a sheet of blue paper bound by an elastic band. Standing in profile, and with Mellish's watchful eyes upon her, she knew she could hardly slip off the wrappings and then hide them.

"Show me!" Mellish commanded.

She held up a bundle. "I don't have a pen," she said.

"What's that in your pocket?"

With her other hand she felt along the side of her thigh. She had forgotten to return her cigarette lighter to her purse. "A lighter," she replied.

"Forget it. I have a pen in my pocket here." He pressed the blade of the letter opener to his right pants pocket. "But you'll have to come and get it. I don't want any fingerprints. Come on."

She walked toward him, her stomach churning with a mixture of dread and disgust. Because he had placed himself on the lower step just outside the vault door, he was eye-level with her and she had to press against his belly to get her hands in his pocket. The heat of him seemed to swim around her; his breath so repugnant she wanted to turn her head but could not, forced by proximity to stare in his eyes while she groped in his pants pocket in a grotesque parody of flirtation. She noted the bloodshot sclera, the pupils shrunk to pinholes, a look, she thought—was she imagining it?—of incipient madness. She considered for a second crushing his genitals with her hand but, as if he had read her thoughts, he raised the letter opener and brushed its cool blade against her cheek. She pulled the pen, a cheap ballpoint, from his pocket and stepped back quickly.

"Run your hand over it a few times," Mellish said. "Just to remove anything of me on it. I wouldn't want to leave any evidence. You never know. The police may not believe your suicide."

She thought: Of course they won't. Suicides seek quick death, or painless death, or both. No one would impose the slow terror of suffocation on herself. The police would recognize the fraud right away. What would prevent her, once locked in, from tearing up her note, or better yet, writing the truth? With this murder attempt, Mellish had crossed beyond the borders of reason. This was desperation. But instead, as casually as she could, she said, "You've been very clever all along, haven't you? For instance, how did you manage to kill Michael Rossiter and divert suspicion? Weren't you with...Nan, isn't it? Is that her name? Did you get her to lie for you?"

"Nan? Good god, no. She probably would lie for me, though. But she wouldn't be very good at it." His voice grew impatient. "You've got the pen now. Start writing!"

"Write what? 'Dear World, I've been feeling a bit low lately. Sorry about Guy, but I had to do it. Yours truly, Elizabeth Elliott.'"

As soon as the words were out of her mouth, she regretted them. The effect of sarcasm on Mellish was immediate. Under the unflattering light of the single bulb, the pale skin of his face reddened anew with angry clots of blood. He stared at her hatefully and she knew only his dread of the confined space restrained him.

"I'm sorry," she said hastily. "I just don't know how to phrase it. Give me a moment to think."

Keep him talking, keep him talking.

"In the meantime, why don't you tell me how you fooled Nan?" She cleared a spot on the shelf nearest her and began to run the pen over it, writing a few nonsense words—whatever came into her head—pausing every so often as if in thought.

Apparently mollified, Mellish said: "As I said, Nan wouldn't be a very convincing liar. But it was easy enough to make her believe I was in my apartment the whole time. When I got home from work, I paid a brief visit to her and told her I was going to take a shower before we went to the restaurant. I knew she would be in her bathroom fussing with her hair or her makeup. Our bathrooms share a common wall, you see, and it's fairly thin. You can hear the shower or snatches of conversation easily through the wall. So I turned on my shower and a tape-recording of me singing in the shower—I have one of those waterproof Walkmans; they're really quite clever—and then just left the apartment by the back stairs."

"And no one saw you?"

"It was the dinner hour. It was so hot for late September. Everyone was inside. And Rossiter's is only five minutes on foot, most of it down a back lane. There's lots of shadow under those big elms and I wore my straw panama to cover my hair and obscure my face. If anyone had noticed me, they probably wouldn't even remember a man with a briefcase. I'm just another chap coming home from the office. There was a bit of a risk, but it was one I had to take. The whole thing only took about fifteen minutes. When I got back, I just dampened my hair, changed my clothes, and Nan never knew the difference."

"You say there was a bit of risk. Why didn't you wait for another day? Or late at night?"

"It was all timing. I only learned what Michael had learned Monday afternoon."

"What had he learned?"

"Liz, don't play me for a fool. You know what's in this file!"

"Then why is it so important to you?" She thought of Michael's incriminating letter, still sitting in the photocopier.

"It's none of your business. Just keep writing." He paused as if trying to control himself.

"Anyway," he continued after a moment, his voice falling into almost dreamy tones, "while Michael was out helping Bunny with something, I was just poking about his desk and I noted the draft of a letter to you. Well, I didn't know it was to you at the time. There was just the body of a letter going to someone. And I knew I had to stop it, and him."

"Why didn't you do something right then?"

"Bunny knew I was there. So the next day I phoned him in the morning and told him I'd left my glasses in his office—which I had. Deliberately. He said he had a couple of people dropping by that evening, but 6:30 or so was fine to come and pick them up. I said I wouldn't be long. And I wasn't." He made a sickly grin.

"That was taking a chance, wasn't it? I mean, he could have told someone he would be meeting you at his house at 6:30."

"Yes, but I already had prepared my alibi, so it didn't matter. I found the file right on top of his desk, and stuffed it in my briefcase. He hadn't sent it."

"Or so you thought."

He regarded her stonily.

Liz tried to keep her voice soothing. "Taking the violin was a good idea, though. A diversion?"

"To provide a motive."

"Did you think it was the Guarneri?"

Roger shrugged in the affirmative.

"And where is it now?"

She looked up to see a shadow of regret cross his heavy features. She felt a shiver of horror for she knew what he had done with the violin. He had destroyed it, even while believing it was a peerless instrument, a thing of remarkable beauty.

"I had to do it, Liz. I couldn't have it lying around. I used my marble rolling pin to crush it. I thought one blow would do but I had to keep hitting it and hitting it."

"And what did you do with the pieces?"

"I had some potting stones. I put them in a bag with the pieces of violin, and later that night, after I left Nan, I drove to the Red, to the Alexander dock, and threw it in the river."

He looked at her as if seeking forgiveness. But she had nothing to give him, nothing to say. In what seemed like the years she had spent between the library and this subterranean vault, she had passed through disbelief, then shock, then fright. Her opportunities for escape had evaporated, her hope for rescue diminished by the minute, yet she found herself now almost morbidly calm and she wondered with an odd detachment if this was the way a live bird felt in a jaws of a cat. Her face must have been blank and ungiving, for abruptly Mellish's mood changed. His eyes had shifted to the paper on which she was writing.

"I want you to come here and show me what you've done!"

She looked at the sheet on which she had written over and over after the first few nonsense words: "Mary had a little lamb, its fleece was white as snow." Its childish cadence played in her head. She almost smiled as she lifted the sheet and then, after a pause, crumpled it, dropping it at her feet.

"No," she said. "It won't do."

"You little bitch," he spat out. "Pick that up and bring it here."

Liz kicked the ball of paper instead. It landed neatly in front of him. He snatched it and quickly smoothed it out.

"Fingerprints, Roger, fingerprints." Her own boldness surprised her.

He didn't reply. He stood staring at the writing as if it were the worst pornography, vile and yet somehow compelling. Without lifting his head he said in a flat voice, "Give me your lighter." She hesitated. He looked up. His eyes were glowing with anger. "Give me your lighter!" he repeated, the menacing tone unmistakable.

She tugged it from her pocket and sent it flying through the air. He caught it in his one free hand, put the letter opener in his shirt pocket, and set the paper on fire. The flame, tentative at first, soon flared and greedily engulfed the paper. The smoke rose in a plume, broke along the ceiling of the vault and then slowly snaked toward her through the dead air.

"Now," he said, letting the curled and blackened ash fall to the floor, "Take another piece of paper from those microfiches and write the following: 'I am responsible for the deaths of Guy Clark and Michael Rossiter.' Short and sweet. And, of course, don't forget to sign your name. Then bring it to me. I think it should be left outside the door."

She removed the elastic band from another set of microfiches and unfolded the protective paper. Her hands shook and she knew her earlier moment of calm had been just that—a moment, an interlude dictated by the body's will to survive, a time for her to gather her resources. But there was still a chance. She was not prepared for darkness, for suffocation, for death. With her heart crashing against her chest, she followed Mellish's dictation. Steadying her voice she said, "Would you tell me one last thing? Can you grant me a final wish before I give you this 'confession'?"

He responded to her quaint phrasing with the smile of a beneficent tyrant. He said, "You want to know, 'why,' the last of the five journalistic double-U's, the most important and the least regarded. You want to know why I'm doing this. You've already asked and I wouldn't tell you."

"But can't you tell me now?"

His eyes focused on her were jubilant. "Do you know," he said, "I seem to have gotten over my little attack of claustrophobia. I feel quite fine now. I suppose it's true that one can overcome one's fears by confronting them. When I was first apprenticing at the Dorchester—in London—I used to dread having to eviscerate poultry or butcher the great sides of beef and pork. I would feel faint. All that blood and guts. But I got used to it. And when I was very young—did I tell you I spent some time after my mother's death on a farm belonging to a cousin?—she made me wring a chicken's neck. I think I was all of six years old. She was an awful woman. She used to lock me in a closet under the stairs when I was bad. I suppose that contributed to it…"

Oh god, Liz thought, he's slipping over the edge. With growing horror she regarded his flushed and sweating face and the two narrowed slits that were his eyes, the flecks of spittle which had appeared at the sides of his mouth. It was though he were somehow fuelling himself for the task ahead while at the same time starting to distance himself in his mind. She needed to stop the incipient frenzy before he whirled around like a fat dervish and slammed shut the vault door like a coffin lid.

"Roger!" she cried. "Roger!"

His eyes refocused on her slowly.

"What?" he said absently, licking the sides of his mouth.

"You haven't answered my question."

There was a silence and when he spoke again it was in a sly, teasing voice.

"I won't tell you because I'm not supposed to tell."

Her heart contracted with his words. All along she had willed herself to believe Mellish was acting on his own, for his own peculiar reasons. Now her mind had to confront the obvious: that he was the instrument of another, the only person who stood to lose if a curtain were thrown back on the past. With great weariness she said:

"Did Paul ask you to do this? Or tell you? Or contract you?"

The question seemed to offend him.

"Of course not," he snapped.

"Then why are you trying to protect him?"

"Can't you see? Can't you tell? Look at me, Liz. Look at me! Isn't there something in my face that gives the answer? My god, I'm surprised no one has ever seen it!"

Liz looked at him with consternation. Her eyes searched his features. What was she to look for? Or at? She saw nothing but the same square fleshy face with the slight lantern jaw, the same white forelock, tenacious before the receding hairline—features with which she had been acquainted for two years, now burned into her memory. She shook her head and opened her mouth to signal, "no," but Mellish interrupted.

"Try this then," he said impatiently and then in a voice lowered by half an octave and laced with familiar cultivated tones narrated: "Roll over Beethoven, tell Tchaikovsky the news."

Liz could feel the fine hairs on the back of her neck rise. The imitation was uncanny. And now, too, she saw, or thought she could see, a physical resemblance. It wasn't much but, yes, there was something about the eyes— their wide separation caused by an uncommonly broad nasal root—and something about the small mouth, too, although Mellish's lips were fuller than Paul's, the lower lip protuberant, the upper a Cupid's bow, a faintly effeminate, Brian Mulroneyesque focus in the expanse of jaw glistening now with perspiration.

"So," he continued, evidently pleased with his performance, "Have you figured out why? Remember, I didn't tell you. You figured it out all by yourself. Not that it really matters now."

His mocking voice seemed to reverberate in her head and she had the sensation of sinking under water, into a wavering prism of shattered light, a smothering confine where there was only the sound of her own pounding body rhythms. Everything seemed unbearably heavy, her arms, her mouth, her eyelids. Slowly she opened her mouth to give voice to what her conscious mind could not now deny.

"Brotherly...love," she intoned.

He smiled at her. "Well, half-brotherly anyway."

"Half-brotherly," she echoed hollowly.

"Yes, we share the same mother. Paul is half-English. His father was German."

She realized she was staring at him, seeking confirmation in his features, trying to find in the one sibling the traces of the other.

"I never knew he had a brother," she heard herself say. "I thought his whole family died in the war."

"I was told Paul had died in the war," Mellish said, suddenly confiding in tone. "But one day a few years ago when I was working at the paper in Ottawa, I saw a wire-service photo of him that someone had tossed in a basket on the entertainment editor's desk. It was an old one of his appointment to the orchestra here. Even after all these years, I could see that he was really Karl Staudt. My mother gave me a picture of him that I've had with me since I was a child, a picture of him as a young man before the war started. I knew I wasn't mistaken. My mother told me he was studying to be a musician. She predicted he would be a great artist and that we would meet one day, when the war was over."

The jubilant expression returned to his face.

"And you know," he said, "we did, finally. Didn't we?"

His gaze seemed to turn inward like that of a child reviewing some secret memory. Liz had already written the absurd suicide note, but Mellish seemed to have forgotten it. He was agitated now in a different way, rhapsodic, and she sensed that as long as she could keep open the portals of his memory she had a reprieve. In as casual a manner as she could muster she said, "Your mother must have become separated from Paul before the war. That would have been painful for a woman."

"Yes," he said. "It was. Oh, it was. I was very young, remember. But my strongest memories are of her grieving for him, worrying about him. You see, it was very confusing for her, to have a son fighting for the enemy. And we were very isolated. My mother's family would have nothing to do with us. She had been married to a German hadn't she? A Hun. They wouldn't forgive that! And then she had left him and returned to London and, worse, had a child out of wedlock. Me! I was a bastard, and when I was six, I became an orphan." His sad smile seemed to ask for her sympathy.

But Liz was repelled. She prayed her repulsion didn't show on her face. Quickly she said, "Children usually go with their mothers in a separation. Especially in those days. Why didn't Paul return to England with your mother?"

"He wanted to. He was in his teens. But his father wouldn't let him, would he? Not then. Not in the Fatherland. Of course, his father forced him to join Hitler Youth and all that. He didn't want to, you know. He didn't want to, but his father made him. And then there was no way of getting out of that system."

"Did Paul tell you that?" She hoped the disbelief did not tell in her voice.

"My mother told me. She said he would have made a much more proper English boy. Like me. Like I would have become, if there hadn't been a war, if my mother hadn't died, if..." His voice trailed off.

"I tried to find him. I didn't believe he had died. In the early 60s, I went to Germany. I knew the name, you see. I thought there might be a cousin or someone who would know. I did find some distant relatives, but they insisted Paul had been killed, that his body had never been found. Maybe they didn't believe I was related to him. Maybe they thought I was some official snoop. But I knew we would find each other eventually."

As he talked he methodically wiped the blade of the knife with his fingers. Even in the pale light of the vault the silver finish flashed and scintillated and she shivered at the memory of its sharp point against her back, at the notion of it piercing her skin. She looked at Mellish's face. It was still flushed and damp—the heat and closeness of the sub-basement seemed worse with each passing minute—but his features had relaxed somewhat and the manic quality had, at least for a time, absented itself from his eyes. She felt safe to probe deeper.

"But you've kept your relationship a secret," she continued. "Why? Was this Paul's idea?"

Mellish started. For the first time he looked uncertain. "Well, yes," he said slowly. And then he glared at her as if she were stupid. "But surely you see why, Liz. He had created a new life for himself, one that did not include a brother in it, particularly a brother who knew something of his past, something different than what he had been telling everyone else. My sudden appearance might have started people asking questions. It had to be kept secret."

"But the two of you could have arranged some other story, surely."

"He didn't want it that way. He thought...he thought inconsistencies would arise. Naturally, I agreed with him."

And yet, to her ears, his voice lacked conviction. Liz imagined that Paul must have been unpleasantly surprised to find a near-forgotten half-sibling suddenly materialize, and she wondered what compromises he had made, what manoeuvres he had used to contain this eccentric, orphaned man and satisfy his need for acceptance and inclusion without drawing public attention to their connection. To Paul he must have been like a ticking time bomb. She asked, "Did you know everything about his past? Did you know what's contained in that file?"

Mellish shifted his eyes downward to the file balanced atop the leather jacket. When he looked up again, his eyes were hard, the uncertainty vanished.

"Yes," he said.

And in that simple affirmative, that merciless stare, was everything she needed to know. She didn't have to ask if he had been shocked or disgusted, angered or frightened, if Paul had denied everything and Mellish believed it, or if he had rationalized his crime to his half-brother the way he had rationalized it to her. It didn't matter now. A few feet from her was a man blinded by a fierce and distorted loyalty to a paragon conceived in his mother's myth-weaving, to a long-lost sibling, to a remnant of precious family. He was like a tortured shadow who, in searching for, and finding, itself, repeats the action of its beloved. This shadow, this larger, coarser mutation of her once sweet lover, was repeating Paul's murderous activity in another form. She knew now that any hope of reasoning with him was gone and her blood ran cold.

Wordlessly, he slipped the knife into his breast pocket and removed the lighter. With his eyes trained on her, he bent down to the file folder, tugged at the top and removed a sheet of paper, waving it before her triumphantly. Then, suddenly, he disappeared from view and her heart leapt with a foolish certainty that he had vanished. Instinctively, she started forward, but he was back in an instant, dragging with him an empty drum, its metal base scraping the concrete floor with a hideous rasp. Robbed in that moment of her last chance for flight, her wits began to crash around her. She stepped back, aware only of her own laboured breathing, her dry mouth as she watched Mellish take the sheet of paper, set it aflame, drop it into the drum, and witness with scornful gaze its annihilation. He followed with another sheet and then another, finally lifting the entire file and tossing the contents in ferociously crumpled sheets of four and five into the blaze. The interior of the drum glowed like a furnace, orange and throbbing, as each new piece of paper fell to the flames. Smoke rose in a column as the fire intensified. Some of it drifted toward her, filling her nostrils with its acrid perfume, stinging her eyes, obscuring as it arched and billowed around Mellish's face, hellishly shadowed in the flickering light. She knew she could no longer bear it.

"Don't do this, Roger," she heard herself beg, forcing back the sob that rose in her throat. "Don't do this. I was Paul's lover."

"You're lying!" he cried above the crackle of flames. But he was lost to sensibility.

"Bring me the note you've written. Now!"

With shaking hands, Liz lifted the sheet from the shelf and willed herself forward. Her feet were leaden. The distance seemed to yawn before her.

He moved around the drum, snatched it from her with his free hand, careless now of fingerprints, and glanced at it quickly. With a grim satisfaction, he moved slightly to set it on his coat. Liz looked helplessly at the knife balanced in his shirt pocket and then, as he bent in his task, she looked past his head and saw through the nimbus of smoke a sight that finally sent the tears coursing silently down her cheeks. But they were tears of relief, for, not six feet away, Leo was staring hard at her, his dark eyes a warning.

42

Abyss

Leo tensed. When Mellish moved, as he did now, with exaggerated care placing Liz's note into his coat, he anticipated with dread the final act: that Mellish would suddenly slam the door to the vault, leaving it locked and impenetrable. Time was running out. The smoke from the fire had already reached Leo, insinuating its way into his nose and throat, forcing him to suppress with fierce concentration the urge to cough, allowing him only shallow breaths when he needed every ounce of nourishing oxygen for his straining muscles. It was impossible to conceal his presence much longer, yet surprise remained his single ally.

He was standing a few feet behind Mellish, between two rows of dusty, half-empty wooden shelves, submerged in shadow. He couldn't make any mistake now. Arriving at his position undetected had already taken him down a treacherous stretch. The passage, narrow though it was, had been left with discarded wooden flats leaning upright against the wall, each of which looked perilously close to tipping. Worse, the floor had been scattered with bits of wood and packing straw and though he had prudently removed his shoes at the stairwell, he had feared a warning snap with every step. Despite the stone walls and their temporary wooden bolsters, the passageway had seemed like a membrane, fashioned to amplify sound. He had realized almost immediately that Liz was not only in the large storeroom to the right of the corridor, but in the ancient vault, the curiosity that had captured his attention on an early visit. Her words, soon distinguishable as he edged his way along, echoed hollowly as though travelling from some remote region while the male voice—Mellish's, he realized with alarm no less diluted by confirmation of his expectations—rumbled and reverberated. The content of their exchange had filled him with amazement and misgiving.

The storeroom had two entrances. The closer one opened onto a short corridor that led directly to the vault. The farther entrance, some twenty feet beyond, marked the back of the storeroom. Leo had had to stop and strain his memory for a recollection of the vault's design. The door, thick and impenetrable, didn't lie flush against the wall when opened. He had known that. He had pushed against it and felt its weight recoil on his earlier visit. But did it open to the left or to the right? He couldn't remember. If the latter, then Mellish would be screened and Leo's chances of crossing the entrance undetected multiplied. If not, then the element of surprise vanished. He would be seen. But there had been no choice. With an adrenaline surge, he had stepped quickly into the pool of pale light carpeting the doorway and then out and beyond. The vault door opened to the right.

With relief he had clutched at a bare bit of wall, grateful for its unexpected and delicious coolness. He hadn't been caught. But in the beat of time it took to cross the doorway he had turned his head and the scene had been emblazoned on his mind. Mellish was in front of the vault, half-hidden by the door, his back to the storeroom and its rows of shelves. As Leo inched his way to the second door past a series of metal drums along the wall, he had felt a surge of confidence. Circumstances favoured him. Mellish was too entirely absorbed in his manic activity to expect an attack from behind.

He had found sanctuary at the end of a row of shelves containing more of the industrial drums witnessed in the corridor, their blunt shapes in the dim light at once sheltering and ominous. Almost immediately, Mellish had moved from view and Leo, barely thinking, had darted into the aisle determined to charge forward and pull Liz from the vault. But as quickly, Mellish had returned, dragging an empty barrel with him, arresting Leo in mid-motion, stifling a gasp, quelling the crash of his heart against his chest. He had not been seen. But he had beheld Mellish's face in profile and been jolted by the transformation, by the blotchy skin, the stubborn set of the jaw, and the singular frenzy in his eyes.

And now the moment had arrived. This fire, this reckless dangerous fire, blazed higher, clouding the room with smoke. Liz, whose voice told him she had been fighting back the panic, broke down in entreaty, anguishing to hear. He pressed forward, his senses sharpened as he closed in on his quarry.

And then, unexpectedly, Mellish bent down and Liz's eyes were locked on his. He tried to caution her with a silent gesture. But her face crumpled and broke, the tears speaking not of horror, but of deliverance. And then there was no choice. With a howl of rage, Mellish thrust Liz backward from the edge of the vault with his left hand, grasping the lip of the door with his right. Leo was upon him in an instant, pressing against his back, as revolted by the man's heated, sweating bulk as he was surprised at his strength as he tried to choke him with the crook of one arm and pry loose his hand from the door with the other. He heard rather than saw Liz fall to the floor of the vault and a shiver ran through him at the vicious crack as her head met the stone. But Mellish was determined. Grunting furiously, he flailed with his free arm, first trying to drive his elbow into Leo's side, then reaching over to smash his fist on the hand trying without success to wrench his fingers from the door. Then Leo gasped in agony as something cold and sharp pierced the skin of his forearm. Instinctively, blinded by pain, he let go his adversary only to hear in the next instant the awful forbidding slam of the vault door.

Hardly aware what he was doing, he ran at Mellish with his shoulder, knocking him away from the door before his scrabbling fingers would find the combination lock, sending him crashing against the drum, knocking it over and scattering in a blaze of ash and spark and flame the still burning contents, saturating the air with smoke. Coughing, nearly gagging, he lunged again toward his opponent. But Mellish was on the ground groping amid the debris, muttering and cursing. And then Leo saw it—the source of his pain, his throbbing arm, the warm blood bubbling from his wound—saw it gleaming in the new flames dancing over the straw and paper. He kicked Mellish's hand from the knife with sudden fury, and then kicked the knife, sending it scuttling toward a stand of shelves all too quickly swathed in fire. Screaming, Mellish hurled his weight against Leo's legs, knocking him to the floor, then tore toward the shelf, half crawling, half swimming through the billowing smoke. But Leo twisted himself around, sending pain tearing through his ancient back injury, and grasped a retreating ankle with his left hand, holding doggedly while Mellish thrashed at him with his free leg, dragging him by increments along the blackened, ash-strewn floor. With his other hand, Leo tried to hoist himself onto his adversary, thwart him in his desperate pursuit of the knife, but he was frustrated by his awkward berth along the floor, by the feet beating about his head and by the numbness overtaking his right arm. He could feel his strength ebbing and then he heard a grunt of satisfaction. Mellish had found it. And then his shoulder seemed to erupt with pain as Mellish, coiled about, thrust blindly again and again through the smothering haze into his flesh. With a groan Leo released his hold and tried to rise to meet his opponent who was heaving himself, coughing and choking, from the floor. But his own progress seemed agonizingly prolonged, like the movements in a slow motion film. He looked up and saw Mellish over him, wild-eyed, saw him lift his leg, saw the advancing shoe, felt the impact along his temple, the shock as his skull seemed to split in two.

And then, as he tried again to rise, to thwart a second blow, there came an explosive roar from the back of the storeroom and suddenly the film regained momentum. Heat rolled over him like a blanket. Everything was bathed in flame. He looked up to see Mellish staggering forward from the impact, his lips moving in a soundless scream. He seemed to forget Leo then. He careened toward the vault and Leo, turning his head to watch, unable to get up, groaned in despair. If he turned the combination, Liz was lost. But, instead, Mellish snatched at the remains of the file unconsigned to fire and with a final half-crazed stare fled the room. As Leo sank into semi-consciousness, lulled by the sweet chill of the stone floor beneath his aching body, one detail floated by like a bright scarf—the white label affixed to the side of the blue drum in whose shelter he had earlier stood. Written on it was the word trichloroethylene. It was the liquid used to clean the presses and it was highly flammable.

The thought pulled him from his stupor. There were other drums in the storeroom and more in the corridor. Battling nausea, gasping in the smoke, he willed himself onto his knees and began to crawl toward the vault, keeping low where the air was least contaminated. His right arm, torn and bleeding, had weakened terribly; blood streamed down his face from the wound to his head. With effort he stood up, thrusting his nose under the collar of his shirt to filter the smoke, aware of the mounting heat at his back, the crackling as the flames consumed the wooden shelving. There was no time. Fearing the worst, that the vault had somehow locked, he pulled on the handle, gasping as the pain coursed down his arm. At first, it would not yield but then there was an almost imperceptible click and, slowly, agonizingly, he pushed the door back on its hinge to reveal Liz, immobile, her limbs twisted in a parody of sleep. And then there was another explosion and a blast of smoke and flame ripped into the vault itself. The storeroom behind him was now a pool of fire.

Desperately, nearly retching in the suffocating air, he pulled Liz to a sitting position with his one good arm. Crouching down, he hoisted her over his shoulder, then, bowed under the vault's low ceiling, stumbled forward into the searing heat. He heard Liz groan, felt her first tentative struggle back to life. Stepping from the vault to the floor of the storeroom his legs nearly buckled under a combination of weight and fatigue. The distance to the corridor seemed to spread out before him, the air between charged with roaring flames like great orange tongues licking and curling, whipping at his clothes and hair. For a moment he doubted his ability to travel the few feet to safety. The flesh on his hands and face scalded. The blasted air seemed to suck the very breath from his aching lungs. How easy it would be to surrender to this inferno, he thought, as his lids dropped over his burning eyes and a vision of cool green gardens and running water bloomed in his brain.

The hallucination was momentary but its power to confound terrified him and that in itself was sufficient to propel him forward. He pressed against the wall, twisting his head away from the bulging curtain of fire, blindly pushing away with his feet fallen bits of flaming wood. And then he felt a sudden convulsion. Liz had wakened to consciousness. Her body tensed along his own. He heard above the fire's roar a terrible retching cough and then her arms began to flail weakly down the back of his legs as though she believed herself still in Mellish's grip. It was then Leo realized his clothes were burning. Liz was not disoriented. She was beating the flames from his trousers. Through the acrid smoke came the sickening stench of burning hair and flesh—his own—and the pain, unacknowledged in the single-minded pursuit of escape, now ripped through him like a barrage of deadly arrows. He plunged forward in a final effort.

And then, miraculously, he was in the corridor. He felt his knees give under him and he dropped to the floor in a heap, half-falling onto Liz. With waning strength, he made himself roll away from her to extinguish the flames still fed by his clothes, each turn along the hard stone a torment to his burnt flesh. A few seconds later, the right side of his shirt and trousers reduced to charred rags, he lost consciousness. The last thing he saw as his mind ushered the awful pain to merciful oblivion was Liz struggling toward him through the gathering smoke, her face a web of black streaks.

But it was pain that awakened him a moment later. At first, his mind, dream-thickened, told him incisor teeth were slashing his shoulder and for the first time a cry forced its way from his throat. Then he realized there were hands tugging urgently under his arms, trying to pull him along the corridor that in the brief time he had been unconscious had surrendered to the fire, the wooden flats forming a blazing gauntlet. He looked up to see Liz, her face contorted with effort, and Stevie, fierce and pale, leaning over him, mouthing words unintelligible above the crackling spluttering flames. Pushing his heels against the floor, he tried to scramble to his feet, but his socks slipped along the slick surface and he fell back, tumbling from his rescuers' grasp, his arm a tattered ribbon of pain.

And then together they witnessed the final horror. As though cloven by an invisible hand, the smoke parted suddenly and raced toward them, swirling over their heads, leaving the fire clear and inviolate in its relentless destruction. At the far end, like an emergent moth at the tip of a flaming chrysalis, Mellish materialized, hugging the remains of the file to his chest. His eyes were distended and glistening, mesmerized by a world of writhing walls. He looked past them, not seeing them, his face all mad glory. Leo had only a second to remember the sub-basement offered a single exit before the explosion sundered the corridor and Mellish, his eyes acknowledging theirs at last, held out the file to the ravenous flames like an offering, shrieking triumphantly as the air burst around him. For an instant he seemed to float in the air like a fiery spirit, his arms two blazing wings, a wondrous aura playing over his hair and clothes, and then he dropped into the hellish abyss. The last thing Leo saw before the sickening smell of incinerated flesh again assailed his nostrils and returned him to the void, was the shock of white hair gleaming like a diamond before it too was consumed. Only then did he hear the sound of running feet, the shouting, the shrill ring of a fire bell somewhere off in the distance.

Monday Edition

43

The Beginning

The room held only one chair for visitors though there were two beds and the prospect of family members and friends descending in clusters on the cramped space and its Spartan furnishings was never far away. At four o'clock, however, most of the afternoon well-wishers had exhausted their supply of conversation and headed for home and the agreeable rhythms of normal life. The patients, well worn for being the objects of their clucking relatives, sought their own relief in sleep, television, or the quiet anticipation of dinner before the evening onslaught of visitors fell once more upon them. Except for the murmur of conversation among the staff at the nursing station, the ward had been mercifully quiet when Stevie passed through on her way to Leo's room. It was what she had expected, and wanted.

She lifted the chair gently from its position facing the unoccupied first bed and set it down beside the second. Leo didn't awaken. Impatient to talk with him, she leaned over to tug on the arm lying outside the bedclothes but then thought better of it. In the ambulance the night before he had bobbed in and out of consciousness, his face, bloodied and streaked, contracted with pain and its suppression. "Oh, for Christ's sake, just scream or something," she had shouted to him at last, kneeling down, stroking his hair, sick at heart for her helplessness, his suffering, the harrowing scene in the *Citizen* dungeons still then crashing through her mind. He had had a moment of lucidity then. "Okay, I will." But his grin wobbled, then a medic jabbed him with a silencing needle.

Now, at rest, in the thin autumn light filtered by the window blinds, Leo's features were smoothed and placid, the pain soaked up in dreams. The empurpled welt on the side of his face filled her suddenly with tenderness. There was gauze dressing along his right hand and arm, and the hair on one side of his head above a line of scarlet skin had very nearly disappeared. Her dread had been that he would be disfigured, but staff calmed her in Emergency, and her father, who had examined him in the morning had phoned to tell her the scarring would be minimal, Leo's face would be spared.

"Finally, a smile on your face," Kathleen had remarked. She'd been hovering like a solicitous shop clerk since Stevie had awakened.

The surge of relief had so very nearly overwhelmed her that Stevie let the comment pass without a retort and instead gave the old doll a big hug.

She knew she had become lost in thought when Leo's eyes opened suddenly, startling her. She was about to say something when the eyes, instead of focusing, rolled back in their sockets and closed again. A sigh escaped his lips. Acting on impulse, she bent over and placed a kiss on his mouth, letting her hair fall over his face. This time Leo's cheek twitched and his eyelids flickered. His eyes opened slowly, fighting to adjust to the object in his field of vision. A smile spread slowly across his features and then recoiled along the line of bruising. He moaned.

"Am I extra-crispy?" His voice was thick.

"Just a little singed around the edges," Stevie replied. "You'll be fine. Really."

Leo gave her another sort of Demerol smile. "I was dreaming about you."

He gazed at her, seeming to drink her in, and she wanted to laugh out loud. He looked all at once so comical with his wobbly grin, bandaged, bruised, pasted against the white hospital pillowcases. And the desire to laugh was itself a balm, a return to normal. She wanted to kiss him again. But she stopped herself, confounded suddenly by the force of her feelings, constrained by the barely private, briskly efficient cell with its starched linens and chrome fixtures. There would be another, better time. Instead she asked the question unresisted by history's legions of hospital visitors: "How are you feeling?"

Leo struggled to concentrate. The question seemed almost abstract. How was he feeling? "Sort of blissful." He grinned stupidly, then winced.

"Painkillers."

"More, please." He tried to fix his attention on Stevie's face, on the dark eyes beneath a brow furrowing and unfurrowing in response to his own wavering attention. The absurd thought came to him suddenly that auras truly did exist. A liquid crown of light, blue and white, flowed in soft currents about her hair with delicate flames drifting up and fading away like a cool and kindly fire.

"And you? Okay?"

"I'm fine. They released me after examination but they kept Liz in overnight for observation. She was lucky. She just had a slight concussion. Leo?"

His head fell back into his pillow as his eyelids began a lazy descent. Dismayed, Stevie wondered if he would be able to sustain a conversation. A glass of water on the adjoining night table next to a basket of cut flowers caught her eye. It looked untouched. She presented it to his lips.

"Drink this."

The water was tepid and to his flannelled mouth tasted sweet. But he was thirsty, thirstier than he might have imagined, and gulped the water down gratefully. With each drop his head cleared a little, substituting the anaemic throb of fading headache at one temple. Stevie's image clarified and with it came the sharp reminder of the *Citizen* basement, of her tugging at his arm, of the pain, and the horrible finale they had witnessed together.

"Mellish!"

"Ash," she replied, watching liquid descend from the drip into Leo's arm. "The fire consumed virtually everything in that lower basement."

"He was Richter's…"

"Brother, or half-brother, I mean. It's in the paper. They were able to put an edition out—the rest of the building, the presses and stuff, weren't damaged. That Alcock character is crazy. He had someone interviewing Liz as she was being put on a stretcher and then that woman we met outside—"

"Julie."

"—tried to climb into the ambulance with us. I practically had to beat her away."

"Ambulance chasing."

"I thought only lawyers did that."

"Either."

"At least you were unconscious through most of it."

"No. I seem to remember something of it."

Leo smiled at her, remembering a moment or two of delicious nurse-like empathy. He winced again. Stevie returned the glass to the night table and perched on the edge of the bed.

"Remember talking about Richter's Bowie eyes with my father?"

"Uh-huh," Leo replied dreamily, barely giving a damn.

"After I left, he told you someone else at the mall had the same thing."

"The same eyes?"

"No. See, Richter's eyes—the different coloured irises—are because of a certain genetic disorder he has. Called Waardenburg Syndrome." She repeated the word as she had earlier in the day when her father had explained it to her on the phone, rolling it around in her mouth, drawling the "a"s.

"It's not dire or disabling or anything," she continued, "at least in Richter's case. It's just an anomaly, something only people like my father would know about. But there's another characteristic that people with the syndrome sometimes have." She studied Leo's face. "A white forelock."

Leo gazed at her, though she seemed at the moment to have become two. "I thought he was just greying funny." He covered one eye with a hand. Now there was one of her. "They don't look much alike."

"They do if you think about it," Stevie insisted. "They both have jaws on the large side. They both have small mouths. And they both have widely spaced eyes. All of these are characteristic of the syndrome."

"But usually it's only *after* you're told of someone's relationship that you look for resemblances." Leo grunted as he attempted to raise himself. The pain that shot down his arm as he pressed his hand against the mattress sharpened his mind. "Mellish and Richter only share one parent, after all. And the differences in their ages, Mellish's weight, the extra flesh on his face—" Leo broke off, watched Stevie as she stared silently through the blinds at the pale sky above the parking structure opposite.

"Who else knows about this syndrome thing?" he asked. "Is it in the paper?"

"No."

New lede, he thought, drowsiness returning. "One had curious eyes, the other peculiar hair. But little did anyone know that in these eccentricities lay a common…something…"

Who says you can't write on drugs?

"Did you bring a paper?"

"No. I can get you one. There was a box in the lobby."

"No, stay."

"Richter and his wife have vanished, no surprise," she said after a moment. "It was on the radio. Did you know?"

Leo yawned. "I have vague recollections of my mother being here. And of Frank shouting at me. Poor Frank, ha ha. No one to arrest."

"I don't know how the Richters could leave without anyone getting wind, but I suppose they've always had some contingency plans."

"Particularly after Mellish entered their lives."

"That must have been a nasty surprise," Stevie remarked. And in any other circumstance a richly deserved one, she thought bitterly. But the reunion of the two siblings had laid the ground for death, and anyone in possession of the damning truth might unwittingly have stepped on it. It had been Michael. Her mind flew suddenly to a rendezvous in some elegant riverside living room north of the city. She imagined the one, Mellish, eager, a little flushed, oblivious to what could only have been shock and dismay on the part of the other. To what length had Richter gone to contain this threat to the careful fabrication of his life, to manage the swarm of potentialities that Mellish represented? When Michael confronted Richter with *his* knowledge of the truth, did Richter then direct Mellish toward his murderous action? It was this thought that had been on her mind since she had read the cursory story of the murders in the *Citizen* that morning. She drew her hand away from the edge of a blanket she had been heedlessly worrying and put the question to Leo directly.

"Mellish told Liz that Richter was not involved," Leo replied. "At least that's what I overheard."

"I wonder." Stevie began doubtfully, thinking out loud. "Maybe Richter had a role after all. "The only way—sort of ironic—that he could have protected his identity would have been to tell Mellish the truth, or at least some version of it. And then instill in him the need for secrecy, making their continued relationship dependent upon it—"

"Which wouldn't be hard," Leo murmured. "You could almost feel Mellish's need for approval at times."

"So," Stevie continued, "when Mellish found out what Michael had discovered he didn't need to say anything to Richter, or ask what to do. He already knew what to do. And he did it."

Leo thought back to the conversation he had overheard.

"'Brotherly love' Liz said last night. It's strange, isn't it, how love can be as destructive as hate? Mellish knew all about Richter's crime and it didn't matter. The need he felt to preserve his brother's reputation must have been so fierce he was prepared to destroy in the process."

Is this a lede?

Nah. Third paragraph.

"A grotesque form of identification," Stevie continued.

"Been reading your mother's psychology texts?"

"No, I got it directly from the source herself. She's been psychoanalyzing it all morning. According to her, Mellish couldn't separate himself from his brother so the threat to Richter became a threat to himself. He resembled Richter—I know you don't think so—and then did what Richter himself did once upon a time—murder."

Unbidden, images of Tuesday evening rushed through her mind. She could see it all now, as it must have been—Michael answering the door, taking him through the house to the study, walking ahead of him, just slightly ahead, talking affably of this or that, then perhaps bending to switch on the computer or pick up some photographs, then hearing a swoosh through the air as... A shudder went up her spine.

"Mellish was orphaned by the war, wasn't he?" she said quickly.

Leo nodded. "Why? Is it important?"

"I was just thinking how shattering the loss of parents could be—particularly if you're still a child."

"I lost my father when I was seven years old. I don't think I was too damaged."

"But you weren't orphaned. You still had your mother and a family around you. Mellish never knew his father. And then he lost his mother. And what about Merritt? And Guy? They were orphaned, too, at a young age."

"And you think this accounts for their behaviour?"

Stevie shrugged. "Beats me. The one arts course I took at the U of M was in nineteenth-century English literature. I remember the prof saying novels then were full of orphans."

Neat, Leo thought. A nice literary bullshit gloss. Ninth paragraph. He was about to ask the name of the prof when an obnoxious squeaking and scraping sounded outside in the hall. Stevie leaned back to look through the door and noted it was the meal cart.

"Dinner time," she announced.

"I'm starved." He smiled as the nurse, her broad features fixed in the patronizing smile of one who had tarried too long in the health care system, placed the covered plastic tray on a portable table and manoeuvred it across Leo's lap. To make room, Stevie moved down to the end of the bed.

"There we are," the nurse said airily. "I hope you're not a reporter," she barked in the same breath to Stevie. "We've been bothered by reporters phoning and showing up at the desk all day. I think we need to rest, don't we?" she added to Leo. "Do we need anything else to drink?"

Stevie sorted through the "we's" quickly. "No," she said to the first question as Leo replied with the negative to the last.

"Oh, well then, we'll look in on you a little later."

"Why are reporters after me?" Leo blinked as the nurse departed.

"Don't be so damned ingenuous. You're today's story in the *Citizen*."

"Oh, hell," Leo raised the lid of the tray. "I guess Liz blabbed."

"You saved her life, you idiot."

"Is this food?" Leo dabbed at the contents with a fork.

"Shall I go and get a paper?"

"Well, okay." Leo examined something pale he'd speared with his fork. "I suppose it might be worthwhile to see what sort of hash they've made of the story."

"I suppose," Stevie drawled. "And maybe I'll check through the classifieds for apartments. I think it really is time to move out of Max and Kathleen's."

"I know a place you could stay."

Stevie gripped the railing and slid off the bed. She turned and gave him a smile. Unfortunately, it was ambiguous.